The Search of
Tristan & Iseult:
A Postmodern Metafictional Travel Romance

{ BROUGHT TO YOU BY }

Bernard, *the Bardic Narrator*
& Patten, *the Producer*

IDENTITY PUBLICATIONS

For permission requests, write to the publisher at:
contact@identitypublications.com

Ordering Information:
Quantity sales. Special discounts are available on quantity purchases by corporations, associations, and others. For details, contact the publisher at the address above.

Orders by U.S. trade bookstores and wholesalers.
Please contact Identity Publications:

Tel: (805) 259-3724 or visit www.IdentityPublications.com.

ISBN-13: 978-1-945884-12-2 (paperback)
ISBN-13: 978-1-945884-10-8 (hardcover)

First Edition
Publishing by Identity Publications
www.IdentityPublications.com

If you ask me, I will tell you
Whence this story, whence this legend
From the mountains, moors, and fenlands
Ancient Cornwall is the venue
In the melancholy forests
Down among the oaks and fir trees
Merlin the magician sang them
Sang of Tristan, child of sadness
Sang a song of love's sad sorrows
Proved again love revives us
Proved again love survives us
Ye who love an ancient legend
Love the ballads of the people
Listen to this Cornwall chorus
Full of wish and tender pathos
Full of hope and tender heartbreak

"I should like to tell you a story that pleases me. It's called *The Woodbine*. It's about two lovers, their romance, and how one day they die together."
—Marie de France, *writing in Norman-French in the 12th century in England in the time of Henry II (trans., B. Patten)*

"The words which are criticized as dirty are old Saxon words known to almost all men and, I venture, to many women, and are such words as would be naturally and habitually used, I believe, by the types of folk whose life, physical and mental, Joyce is seeking to describe. In respect of the recurrent emergence of the theme of sex in the minds of his characters, it must always be remembered that his locale was Celtic and his season Spring."
—John W. Woolsey, *United States District Judge Lifting the ban on "Ulysses"*

"New things and old co-twisted, as if time were nothing."
—Alfred Lord Tennyson, *Idylls of the King, Gareth and Lynette* lines 222-3

CONVERSATION WITH THE READER

Our ideas of our ancestors must not be solely gleamed from musty records and chronicles, the authors of which seem perversely to have conspired to suppress in their narratives interesting human traits and details, in order to find room for flowers of monkish eloquence or trite reflections on morals.

Let them, not me, find amidst the dust of antiquity nothing but dry, sapless, moulderings, and disjointed bones, such as those which filled the valley of Jehoshaphat.

Let them in the office of antiquary, in toilsome and minute research, incapacitate themselves from compounding a tale of this sort, my tale, designed to amuse the enlightened public.

Let them, the severer antiquary, think that I am polluting the well of history with modern inventions and impressing upon the rising generations false ideas of the age I describe.

You, dear reader, I hope, will judge that you should not be trammeled by the repulsive dryness of mere history. You, I hope, will not forget that in distinguishing what is ancient from modern, there exists that extensive neutral ground, the large proportion, that is, of manners and sentiments which are common to us and to our ancestors, having been handed down to us, or which arise out of principles of our common nature, and must have existed alike in any state of society. The human passions from which spring out feelings and actions are generally the same in all ranks and conditions, all countries and ages. And it follows as a matter, of course, the opinions, habits of thinking, facts, and events, however, influenced by a particular state of a certain society, must still, upon the whole, bear a strong resemblance to each other. Our ancestors had eyes, hands, and organs that we have; they were fed with similar foods, hurt by weapons, subject to diseases, warmed and cooled by the same winter and summer as ourselves. The tenor, therefore, of their affections must have borne the same general proportion to our own and will help us understand ourselves.

I may have, it is true, in aiming to encompass complex human situations, confused the manners of two or three centuries, or two or three decades, and introduced, say, during the reign of Richard I, circumstances apagogical to a period either considerably earlier or a good deal later than that era. It is my comfort errors of this kind will not matter much to the majority of you readers because the purpose of this work is merely to have some fun while holding a mirror to ourselves.

Thus, this is not a novel. It is an entertainment and a travel log pointing out interesting places you might like to visit in Ireland and Cornwall, and it is a philosophical disquisition on life, love, death, logic, knowledge, truth, and everything we try to deal with in our little lives which, unfortunately, are simply rounded by a sleep.

So, partake, if you will, in this delicious Irish stew into which delectable items have been cast for you. Go ahead! Release the cork from its wire prison, aim the bottle at the ceiling, let the wooden mushroom shape fly up with the pop of a small air gun. Then, backed by centuries of sophisticated tradition, wrap the bottle in a white napkin, chink, and clink with friends, feel the ice-cold bubbles of Mumm Cordon Rouge, tres sec tickle your throat and electrify your stomach. Irish stew and champagne—quite a combination, not to be missed.

To display a more natural form of literature growing out of life in which characters are hounded, as are we all, by time, age, and fate, the Bardic Narrator, Bernard, tries to slice the events through different angles rather than through one person or place making the story ring true even though it isn't. Thus, events are a congeries of elements, uncentered and unfocused from a single viewpoint, so that the view is about dispersal and complexity, real-life chaos, human sizzle, and its magic. Such a change is fundamental to the complex realism basic to the postmodern metafictional travel adventure romance entertainment's role as a distinctive medium for modern thinking. And by the way, forgetting the idea of linear construction into a story or into an event or into the plot puts you where the edge is and where the fun is. Otherwise, there's nowhere to go, like being stuck in a bowling alley—at night.

~BMP, Houston, 2019

WHAT THE READERS SAY ABOUT DOCTOR PATTEN'S NEW BOOK,

The Search of
Tristan and Iseult:

◆————————●————————◆

"It brought on my period a week and a half early."
—C.C. Typist

"This ancient romance denigrates established religion, fosters disrespect for authority, undermines TV and other well-established excellent media of our era, and most offensively proffers a spurious and fake hedonistic philosophy of life."
—Rev. Billy Sunday

"A page-turner. Once you pick it up, you can't put it down."
—E.P., *Author's wife*

"Too cute. So bad, it's good. The only book I know that is 100% blarney."
—H. McDonald, *Author's friend*

"Wonderful. Just right for my insomniac patients."
—Dr. D.R., *Neurologist*

"I don't know, but the author, he in trouble."
—S.W., *Upstairs Maid, Riveroaks*

"If this book has any real significance, it is that of a Rorschach test. The meaning is whatever it provokes in the reader. As far as I am concerned, there is no given 'right' reaction, and I doubt even literary scholars would get more than half the allusions the author has crammed into his magnum opus."
—K.J., *Jungian Psychologist*

"For me, Bernard and Patten are warm, living, breathing, futile, half-baked, incredibly alive, and endearing boneheads."
—D.B. Wyndham Lewis, *Satirical Essayist And Journalist*

"This is the funniest book in the world, and I have annotated my copy of it in minute detail."
—Evelyn Waugh

"About the character Lupin: He is the forerunner of modern youth still living at home under the parental roof. He treats the house as a hotel, staying in bed all morning and then going out with friends at 11 o'clock. He is insouciant about money and drinks and smokes too much. His taste in music, art, literature, entertainment, and friends seems specially designed to irritate. Lupin suffers from an incurable condition he cannot help: **YOUTH**."
—Peter Morton

"Take a tip. Freeze on to this book for it is the book of the future.
Stagnant dummies have been standing still for years, and now are moving back.
Go off—move ahead to the future."
—Luping Pooter, *Broker of stocks and bonds*

"Sexual chicanery and self-interest know no bounds. Neither does Dr. Patten's
barbed humor as he mocks preconceptions, lifestyles, and everything sacred with
total abandon—rude epithets and all. This unique version of Tristan and Iseult
(note the Irish spelling, Iseult not Isolde) stands up as a busily plotted, nicely
unpredictable, adventure romantic travel sex comedy with a sarcastic edge. Its
most enduring and endearing feature is that it takes no prisoners."
—A.P., M.D., *Author's daughter*

"T&I strikes me as best fitted for reading in a train. It is not so funny that an
occasional interruption would be resented, and such thread of story as runs
through it can be grasped and followed without much strain on the attention."
—The Literary World, *July 27, 1892, 7-8*

"It is the shortest long novel I have ever read."
—C.S., *Obsessive reader*

"There is in the first tableau alone more life and movement
than in all of German literature."
—Carl Marx, *Political philosopher*

"It's fun when the poignant and the absurd are conjoined."
—V.K., *Creative writing instructor, Rice University*

"Literature at its finest! It frees us of ordinary nonsense
by taking us into a realm so weirdly absurd that it is ultimately settling."
—O.P., *Author's Mother*

"On the one hand, as his poems are highly aware of audience, extroverted, and
broadly theatrical (employing direct address, monologues, characters, zany
action, colorful mise-en-scenes, absolutely correct meter), so there might be a
fine line between what constitutes his poetry and what constitutes a tableau in
Patten's oeuvre. But his erudite (there is no other word) knowledge of art, science,
literature, history, etc. belies any simple reduction."
—Alex Cats, *Italian futurist*

"It must be confessed that the book had no merit to compensate
for its hopeless vulgarity, not even that of being amusing."
—The Athenaeum, *13 August 1892: 223*

"Your book is nonsense. No use. A waste of time.
You should be talking to a psychiatrist, not a publisher."
—Rejection letter, *One of many*

"The great tragedies and romances exalt unpragmatic protagonists like Tristan and Iseult inhabited by a reality they can neither abandon nor escape."
—F.B., *literary maven*

"Bernard and Patten are capable of melding science, philosophy, poetry (modern poetry, not the sort you can remember), and sheer whimsy into an elaborate meditation on mankind's mysteries. Starting simply, they build to unexpected metaphysical heights, achieving the redemptive quality of art.
—F.S., *Steelworker*

"What I like the best is the weird sense of non-direction and bizarre humor singularly lacking (probably for good reason) in so many other books. What I liked the least was the lack of vampires, zombies, and white and green dragons (there is a red dragon, however, when the Vikings attack the Irish, and a fiery red dragon gets extinguished in tableau 16)."
—S.S., *Correspondent*

"In Doctor Patten's book, we find ourselves in a surreal, time-collapsed dream murderously supercharged with virtual reality where postmodern characters loom large as historical and cultural archetypes."
—K.H., *Author's Friend*

"As this ancient story carries its strange preoccupations to their fullest expression, it's clear at times that the author is as naked as the characters who bear his writing. The book is best read as a richly sensual stylistic romantic exercise filled with audaciously beautiful imagery, captivating symmetries, and (sometimes) brilliantly facile language.
—Cinnamon Toast, *House Cat*

"This fluid-filled time-travel fantasia on violence, revenge, and sex discovers many unsettling contemporary resonances and has the look, touch, and feel of a sophisticated video game."
—J.P., *Author's brother*

"When the smoke has cleared, I predict this version of Tristan and Iseult will remain as one of the lasting monuments of American scholarship. Its loveliness and readability should not prevent us from recognizing what solid work has gone into it. This timeless classic will be read, reviewed, and studied for decades."
—Jeanine Jones, *Author's friend*

"His points are about society, the inability to love, the inability to perform sexual love in a creative way, the general fake nature of most of the stuff we are handed. Great comics throughout history always disguised through laughter, through jokes, an underlying theme which is of utmost seriousness, and which, perhaps, needs laughter because it is so painful."
—K.B., *high school English teacher testifying as an expert witness in the author's defense.*

"He's no Lenny Bruce, but he is in that tradition of nakedly honest rage at the deceptions all down the line in our society. Bernard and Patten share Pirandello's preoccupation with the elusiveness of any absolute, including absolute truth. After Vietnam and Watergate and Clinton and Little Bush and spin control, Enron, Global Crossing, PR, PC, scripted reality, and all that Mad(ison) Avenue deception and finally—Humpty Trumpty as president of the United States of America—is there any other reasonable position?"
— R.J.G., *jazz critic and columnist for the Enquirer, testifying as an expert witness in the author's defense.*

"At last, Mickey has produced a book that represents literature and not its antipodean opposite, commerce."
—S.P., *Author's sister*

"My God, Bernie! I'm wrung out. I'm amazed and incredibly jealous. This is a masterpiece. I'm agog—but I have much to say when next we meet. You are the only person I know who has a bigger, better vocabulary than I. And your courage in writing! Thanks for allowing me a small part in this. Much love."
—Earth Mother B.K. Reeves, *creative writing instructor, San Jacinto Junior College*

"Mick, in his compositional powers, confers greater and greater mental scope on any whim of the imagination so that the experience of reading becomes the experience of pushing back the horizons of thought. It leaves no doubt that Mick's achievement was one of combining, shaping, transforming, adapting, translating, and, in the final analysis, recreating material which already existed to proleptically approach true literature and the redemptive qualities of art."
—B.P., author's father

To which the author replies:
"The tableaux of this book are regressive, inexcusably innocent, too literary, overwrought, eminently Victorian, enigmatically and romantically sensuous. The characters have handsome androgynous figures wearing Gallo-Roman attire. Some are usually decadent or morbid like a Burne-Jones painting. Relentlessly busy, frequently sentimental, they help comprise a picture of a beautiful romantic dream of something that never was, never will be, in a light better than any light that ever shone, in a land no one shall visit, define or remember—only desire. All in all, this work signifies abstract airy nothing. But as we all know, signifying nothing can signify a great deal, not just a local habitation and a name, but the heart and core of Western literature and culture."

"Because my T&I demands considerable education and reflection, it represents the high culture that is now in some jeopardy. Absorbing as it is, its chief virtue is that it can be absolved of Dostoevsky's invariable flaw, tendentiousness. Nevertheless, reality in America is more grotesque and hilarious than any parodist could hope to trump. Contrasted with the truth of multiple modern corrupt practices in these dog days when lawyers and psychopaths rule the universe, my story is as tame as a holiday postcard."
—Nemo, *Houston, 2019*

"Cannot fiction devise a framework that is not so logical yet more suitable to its genius?"
—EM Forster

"A great while ago, the world begun,
With hey, ho, the wind and the rain."
—Shakespeare

To Arnold J. Toynbee, who (first?) awakened us to the
benefits of postmodern thinking.

&

To William H. Glass, who described metafiction as the product of authors who
better understand their medium.

IRISH BANTER

We waited and waited and waited, like those people in the Warner Bros. movie Casablanca. Bernard was to tell the story of Tristan and Iseult, their love, lives, and deaths together, the ancient romance while unlocking the adventure mystery of the pink martini. And we knew the conflicts: Tristan loves Iseult, and Iseult loves Tristan, but she also loves her husband, King Mark, Tristan's uncle, whom Tristan also loves and to whom Tristan owes his fealty and service. We expected plenty of sex, action, unusual plot twists and turns, rising action, climax, resolution, etc. but so far, we got nothing. Something is wrong. Hey—here comes Patten. He'll explain.

Patten, the producer, pushed through the crowd, headed to the podium, got there, cupped his hands and yelled, "The rumor is true."

No attention. In fact, the general uproar increased. So, Patten shouted all the louder, adding cadence and pace and distinctly emphasizing each word, **"I regret to inform you the rumor is true!"**

As this ominous message filtered through the throng, the din dimmed down. And on that stricken multitude, a sickly silence sat.

A young woman in the first row, an Ursula Andress look-alike, vintage 1964, rounded up her two talents, women's weapons to vanquish fate, and, pointing them in the right direction, (that is) straight at Patten, smiled like a big cat, adjusts her hair and asks in a Brooklyn accent, "We get our money back—when?"

Patten went red to the gills.

Well, he had fixed up a nice mess for himself. Looking at his Rolex, he muttered, "Not yet, sweetie. At the moment, Bernard's attorney, John Raley, is fast at work trying to get him out. Out on a technicality."

Her eyes became round as saucers. Her eyebrows rose in prodigious arches. Her jaw dropped. It was straight out of summer stock—the star turn of some ham actress playing melodrama in rep.

"Typical!" she cried. "My last boyfriend jilted me on a technicality. He claimed the pillows on my chest had driven him crazy."

Patten eyed her suspiciously and thought: She speaks truer than she thinks, for love and psychosis look pretty much the same on functional MRI (magnetic resonance image). Authors too numerous to list gave it for fact that love is a madness.

But who is she? And what is she? Oh, God. Is she another of these modern Western women dedicated to the destruction of male egos and, indirectly, masculinity? I know them. They have black bras with scalloped edges, multicolored condoms in their purse (some condoms even glow-in-the dark—neon—interesting effect), and they know exactly what they want in bed and tell you. They are not afraid to push your mouth in the right place and tell you, "Eat me!" And then some hit the #metoo trail with a press conference, followed by a lawsuit.

Or? Or? Or is she a BABE?

Patten put on his TV MC face, gazed at her lovingly, as a miser loves treasure, a glutton food, a king his crown. Miss Ursula look-alike looked good in that blue micromini. Just enough wrong to make her look right. And the two items on her chest did give her what Patten used to call in high school "personality." Was there anything more important than love? If there were, Patten couldn't imagine it. And just like that, on impulse, he wanted her to license up his roving hands and let them go before, behind, between, above and below her everything. She would be his America. His Newfoundland. His mine of precious stones. His empery. Where his hand would set, his soul would be.

"Let's talk about them, baby doll, your pillows, and your whole sad story. Let's talk over drinks—later."

Patten turned toward the crowd. "In divorce and in the law, technicality counts. Some say most of the law is technicality. Bernard's technicality was that he signed the voluntary commitment papers as Lord Motor-On. The clerks didn't pick up on that. Consequently, attorney Raley is making much of it."

(Patten resisted the temptation to launch into his diatribe about Law, which, though backed by (legal) force, has grown so hopelessly inflated and complex that not even a trained lawyer can be conversant with more than a single branch of it. Much of the complexity deliberately invented by Pluto, the god of wealth and Mercury, the god of thieves with, unfortunately, little or no contribution from Apollo, the god of science, wisdom, and knowledge.)

Some red-faced man in the audience cried out: "Was his motor really on? Ha ha ha!" He was laughing so much at his own joke he started choking, and it was some time before we could get the fit under control.

Patten: Very funny, a play on words. For those of you who are not familiar with the expression, "motor-on" is Irish slang for sexually excited. And the answer, dear Jimbo, is yes. Bernard's motor was on, is usually on, and will usually be on, now and forever. And his motor was on then—grandly and brilliantly on!

Patten drummed his fingers on the podium. They'd be wanting a refund. Merde! And double merde. Unless, unless.

He decided he'd fill the time with (what else?) a story. "Energy is sometimes grainy (quanta) sometimes a wave depending how we look at it!" Patten announced. "We don't investigate reality anymore. We make it. Make it up in our minds, our minds and wills in the form of stories, often little stories to explain things and make us feel better. Some say we make up God. That God is a story. A story we make, or we made, or both. You could say God, the story, exists to help us feel better."

That's what we expected from the likes of him, from Patten. Not from God. From Patten. We didn't expect God from the likes of him. No. From Patten, we expected bullshit. We expected bullshit, and that's what we got. But we expected a story, also. And more than that, we expected an Irish story. And, of course, we expected Patten to Irishly stretch the truth somewhat, as was his habit, in a story when a little stretching would improve the tale. The story we got—it wasn't the usual Birth, Initiation, Consummation, Repose, and Death. No, sir. It was just the facts—cold bloody facts:

"Here is what happened and why Bernard is not here to tell his tale. The most recent trouble started two weeks ago at the time that I (Patten) was crouched on the floor of my psychiatry office, trying to forget the hundreds of yellow phone message slips that littered my desk like autumn leaves on an unraked lawn. I was ignoring the fax machines that did not stop bleeping and squeaking and spitting out requests, complaints, demands, avowals, acknowledgments, declarations, unconstrained admissions, confessions, subpoenas, testimonials, and reports."

"All that meant nothing, for I had finally mastered the Asana. I had reached the astral plane. I had achieved union of myself with the universal spirit. And just as I had begun to meditate my thoughts away to nothingness, that little piece of dipshit, Bernard, interrupted."

"It's me, Patten. Got to talk."

"Listen, Bernard. I told you: Don't call. Especially don't call my cell."

"Emergency! Come to McHugh's. The Catholic mafia are after me."

"'Is after you.' 'Mafia' is singular. Furthermore, there is no Catholic mafia. JFK filled his cabinet with what he called the Irish mafia, but that, of course, was a joke. So, you don't have an emergency. An emergency means significant loss of life or limb is imminent. What you have is a paranoid delusion, one of many."

"Help!"

"Bernard, you're over the line."

"I'm on the verge, at the brink, but not over. Did you know that it is a proven fact by the Irish nationalists that an Irishman reached the moon long before the Americans and planted a statue of the Blessed Virgin Mary there, which powerful telescopes see and photograph every day? And that the fairies had their last convention in Dublin, Ireland in 1859 and decided they were no longer needed, so they moved no man knows where, but I think maybe they moved to San Francisco. I don't believe in fairies, but nevertheless, they are there. You have to speak nicely about them, or they turn nasty and ruin crops, water the whiskey, and cause inflammation of your knees. Most of these facts are quite unknown, mainly because they are boring, as boring as algebra."

"Put Himself back on. Too much learning, Bernard, hath made thee mad. Shut your fugghan mouth before they lock you up."

"Listen, Patten. I can't do it. For God's sake, let me skip Tristan's childhood and all that David Copperfield crap. Let me start the story in the middle, at a noble sirloin of beef when Tristan gets kidnapped by the Vikings."

"They were not Vikings. They were Norwegian pirates. Keep the story straight And don't insult the Vikings."

"Vikings, schmikings. Who cares? Does it matter? They were Viking, but they were not Vikings. Ha ha. Get my point? Verb versus noun. Let me entertain the group with action. Let me loosen the grip of reality on their human spirits. Let me take them out of themselves. Let me lift their souls to God. I promise I'll be great. I'll sing the peasantry, and then sing hard-riding country gentlemen, the holiness of monks, and, after, porter drinkers' randy laughter. Let me cover seven heroic centuries of the indomitable Irish, who refuse to know defeat even when it looks them straight in the face."

"Whoa!" moaned Patten. "It's straight in the eye. Eye contact! And who do you think you are? A reincarnated Yeats? I hired you to tell the story of Tristan and Iseult, their high tale of love and death in ancient Cornwall. Ancient Cornwall—the House of the Sun, Kanoël in Cornish. Do that. Nothing else. Start the story after Morgan conquers Kanoël. Take it straight through to the lovers' deaths. No, wait! That's too long. Take it through to Iseult's trial for adultery. Then we'll break for intermission and take up their exile and romance later. No, that won't do. Of course, end with their death. Every real story ends in death, and this story is real. And, oh yes, along the way, unlock life's greatest mystery. Teach these people that words are one thing, the raw force, the titanic personal passion we call love is another. I don't want them to hear about passion. I want them to feel it and see it in action. Prove your thesis: Love is stronger than death! The spiritual history of the indestructible Irish race must remain secondary. Capeesh?"

"I shall tell, and I shall not tell," said Bernard. "It's me own neck, so it is. The hand that knows its business can't be told to do work better or faster... those two things. Every real story ends in death. That's bullshit, an overgeneralization. Look at *Alice in Wonderland* and *Good Night Moon*. No deaths. *The Monkey's Paw* says Hebert died, but the story did not end with his death. It ended with wind blowing in the doorway."

"Bernard, you're around the corner. Put Himself back on. Whenever you misquote Frost and Hemingway and Yeats in the same sentence, I know you're gone—around the twist. But the logic does remain. Your counterexamples prove I overgeneralized. Part of you is sane."

"I'm as sane as you, Patten—and as sane as any parish priest."

"Patten, did you realize in Frieberg in the center of the city there are duck statues in honor of the ducks who came and quacked their heads off prior to air raids. Frieberg was bombed many times but never by surprise."

"That's it. Around the twist. You're off. Around the twist."

"No, nothing like that. Perhaps a little too much of the drink taken. I did stand a few rounds of Patty's for the group. But nothing like that. And I made some new friends named Harry and David. They're trying to organize a cheese of the month club with real cheeses sent from Israel. They call it *Cheeses of Nazareth*. And if that fails, they'll do fruits of the month.

"Patten, do you believe in fairies? The smallest thing in Ireland used to be the fairies. Now it's my bank account after a binge on the town. You must call them by affectionate names like "piskies or pobelveen"(Cornish: good people or good wee folks, Ed). When I asked an old woman whether she believed in fairies, she replied that she didn't, and then she spontaneously combusted. No, kidding."

"Zip it, Bernard. Your obsession with fairies proves you are insane. More ECT and Paxil is wanted. Put Himself McHugh on."

"He's not here. MacAdoo's bartender. Here's Hisself: Merciful Jesus, and he's abringing more of the creature, Black Bush from the Black North. God! Them's a great drink altogether. I'd go to jail for another."

And then, as usual, completely out of context, Bernard proceeded to tell his favorite joke:

"And did you hear the one that's going 'round about Peanuts at the confession: 'And you, did you, like the rest of them, throw peanuts in the river,' said the priest. "No, Father, I am Peanuts!'" (Believe it or not, that gem was one of Bernard's favorite stories, and he rarely missed an opportunity to hit its side-splitting hilarious punch line. Spare us, sweet Jesus, spare us. But the story reminds me of the old Irish joke about the new arrival in Hell. He was ushered into a room where thousands of the damned were standing waist-deep in excrement drinking tea. "Not as bad as I imagined," the newcomer thought. Then a little devil dashed into the room and shouted, "Teatime is over. Everyone back on their heads.").

"MacAdoo, watch Bernard. He's one sicko man. Last time he went off, he checked into the Great Southern Hotel in Galway City under the name "Lord Tristan" and ran up, on his American Distress card, 3,700 Irish pounds worth of long-distance telephone calls to a 900 sex number in San Jose, California. When I checked it out, I found that that number was run by Introservice, 1153 North Dearborn Avenue, Chicago. Intro is a dateline for women in prison, dealing exclusively with those about-to-be-released so men can meet them. Bernard kept asking the girls over and over the same obsessive question—"Have you an opening I can fill?"

"Ah, sure, t'was sex he had in mind," said MacAdoo, the shrewd. "And he might have a bit of trouble in that way as there is a huge woman here by the name of O'Hare who is waving her fists and shouting about neglect of promise and the guards and the gardai. She's a darling face, and those bouncy, high-gloss fire-red curls are worth all the money in the Allied Irish Bank. But I don't like her tongue bead. I have the feeling that she and Bernard had already been very, very wicked together because Bernard probably promised, you know. Jesus, I guess you can't have everything without giving something in return even if it's a fake promise."

"Right, MacAdoo. Sex and ultimate unemployment. Those two things—Bernard's downfall. And always with the girls. That's why I, for one, never believed what they said about him and the sheep."

"Besides, having reviewed various career prospects, he settled on becoming a saint. I advised that he not learn his saintly trade from women, although women are among the prime authorities on monastic life as they do frequent the places on a daily basis. But then, Bernard, finding monastic rules not to his taste, he decided to write his own or, rather, claimed they had been dictated to him by the Archangel Gabriel, just like the Koran, which came from the same angel in Arabic *Jibril*."

"Last week, in the lobby of the Shelbourne (Dublin), he accosted a novice nun, called her Iseult, and asked her the same question: "Have you an opening I can fill?""

"Poor girl, she took it the wrong way, complained to the gardai who brought Bernard to the hospital. He needed 32 wallops of ECT (electroconvulsive shock) to straighten his crooked brain. After the elative phase, came a massive depression, for which he needed eye-bulging doses of Paxil—*Pax ille*—peace to him—Paxil. Ought oh! No! I hear him singing. Is that he? Is His-self singing?"

"Nothing much; he's just giving his own Latin version of 'Galway Bay.' Now and then he stops and shouts, 'Fuck the begrudgers and the technocrats, ha ha ha.' Some of the regulars have called the gardai. Fat Lady O'Hare of the fire-red locks is screaming for them too. Neglect of promise—sounds like him, brilliant already. Bernard has a hold stable of neglects; Bernard does. Yes, drink has been taken."

MacAdoo displayed swear-sign fingers at the patrons. "Oh, pipe down, why don't you. You disgrace yourselves—once again. Pipe down. Else, no more drink."

Oh, God, that fixed 'em. The background noise dimmed down. The Irish fear no drink as much as they fear death—No! That's not exact: They fear no drink much more than they fear death or even Hell. Open a bottle of Jameson, and you get the fastest way out of Dublin. The creature is the Irish solution to a variety of problems, if not every problem. And it is getting bloody worse, for drink remains a refuse among the swelling army of the poor. With them, there isn't much else to do. It's an escape from poverty and hopelessness. Next to emigration, the bottle remains the quickest way to transcendence happiness. And some say God made alcohol for a purpose: To keep the Irish from dominating the world.

"MacAdoo, did Bernard make any calls?"

"No. He asked me to ring the Vicar of the local Church of Ireland. He said he was inspired to embrace Protestantism. Naturally, I did not place the call."

"O, Saint Dymphna, pray for him. (Saint Dymphna is the 7th-century Irish patron saint of lunatics—Ed)."

"That's it. He's off. Trapped again by the Irish Mental Health Act of 1947. The choice lies between voluntary insanity and compulsory insanity. Advise him to choose the first. Tell him that voluntary insanity will make him think better of himself, for it has a certain poetic ring to it. Voluntary insanity sets him apart. And integrates him with a group we know so well—romance writers, poets, tap dancers, copy editors, editors-in-chief, literary agents, book publishers, and professors of English."

"According to a recent ruling by the lunacy commission: Anyone can be insane by compulsion, but usually it's only writers and poets that volunteer."

Hey, wait! Raley's coming. Raley? What kind of a name is that? Sure, at some time, it must have been Reilly or O'Reilly until some drunken ancestor mispronounced it to some official, probably a hangman or judge. Don't let Bernard leave. For God's sake, don't let him *sign* a blessed thing. Tell him to keep his stupid mouth shut, for there is nothing in the language to match Irish poets in vindictiveness, except what has been said by the Anglo-Irish."

"Sorry, Patten, too late. *Commedia finita est.*"

"Attendants are arrived. Strangers in white. They're waving a paper, a paper in his face. They say he comes quietly, or they take him by force. And now, he's favoring them with a loud and slightly off-key rendition of "The Wearin' of the Green," which, I must say, he does better than that lugubrious lament for Robert Emmet, "She is far from the land where her young hero sleeps.""

Here Patten broke off his tale and fell into an apparent inner colloquy that itself held us, his audience, spellbound with curiosity. What the devil was he thinking?

What Patten was thinking I don't care to recall, so let's skip it. It was a box of stuff in the desk's bottom drawers: the lint in the navel of his private civilization, hinting with the usual Irish fatalism at an apocalypse that was nothing other than personal and private. It concerns us not, and I will not tell it for fear that the impatience of some readers would be so much fretted that they might hang themselves.

[Note from Editor: This isn't fair. Baiting the reader and then leaving her flat. So, here's a summary of what Patten was thinking. It's an escape from poverty and hopelessness. Next to emigration, the bottle remains the quickest way to transcendence happiness. And some say God made alcohol for a purpose: To keep the Irish from dominating the world. I don't have time to edit thoughts. And why should I? That's Patten's problem, not mine. But note that none of these thoughts match up with the description of them by our narrator (that is the narrator in the audience—this story has several narrators, and the one in reference here is in the audience reporting to us what she sees and thinks she sees, proving her unreliable, like most of us].

Here they are: Patten's thoughts at the moment:

1. That song (not The Wearin' of the Green, the other) reminded me of Sarah Curran, and Sarah reminded me of other beautiful women. And that association returned my attention again to the simpering and coquetry of the Ursula Andress vintage 64 look-alike *devant*. Although she had not directly accepted my invitation for drinks, the doe-eyed creature has been repeatedly crossing and uncrossing her long, sexy, darkly tanned legs. Now, she holds in her hand a gold Dunhill lighter (which I presume had descended from Mount Olympus disguised as a matchbook bearing an advertisement for a correspondence school in stenography). Anon, she lights one of

those ten-centimeter thin, low-tar things women smoke, drags, and exhales a pale white cone of smoke directly at my face. This is a good sign, for my psychiatry training fails me not: She is using the cigarette as a powerful erotic metonym. She is saying, "You are welcome to my cave. But first, you must negotiate with my dragon."

(At this point, the women in question, as if on cue, put her cigarette to her lips and took a long, deeply satisfactory drag. She looked like she was eating, not smoking. Had she taken her medicines today? Were they wearing off? Perhaps the cigarettes were her meds. The filters are mainly white in the United States, but yellow in Europe. Why? Probably so smokers can tell at a glance what continent they're on.)

2. "Poor soul," Patten thought. "She's no quitter. She's trading five minutes of life for five minutes of serenity. Yet, she's part of a lost American generation that doesn't know a real cigarette from a fake one; dolls who think they're smoking when they're just blowing whitened air. It's part of the general tendency to dilute experience. Decaffeinated coffee, low-nicotine tobacco, no-fat ice cream, sugarless gum, condomized sex, hot tubs that are not truly hot, medical students who get practice from actors and not real patients—all part of the one self-same wild rush to the blandness of TV melodrama. And what about dealcoholized alcoholic beverages? There was a champagne and a beer and (God help us) a virgin daiquiri. But so far, the conspiracy had not produced an Irish whiskey without alcohol. Thank God."

3. Would she, could she be a Molly? Yes, a Molly-pull-me-down to feel her breasts all perfume yes and my heart going like mad and yes she said yes I will yes I will yes!

4. That's it, babe. I'm kidnapping you. You're going home with me. Wonder what Andress would look like undressed? Naked! That's what women are made for. Big tits and hips. Lucky day for me.

From where Patten stood, he smelled her perfume. Sweet and lovely with a high note of gardenia, a middle faint note of citrus—a combination of lime and oranges—a bass note of earthy red beet.

5. And as usual, before his thoughts stood ever the same problem: How would it turn out when the trolls came? Would he be able to hack off their heads and wrest the kingdom from their power? It might happen that he would be going about with some object in his hand and would suddenly grip it hard; all his strength would be needed to wield the enchanted sword. For these would be archtrolls, no less.

6. She might be married. Never smoke another man's pipe: (Ed. that Irish adage is not about smoking or pipes) A more heinous crime than meddling with another man's wife can hardly be imagined. In fact, the crime was so dark that a special punishment after death was meted out to it. The visionary literature of the Middle Ages gives many examples, as does Dante. No need to illustrate such horrors. But if the husband says OK, is it OK? Condonation exists as a legal principle, why not in real life?

7. Was he in his body or out of his body? He scarcely knew. For Patten was trying to move in a great bubble of imagination that he had never known the likes

of in all the years (about 40) of his life that he had been trying to escape the fetters imposed by writing class protocol and the stupid conventions of literature. At last, he approached the redemptive quality of art. Here was his chance to walk the walk, talk the talk, balk the balk, cork the cork.

8. No no no. Stay logical. No clang associations. No rap. Liberate the human spirit with power and freedom. Temper imagination with judgment. Grasp the artistic power of constraint. Free the human spirit with power and pathos. The freedom is implied in the word liberated. Oh, fuck. Don't think. Just have the experience. See where it goes.

(Editor's note: Here ends the summary of Patten's thoughts, a bunch of fantastic assumptions and extrapolations thereof. Mostly a pack of lies. And all the while this was going on, Patten felt he was on the ceiling looking down at himself and the audience. Derealizations of that sort are not unusual in those with weak and weakening egos and, of course, are characteristic of psychotics.)

"Bernard is unreliable. The day of his ordination, sacred oils were not dry on his palms when he used those lubricated hands to commit heinous cardinal sins by fiddling with his you-know-what. Bernard stupidly confessed the dirty details of his decline into depravity, and they exiled him to Craggaunowen, a small, cold, bare, dark, dreary, dull, dirty, monastery on the Burren, that Irish mess of stony rubbish in western Ireland, 3,612 miles from Brooklyn."

"A tree may grow in Brooklyn, but nothing grows in Craggaunowen Burren except a few wildflowers in the crevices and crannies between the crags, grikes, clints, fissures, and sink-holes and then only after exceptional rains that rarely come."

"Bernard hardly spoke to the monks, reticent mystical men, holy water addicts, mostly culchies, who seemed like dozy humpback whales occasionally surfacing from the abyss to periscope the horizon, and sing Gregorian Chants, and then submerge themselves again in the fathomless depths of Irish (un)consciousness."

"How do you know this stuff?" asked Miss Legs waving her cigarette at Patten.

"He told me. For God's sake. I'm his psychiatrist, and I am trying to give you backstory so you will understand him, and I am trying to fill the time while hoping Bernard shows. OK?"

"He needs a woman, not a psychiatrist."

"Great insight! How did you know?"

"I've been around."

"What's your name, baby doll?"

"Sinéad (pronounced ShaNADE ed.). And don't call me baby doll."

'Sinéad! Must be Irish, what.'

"OK, Sinéad, no more baby doll for you. What say you, honey buns? Let's see where Bernard's headed and why."

"Each morning, Bernard continued to empty himself, claiming if he did not, there would be no room in his mind for God. Even then, he was plagued by a sexual thought every 27 seconds. The silence of God bothered him, so the devil approached, spoke to him in pictures (in dreams) of naked women and images of magnified breasts that appear and disappear with every speck of nipple russet showing clear. Usually, Bernard awoke, unable to move. Short of breath. A night terror, but the abbot thought it a medical emergency, possibly a heart attack, which it was, but an attack of the heart of the natural propensities related to the command of God to be fruitful and multiply.

"A Catholic nun, a certain Sister Lucy, came and examined him in his monk's cell. He remained seated in an osier wicker chair while Lucy stood beside him close up, taking his pulse from his limp right wrist. Her breasts, as in the dream, close up and gigantic, projected out at the level of his mouth, nice shapes despite her nun's habit. He looked up at the mounds and then at her face and herself. She flashed bright green eyes, Irish eyes, licked the corner of her upper lip, moved her index finger along the rim of her right ear, and smiled. 'And how would you be liking the scenery here on the Burren?' says she."

"Lucy puffed her chest the more. Doorbell shapes pressed tight against her white cloth, nipples erect.

Desperately, Bernard clanked away. Prayed again, what he had so often prayed, Our Fathers in Latin with emphasis on the ne nos inducas in tentationum (lead us not into temptation) but deliver us from evil. He tried to focus on the bright yellow crucifix that hung on the opposite wall. He tried to think of Jesus Christ and the sacrifice Our Lord made to redeem the sins of the world and, by logical extrapolation and particular subsumption, the sins of the likes of him. But his infirm mind kept returning to the obsession. His undisciplined and undisciplinable roaming and Black Irish eyes (Bernard is Black Irish) now smiling, focused again on Lucy's mounds.

"Scenery, I like it fine," he said, eagerly appreciating the wrong scenery. "I like it fine, indeed."

"Lucy took his hand and coached it under her garb. "I was thinking in my mind that you were the kind of man that appreciated beauty," she said.

"And so, they both, Bernard and Lucy, monk and nun, man and woman, lover and lover, fell into grievous mortal sin."

"Time runs on. Lucy visited daily. She gave him her special nursing treatments, her special nursing service. The other monks marveled at the effectiveness. The abbot knew the therapy worked because Bernard no longer confessed self-abuse. Lucy had cured his nasty habit.

"Oh, well, a secret love often desires to be free. They were discovered and Cardinal Spellbound, with the full approval of the archbishop, (who, by the by, had to be disturbed from his weekly Sunday visit with his sister) sent Bernard to exile in the Arans, those desolate islands on the bleak Atlantic coast off Galway Bay.

"We Irish know the Arans as Arana Naomh, literally *Aran of the Saints* because so many Irish saints have passed time there, particularly in the fifth and eighth centuries. The Arans are typical of western Ireland, desert without man, desolate, forsaken, naked, uninhabited, with wild tracts of purple heather, grey rocks, tall salt grasses, sea, sky, and nothing."

"Bernard lived in Kilronan on Innismore, the capital, population 42. He lived like the hermits of old in a stone hut, the Clochan, shaped like a beehive, or the nose cone of a rocket."

"He lived in the same way Saint Edna lived when he taught school there in 814. But he did something the saint (probably) never did."

"Mrs. O'Biataigh (O'Beatty in English), a widow of some five years of the much-lamented Price O'Beatty of Bride street, supplied Bernard his breakfast. And, the archbishop, in his kindness, allowed weekly visits from Bernard's sister, Lucy McCabe, who arrived each Sunday afternoon by way of the ferry from Galway across the bay."

"These halcyon days lasted three months until widow O'Biataigh declared in the confessional that the Holy Ghost had made her pregnant. That became the talk of the town, for the Holy Ghost had not visited a woman of Aran for over two years since Maureen O'Hara had gotten in a family way while attending the Irish language school at Innisheer, the smallest island of the three Arans."

"O'Beatty swore it was the Holy Ghost, so the church sent investigators from Rome to study the miracle. But they concluded that O'Beatty had fallen into grievous mortal sin. Then, O'Beatty, under pressure from the one attorney in town, Mister Tulkingtorn, filed a paternity suit against Bernard and named as correspondents the Holy Ghost and the One Holy and Apostolic Catholic Church. Among other vile things, she alleged that after Bernard ate the black and white puddings and sour brown breads she had brought, Bernard would take her every day from behind "like a heifer.""

"The all-male jury came in with the verdict 'not proven' because they all knew O'Beatty, shall we say, had been user friendly to other men of the Arans including Sean O'Flaithbheartaigh (John O'Flaherty), between jobs, Terrence O'Toole, the fishmonger, and a certain obscure man named Jude Fawley, the stonemason who was already married to Susan, a nice but passionless woman from Christminister, England."

"So, Bernard won his case, but as often happens, lost his reputation. Cardinal O'Brien deflocked and defrocked Bernard straight away. And that ended his job, or rather his meal ticket, for he never did any useful work either at Craggaunowen or on the Arans or anywhere for that matter. A defrocked priest is a pitiable thing. He can't say mass, he can't hear confessions, he can't exorcise devils, he don't put a bolt to a nut, he don't tell you the law, he don't give you medicine. He has no saleable skill. He... Well, I think you get my point. My point is that..."

Before Patten got to his point, whatever it was, if indeed he had a point, the group jumped to their feet, mad with a general ovation, for Bernard, the Bardic Narrator, who had just entered stage right, was full striding toward the podium.

(At this point, a real writer might have shown you, readers, how Bernard was bizarrely dressed in a long blue flowing robe and wearing a black conical hat on which were embroidered yellow suns, moons, and stars. His rough disheveled look might have suggested he had too much of the drink taken. Such descriptions are OK, I guess. But they rarely get to the heart of the matter, rarely tell us what the character is really about. So, let's skip it.)

Bernard nodded, pumped several times with his right arm, reached under the podium, and took a swig of Black Bush, the whiskey made in Antrim in the Black North.

(Black North refers to the six counties in northern Ireland that should be part of the Irish Republic, but that are under the control of the foe of mankind, the British. Ed.)

Password of the Irish Republican Army: Question: Do you believe in a united Ireland? Answer: The island's united, the people divided. At last, a password which expresses meaning and truth!

The house lights dimmed.

The audience sat hypnotized for a minute, silent and motionless in their places as though drunk or in a transport. All this, with what preceded and what followed, occurred with such involutions of rapidity that past, present, and future seemed one.

Happy they were, for they, like you, dear reader, are now about to enter the magical world of narrative time.

Suddenly the room held a predawn dark. And in that stygian gloom, we heard rapid roll and roar of deep-mouthed thunder. And then, (showing its fictional tag by) reversing the order of nature, there followed vast displays of refulgent lightning, with a wind that had a howling edge to it, loping oak leaves, the smell of ozone, and the heady reek of cold, wet stone.

And amid the chaos of wrack and storm, Bernard let out his own thunderous bark and bawl: "Tristan and Iseult, their high tale of love and death in ncient Cornwall, House of the Sun."

"Have the scene arrange itself as it will seem to do. Earth is the right place for love. I can't think of anywhere it's likely to go better. And in an atmosphere of Juliette's tomb, too, for Earth is the right place for death. I can't think of anywhere it's likely to go worse. So, love and death—ancient themes of ancient Eire, the Western Isles, O favored land. Muse of history, Clio, is it? O honored Muse, tell the tale."

TABLE OF CONTENTS

Tristan Kidnapped

◆———————◆———————◆

Tristan mated with his queen.

(Get it? This double entendre is foreshadowing, a play on words, and an inside joke. Eventually, that's what Tristan does: mates the Queen Iseult. Pretty stupid, n'est-ce pas? Ed.).

Tristan mated with his queen, looked up from the chessboard, and smiled. That smile turned to chagrin as the universe contracted, and its exact geometric center floated before his mind. Inexplicably, the ship had left port and was now far out upon the wine-dark sea. Or was it now far out upon the snot-green sea? Homer or James Joyce? Wine suggests fun and life. Snot suggests sickness and death. Take your pick. The sea can be both. Often is. Just like life.

Tristan, as the chronicles of the time inform us, was a year or three on the right side of 20 in the year of our grace 525. To be exact, it was Tristan's 17th birthday. Does it matter? Past and future are equally nonexistent—nonexistent nothings, for the past no longer exists, and the future does not exist either—not yet. So, the one thing that exists, the only thing that exists is the present. And that present is with us, but only for an instant. Even the present soon becomes nothing. Clicks away, flies from us. Yes, flies, like migratory birds, headed south. But in this, our narrative present, things are artificially prolonged and thus a bit more stable, so let's get back to it.

It is an evening peculiar to the Brittany coast: mute and calm, gray surtout, troubled leadened vapors low and fitful over the waters, shadows present, foreshadowing deeper shadows to come, and the sky above—the sheltering sky above is the color of a TV tuned to a defunct channel.

Considering the lawlessness and loneliness of the spot, and the sort of stories at this era that are associated with the seas, Tristan's jolt might have deepened into notable uneasiness had he not been a person of a singularly trustful nature. He was a youth not liable, except on extraordinary and repeated incentives, and hardly then, to indulge in personal alarums anyway involving the imputation of malign evil in man or nature. In this respect, and in many other respects, Tristan differed from his contemporaries who feared and feared and feared. Remember, these are not medieval times. These are pre-medieval. The past is a different country. They did things differently there. They also saw things that we don't. Christ at dinner. Ghosts and devils and angels flying about. That stuff.

Were they all batty?

Doubtful.

Think about this: They lived in one shitty town their whole life long. Their kids got the runs and dropped dead. By age 18, if they lived that long, they had six teeth left in their heads. Most were coughing blood from cavitary TB. One year later, like Keats, arterial bleeding from the lungs seals their fate. Historians consider it would have been better, a lot better, just committing suicide. But there was really no need to kill yourself since disease was very likely to do it for you. Major epidemics of smallpox, rabies, and famine fever struck every generation from the third to the sixth century. The only cure was prayer and applying saintly relics to yourself. Relics were expensive and surprisingly didn't always work. To the peasants of old times, the world outside their own direct experience was a region of mystery, a mystery as dim as the winter life of swallows that came back with the spring. You would think this hard life would shake their trust in God. Nope! To people like us who are accustomed to reason about things, it is difficult to enter into that simple, untaught state of mind in which form and the feeling have never been severed by an act of reflection or elementary logic.

Sic transit gloria mundi.

These people, our-not-so ancient ancestors, had to do something to jazz things up; they had to do something to amend their miserable existences when tired at looking in fear and sullenness at their unpropitious deity. Not having TV (which is silly and fake) or drugs to escape, they made up stuff to keep their little minds from going ga-ga. They made up stuff just the way those guys locked in solitary at Gitmo get hallucinations.

From the back of the room, a white rabbit, dressed in tux and tails, who seemed to have wandered in from some other story, opened a parchment scroll and read, "More story, less lecture!"

"Captain Cereno, sir," said Tristan, for the Captain's name was Bjornito Cereno. "Sail back to shore."

The Captain's manner conveyed a sort of sour and gloomy, faintly amused disdain, which he seemed at no pains to hide or disguise. Bjornito Cereno made no reply but stared at Tristan and then wrinkled his nose in disgust as if Tristan were a smelly piece of warm black shit.

Tristan felt an apprehensive twitch in the calves of his legs. He looked down to check them. The shadows of his legs were cast precisely by photons that traveled 93 million miles to this exact spot. Think about that! Such photons were generated one million years ago, scientists said, in the center of the sun. Those photons, the message carriers of the electromagnetic force, escaped the sun's surface only eight minutes and 18 seconds before, and by not passing through Tristan's legs have cast the shadows which Tristan is now pondering.

To think too much about light is to think too much. Was light refrangible before the flood? How could it be, else God could not have created the rainbow as a sign of his promise not to flood again. On his deathbed, Einstein said that the speed of light was the secret of understanding the universe. He was about to explain, but he croaked. Too bad. The autopsy showed a ruptured aortic aneurysm. Therefore, an aortic aneurysm prevented mankind from knowing the secret of the universe.

Tristan's mouth went dry. There arose a vague ache in the pit of his stomach. A feeling of nausea that had nothing to do with the sea. Do fish get seasick?

An alteration of courtesy and gross ill-breeding in the Captain seemed unaccountable, except on one of two suppositions—innocent lunacy or wicked imposture or both, taking the logical operative "or" in its inclusive sense, meaning both things were possible.

Tristan thought: The Captain lost the chess game. Big deal. Does he have to turn sulky? Some people these days are such complete sore heads. They take games seriously, too seriously. The Captain and everyone need to lighten up.

Tristan tried to follow his own advice (lighten up) and tried again, this time, in that stilted formal form of address in common use in those days and in common use these days in legal documents and both houses of parliament (and other cultural backwaters like the U.S. Senate), "Captain, sir, I am afraid I must insist on being returned forthwith to shore so as to not be late for my birthday party."

Captain Bjornito Cereno faltered, then, like some somnambulist suddenly interfered with, vacantly stared at his visitor, and ended confusedly by looking down at the board and then at the aft deck.

Tristan felt a chance phantom cat's paw—an islet of cold breeze, unheralded, and unfollowed—come fanning at his cheek. His glance fell on the passageway near a dark hatch leading down into the steerage, perceiving motion there. In the same instant, he saw one of the prowling sailors hurriedly place his hand in the bosom of his frock, as if hiding something. Before Tristan could be certain, the sailor slunk out of sight.

What was that which so sparkled? thought Tristan. It was no lamp, no match, no live coal.

"It's a knife, stupid," shouted an old man from the back of our room.

Bernard nodded, "Yes" and took a swig from the fifth of Black Bush, which he produced again from under the podium. No, No. Swig's not right. More like a draught, a big draught. This is a violation of protocol as Bernard is a poet, and as everyone knows, wine is the correct drink for poets. Consequently, Ben Johnson, as poet laureate of England insisted on being paid in Sack. He was. Also got a free coach to drive him around London. Those were the good old days as opposed to the bad new days we have now. Poets had respect then, lots of it and, believe it or not, got paid.

Tristan's vision moved jerkily back into focus but sweat dripped into his left eye. The fingers that wiped it shook like a drunkard's. Before he could tell himself to be careful, the Captain fell at Tristan's feet and shouted, "Give way for your life, m'boy!" (there was a second of charged silence) "and save me too, for God's sake save me!"

The Captain's lunge and shouts added wildly to the atmosphere and started a clattering hubbub in the ship, above which now rang the alarm tocsin.

The Captain roared, "These bloody plotting pirates mean murder, murder most foul as in the best it is, but this one most foul, strange and unnatural!"

Tristan had no chance to draw his sword; two sailors, each the size of a beer truck, grabbed Tristan from behind, took him below, and locked him in the hole with Gorvenal, his wise squire. Later, the Captain was thrown in with them.

I won't describe the hole except that it was dark, littered with used condoms and beer cans, and had the reek of a crack den that I once had to remove my friend Larry Elmer from. Squalor. Terrible squalor. Yes, squalor. But more than that, it smelled of death.

In the inky blackness, the Captain explained. "We are Normans from the Nordland who pursue a new kind of economic enterprise called Viking, designed to generate higher than the usual hedge fund's rates of return on invested capital by employing risky procedures called 'pillage,' 'plunder,' and 'burn.' In that order. If you burn first, there isn't much left to pillage and plunder."

(Note: Vikings helped to preserve a lot of precious Irish objects by a technique known as stealing. The objects were kept in treasure-hoards, which we will stumble upon later in this story. Ed.)

"Our *modus operandi* involves nosing our longship through mists that lay on the coast. Our prows are painted ferocious with wooden dragons in colors of fire and blood. These are designed to strike terror in the hearts of those who watch from cliffs and drumlins. When the frightened multitudes flee, as they almost always do, the crew takes whatever they can. Simplicity itself—mean and bold stealing from others, as told in the Sagas and Donald Trump's latest book, *The Art of the Steal*."

Gorvenal, Tristan's squire and teacher, as usual, used the opportunity for a lecture:

"Those unskillful in black arts," began his discourse, "have always found it easier to supply their wants by rapine than by industry, and from time to time pour in upon the habitations of peaceful commerce, as hawks descend upon domestic fowl. Their celerity and fierceness make walls, locks, and weapons necessary, and their ignorance makes such devices efficacious. Pretty much like the Wolf of Wall Street, they make no useful product, produce no useful service. They merely steal." Thus spoke Gorvenal, The Worthy.

Tristan's squire and teacher was right, although his voice was toneless, and his language wordy, pleonastic, and supererogatory. In a nutshell, he said that some people would rather steal than work. That certainly is true on Wall Street, where their version of the golden rule is "Do unto others before they do unto you." Wall Street needed, during the last crisis, a bailout of 7.7 trillion dollars. Good thing the dollar isn't worth much nowadays. Otherwise, that would have been real money.

Gorvenal again: "We have Vikings here too. There are more millionaires in this country than in any other and at the same time more robbers and killers and more people in jail. Extremes in riches make extremes in crime. As long as the social system permitted the acquisition of extreme riches, there would be equalizing crime, and the government and all law-enforcement organizations might as well fold their tents. Prisons are pimples on a corrupt world. The great criminals, the real enemies of man's welfare and peace and happiness, never go near a prison. They have the highest tombstones over their heads. Them capitalist fellows are thieves; they rob widows and orphans. But they're smart enough not to use guns. Behind every great fortune—a crime."

The Captain scratched his head and seemed to agree with Gorvenal, but he wasn't quite sure what he (Gorvenal) was driving at. Was this all part of some long-buried tribal Jungian memory prompting us to get ready for a tougher future?

The Captain continued his exposition:

"Due to too much competition, and too many exhausting raids, the towns and villages in Anglia (old England), Eire (Ireland), and Transalpine Gaul (France) have been depleted. In short, the Viking business has turned frosty and is lousy. Consequently, the able-bodied seamen, who had been promised much and who had got nothing, mutinied, killing all the ship's officers except the few, like myself, who are needed to navigate."

"Whoa," shouted an old man in the front row center while jabbing the spittle laden stem of his Petersen Classical bent apple smoking pipe. "Back to the story, creep, or we walk. What the devil do the Viking problems have to do with the romance of Tristan and Iseult? Move from the intellectual to emotion, from summary to experience. And don't forget the four C's: Conflict, Character, Compassion, and Change."

"Thank you, Mr. O'Casey," said Bernard as he reached under the podium again. "In a certain sense, you are a conflict and a character and a change. But I agree with you that this seems not related to the Tristan story, except all the ancient texts talk about the Vikings and how Tristan was kidnapped. This must have been on their minds, the way we moderns are concerned about the World Trade Center thing, the Boston Bombs, multiple mass shootings, the opioid crisis, Trump's simplistic thinking and so forth. In telling you about the Vikings, I am merely following the ancient storytellers."

(Why, oh why, oh did I take 55 writing classes? I thought I had a calling. A calling to do literature, not litter-a-ture. When I visited Yeat's grave. I knew it. You know the one under old Ben Bulben: "Cast a cold eye, on life, on death, horseman, ride by.")

The caretaker played a tape made by the poet just before his death: "It is the duty of every Irish poet to rework the legend of Tristan and Iseult." That was Yeats speaking to me. The voice of the dead poet was alive and speaking, speaking to me. A shiver went down my spine. It applied. No choice. I have to do it. *N'est-ce pas?*)

Do you understand?

You? Who the Hell are you? That's what someone must be saying now. Is that you? Is that what you, dear reader, are saying? "Who's this?" Or thinking? "What's up? What's happening? Who's telling this story? What time is it? Where are we now? How many narrators do we have? Bernard? Patten? The author? Someone in the audience? One or more editors? The monk who is transcribing the manuscript and translating it? Who?"

Whew! This really is metafiction, postmodern metafiction at that. Some people like it; some don't. It takes all kinds to make a world.

Now for a confession:

OK Reader. Hell, I'm the guy pulling the strings on Bernard and Patten, who are pulling the strings on Tristan and Iseult and the others. I'm the guy talking. I'm the guy making the story. It all goes far, far back to the primitive origin of our race. Around the campfire, someone is talking telling stories while the dopes nod off from the day's fatigue of hunting and gathering. And I am addressing you directly, dear reader, with my reasons for writing this book. So, pay attention, please. I am telling you this story because William Butler Yeats came back from the grave and told me in person to rework the story of Tristan and Iseult. Notice Yeats said rework not retell, but, of course, I do both by intermingling fiction with truth about love, death, and various other assorted aspects and topics of interest to you humans.

Speaking of which—let's get back to the ship's black hole and see what's what.

Into that stygian darkness, a delegate of the desperadoes, a man named Dunstan (or was it Dylan? I'm pretty sure it started with a D. Or was it an F? No matter) who was born in a small town of La Mancha, the name of which I don't care to recall, had a broken nose and a battered visage which looked like a potter's error—a "reject for export" face—confirmed the Captain's grim story and added that the crew intended to collect a ransom or, that failing, sell Tristan in the Middle East as a sex slave. As for Gorvenal, Tristan's mentor, he was dead meat, useless to them. Him they would deep-six. (Ed. Old navy slogan: If it's dirty, paint it. If it doesn't work, deep-six it, meaning, Heave it overboard into the deep six (fathom) sea.)

And speaking of the sea, as if on cue, suddenly, a great storm blew up, for the weather on the French coast was as risky as a dot com stock or a subprime mortgage for 756 thou issued to a Hispanic maid in Merced, California who earns $7.25 an hour.

The sailors, superstitious lot that they were, said that the god of the sea who hates all felonies and rapine was angry and about to punish them.

"Poppycock! Utter poppycock and gimcrackery" chortled Dunstan, his small brown eyes nested deep in wrinkled flesh. (His ugliness was the stuff of legend, for this was an age before affordable beauty, before plastic surgery).

Dunstan chortled, dismissing such talk as gimcrackery; for they had not seen the "blood light," the sky's otherworldly red that deeply frightens Nordic people as it foretells war or misfortune or both. What, me worry?

(Editor's note: Chortle is a factitious word introduced by the author of *Through the Looking Glass* applied with some suggestion of chuckle and snort. I was unable to find Gimcrackery in my Oxford English Dictionary, but I have seen the word used in Neuromancer, where it seems to indicate a kind of scamp. It is playfully used as a mild term of reproof.)

Dunstan was absolutely sure he was right. But the other sailors seemed concerned. Blood light or no. Trouble was coming, and they feared it might arrive soon.

But when the mizzen and then the mainmast blew off and the day turned stygian, atramentous, and starless, two sailors were sucked (poor souls) off the deck and into eternity. 'Tis a serious matter to lose a ship when you are on it, so the men refused to obey until the boy was put ashore.

Dunstan smelled his own stale sweat.

Dunstan or Funstan, whatever, poured the sumbel, a ritualized toasting to the gods, first to Odin, then a few drops for Loki (the trickster to ward off nasty surprises), then to ancestors and the honorable dead, and last to whomever members of the crew could think of. After nominations had closed, nothing happened.

Shit!

Once again, the libations failed. Those Norse gods never did measure up or put out, which is the reason that they were replaced by God the Father, the Son, and the Holy Ghost, who never did measure up or put out either but were said to. Good PR makes all the difference—for a time, for a time. Take away the mumbo-jumbo, and you got nothing. Religion is often like that—GIGO: garbage in, garbage out. Praying has been studied scientifically. There are ten controlled studies in the medical literature, each with age- and sex-matched controls, each showing no effect on the health outcomes of prayed-for patients, except one study which showed the prayed-for group did worse than the patients not prayed for. People dislike atheists, but you know, atheists don't bomb anyone, behead anyone, stone anyone, burn anyone at the stake, crucify anyone, or fly planes into skyscrapers.

A giant rogue wave pooped the deck, almost broaching the boat, causing Dustan to change his mind. "Discretion is the better part of valor," he remarked. "And I take the better part. Lads, put the lad ashore."

This decision made, the sea calmed. The winds ceased. The air cleared. And the lonely moon's light returned with an eye-squinting brightness, radiating nine beams, broad as planks.

Because of shoals, and a lee shore, the pirates couldn't get close in. So, in the cold and in the sheer, unremitting loneliness of that moonlit night, Tristan dove over the taffrail and swam furiously against tide and hypothermia. A tremendous wave swept him forward to the rugged shore, where his skin would have been torn off, and all his bones broken, had not he got it into his head to grab hold of a rock with both hands as he sped by. He clung there groaning while the great wave passed.

No sooner had he escaped its fury than its backward rush caught him with full force and flung him far out to sea. For Tristan, it was like a blow in the stomach with the end of a log. Pieces of skin stripped from his sturdy hands were left sticking to the crag like the pebbles stick to the suckers of a squid when it is torn from its lair.

Tristan prayed to Albertus Magnus, teacher of Saint Thomas, and patron of men of science, who, though religious, believed that objective evidence is the ultimate authority. According to Albertus, humans may lie, but nature is incapable of it. What he was saying was that reality is real, and everything else is not reliable. Without actual evidence, you just don't know.

Hey, reader, still awake. Still with us?

There has to be a way out of this mess. The story has hardly begun. Please, Heaven, intervene in an unobtrusive way. Thou who strengthened Jacob so that he overcame the angel on the rock, please, pretty please, strengthen Tristan.

Sometimes, truth be told, Tristan felt the saints were laughing at him. Do they laugh at us in Heaven? Saint Maisie of New York herself—remember her—she died of a laughing fit. Today might well be Maisie's feast day, for Tristan thought he heard a woman laughing. And then a chorus of Greek Gods and Goddesses who, we are informed by Homer, laughed their heads off at all things human. And our God himself does the same. Our God must have a cosmic sense of humor to let J.P. Morgan Chase lose 2 billion dollars on bad trades and also have to pay 13 billion dollars in fines about bad mortgages. Serves them right. That's what you get for being money-mad instead of production-oriented.

Vexilla regis inferni prodeunt.

(Editor's note: Smarty-pants author again showing off. His is a quote from the famous Commedia: "Forth come the banners of the King of Hell." It nagged in his head like an earworm tune and means in this context that more Hellish trouble was expected soon. He was right, of course, because he is writing the story and presumably knows what is going to happen next.)

Story question: At this point, can Tristan take care of himself? Which entails a larger question: Is a single man alone, able to look out for himself? A million years of human history refutes the ridiculous Hemmingway idea that one man alone ain't no bloody fucking good.

Tristan struggled to the surface, swam clear of the coastal breakers, and then swam along outside them, keeping an eye on the land, in the hope of lighting on some natural harbor with shelving beaches. His progress brought him to the mouth of a fast-running stream, which seemed to be the best place because it was clear of rocks and sheltered from the winds. The stream's current checked the forward thrust of waves and allowed Tristan to wade in safely.

Tristan's knees gave way, and his sturdy arms sagged. And at a short distance from the water's edge, exhausted by his struggle with the sea, he collapsed. His flesh was swollen, and streams of brine gushed from his mouth and nostrils. His head was bloody but unbowed. Winded and speechless, he lay there too weak to stir, overwhelmed by terrible fatigue.

The forces of nature are indifferent to human plight. The sea has no appreciation of great men, not even of Tristan, but knocks them about. Often, too often, humans aren't much help either, for they are as indifferent to human plight as the indifferent forces of nature. Blow, blow, thou winter wind. Thou art not so unkind as man's ingratitude—something like that. Shakespeare, right?

An English dog walker, unfazed by watching these events, asked Tristan in a crisp British accent, "Been swimming, then?"

Blue-lipped Tristan managed to nod while gesturing with both hands out, begging for help, palms up like a suppliant. "Jolly good show," the man said as he and his dog disappeared into the fog, ignoring Tristan's distress.

In that moment, if he had any taste for the niceties of language, any insight into how language reveals the character and psychology of a race, Tristan would have experienced something of the thrill of contact with his first real Englishman. Jolly good show indeed.

The river wound in and out in its pretty delicate curves, looking like a silver serpent beneath the glittering rays of the moon. Not far from the river, Tristan found a copse of trees in a clearing. Here he crept under a pair of bushes, one a hawthorn and the other a woodbine (a type of honeysuckle). These two shrubs grew together with their branches so closely intertwined that when the damp winds blew, not a breath could enter, not the rays of the sun penetrate their shade, nor the rain soak through. The plants in their private world on the entwined bank were as two lovers, intimately and intricately folded together, not separable, except with greatest difficulty and then only with the destruction of both.

(Editor: This beautiful poetic metaphor of passionate love is foreshadowing, predicting—oh Hell, I'm not about to give away the spectacular ending of this great romance. Hang in there, friend. It gets stranger, and better.)

Tristan crawled into his shelter, and at once heaped up the dry leaves into a wide bed—the ground was littered with piles of them, enough to provide covering for two or three men in the hardest coldest worst winter weather and the wide weltering waves.

In this dry bower, Tristan slept listening to the dull low-pitched rhythmic concussion of waves against the granite teeth of the Cornwall headlands. The pitch was an A (440 Hz), concert A, the same that haunted syphilitic Robert Schumann at the end of his days.

To learn what Tristan did when he awoke, turn to the next tableau, Tableau Deux.

Tristan Meets His Uncle, King Mark

ZZZZZzzzzzzzz.

In the morning, hungry and chilled, but refreshed by sound sleep, Tristan climbed the cliffs on the southwestern coast of Cornwall at Land's End about 40 miles south-south-west of King Mark's summer castle at Tintagel. Here at Lantyan were forests ancient as the hills enfolding sunny spots of greenery with gardens bright with sinuous rills, where blossomed many an apple-bearing tree.

Apple trees at Lantyan. Tristan and Iseult met here often in secret.

The author and his wife Ethel were here to get the feel of the place.

(Editor's note: The allusion to Eden appears deliberate and was probably copied directly from some English poet. It is a fact that the main apple orchards were at King Mark's winter castle (castle D'Or) at Lantyan, not at the summer palace Tintagel. The apple orchards at Lantyan may be visited on the eastern side of river Flowey by following the ancient now grassy road one half-mile southwest of Castle D'Or. Whoever originally wrote the Tristan story must have known the area well as the geography of the ancient texts is exact and does not fail to mention the orchard looking lazy with neglected plenty, just as it does to this very day. Bernard and Patten have been there many times, and that is why the description is so accurate and how they (Bernard and Patten) know the ancient writers were there as well.)

(Author's Note: Adequate historical investigation failed to reveal the exact place Tristan slept, but it is thought close to Gwennap Head where the Cornwall Minack Open Air Theatre and Exhibition Centre stand at the present time. If I have the time, I will insert a picture. I'm pretty sure that my wife took a picture of the place on our last visit to Cornwall. Better yet, dial and query the internet "Minack Theatre" making sure you spell theatre the British way with an re not an er.)

The road was deserted as ever: the sea this morning, not wine-dark and not snot-green but mackerel-blue, swelled sleekly between the breakwaters. At the edge of the sea, you are in a liminal space where everything is shifting, nothing fixed, no stillness, no silence, just the rasping breath of waves and wind.

Here and there, a gull on a post floated off by the swell, looking silly. There was the usual breakwater smell, a smell of pickled seagrasses, and slimy green boards sucked by the tides. Farther in, there was freshwater in the fens, some open grassland, mixed woodlands, and among the trees ouzel, song thrush, redwing, nuthatch, starlings, and jay.

Walking along the margin of the forest east of the beach, near the ancient village of Carn Euny, Tristan came across a group of hunters who had just slain a white hart (Ed. a hart is a male deer after its fifth year).

Tristan, seeing, by a gesture, that the main huntsman was about to cut the neck of the beast, cried out: "May it please my lord, don't cut up the white hart, the king's property, like a farmyard pig."

(Ed. Tristan is a smarty-pants. He's smart, he's funny, and he knows all sorts of useless information, and he had an open mind about music and people. Here he is trying to show off his knowledge of dissection and his understanding of medieval law.)

By medieval law, white whales and white deer and for that matter any white animal belonged to the king and could not be killed without royal permission.

"It is the custom here, and we are agents of the king and have his full and legal authority to do this thing," answered the huntsman.

"I wasn't thinking of legalisms so much. I was questioning technique."

"If you know a better way, why please show us, for we are Britons, ignorant people who are eager to learn."

Tristan did as Gorvenal the wise mentor had taught him and turned the whole scene into slasher flick:

First, he skinned the entire animal, then cut it into pieces, according to the principles of correct anatomical dissection. He was not equal to Saint Thomas Aquinas and could not recite the 55 reasons he made to prop his method up, but Tristan knew how to do it. And more importantly, he did it. Theory is one thing. Practice another. It's best when the twain meet but given the choice... Hmmm.

The huntsman and the kennel masters were delighted. They said, "Friend, your way is good. What you have shown us is meet. In what land did you learn this? Please tell us, kind sir, your nation and your name."

"Good lords, my name is Tristan. I learned from my mentor Gorvenal, Squire of the Lyonnesse, at the Castle of Kanoël in Brittany."

"The Lyonesse submerged ages ago?"

"That is correct. Gorvenal hails from ancient families of the Lyonesse. He doesn't live there. No one does."

"Tristan, good fellow, come with us to Tintagel so that King Mark may examine you and learn more of your skills," said the huntsman.

Then the huntsmen thrust pieces of the white hart upon pikes and put the main carcass on a travois sled. The heart, offal, and ears he fed to the dogs.

In twos, by rank, the party started marching northeast upon the forest path until they hit the Saint's Way, now used by locals and tourists as a nature trail, but still to this day called the Saint's Way and still to this day consist of bending trees over a silent sylvan passaway occasionally adorned by full-flowered eglantine and honeysuckle.

The train marched along the Saint's Way to Lanwethenek (modern Padstow), and thence along the crumbling Roman highway toward Tintagel, that great castle girded with fields and orchards roundabout, living waters, fish ponds, buttercups thick in the meadows, daffodillies, shepherds, and ploughed lands considered sacred by Dun Waldo Mulutius, the first King of England, who had declared:

"A ploughed field is sacred ground;

Man was lost in a garden

And in a garden will be found."

Coming the other way, they met a procession of mourners carrying a dead child on a litter. They had draped the small corpse in white twill lace, its doll-like hands clasped on its breast. There was another child, nearby, an attendant, whose duty it was to fan flies away.

Tristan saw a child fall on the wayside. He was gathered up, dusted, cuffed, and cherished by its mother. On the line of march, somehow, one lost touch with such humanities. Never before had Tristan been so intensely aware of what it meant to be young and healthy in fine shape in fine weather. It may not be of interest to anyone, but what he wanted now was a good bath and a real meal of mutton or beefsteak.

More drifts of people. Grey old men mainly. But there was a woman with a stroke. Half her face looked sad, and the other half glad, a tragic-comic mask. She was carrying a bag which said, MAKE THE WORLD A BETTER PLACE.

The traffic thickened: The road jammed with dirty people and crawling animal-drawn carts. Overhead thunderclouds raced in a blackened sky. Weeks of dry weather gave way suddenly to a vicious downpour of rain mingled with quarter-inch hailstones.

They proceeded farther northward over bleak moors, littered with forbs, sledges, swales, rushes, reeds, and rough grasses, feet slipping and sinking in sweet- and sour-smelling soggy soil, until on the evening of the third day, when they smelled the salty sea, and came out from the old dark oak forest to see ahead of them a great turf-and-timber fortress standing high on a headland, with many long thatched halls, byres (these are cow sheds), and barns huddled among sheltered citrus orchards warmed by the Gulf Stream. All was hazed over with the smoke of flambeaux and evening fires, mixed with sea spray, sea spume, and sea fog.

This was a great castle—but not all that great, really. It was only one-fifth as large as Dunstanburgh Castle in Northumberland. It had fewer windows than the Chrysler building. As for luxury, it couldn't hold a candle to the White House in which the fabled George W. and Laura Bush once lived. But in summer, for King Mark, at that time and in that place by ancient standards, Tintagel was a pretty spiffy home. Living in the dark ages was like camping out, only worse because you didn't have a nice modern home to come back to. What you got was what you had to live with, and, often, that wasn't much. If you are like the average American, you now live more than a thousand times better than the kings and queens of old. Dial into the internet looking for "Tintagel Castle Top-Rated Ancient Ruin" to get many photos and great views of what King Mark's fortress looked like. Ed.)

The hunting party approached the castle wall starting at six-mile-bridge, just beyond four-mile-water, winding their way through the protective marsh. As they got closer to the moat and prepared to cross the drawbridge, the head huntsman pointed to a small stone marker on the northeast corner of the wall on the castle side and intoned, "One front, six left, and nine front going out. That's 1-6-9. Easy to recall, right? That was the secret of the stones, the escape route of last resort, which Tristan will need to use when he has to flee for his life. I hope he memorized the code. Otherwise, he's doomed."

Four-Mile-Water reminded Tristan of Four-Mile-Water, Wexford, where there is a graveyard of fastidious Irish Saints. Once two items are connected in the consciousness, each tends to recall the other and in that order, for that is how the human brain works. If I say A, most people will think B.

The Saints' graveyard at Wexford used to be on the other side of the river until, once, they buried a rogue corpse there. That night, the Saints all moved to the other side, leaving the rogue corpse to lie in solitude. It might have been easier to merely move the rogue, but they were Saints, and Irish you see. Irish Saints do things in style.

About 69: Tristan, who, in the innocence of youth, had no idea of the sexual implications, gave the huntsman the thumbs-up sign, and committed the combination to memory. Some castles in those days came with certain luxury items, like unto those at the Trump Tower on Fifth Avenue in New York City. Here the stylish idea was to provide an emergency means of crossing the moat by secret submerged stones. Piles had been driven into the moat, and a flat stone fastened to each pile just below the water's surface so that no one, through the murk, could see the stone path. If one knew where to start and knew the combination, he could cross the moat without using the drawbridge. The invention was none other than a modern application of the ancient stone-step system used by age-old Celts to cross their lakes while exiting the cannogs. Tristan will soon need to recall the escape combination when he flees the castle. He will be under extreme stress and duress, so I hope he can get the combo right. If he doesn't, he will fall into the moat, and that's all she wrote.

The walls of Tintagel stood about the sea. It was an ancient city without orderly patterns of streets. In fact, it had grown over an ancient city, which had grown over an ancient city, as perhaps someday another city would grow over the ruin of it. The keep, towers, moat, palisade, ramparts, motte, and bailey were finely fenced and fortified against all engines of war. On towers and turreted tops flourished flags and banners and pennants, vert and azure. There was the smell of cooking and the faint sounds of clattering pewter plates in the sizzling kitchens.

But, as the horns blew to bring the barons to the gate, Tristan looked up and saw beautiful women and maidens, with and without white married women's wimples, as they peeked out over the walk above the moat and gate. They were, these women, contemplated with awe not so much for what they did, as for what they had done. They then had the knack, with the gentlest of pressure, of bending men to their will. So, even before women's' lib, women could and did get their way.

One woman particularly attracted Tristan's attention, Morgana le Fay, also known as Fata Morgana, Italian for fairy mirage. This figure, mysterious even by the standards of Arthurian legend, commanded supernatural power. A premedieval red-headed karma queen, she could conjure tellurian energies, so say the ancient texts. And she was an independent girl. She had lost her virginity at age 13—a remarkable feat given the time and place. But that was long ago. Now, 73 men later, Morgana was probably 40 years old, though, through a miracle of plastic surgery and breast implants, she looked only 39.

Come to think on it, without the high heels, fake eyelashes, tattooed eyebrows, trinkets, bling, and foundation makeup… oh, yeah 40, yes, 40 would have been more like it. The gloomy truth is that there hasn't been in Cornwall an officially recognized miracle here since 1976 when the Virgin Mary moved the Tristan stone to a parking lot to make room for a high-density housing development.

Morgana—as she, this woman, was redheaded, Tristan thought about something Gorvenal had told him: "From my personal experience, I know that Redheaded women buck like goats." What the devil did that mean? Next time I see Gorv, I'll have to ask. We left him in the hole on the pirate ship. We hope he's OK. He needs to escape to help Tristan slay the red dragon.

Morgana—ruthless as the goddess she was, stared down at him from the bastions. Tristan stared back. Then, she left her position by the wall and followed him along, smiling with a funny look in her eye. She was giving him the good eye and, some thought, eyes of desire. Morgana is the cleverest woman in Europe as her friends unanimously called her. She is said to have a golden key that opens every door. About that and her more later.

Well? What was Tristan supposed to do? It's as natural for men to ogle women (and vice versa) as it is for both of them to sniff the air when they smell a steak cooking. Whether politically correct or not, both behaviors will continue, on and on for the next four billion years until our sun becomes a red giant and burns out Earth. By that time, it is to be hoped, humans will have left earth to pollute some other planet.

Answering the watchman's shout in full stride, the group thundered across the moat, beneath the spiked portcullis, into the barbican and bailey, through streets paved with dust, horse dung, and comsumptives' spits.

So many marveled at the good order of the cavalcade that King Mark himself came to see the assemblage. The king recognized his liegemen, but he didn't recognize Tristan. Yet, somewhere deep in his heart, he felt a sense of affection, even love—love for the boy and, in his (Mark's) deep heart's core, on some emotional plane, ineffable and vague, yet real, he recognized and cherished Tristan as if the youth were directly related to him, which, of course, he was. Mark is Tristan's uncle. Blanchefleur, Tristan's mother, was (she died of myasthenia gravis) King Mark's sister.

[Editor's note: Tristan's mother, Blanchefleur, now dead, was Mark's sister as stated. Noirfleur, still living, is Mark's other sister and the mother of Andread, Tristan's cousin, and soon to be Tristan's rival. The names are the names in the ancient texts. The names are French (Tristan = child of sadness; Blanchefleur = White flower; Noirfleur = Black flower). All this was way before the Norman conquest, proving the continent and England were closely connected in the fifth century. In fact, scientists tell us you could actually ride a horse from Cornwall to France over a densely forested land bridge. Several texts from different travelers attest to this fact. Land also connected west England with the Isles of Scilly. Extreme low water gives people in Penzance glimpses of sunken forests in Mount's Bay. The ancient name of St. Michael's Mount is Karrek Loos y'in Koos, meaning grey rock in the woods. Deep-sea trawling nets catch not only the bones of mammoth and other extinct beasts but ancient weapons and pottery. Doggerland was also a forest that connected England with Europe. It is now under the North Sea. For more info consult Julia Blackburn's book *Time Song*.]

(Editor's footnote: That reminds me. Mark in the ancient Cornish tongue means horse—for which reason there was a story told of him that he had horses' ears and a horse's snout. This was rubbish. His ears were long and did stick out, but in general, he was a man like other men, and a warrior more than most. He did have a throne, which may have been the source of the confusion because on either side, where the armrests would have stood, there were two large horses carved of wood. These were finely wrought and world-wide known as the stallion fore posts at Great Mark's throne.)

Ho-hum! Who cares?

Bernard, the Bardic Narrator, looked up. He sensed restlessness. It was the usual problem caused by the tendency to explain too much.

Patten stepped up to the podium. "Bernard, if you weren't one of my own, I'd kick your ass all the way back to Carrick ma Cross. But, that's it, kid. We're taking you away from anything having to do with human beings and putting you in the nut hut with the other loony birds."

Bernard took another swig of Black Bush. "OK, OK, simmer down." He flipped his hands' palms up and then down and shrugged his shoulders. "That's enough. Henceforth no sidebars. Back to the story and nothing else. I promise."

Tristan and the hunting party entered the castle at the second story via the drawbridge. Toward the left stood the main guard where soldiers ate and slept and held court. This guardroom had a stone fireplace on its south wall, along which a blind man admired himself in a mirror. An Eagle Scout, in uniform, sat off to one side playing Tetris on his Gameboy. An amnesic busily wrote his memoir. A clerk worked feverishly on some crucial document, a lost epic, the diary of a famous aviator, translating a language he had not mastered. Even more strange, a poet, eye roving in a fine frenzy, composed verses about (of all things!) the stock market. Someone on the side was watching a video of the French movie Caché for the 453rd time, trying to figure it out. And a clergyman put the final touches on his disquisition on the important subject of Filioque. Yes, Filioque? Who came first? God the Father or God the Son? Who is more important than God? God the Father is God and the first person of the blessed Trinity. God the Son is God and the second person of the blessed Trinity. The Holy Ghost (no kidding—that's the name) is God and the third person of the blessed Trinity. The disquisition on Filioque handled just the relation of Father and Son. In fact, there had to be, and there were massacres to decide the issue. Look up the Thirty Years' War, and not the officially sanitized view. We now know that God the Father and God the Son are absolutely equal and existed each the same for all time. That issue and the Trinity thing were both settled once and for all on the battlefield. So, there is only one God, but he is three equally divine persons. Get it?

(Author: Skeptics say the true meaning of the Trinity is that it is a fiction and that so many believe it shows the enormous power fiction, for better or worse, has over the human race.)

Next to the fireplace, small spiral stairs led down to a dark room with no door, no other exit. This was the dungeon. From it came the odor of human meanness and injustice: the smell of a zoo, of sawdust, excrement, and confinement. At the bottom of those stairs, three soldiers were strangling a convicted prisoner who looked like Tim McVey. No! It was Tim McVey, the same hero named in several pagan hagiologies. Headed to the oubliette. No question.

Whew! Can you believe that that brute is the lineal descendant of men who supposedly flew in machines, traveled to the moon, harnessed the forces of Nature including electrical essence, built mechanical devices that seemed to think, and blew up entire buildings and eventually entire cities with a single bomb? Can you believe that there were such men? Headed back—iron, bronze, silver, and then the golden age.

Tristan saw the neck veins sticking out. The guy was really getting it. "Oh my God," Tristan thought, "Am I in a snuff club? Is Tintagel into torture? This is a definite violation of the Geneva Convention."

The limp, but still breathing, McVey was pushed through a tiny opening in the floor, dropped 16 feet to the dirt below, where he (It? Before the flame out and the simplification they had robots that looked and acted like men. Thus, this McVey could have been a machine) remained without food, without water, without heat, without sanitary facilities. The prisoner's prospect was zero, like those people sealed in Nazi trains to Dachau, and worse, without hope, they were left to rot and die and knew it. Gitmo: ditto.

When the stench from the dungeon got bad, soldiers dropped quick lime, if available, through the hole. Otherwise, they stuffed their noses with pine or simply suffered the stink.

In the guardroom, there was only one chair, the Chair of Estate, its high, engraved back made of black bog oak. That seat was for the Captain of the Guard, who gave the orders for the day while so ensconced. The captain seemed to be waiting for orders himself as the thin grey afternoon light silently fell on the walls decorated with crossbows, whips, foxes' brushes, on fustian coats and on hats flung on the chairs, on tankards, sending forth a scent of flat ale, and on a choked fire, which did not abate the look of gloom.

Toward the right, opposite the door to the main guard, another staircase spiraled upwards to the lofty hall above, where King Mark held court.

Tired of anxious, weary waiting? Let's go there with Tristan and see what's what.

Ready? Climb!

OK We have ascended with Tristan and are now entering the large chamber. Let's pause here and catch our breath.

Wow! This room is much larger than the parallel room at Kanoël as befitted a great king like Mark, who reigned over all Cornwall. Still, despite its size, I wouldn't want to live here. No, sir. It looks too grungy for the likes of me, with an Edgar A. Poe atmosphere, the usual quality for early gothic.

What do you expect? After the great flame out and the simplification that followed, civilization reverted to primitive ways. (Ed. This story takes place in the future after World War V caused a gigantic hydrogen bomb destruction of most things on this planet, resulting in reversion to customs and habits for humanity usually associated with the Middle Ages.)

Much of the squalid appearance was due to that hole in the roof (see it?) and the large central fire on the north wall, which steeps this place in shadow and smoke, making the room look like a cave with a campfire at one end. A similar scene occurs (without the soot) in the modern family room, its TV flashing and fading like the flames of an ancient hearth. TV exists to keep you watching. You probably thought it exists to keep you informed.

Tristan noticed that, next to the fire, a strange standard stood, a sculpture of a nude woman with legs spread wide. Her breasts were like perfect doorbells like those silicone augmented baubles you see on the centerfold models of Playboy®, only more realistic. With her hands, she was displaying her vulva. This totem was the Sheela, the good luck and fertility standard that the most up-to-date modern castles of the time displayed. By her attractive sexuality, people thought she drew away the evil spirits and prevented plague. There are plenty of pictures of Sheela on the internet. Dial in "Sheela Celtic Goddess or Sheela na gig." Do that now. Very interesting and important. There are 101 Sheelas in Ireland and 45 in Britain. The one Bernard likes best is in the Round Tower at Rattoo, in County Kerry, Ireland. She has small breasts, and that's what Bernard likes.

Sex in itself, according to our ancient ancestors, simply taken like food, or drink, or sleep is an affair neither good or bad or shameful or otherwise.

Supper consisted of large helpings of grilled meat, mainly freshly killed white hart and wild boar, accompanied by barley bannock, and lots of mead. Ah, mead! Nothing like it; a honey-based sweet drink that was 14.7% alcohol (our wines have only 8-13% except Gallo cabernet, which is 15% alcohol by volume). Mead got you where you wanted to go and fast. In those days, the helpfulness of alcohol in human affairs was a fact.

All classy medieval food tastes like Christmas. Meat pie with dates and raisins and mace and ginger. Vert juice was the universal condiment like our ketchup, but it was fermented. Also known as verjuice and verjus (middle French for "green juice"), it was and is a highly acidic juice made by pressing unripe grapes. The usual use in Western Europe during the Middle Ages was in sauces, as a condiment, or to deglaze. Verjus (called husroum in Arabic) is still used extensively in Syrian cuisine. Verjus (called ab-gooreh in Persian) is still used extensively in Northern Iranian and Azerbaijani cuisine.

The other condiment at Tintagel Castle was Worcester sauce, the oldest condiment in Europe. Worcester sauce has been in use since the Roman occupation. Worcester sauce is more expensive than Vert juice, so most people assumed it was better. It certainly takes longer to make, for it is fermented anchovies aged for three to five years. Almonds were also widely used, and pudding was stuffing made of bread. Bread pudding is a retronym like daylight baseball. In fact, the meal they ate that night at Tintagel exactly duplicated what Henry VIII and his courtiers consumed in a single day of feasting in 1518:

- 11 beef carcasses
- 6 sheep
- 384 pigeons
- 648 larks

- 72 geese
- 4 peacocks
- 3,000 pears

- 1,300 apples
- 3000 loaves of bread
- 400 dishes of butter

The menu only goes to show that things don't change much in Europe in a mere 1,000 years. Not only that—as usual, nobody said anything memorable at supper. One usually doesn't, then or now, in any part of Britain. Some people are not meant to say anything of consequence. As in life, so also in stories about life. Which only goes to show…

What?

Answer: It goes to show that this story is about real life, not some invented fiction.

An old woman shouted from the audience, "Time goes on. Change doesn't."

An old man shouted from the audience, "If you have nothing intelligent to say, old bag, keep your mouth shut. Zip it!"

"Look who's talking!" the old bag shouted back and gave him the finger.

Bernard, the Bardic Narrator, looked up and admitted, "Lost my train of thought." He removed his bardic hat, scratched his head, squinted into the distance, and said: "Where was I?"

I raised my hand and told him from my notes, "You were describing the throne room at Tintagel and had just mentioned the Sheela and supper. How about the people, our ancient ancestors? What were they like?"

About the people: Tristan found their thoughts narrow, their wishes low, and their merriment artificial. He got the impression that many of the barons, who surrounded King Mark, were there to line their pockets or watch and report his conduct. Every tongue muttered censure, and every eye searched for fault. The barons wished for and awaited letters of revocation from Arthur so that Mark would be carried off in chains to Camelot: His name mentioned no more. After that, the barons planned to take over. Sound familiar? The sword of Damocles hangs over the head of rulers, indicating imminent and ever-present peril faced by those in power.

The antagonism was a fact, hard as a pebble. Mark's breezy manner suggested a lack of clear vision that is imperative in a king or leader for the perception of truth. Consequently, Tristan thought that Mark didn't know how much he was hated or what bad things the barons had in mind. And that was probably true and not true, depending on how you defined the quantifier "how much."

But in fact, I think, Mark slept badly, had suffered recurrence of the old gastric trouble, and currently spent much time brooding overmuch on the past because he was looking for something that might have been done differently to avert the future that he now prefigures. For him, for me, for you, there exists no difference between an atomic bomb attack and a fatal stab wound of the heart or a heart attack or a drug overdose. If you are dead, regardless of the cause, you are dead. Recall it was only a fine horsehair that suspended the sword of Damocles over the head of King Dionysius II of Syracuse.

The men finished eating. A gong rang, and the women of the court entered the room. The part of the meal called "the carousel" had begun.

Wow! What a great idea! Women and men eating together. Isn't it swell? Isn't it grand? Isn't it wonderful? Nowadays.

Tristan loved it. Men and women happy together, something about it, especially with the music from the gallery, sweet and lovely music, wonderful music of a lute, and the tready entwined voices of recorders. It thrilled Tristan, thrilled him to his deep heart's core. It whirled him farther than Uranus flies.

With the women there, the party progressed rapidly. Women are the catalysts of real fun. They always will be. Every party needs lively female voices, not to mention a few willing slits. Where would we be without them? Modern physics teaches us that there is no solid matter, only bundles of energy that appear solid. But I know women are different. They are solid. They are something to believe in. About their divine nature, there is no doubt. About their animal nature, ditto.

Soon there was loud music. People everywhere. Drinking. Drugs. Moods brightened by chemicals. All this typical of that age and, for that matter, every age.

Everybody wasted: a different flavor of stoned. What's your bag? What's your fix?

In the stairwells. In the garderobe. Peeing off the balcony onto unsuspecting heads below—on to people who thought it might be beginning to drizzle. A number of rooms bathed in a strange purple glow. Beds set up. All around him couples stroking, licking, kissing, sucking. A few women naked. Some clad in a blouse or a concert T-shirt or simply with their skirts hiked up and panties down.

Tristan noticed his vision became disconnected, moving in jerks like those old-time silent movies of the Keystone Cops. Everything was funny. Too funny. Too, too funny.

The party expanded on entropic waves of laughter into chaos, the real chaos of real-life chaos, the endearing chaos of freaked out parties. Your generation knows nothing about these... But of course, you think you do. How different was the chaos of real-life from the ordered arrangement depicted of it in some books? Not here. You bet. This is real chaos. Tristan slipped and fell and laughed and laughed. Some girl helped him up and kissed him hard on the lips. If it were not for parties, how could anyone endure, on a daily basis, our cultural wasteland?

"Why did you kiss me so hard? You cut my lip!"

"Let's pull some crackers," she shouted.

They seized the little strings and yanked. Detonations splendid and prolonged followed. See them explode and fly! Whee!

The noise joined the thunder outside to produce a terrific salvo. Guests put on caps, forage caps, Roman helmets, crowns. Tin whistles shrilled, voices shouted toasts, "Long live the king! To joy! To love! To joy and fresh new days of love! To all, our dreams doubled. Here's looking at you, kid."

Tristan took two or three swigs from a bottle of gin. The gin burned his throat. Coughing a bit, Tristan carelessly cut himself a piece of cake, stuck it in his mouth, but couldn't swallow it. It stuck in his throat.

Andread, King Mark's other nephew by Mark's older sister Noirfleur (remember her, the mother of him?), was in antic form, surrounded by his crowd of brainless, empty-headed young fops. Andread had gotten his face smacked more than once by offended ladies. He now came over to offend Tristan.

"Look at Tristan. He'd rather have his cake than eat it," roared Andread. "No fit yet, but probably guilty as Hell. Ha, ha, ha."

(Author's note: This was Andread's obscure reference to the corsned or "the ordeal by bread," a medieval test to determine guilt: An ounce of bread was placed in the accused mouth. If he had a convulsion (fit), he was guilty. If he swallowed it, he was innocent. Other things were sometimes used in the same way. When a large pear was stuffed in the victim's mouth, death always followed because of obstruction of the windpipe, proving those accused were always guilty. Scholarship can find no explanation of what would happen if the accused neither had a convulsion nor swallowed properly. Probably a mistrial. Reportedly, the result was just as accurate as our own trial by jury, but faster and cheaper. But who knows for sure?)

Question from Miss Andress Look-Alike. "Was he handsome?"

"Who?"

"Andread."

He wasn't what some women would call handsome. Andread is a tall, heavily built man, with a dark complexion and rather good looking, but loud spoken and given to bragging. He likes to be right about small things, like foretelling the change in the weather. In general, his words and actions have an irritating arrogance: He was always right; at times, he got on everyone's nerves because he talked so much and with such cocksureness—he was like Patten. No, change that. He was worse. He was like Donald Trump.

Andread, who was becoming odious, wouldn't recall his last remark or much of the latter part of the evening, which he would top off at his favorite bar, the Chthonic. Rumor had it that he was homosexual, but that was only because Andread liked to dress up as a nun and go bar hopping. In reality, he was simply a garden-variety alcoholic.

Aside from drink, Andread's drug problems were a thing of the past, though he often thought back (with nostalgia) to the good old days when a Bolivian white powder was part of the energy plan.

Another question from Miss Look-alike: "Is he manageable?"

Andread had been the Peck's Bad Boy of three universities, thrown out of each in turn for reckless escapades as vicious as they were inane. Twice he had been dragged into the spotlight of the courts for breach of promise. Once (on Long Island?), he had run over and killed a pedestrian in his reckless roadster and had been saved only by the hasty and lavish bribes of his mother's attorneys.

Another question: "Is he, is he... You know."

Andread's criminal record was now expunged (legal term for artificially cleaned up). He had served his time for the desecration of the Jewish cemetery (toppled over 100 headstones), and his gun collection was mainly legal. Like Nixon with Vietnam, Andread favored bombing people, especially the Western Isles (that was their name for Ireland) back into the Stone Age (if it refused to see reason his way). Nixon had been known among the eastern academic elite as the antichrist. Andread, ditto.

"What about his religion?"

Andread's patron saint was Kievan Prince Vladimir, who converted in about 988. Later canonized (I am not making this up—this is fact, historic fact), Vladimir was not in every way a saintly figure, for he was reputed to maintain a harem of 800 concubines (yes, madam, 800!), and is even described by a German chronicler of the period as a fornicator *immensus* and *crudelis*. Saint Vlad promoted the doctrine of caesaropapism and the extermination of all Judaizers. Andread, ditto. But Vlad got the nod from the pope, and Andread didn't. So far, Andread hasn't been beatified or beautified.

OK, OK. The part about Vlad was fact, but the part about Andread was made up. Or was it? In fact, the pope didn't make Andread a saint, and he was not beautified or beatified. Andread isn't even real. He is just a character in this and in the ancient versions of this story.

King Mark thought that Andread's main character defect, however, was that he floccinaucinihilipilificated (accent on the cat which is pronounced like the name Kate)—that is, he belittled the achievements of others. Try to remember that word—floccinaucinihilipilificated—you might need to impress someone at your next cocktail party or on your next blind date.

Another negative: Andread's Jesus joke: I don't even have to close my eyes to hear it: The good Samaritan came by and volunteered to remove the nails, and did, but started with the hands. And Jesus shouted, "The feet! The feet, man!"

Ursula look-alike stood. "What's funny about that?"

"Not much," said Bernard, "especially when you have to explain it. It involves sequence, honey. The proper sequence: Socks first, then shoes. Plunder first, then burn. Ask if we will have sex, cutie pie, then ask if you can be on top. That sort of thing. When the nails come off hands first, Jesus falls over, and his feet get ripped. Some Samaritans make things better; others screw up. Explaining a joke is like dissecting a frog. After it's over, you know more, but the frog is spoiled."

A beat while Ursula lights a cigarette and takes a deep soul-satisfying drag. She blows a nice cone of smoke at Bernard, who nods and continues to expostulate about Andread.

Another negative: Andread accepted deference benignly while giving nothing back. An hour into dinner with him began to feel endless. So, I tend to drink when around him and tend to drink like young people: stupidly. After that and after, laughter piles up. And then I'm out on the street, still flush with that body glow, but no memory of how what had connected with what. What's the fun of getting drunk when you can't remember what's the fun?

There was also an objection to Andread's favorite tie, which pictured a silver-colored screw screwing into the yellow-colored letter U. Mark didn't like it. Nor did the barons. Screw U!

Of course, evil never exists in a pure state. Even Satan had been an angel. Every morning, without fail, Andread fed Sidney, his iguana. Sidney, the iguana, was very dan-ger-ous. Cannot pet him. Sidney bites everyone, even Andread. And Andread bites Sidney back. But Andread loved him, and Sidney loved Andread.

Andread especially liked carnivorous plants: the sundew (Venus' flytrap), the pitcher-plant, and the teasel.

Another positive according to some and a negative according to most: He had become, despite frequent migraines, passionately addicted to the study of literature. At 40, he had attained such a degree of scholarship that he dared accede to his venerable father's dying request: "Teach, Andread! Teach English Lit!"

It had been whispered that Andread had badly burned his fingers in the fires of Wall Street, the adverse effect of which had been partially compensated for by that corner in stamps. Picture on one side; sticky the other. Farsighted, that was. A great invention. You stick them on the letter, and someone carries it to the address on the envelope.

Andread still made seriously generous donations to AA and to the society for the historic preservation of *pied á terre*.

The court psychologists claimed they did not have enough information to be pessimistic. Nor did they ever discover a cause of Andread's aberrant personality. There is always a psychopomp around the corner, isn't there? The four years spent on the locked ward of Rusk State Hospital for the criminally insane should not be held against him. There were lots of nice people there, most of them born-again Christians. His scotch: Dewar's. His quote: "I am not crazy. I have just been in a very, very bad mood for 40 years." His motto: "If you can't eat it and you can't screw it, what good is it?"

(Author's note: As for me, I wonder if a lot of Andread's problems didn't relate to masturbation, overvaulting ambition, the influence of Jewish friends, and hanging around creep-joint bars where all sorts of nighttime flotsam and jetsam made their way. The best that anyone could say about him was that his tattoos were spelled correctly, except for the one over his right deltoid: FURK IT ALL. If you looked closely, the R should have been a C except the dude who did the tattoo didn't know much. FURK IT ALL.)

The lights of high Tintagel, the gay music, the unhappy people had whipped Tristan like a lash and had driven him out into the misty night, which held for him a premonition and a probing mizzle chill. When tired of feasting, of too much talk and too much mead, may not the royal nephew have some air?

To learn what interesting romantic thing happened there while Tristan is taking air, turn to tableau three.

Tristan Courts Morgana Too Slow

Under the silver nail-paring of a moon that looked like a small slice of honeydew melon (the moon is older than TV, and in the old days they used to watch it more than they do now), Tristan felt a deepening melancholy, that sense of existential solitude, the being-and-being-alone in a universe that still nights sometime give. He stood gazing at nothing, down through the gloom, save a moving blur where foamed the sea (Thalatta! Thalatta!) on the eternal Cornish rocks, the moan of Cornish water, the plankton-lit surf, and the sea face of moonlit spangles, dancing silver coins. This is the sea out of which we evolved. She is our own great mother, alma mater, the ancient beldam of life.

Tristan, at the rocky bulkhead, kneeled and ran the cold ocean water through his hands. Why have so many poets preceded him to the water's edge to make obscure offerings to the tide? The sea is the land's edge also, a boundary. And boundaries, as all poets know, are meant to be tested, probed, and, when necessary, crossed.

(Ed. Oh, God. Obvious prefiguration. Tristan is going to take a sea journey soon that will lead him to Ireland and to Iseult the beautiful and much more trouble.)

Staring at emptiness for a long time, Tristan scarcely heard, coming down slowly toward him from above, a troubling sound of… cloth.

He (*mezzo forte*): "Hullo! Who's that? Saxon or Celt?"

The kind of over-smoked voice that sounds automatically intimate said in *piano forte*, "Good evening, sir. Perhaps you do not know me or remember that once you gave a lady such honor by your special look as to acknowledge her obscure existence. Why do you stay away from history like this? A celebration is going on. Come celebrate with us. Come celebrate with me."

"History?"

Perceiving beside him, a slim figure provisionally cloaked in clinging green against the cold, he bowed as in a weary deference to his fate. "Yes, I know you surely, madam. You were among the creatures of distinction whose quality may be seen even now, even in the dark."

"It is not dark," she said. "Or it is not so dark but that a woman cannot see or does actually see—if she be careful not to fall down these caliginous stairs and break her neck at Tristan's feet."

What the devil is she talking about? Is she drunk?

Morgana came closer and put a small and cat-like hand on Tristan. "You, sir, lay a puissant burden on my virtue and turn my wits inside out. By Isis, I shall give them bloody teeth who paragon again Caesar or anyone else against you, for you are my man of men. This has never happened to me before. What I mean is that you and I are the first people who have ever been us."

Tristan thought: 'Lead us not into temptation!' Then he said aloud, "*A spiritu fornicationis, Domine, libera nos. A morte perpetua, Domine, libera nos.*"

(Translation: From the drive to fornicate, Lord, free us. From eternal death, Lord, free us.)

Close up, she smelt of woman, of powder, nail varnish, nightdresses, female things plus cigarette smoke. She was *bellibone* (an interesting word from the French belle et bonne, meaning fair and good), and he found her so. Her red hair tumbled down her back like the sun kissing the river Flowey at twilight. She would make a good jammer in Roller Derby, where her name would probably be something like Tinker Hell, or Malice in Wonderland, or Wild Cherry Bomb, or Dinah Might.

"Madam, must we continue to talk in a lost language found in runes in our stilted and artificial northern manner?"

Morgana laughed, showing her straight white teeth and shining jeweled eyes and shrugged herself a little nearer to him, having not far to come. "It's an old habit. Silly men pursue me and make songs about me in that tongue. You may have heard some. They are based on legends that I am strange. I am not strange—not half so strange as you are and not a fifth as strange as Patten."

Patten? Who's he? thought Tristan.

Tristan had before him a white neck, a white bosom, beneath a fair and feline face whereupon demure determination was engraved. It was difficult to concentrate while looking at cleavage, especially cleavage of that kind and magnitude. Women have a switch in their heads. The switch is usually in the off position. But once turned on, oh my God—watch out! Tristan was feeling faint with interest. He felt like springing on her or falling at her little feet and crying.

"You are strange," he breathed, "and, methinks, a sagacious peril to men like me."

A wry twist, all but imperceptible, disfigured for an instant her small mouth (the micro mimic movement discussed in Psychology 301. MMMs betray the real underlying emotion, so we are told).

"Women are both perils and slaves to the men they honor," says she. "Men worthy of their reverence know this well and honor them, sometimes to humor them. Thus, we are their slaves and their impediments, one and both. Much is to be forgiven once that fact is clear. Remember—with such forgiveness, comes the thing men seek, woman's special service, the special service that men need. A service I offer you, for each man must have his mate. That no one can deny."

Oh, God! Jesus wept, and no wonder, by Christ. What a world this is! What a world! You don't believe me? Well, I'm sorry. I don't care. Believe what you like. The fact is Jesus has good reason to weep. Look around you. The forever are there. This is a bawdy planet. Love is all around you. Look around you. It is there. Everywhere.

Why the devil am I writing this crap? For money, of course. But what else? Hmmmmm. For amusement. To me, this stuff is fun to read, and I can't find anything like it anywhere else, so what can I do? I have to make it up myself, creating a literature that I like and love. Why not? If Shakespeare can put an ass's head on Bottom and a Nobel author can fill the room with butterflies when a woman has an orgasm, why can't I write my stuff as I please?

Dear reader, excuse me for a moment. There is a loud amusement park across the way, and I must get up to close the window.

Tristan drew the fringes of her cloak together, brushing her breasts ever so lightly, while she gave him her gamey eye. "I fear that you are taking cold," he said as the thin haunting piping of a recorder (tuned to the soprano human voice) sent a shiver up his spine.

One fact was clear: In bed, it was she, Morgana, who would do the teaching.

"Warm me, then. Come away to yon tower top to play. I have a treasure that I would show thee. My treasure's there."

Tristan's snifter fell from the rail and smashed onto the rocks below. He regretted the loss, but there was no sense crying over spilt brandy, *Sempé Armagnac*.

(Editor's note: Adequate historic research indicates *Sempe* was not served in King Mark's court. The *Armagnac* under discussion is more likely *Cerbois Bas Reserve Personell, Apellation d'origine controlée*, from Ars, France.)

Let's hear about and see Morgana's treasure in tableau four. Can you guess what she means?

Tristan Ascends the Mountain;
Sees Morgana's Treasure

◆●─────────────●─────────────●◆

The stairway ascended what could have been a mountain. Not an easy climb. Tristan and Morgana scaled 40 flights. To give an added fillip, the steps themselves were not of equal height. And sometimes the stairs were not even stairs, and sometimes the stairs were not even stairs. (Dig? Even vs. even, same word but the sense equivocates.)

So, the pair, Tristan and Morgana, clambers over slopes of pebbles and small rocks that used to be stairs and over flattened irregular surfaces that used to be even stairs but now are not even stairs. And sometimes, the entire route is just a scrabble.

Breathless, at the tower top, they see a small, unutterably drab (except for the wall frescos) columbarium where the guard keeps pigeons for food in case of castle siege.

Morgana smiles and sits on a pine long-seat littered with pigeon doo. She closes her eyes and begins scissoring her legs open and closed while massaging her crotch. Her face reddens. Small beads of sweat appear on her upper lip as she tilts her head back. Faster and faster, she moves her legs. She moans and then moans louder and more frequently.

Tristan, blushed with confusion, clasped his hands together as if taking a vow.

"What are you doing?" Tristan asks.

"Making a thrill, silly," she said, for women are great explainers.

She stops only to pull down her cotton thong, spread her legs, and show her THING. "A thong of beauty is a joy forever," says she grimacing, as, with her thing, she beckons to him. "Come on, Tristan. The panties are over, it's time to call it a lay."

(Editor's note: I am leaving this in because I want to show how the author gets carried away. A thing of beauty is a joy forever. The party's over. It's time to call it a day. Morgana is clever but not silly. This stupidity comes from Bernard or Patten. It has to. Morgana is not capable of such gross want of intelligence. She is not a freak show, a goth, a raver, a rocker, a punk, a hippie, or a dork. She's a mod. She got one of those MacArthur genius awards awhile back and was summa cum laude from the Irish College of Necromancy, Dublin.)

What was Tristan supposed to do? Admire it? Touch it? Smell it? Lick it? What?

It did look like a beautiful complex crimson rose, as multiple novels had told. Suddenly, stunned by its magnificent splendor, it seemed the most beautiful thing he had ever seen. And as mentioned in that famous painting: It was the center of the world.

As if this weren't lure enough, there were her enormous breasts (the right one of which had a nipple ring), her hair braided with flaming snakes, her death row jewelry, all right out of the comic books like Sin City of his childhood. You would be surprised how many childhoods each of us has had—especially in comic books, which with their depictions of cultural superheroes that review an ancestral memory such that in the logic of myth, Hercules is equivalent to Spiderman and Superman and Ironman and so forth.

"Come take a look, come closer!" Morgana said, kind of cocking her head to one side and rotating her thighs. "Hmmmm," she groans. "Eat me," she commands, pointing to her THING. "Eat me."

What about that, eh?

What about naked women? What about naked women out of control in heat? What else were they invented for? This is the female form. It attracts with an undeniable attraction. Morgana seemed to be looking right through his soul.

"Eat me!"

Extraordinary. The points in a situation that men miss. Tristan had been thinking treasure, gold, and silver, pearls, perhaps, or jade—stuff like that.

But this? This?

This he had not even considered. Morgana had said she would show her treasure. This was it. This wild rose with a small but enlarging cherry on top. Tristan's brain, momentarily over-computed and stunned, refused to work. The language of the brain is not the language of math. The reason that no computer can imitate the human brain is that thought is a never-ending process of change, and the brain is in a never-ending process of change induced by thought. She wasn't wearing stunt boobs. But she was Barbiefied unknowingly and (probably) against her will by Tristan's brain.

Tristan fled.

Yes, fled.

This was the summer of a virgin's discontent. And Tristan was that virgin. He may have heard the voice of his good white angel, inviting to industry, sobriety, peace, and celibacy. Who knows? What is known: He was not yet equipped to deal with the slippery truths of real-life sex, yummy lips, and bliss. Too bad. He missed his date with destiny. And let us not forget that warning about the hell and fury of a woman scorned.

He wanted to call his mother and tell her that he was alive and well and ask her advice. But alas, Blanchefleur (his mother, remember?) was dead. She had been dead 17 years, and she would issue no more advice—to him or to anyone. Rivalen, his father, was dead also. The kid was on his own. A pity. But, you know, Rivalen lost a father and that father lost, lost his, and the survivor bound in filial obligation for some time (you know the rest—Shakespeare, Ham I ii 93) to do obsequious sorrow, but to persevere in obstinate condolement is a course of impious stubbornness, shows a will most incorrect to heaven, an understanding simple and unschooled. In other words, there isn't much you can do with the dead except bury them or burn them. If they died in the state of grace, then put them in sacred consecrated ground. If they died in the state of mortal sin, then they would have to be buried in unconsecrated ground among Jews, Protestants, and vegetarians.

Tristan's black angel then got the better of his white angel. So, not much later, Tristan reclimbed the mountain, returned to the columbarium. He was looking for Morgana, and he was looking for her thing. And yes, he had in mind that he would eat her thing as commanded. He was not a germ phobic. No sir. In fact, for reasons he did not understand, he wanted to eat her thing, and he wanted to lick her thing, and he wanted to lick her tits, kiss her lips, dive into her inner spaces, explore her every female orifice. He wanted to fill her compact and delicious body. But he didn't for the life of him know why he wanted to do these things.

"Passion!" shouted Sinead.

Out of breath, he stepped onto the last platform, and it was then that he saw them, together on the floor, Morgana on her back and some man face down into her nape, two bodies moving like one. Plato's double-backed beast. Tristan was mystified. A shadow on the wall opened and closed like an umbrella.

Again, with a movement of compunction, as new and strange to him as everything else that day, and especially all that within the last hour, he fled.

Compline seemed especially profound that night. Tristan, shaken and shaking, recited the Athanasian Creed. And then he prayed Morgana would give him another chance.

Tristan would have some more chances to get laid that night as you will see if you go on to the next tableau, tableau five. The more I tell his official story, the more it feels true.

TABLEAU CINQ

The Party

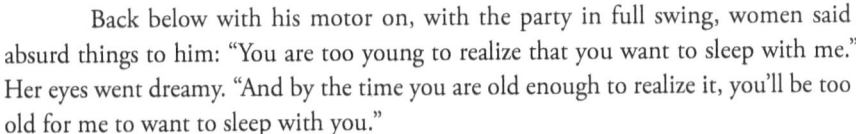

Back below with his motor on, with the party in full swing, women said absurd things to him: "You are too young to realize that you want to sleep with me." Her eyes went dreamy. "And by the time you are old enough to realize it, you'll be too old for me to want to sleep with you."

That was a good line, but he didn't get it. He didn't get the action expected. Why would she want to sleep with him or he with her? That dame had slipped her foot out of its narrow black shabby little black satin slipper, and her teeny tiny toes ran caressingly up within his trouser leg, the two little toes pressing and twiddling delicately on his calf muscles as her fingers were on his right thigh. Still—he didn't get it. All he could think of saying was, "Let's go get more Harp."

(Editor's footnote: Harp is an Irish beer.)

A professional came up and asked, "How about a quickie for five dollars, Gov'ner?"

He shook his head, "no."

Another asked, "Five dollars for a quickie?"

No again, but he realized he didn't know what he was refusing, so he asked the mother superior who was by the Sheela talking to a young woman who had just entered the noviciate and who differs from the Medici Venus only in that where the goddess has a bosom, she wears a cross. "Excuse me, Sister, what's a quickie?"

"Five dollars, same as the others. Ten with this novice."

Another lady addressed him, "Today I read an interesting article in Cosmo entitled *15 New Sexual Positions You Should Test Drive Today*. Want to go for a ride?"

"I don't have a car."

"Jesus, some men are so dense they are pathetic. I think I will set fire to your hair."

Another lady of uncertain age, a literary type, had offered, "Now that you've had a single malt scotch here, (the scotch in reference was Oban, I think, but I am not sure as I lost that page of my notes. Later, if I have the time, I will check with Bernard. Oh Hell. Who cares?) how about another in my apartment?"

Tristan's eyes widened.

She says: "Don't get me wrong. I don't sleep with book characters I work with. We're just friends. You are my friend but without privileges."

35

After dark, she was like a second-grade teacher gone to the bad, in a Woolworth tiara, started up all wrong. But you can bet the glamour she had lives on in the dreams of the many men she has loved who have slept with her.

Ugh! There it was again. That sleep thing. But more puzzling was the idea that Tristan was a character. What does she mean by that?

This was the first time that Tristan had heard the allusion to the idea that he was a character in a book, which, of course, he was. He wasn't sure being a character was good or bad. Like most facts, it was neither. It just was. But the way she said it sounded like being a character wasn't as good as being a person. So, he wondered.

There are probably advantages and disadvantages either way. For most things, there usually are.

Tristan looked in a mirror. He decided to make the best of his status, which he couldn't change anyway:

He self-referentially says to his reflection in the mirror: "So what, I'm a character. Everybody is a character in their own right in one way or other. Even real people are characters. But I am better than they. My story is worthy of a place in imperishable folklore. Other characters have accomplished less, far less. Take, for instance, that character in Homer's Odyssey, Chapter 10, Circe—the character, Elpenor, his name was, the youngest of the Greek party, not much of a fighting man and not very clever. Elpenor got drunk and longing for fresh air had left his friends and had gone to sleep on the roof of Circe's enchanted palace. Roused in the morning by the bustle and din of the departure, he leapt up suddenly, and forgetting to go to the long ladder and take the proper way down—No! Change that. Probably forgetting he was on the roof, he toppled headlong and broke his neck. And according to Homer, his soul went straight to Hades. Stupid right? But we see things just as stupid these days like the death of Philip Seymour Hoffman from an overdose of self-injected Horse. Plus, ca change. Plus, c'est the meme chose."

Next was Miss Posh. She looked about 30, but I didn't like the way she kept giggling and giving Tristan smacks and punching him. Her laugh was a sort of a scream that went right through my ears, all the more irritating because there was nothing to laugh at. In fact, she smoked cigarettes and startled Tristan by asking: "Don't you smoke, dear?" Tristan replied that he had not yet arrived at it yet, whereupon Miss Posh gave one of her piercing laughs again.

Bernard, the Bardic Narrator, looked up. They were on the edges of their seats. So, Bernard figured that this was the iguana, time to break the illusion with a Bardic intrusion. The Ursula Andress look-alike had lit another cigarette and was blowing rings. She was a tease and probably a rover. Bernard pondered how a gesture of nominal exclusion and self-sufficiency could turn into a sexual challenge, in which every nuance was pregnant with significance. There is no possible communication from her that does not entail a string of meanings, all of which attracted him like a magnet. It all resided in the beholder and the beheld, of course, just like the meaning of a story. But still, he was of the opinion that this woman had more sex appeal on the tip of her nose than most women had in their whole body. And at the moment, he had an insight: He was beginning to realize what bodies were made for. Hint: None of the body is designed to play football, for instance. But much of the body is designed to make love and eat and manipulate weapons.

Margaritas and Harp pass through the hands of the partyers like Pepsi at a four-year-old's birthday. If she were there, Miss Andress would waste no time helping herself to the alcohol and to the boys.

She's hot as Hell, and she knows it. The kind of woman who can sashay down the Saint's Way like she owns it, walking tall in her fuck-me black pumps and charming the socks off the men she meets. She's a lot of woman. Most people will agree, especially men, especially me. I bet she's a minx between the sheets. In short, she's a sex goddess, a white-hot femme fatal, a priestess of passion. My type?

Oh, my God! Look at that: Just the right tongue position and upward thrust of her jaw had propelled a wonderful three-dimensional white whirling vortex that drifted upward on an entropic gust of air. Smoke rings—nothing like them.

Bernard thought, "She spent lots of time learning how to do that, how to blow smoke rings, time that could have been better spent in reading ancient history or learning physics or fashion merchandising. Still, there is nothing like watching a goddess who's got her game on. Perhaps she'll let me kiss her feet or lick her pussy."

"But what if she belongs to the branch of society in which there is always a crisis due, like the redhead—what was her name? O'Hara? O'Hair. Fat lady O'Hare—that's she. I have had my fill of the likes of her. Please, Jesus, keep the bipolars away from me. She was a pleasure. A pleasure from everything that smelt of lavender and rose leaves, to clasping her small coral necklace that fitted closely round her little white neck. Everything about her seemed of delicate purity and nattiness."

But where was he? How could he get out of this fucking kip? Tattering a kip. What person in his right mind would... would do such?

Oh, yes. The intrusion. He wanted to tell them about Homer and the Elpenor digression. About how Homer couldn't resist mentioning it because it must have happened in real life and made an impression on the Bard. The lesson was, don't sleep on the roof. And watch out when you get drunk. But more than that, it showed that the greatest of storytellers, in this, *The Odyssey*, the first and probably the greatest of Western novels, couldn't help putting in some private information, even though it interrupted the narrative flow and was of minimal interest to the readers.

That's the problem, man.

The problem with storytellers: they have to tell. They have to tell as much as a salesman has to sell. It goes with the territory. And if Homer can do it, why oh why can't I?

Back to King Mark's Party:

Another young lady, a little dorky, had had only two Tanqueray martinis, but something seemed to be happening to her. The high beams were on, but no one was driving. "Oh yeah," she said. "I love that filled-up feeling. Give it to me, baby. Give it to me, baby. Do me. Do me now. Please do me."

Another woman shared a confidence: "Mark's unmentionable is too small. Grape size," she sighed and wiggled her pinkie. Then she added, "I'm ready to do something foolish. Will you join me? Let's have fun tonight. Next month I will worry myself sick whether or not I am going to miss my period."

A brunette confided, "I tried to pick up Andread tonight. He wasn't up to it." She bent her head low and whispered in Tristan's ear while running her hand ever so lightly over his thigh, "Rather, he was up to it. But his thing wasn't. His thing wasn't up at all. Get my drift? Consequently, I'm hot to trot. How about you?" She got distracted by the shadowy figure of a parish priest with his soutane hiked up and his great you-know-what glaring out. To him, the priest, she went—leering.

Tristan tried to talk with some girls who flicked back their hair. Not really listening. Having too good a time chatting, smoking, drinking—a merry crowd. They scarpered.

With the next woman, Tristan felt that he had wandered into a TV moment, a problem worse than a senior moment. She snarled with a particularly breezy nastiness: "What's wrong with you? Are you a man or not? Let's get it on."

"It?" inquired Tristan.

"Yeah, don't you know what it is?"

"I know what it is when I see it. It is something solid like a chair or a frog or a sword."

"Get the show on the road, baby. *Capisce?* God damn! You're just another nothing doing nothing. I don't have forever. My biological clock is ticking faster than the hands of the handsome Louis XV clock upon its ormolu bracket on yonder wall. I'm probably going to die soon. Like in 15 years. But it looks like clueless you are not going to do much of a job here. I'll get more loving from a dead Republican."

There it was—Death, the second major theme of the Tristan Iseult story. What is at the bottom? Do we die? Yes. But thank God, that always comes later than now. Death doesn't worry me. I just don't want to be there when it happens. Is there sex after death? I hope so. I don't want to miss out entirely.

The next She was a virago named Emma Geddon.

This virago lit a cigarette. The whole atmosphere, with the mere presence of that white cylinder, changed—became charged with a nonspecific potential for arousal. Almost as soon as cigarettes were invented, there were collectors willing to pay money for photographs of women smoking. Several websites are devoted to the subject.

Next Lady Archer, a women of fragrance, elegance, and, if she had not had the strain of the situation upon her radiance, said, "How about some cold, unloving, rubber-insulated sex in a seedy hotel—Dirty Sally's DaySinn just down the street?"

"DaySinn? You mean Days Inn."

Then Tristan noted the ring. "But you're married."

"My husband and I, dear boy, explore the further reaches of 'for better or worse' a little more adventurously than most other couples." And then she recited that famous speech at the end of The Shrew where Katharina makes a brilliant and moving *volte-face* that some husbands not only in Shakespeare's time but also today might welcome, and which a great many wives then, as now, would find exceedingly difficult to speak. At the center of it is the thought: 'Thy husband is thy lord, thy life, thy keeper, thy head, thy sovereign...'"

Lady Archer—I can find no better way of defining her charm than by comparing it to that of certain women past their prime but who will never grow old—women whose beauty seems to hold some of the poignant magic of old classical ruins even behind a parchment cheek too much rouged. They still have it.

Some of them still have it, and some of them that still have it can make it, and some can even make it pay.

At the time, Lady Archer's words (and Bernard's sidebar about the beauty of older women) seemed profound. Though in the cold light of day, Tristan doubted that he understood the true significance. And he did well not to see them as all that relevant. Persons and characters in books who doubt themselves seldom doubt amiss.

How about you, dear reader? Do you ever doubt yourself? Le Je est un autre.

Then came Sally and Mary, who looked like they had wandered in from some other book. Sally was a big woman, but well-proportioned and sexy too. Mary is small but could compete with Miss World or Miss Bikini of South Africa. Both were hot. Very hot.

Sally smiled and gave Tristan the eye. "I am normal," she said. "How about you?"

Jesus Christ, don't they realize this is the 21st century where normal is not normal! LBGTQ or something seems to be the norm.

"What's normal?" came his reply, for the dumb fuck didn't realize she (Sally) and Miss World (Mary) were checking him out and were inquiring about his sexuality. To be explicit, she was telling him that she was heterosexual, and she wanted to know if he was the same.

"We can be discrete," she said in saint-like patience, glancing around and licking her lips and then her upper left molar.

Tristan had trouble figuring out whether the "we" meant she and he or she and Mary or all three of them together. While he tried to figure it out, Sally looked away and with her eyes, followed the Captain of the Guard as he crossed the room to bring some gray-headed woman a drink.

(Author's aside: I wonder what it feels like, during intercourse, to be a woman, whether their pleasure is keener, etc. It must be, else why do they always push so hard? Tireisias said the time he spent as a woman was better and the sex more intense.)

Sally turned to him. "Don't use your body as a briefcase to carry yourself around. Use it to live with. Last chance, Tristan. Else, we go after the Captain."

Tristan shook his head, "no." Mary and Sally didn't leave. He left them just before a busload of bad-ass Catholic school girls arrived. They, too, have cool monikers: Annie Social, Helena Handbasket, Jeckle and Heidie, Babe Ruthless, Eva Destruction, Kami Kazzi. Oh, God! Their uniforms consist of—you guessed it—plaid micro-miniskirts, set off by torn fishnet tights, and lots of brilliantly colored tattoos. They look lustworthy, but some are underage—a no-no.

Another, rather pagan young lady, ready to dip her toes into the water of real fun, who the night before had been out on what used to be called a bender approached and told him that she liked to do it with her high heels on. "Will that bother you?"

"Why do you ask?"

"Because the Captain of the Guard freaked out when I asked him."

(Author's note: Hell, you get the idea. Why should I continue with this crap? Why should I tell you about the white-haired old men and women who were at the party when they should have been home preparing for their ultimate journey? Let's not get carried away. Bernard, the Bardic Narrator, put people in his story because they and their things were real. It was a slice of his life. The chaos, all that was real. All those pick-up lines were real, fueled by alcohol and party spirit, but still real. So, let's have mercy on him. The dumb fuck is just a cunt-struck storyteller with lots of private information that he must unload. He can't help it. I repeat: A storyteller has to tell. It comes with the territory.)

Back to Tintagel and the party: King Mark, too, had had too much to drink and was rattling on, as he usually did when in his cups. His usual complaint was he didn't have enough space. "Mostly, life is a series of disappointments. I wanted all England. All I got was Cornwall," he announced, "mild climate, true, and picturesque, but a disappointment, nevertheless. It is high time I had a fan club. I never get enough respect from my children or enough love from women."

Mark was a little over medium height, well fleshed, with a rather handsome sun-tanned face and graying hair. He looked rather like an aging French actor, but there were differences. His expression when he smiled was very close to the ruddy, complacent, hard look of any number of American senators and businessmen. This tough good guy aura never quite remained, however. It always gave way to a certain vacancy in his face, like the vacancy of actors who play American congressmen pretending to act in the public interest. His eyes gave it away: They were large and gray, and baleful, like glass on fire; the eyes were there and not there at the same time, for Mark from the get-go had plenty on his plate and plenty that he should be worrying about. The politics of a premedieval court: About that, more later.

"Politics is war without bloodshed. War is politics with bloodshed," said Chairman Mao.

Looking over the people in the castle at the party, I know that all of them are God's children, but you can't help conclude that God has some seriously fucked up offspring. It is difficult to explain how a perfect all-powerful God created or even tolerates imperfect humans.

And speaking of imperfect humans, here they come.

Denoalen, Andread, Guenelon, and Gondoine, constituent members of the DAGG, approached Mark. Get it? Each first letter of their names.

What could they want of him that couldn't wait until lunch tomorrow, or for that matter, until Judgment Day? Boys and men always love playing at Secret Societies, and the DAGG was theirs.

Mark saw through this bunch like a CAT scan, suppressed a belch, and eyed them sternly, meaning to warn them even at that ultimate moment that he was not to be disturbed frivolously.

Looking at the DAGG, Mark realized that significant reform of the human race was out of the question. Perhaps that was why so many old men (like him) became embittered. The whole fucking thing is impossible, beyond hope and beyond the beyonds. The decadence and corruption are beyond imagination. The way to deal with it and them is by execution after ordeal by strappado, knout, and fire.

Such were his methods, though it must be conceded that for Mark, as for Arthur, terror was always a rational means to an end—never an end in itself. Rational terror is much better than irrational terror. The brutalities of Peter, Catherine, and even of Lenin, were not wildly out of proportion to their political aims, whereas Ivan the Terrible and Stalin practiced extravagant overkill, slaughtering subjects on a scale defying rational explanation. Ivan's chief instruments were the Oprichniks, a private army formed in 1565. They amounted to 5,236 murderous ruffians picked for their loyalty. Clad in black, riding black horses and carrying special emblems (a dog's head and broom), they were legally entitled to rob and slaughter non-Oprichniks with impunity. About Trump, we have little info as all documents, including his tax returns, have been repressed by his command or for reasons of national security sealed forever as state secrets and all that jazz.

(Editor's note: Everyone knows about strappado and knout, but I have to tell you that in this context, fire meant roasting alive. Not nice! But Mark and the Catholic church did use fire quite often. Church records show that over one million women were burned at the stake. All had confessed, of course. They confessed that they had had sex with the devil, could change themselves into bats and black cats, and could fly about on broomsticks. As versatile as women are they cannot do such things. Their confessions were made to protect their children and husbands from the seizure of property that would have occurred if they didn't confess. Church officials had their hearts in the right place. The idea was to reform the sinner and save their soul. Inquisitors envisioned each person as a battle ground between the evil of the flesh and the good of the spirit. The flesh must be punished to allow the spirit to be happy with God forever in Heaven.

(Modern legal systems hold confessions under duress as invalid. Most modern enlightened jurisdictions require confession in open court, and even then, the confession must be accompanied by proof of guilt.)

Mark held up a forefinger of warning, seriousness settled on his monobrow like crows in furrows of a cornfield. But before he could speak, he was spoken to.

"Sire," Andread whispered. "What do you really know about this Tristan fellow? Could he not be a spy sent by the Irish?"

Mark waved them off, saying, "You guys are going to have to come up with a lot of wonderful new paranoid theories, or people are going to stop believing you. Foreigners and immigrants are a welcome part of our society. Why not show a little courtesy to this guest from Kanoel, a name that declares the ancient affinity of Brittany with our beloved Cornwall, for it is none other but the Frenchified version of our own appellation, which derives from the ancient Celtic word Kanoel, meaning home of the sun (kan = home, noel = sun).

At this point, many of the DAGG were scratching their heads, trying to figure out what Mark meant.

Mark continues: "Fellers, this Tristan fellow looks successful. That makes you jealous, methinks. You see him as a potential competitor for the ladies. Right? Perhaps his looks bother you some as he does resemble my dear departed sister, Blanchefleur. Come to think on it, his face resembles mine and that of Noirfleur, Andread's mother."

Andread's nostrils flared. He and his mom, Noirfleur, never got along. Andread's head tilted back. He enunciated like a poet in the Parthenon. "No, Milord, just concerned for my king and for my kingdom. But admittedly, success often comes from dishonesty. Here might we find bold example sure. Your security forces should keep this interloper Tristan under close scrutiny, perhaps even tap his international phone calls and read his email."

"You misspeak and betray the workings of your unconscious mind, even display, perhaps, your own dishonesty and secret wish."

"Sire?"

"A slip of the tongue, Freud said, reflects the psychological state of the speaker. You said, 'my kingdom.' You meant 'the kingdom' or 'our kingdom.' Are you worth so much that you have the nerve to sneer at a fellow human who comes to us as a friend and guest? And then in your complaint against him, tip your hand and insult your king by calling the king's kingdom yours?"

Mark removed a fly from his wine and drank a draught. "No poisoned chalices here. Please! No eternal doom, not yet—no conspiracy, either—I hope. And no black sails. I'll have none of it. Men, don't let's play-act. No head games. They're no fun, ex-pecially (sic) at my age. From the very beginning, I knew there was something wrong with you, Andread, when your imaginary companion refused to play with you."

At this point, Andread asked for the Hall pass and used it. When he got to the bathroom, he tried to play with his thing, but it wouldn't work. It wouldn't work.

It was a frustrating night for him. But he was too drunk to remember it.

When Andread returned to the scene, he witnessed Tristan's big error. You can see it too if you look at the next tableau, tableau six.

Tristan's Mistake

As was the custom, Mark asked his visitor to recite for the group and sing and play the harp. Tristan, well-skilled in recitation, had memorized all 12 books of poesy and the fillid, the nine-score tales, only five of which belonged to the Fenian Cycle. He held the court spellbound for two hours, not only because of his skill but also because the human attention span in those days had not yet been seriously degraded by MTV.

His was a true *chantpleure*, a lovely word, a chiaroscuric doublet from the French meaning to sing and weep at the same time. It's like the modern music of Shostakovich and the ancient music of the Jews, music that superficially appears joyful, but conceals deep sorrow.

When Tristan finished, the group retained an awed silence—the greatest tribute a performance artist can receive. No one looked at his watch either or popped popcorn into his/her mouth or checked their pagers or iPhones. And no one clapped.

Andread laughed with unnecessary loudness, but in the midst of the laugh, he stopped, a wave of anger suddenly surging over him. Slowly, ceremoniously, he raised his arm, turned the knuckles of his closed fist toward Tristan, and levered up the middle finger of his fisted hand in an obscene gesture.

Tristan, who'd sung for his supper, slumped on a couch across the room, staring at his Guccis, wondering why major league ballplayers are rewarded so extravagantly for their skill as compared to poets, the unacknowledged legislators of the world. Oh Hell, it all meant nothing compared to the Shakespearean fate of us all, which is—well, you know what—so why mention it?

(Ed. Dusty death, of course.)

Speaking of which.

Woe to Tristan. His sands are running out. So great a tribute inspired in the four young nobles, The DAGG, a hate that hung over the evening like boredom. They were the four powerful barons D, A, G, & G—Denoalen, Andread, Guenelon, and Gondoine (DAGG for short), all of them of noble ancestry, distant relations of Erik the Memorable who had defeated Niels and his son Magnus and who, meaner than a junkyard dog, had treacherously murdered Duke Knud the Winegiver, conqueror of the Wends. In trickery, evasion, procrastination, spoliation, botheration, false pretenses of all sorts, the DAGG's influence will ever stand a measure for infamy. The evil that they did, as unbelievable as this sounds, exceeded even that of product liability attorneys, HMO's, Enron executives, Hitler, Iron Man Joe Stalin, and Duke Morgan himself. This I state advisedly because I know Hitler killed over 30 million people, and Iron Man Stalin killed over 60 million.

Lady readers, you wouldn't want to hook up with nor marry into this lot. They're worse than the Borgias. Envy, morbid suspicion, a fatal jealousy afflicted them as they collectively waltzed off to dusty death—after which, for their evil thoughts and for their evil deeds, they were to remain forever in thrall to the devil. Too bad all the injustice the DAGG would commit, and all the misery it would cause, couldn't be locked up with it and the whole burnt away in a great funeral pyre. How much the better would it have been for all parties involved, including King Mark himself! Except, of course, that without these villains, we'd be left with only the usual obstacles. We wouldn't have this entertainment, an exciting Postmodern Metafictional Adventure Travel Romance. For it was the DAGG that engineered the ineluctable subplot of which Tristan and Iseult are and will be the victims.

The DAGG were like Muslims (who are in turn like Baptist fundamentalists because they don't care if they die), exuding the same sullen tension as of distance runners who have trained too long and need relief. Their sin would be mortal because when a king falls, more than a crown is taken. The idea of divine right, and medieval belief that a king was appointed by God and was, therefore, God's symbol upon earth, until the DAGG unquestioned, is also violated. Anyone who rose against the king, or even so much as countered his wishes, was considered to be committing heresy.

OK Let's get this clear if you are having trouble following: Tristan is in big political trouble with the DAGG.

Tristan collected grudges—and enemies—as surely as a millpond accumulates silt. But there was more to it. Much more.

Two days later, the greater misfortune befell him (Tristan). And according to the manner of such events, it came while everything seemed safe and serene. Even the thought of ill luck was far, far away. Still, it happened.

Tristan's second big mistake is coming up in tableau seven. Read about it if you wish.

Morgana's Curse

A muted trumpet sounds. King Mark stands. Signals silence. "By my wish and command, I award Tristan a four-year scholarship to study at knight school."

"Night School? Why can't I go to school during the day like everyone else?" asks Tristan.

But before he and Mark get into an Abbott and Costello Who's-on-First-What's-on-Second type of exchange, the dancers arrive.

Wow! They look smart, sexy, glamorous, and hip. Sex goddesses—capable, confident, and beautiful.

Their show starts with their signature style: traditional singing of "The Girl from Ipanema" (which is bossa nova or jazz samba) and then "Brasil, Brasil," a true samba. A couple in their early twenties from the Blue Samba School in Rio De kick things off. The woman, dressed in a white gown with white satin fringes (actually ledges), featuring embedded aquamarines and multiple layers of ostrich feathers, holds and swirls around the stage a beautiful blue-and-white flag as she dances. She and her partner flawlessly sway to the music, making wider and faster gyres, gesturing gracefully with outstretched hands. "She holds a most expressive face," thought Tristan, with eyes squinting into the distance and mouth opened in a wide horizontal smile revealing glistening straight, bright white Regis Philbin teeth.

The pair are vogueing. They are vogueing long before vogueing had been invented. For the moment, they had transformed themselves and those like Tristan, who dreamed with them, into the queen and king of carnival.

(Ed. The carnival celebrated in Catholic lands is actually an adaptation of an ancient pagan whoop de doo, the festival of Dionysus, which in turn was adapted from the older Thesmophoria, the fertility festival of the mother goddess Demeter. Hestia and Demeter, when replaced by Dionysus, their carrus navalis, cart of the sea, became the Marti Gras float.)

"Give them a big hand," says King Mark. "The samba champions of the world from the Blue Samba School of Rio."

The previously hypnotized audience goes wild spontaneously and not on cue, for this is an era before the invention of the applause card and canned audience responses and an era before anything and everything became scripted and fake. An age before claquers. The audience went even wilder during the next act.

Four women arrive in sinuous, shimmering resplendence. Close up and real—in three dimensions, on stage, one at a time, they dance their personal versions of samba. They are muluakes (mulattos), dressed mainly in their brown skins, as scantily clad as fantasy women on the beach at Ipanema. Each shows her stuff making her bottom whirl and shake. The targas, that Brazilian swimsuit made of a single string of dental floss, apparently disappeared in the frenzy. The group thinks they are looking at naked orbic flesh, because, for the most part, they are. A targa of beauty is a joy forever.

The sensuality, the sight of all that animal health, female pulchritude, all that reproductive potential, amazed the knights and lords—awed some actually, and intimidated others, frightened some, and led to resentment among the older ladies.

Raw sexuality! Large gyrating hips! Beautifully rounded brown bottoms! Some at King Mark's court can't handle it, especially the evil barons of the DAGG. The dark side hates sex as much as it hates humor. Why? The DAGG is the chorus of the unloved. They are jealous of those who are and do love and all too willing to dish the dirt and stir the shit pot.

Bernard smiled and shouted the same again: "The dark side hates sex and humor! Don't forget that. It's key."

Not Tristan. He'd been up to the mountain. He had learned his lesson from courting too slow.

Tristan volunteered at the ladies' request to dance with them on stage.

With the insistent beat and under the spell of such beautiful partners, it all came back, the lessons he had had at Kanoel in samba gymnastics. He pushed himself to the edge of the envelope, straining every nerve, every muscle, every sinew of his body. He wouldn't need a thallium stress test. The vigor of his dancing proved his heart OK

Tristan picked another partner, or she picked him, or they both picked each other or something.

Faster and faster, in widening gyre they moved, the center wouldn't hold, by the kind of primitive frenzy that has its origin, pure and simple, simple and direct, in some time out of mind, and mind out of time ritual, deeply and essentially concerned with (what else?) human mating.

And as in mating, Tristan's bottom now had a mind of its own, moving faster, faster than a ship's propeller spins. The audience goes wild with cheers and applause. Tristan's mulatto beauty turns tail, faces the audience, and moves her frenzied backside toward Tristan. He responds by pushing his arms and legs and pelvis to faster and faster cycles. He grabs her waist. Now she and he move doggy style across the stage. His brow pouring sweat and his breathing rapid, regular, and deep. His pulse pounds in his headache as if he were running 26 miles 285 yards cross-country. But he stays with her, moves in unison, on the beat. Strutting his stuff while she struts her stuff, while they strut their stuff—together.

Suddenly, she stops.

She turns. She hugs him. She kisses him on the lips, on the neck, on the cheek, on his blazing brown eyes. She licks his neck, sucks the tip of his earlobe. Then her tongue finds its way into his mouth. He feels her lips, big, warm, soft, and smooth. Feels and knows her. Unforgettable!

He reaches, by instinct, with his right hand, grabs the right cheek of her behind, and pulls her close. He doesn't care who sees, who thinks what, who comes, or what happens. He is in her arms. She is in his. He is happily connected, willing to die. Willing to die for love, for her love. For her.

She doesn't resist. She's his—soft and compliant in his hands. In fact, she nudges closer. The idea of this female body seeking to slake its appetite on him affects him like an earthquake. He loves her. She loves him back. Her face reddens (just like Morgana's had when she was petting her crotch). She clutches him hard while her body shivers.

Suddenly, it's over. Her body softens. She releases her grip. She pushes away. Something happened. What?

Tristan didn't know. It looked like the thrill Morgana spoke of. Can women get it just by dancing and kissing and hugging?

A jazz sadness quivered in her nerves. She bit her lower lip and, wiggling that beautiful professional bottom, her private treasure, at him—wiggling her private treasure at him, she disappears behind the reredos backstage. She vanishes out of his life forever.

Some loves were never meant to be. And sometimes, mysteriously, we never know why.

Tristan was distracted from so abstruse a thought by a loud declamation issuing from King Mark. "Friend and stranger, you remind me of my sister, Blanchefleur. The way you danced made me think of her. Stay with us in Tintagel. Stay as long as you wish. Enjoy your studies in knight school while you determine what interests most centrally concern you and what you wish to do in life. Master, if you can, the medieval basics:

Apple Feat

Cat Feat

Blade Feat

Dart Feat

Rope Feat

Wheel Feat

Shield Held

Flat Feat

Hero's Salmon Leap Feat [This would come in handy later when Tristan was trying to escape King Mark's guards. Ed.]

Wiftness Feat (to avoid stabs, thrusts, and lunges)

Over-Breath Feat

"Then, after you have acquired the complete fleet of feats, consult with Professor Flannagan, my In-House Natural Philosopher who has a mind that joins one thing up with another. He has more intellect in his big toe than most people have in their entire bodies. He may have an opening for you in the Alchemy Department. Flannagan, a man of eminent renown for his knowledge of mechanic powers, has contrived many engines both for practical use and for recreation. By a wheel, which steam turns, he has forced water into a tower, whence it is distributed to all the apartments of the palace. He has erected a pavilion in the garden around which he keeps the air perpetually cool by means of artificial showers."

At this point, an old woman in the audience stood and waved a sign that said, "Impeach Earl Warren." Bernard nodded to her and continued Mark's encomium about Professor Flannagan.

Mark continued: "I trust Flannagan, implicitly and explicitly, despite the current controversies, and I disagree with him on some things, particularly his relentless stand against scientists at Princeton's famed Institute for Advanced Studies who have stunned the world by presenting absolute and undeniable proof of life after death. If there is no life after death, why would we all want to go on living? It just wouldn't make sense. If there were no transcendence, then all we humans would have are ourselves. And that's not much."

Mark, not noticing being not noticed, went on:

"A researcher at that world-famous institute (he is still talking about Princeton, I think, but I'm not sure) has used hypnosis to induce hundreds of people to recall their previous life experiences as pyramid builders, exchange students, and extraterrestrials. Weird how the obvious sometimes escapes even scientists like Professor Flannagan."

"Flannagan's latest project, aside from the consubstantiality problem of God the Father and God the Son that he has been working on for decades, the project which I fully support, involves flight. Flannagan has been long of the opinion that, instead of the sluggish conveyance of ships and chariots, man might master the swifter migration of wings. Alas, alack, Flannagan can't explain things in simple language. That's his main trouble and what alienates him from the rest of us, and that ultimately will be his undoing."

As if on cue, a pigeon dropped its mess on the royal shoulder.

Mark, unaware of the desecration, mistook the roar of laughter for high spirits. The mirth bursts had had something skiddy and out of control about them, meaning there was liquor involved, which, of course, there was, lots of liquor, most of it Irish whiskey.

"Every animal has his element," said Tristan. "Birds have the air. Man, the earth."

"The natural argument: another fallacy. Fish have water," said Mark. "But, by art, men swim in it. Who can swim need not despair to fly, for to swim is to fly in a grosser fluid, and to fly is to swim in fluid subtler and thinner." (Mark was quoting

Flannagan polly parrot style. And like most leaders, President Trump included, didn't know what he was talking about. For an untrained mind scans a scientific paper and thinks: Why can't he explain this stuff in simple language. He doesn't realize that what he tried to read is the simplest possible explanation in the simplest possible language for that subject matter. A great deal of science is a process of linguistic simplification wherein half a page of advanced calculus expresses an idea that could not be stated in less than a thousand pages of text.)

"Is it natural for us to drink wine or cook our food or wear clothes? If God had wanted us to walk, he would not have permitted the invention of roller skates. What is natural is not so great else we would not need to build houses and castles."

"No more and no less than it will be for us to fly. All this and more will you learn in knight school with Flannagan as your mentor."

"Very well, sire. And I thank you for the scholarship." Because King Mark had this time pronounced the word knight the old way with the K sounded, Tristan understood that Mark had given him the equivalent of admission to Columbia, Harvard, or Princeton. Or the commensurate equal value—a full tuition, room, and board scholarship to Yale. Too bad Tristan wasn't black. He could have gone to those schools for pay, especially if he could pronounce the word multiculturalism.

Tristan addressed King Mark: "Willingly will I serve you as your liege and in any other way you desire. By a strange coincidence, my mother's name was Blanchefleur. It was she who married, here, at Tintagel Minster. Rivalen, my father, King of the Lyonnesse, died while jousting with Duke Morgan. So said my mother to wise and trustworthy Gorvenal, my Squire. My mother died of Myasthenia Gravis. The proof of my matrilineal relationship thereof I have here: her golden ring."

"Oh, my God! That's her ring, Blanchefleur's ring. You are her son. You are my nephew. I am your uncle."

Tears came to the old king's eyes. Mark embraced Tristan as his nephew and acknowledged the relationship before the court and the barons. All (except the evil DAGG) applauded as Tristan knelt before King Mark.

Mark's squire came, leading the favorite bard, whom the muse loved above all others, though the muse, she, had mingled good and evil in her gifts (as usual), robbing him of his eyes but granting him the gift of dulcet song.

Mark placed a gold-studded chair for the bard in the center of the company, with its back to the Sheela. The tuneful lyre hung on a peg just above his head, an easy reach. At the bard's side, Mark had a servant girl put a bowl of sweet meats and a cup of wine to drink as the spirit moved.

The muse then set the bard to sing some tiresome, worn-out common song, which told a ridiculous story about famous Greek heroes involving the quarrel of Odysseus and Achilles son of Peleus. It informed of how these two had clashed in an altercation bizarrely engineered by gods and goddesses, signifying nothing except perhaps the fulfillment of the sacred prophecy that Phoebus Apollo had made in Pytho.

Fantastic stuff, really, (was Homer drunk when he wrote it?) but hardly worthy of Tristan's attention or for that matter, anyone's attention. The wonder was that the old bard himself could get through it without yawning. In the old days, poets got away with a lot of stuff, including chloroformed crap like that. Tristan began to nod off. And yet, this is considered a classic, which it is most definitely. The classics, according to Mark Twain, are literature that everyone would have liked to have read, but no one wants to read.

A beautiful young woman, dressed in green and looking like a 17-year-old dancing queen, interrupted the boredom by slipping a note into Tristan's right hand. It read:

> Crown your head and come away
> In my garden, dare to play.
> Come beyond the pillar stand.
> Beyond the sound of choral bland.
> And touch my hand
> And all you can
> While I you kiss
> And please don't miss
> my special brand
> Of woman's service.
> /signed/
> Morgana, Princess of Lothian,
> Half Sister of King Arthur Pendragon

Tristan folded the note on end and scribbled:

> Dear Morgana,
> Your poetry (and spelling) needs improvement, but your bodily charms need none. I am a stranger here and not to the manner born. Having been in the castle yet only sex hours (sic), I must watch my step and play things cool. Some other time. Not now.
> /signed/
> 5

Tristan reread his note. It was an indictment of circumstance and savage, even. Not now. Not now! Man, more opportunities for love are missed by that "not now" idea than are dreamt of in any philosophy. By choices, people change the probability of a future event happening or not happening. They collapse the wave function, as the saying goes.

Tristan looked over the note he had written. He corrected his Freudian slip of sex hours to six. He crossed out the red five because Morgana might not get that he was pretending he was Luke Skywalker (code name red five), a character in a famous movie called Star Wars vintage 1977. Besides, she knew who he was. No signature required. Besides, it wasn't fit for a character to pretend to be still another character. That's not Kosher. But, you know, there are usually two reasons for the things we do: The stated reason and the one that's true. Although the idea of a woman hitting on him affected Tristan like an avalanche, he wasn't that kind of young man. He had barely (The… umm… samba… the thing on the mountain) begun to experience sublunary pleasures. Before he could even think about kissing a woman, much less loving her, he had to love her. Or, which is (more often) the same, think he loved her. And before he could love her, he had to know her. He didn't know Morgana, who she was, where she came from, what her reputation was… or if she was clean. In fact, all he knew was that she was beautiful and wore green and that she had somehow shed 23 years in the last few hours (was she a selkie from Irish folklore?) and that she had something strange and mysterious between her legs, a little thing which he had seen, and in mental flashes, kept seeing. Beauty speaks for itself in this wide world, but the wearing of the green meant she might be involved in magic, white or black or both. A Glinda or a Wicked Witch of the West? Which witch was best? Which witch was she? A crazy melody started to drum inside his head: Which witch would which witch watch?

To be honest with you, how the fight started I haven't the faintest idea. To be honest with you, I don't care! I do seem to remember someone pushing my shoulder and digging his hand in there and enquiring if I were from the protestant north. And Tristan taking off. An icy cold wind from somewhere. A Nation Once Again in full swing. After that, someone cried SKTEE! And kicked my bollards. You can picture the scene, I'm sure. Black hefty books out of nowhere. Men with fists now squared and, lit with drink, at the ready. Real real-life chaos. Time to blow.

That night a note slid under Tristan's chamber door:

"If it may please my Lord, I await your touch, pleasure, and command. You may come up at this very moment. Tomorrow is too late, for I leave for Sorcery School in Dublin. In case you are as dense as most men are about these matters, I allow myself to state things quite explicitly, for I am languishing in my bed:

By now should come as no surprise

My grassy garden, the thing men prize,

Awaits your presence between my silk-white thighs.

Doubt not, honored sir, the accounts of primeval pleasures fabulous and right:

They be real, as I wish to prove to you this very night. Morgana

PS. I love you so much I am sick with it.

Unfortunately, or fortunately, as you look at it, Tristan was such a sound sleeper he did not hear the message delivered. So that morning, a strange ache and wistful regret suffused the core of his being as he belatedly scanned the note.

Of all the sad words of tongue and pen, these are the saddest: It might have been!

"Poor Morgana!" Tristan thought. He glanced up at the wall. Oh, dear, guess who he saw there. Guess who was on the cross on the wall as usual. Looking down as usual as if to say: Ah, humans. Ah, women.

Ah, women, what? For as long as he could remember, there He had been with His crown of thorns, bloody hands, and feet, all that, just hanging there looking down and looking real petered-out and real dead. Why do they have such disgusting things on the walls? Children are around.

She had pined away, poor soul! Probably believing that he had not even had the courtesy to reply. Rejected women tended to the cloister, a special tragedy in Morgana's case since she seemed psychologically and physically unfit for the convent. Morgana, cloister? Unlikely. Revenge was more probable. That was more likely. Her cup of tea. Ah well, the future is never dead as long as there is a present. Perhaps she will get to love him. Perhaps she will get to kill him. Perhaps both. Perhaps. Perhaps. That's the great thing about the future: it is contingent. We never really know what is going to happen. The consolation, though, is that in fact, most of the bad things [with one big exception (the big D)], that always happens sooner or later) (yes, the big D is death, stupid!)—most of the bad things that we worry about never do happen. Most worry is a waste of time most of the time. "Je ne regrette rien," said Edith Piaf. That's the spirit.

"Today is the tomorrow we worried about yesterday," a woman (not ShaNADE) shouted from the audience.

Tristan established eye contact with himself in the mirror and committed himself firmly to a reformation of his ways in this respect: "Let us not imagine evils which we do not feel, nor injure life by imaginary misrepresentations." Thus, he resolved to lose no more time in meditations about Morgana. He was confirmed in the direction of his decision by hearing a maid at breakfast, who had broken a porcelain cup, remark that what cannot be repaired is not to be regretted. Then among the smells of apples and bacon grease and lamps, the maid looked longingly at him with eyes of desire and said, while moving closer, "I love to see men eat. Would it please my lord to eat me?"

The two other little kitchen maids bustled about, eager to listen, hot and panting, with white cotton sleeves well tucked up above the dimpled elbows and giggling over some private jokes of their own and no doubt their vulgar image of "eat me."

He refused her, too, and her face took on a crushed pansy look. Women are like that. Beware when you offend them! Trouble usually follows.

In fact, right after, by some weird coincidence, Sally, the maid, spilled ice-cold milk onto Tristan's crotch.

"Lud, bless my soul!" exclaimed Sally, with a good-humored laugh and an evil smile. "What would my lord be wanting now, I wonder? Beer?"

Sally thoughtfully rubbed her hands against her shapely hips; her palms were itching to do more damage. "I 'xpect one Jimmy Pitkin pewter tankard will do ye and in the same place, mi lord?" Whereupon started the little maids on a round of short and suppressed giggles. Young people have a way of understanding one another, as young people have a way of doing all the world over and have done since the world began.

"That's not funny," said Tristan, trying to hide his feelings, but only succeeding in looking immeasurably sheepish.

Too bad Tristan, as yet but rudimentarily schooled, had not read Shakespeare. He did not know about the Chick Revenge thing, that Hell hath no fury like a woman scorned. According to the Shakespearean school of thought, Tristan will feel Morgana's curse and wrath—and feel it soon. Part of Morgana's problem, and that of the other dames in Shakespeare, we now know, was premenstrual syndrome. In those days, there was no effective remedy for PMS the way there is now. But of course, I don't know what it is. I'm just repeating what I heard in the school yard. Look it up on the internet if you need to.

United States Government spies on Morgana:

Consider this NSA image recently downloaded from Skylab spy cameras:

Morgana, the prime devotee, is seen in a video depositing on Diana's temple door, a curse that will cause Tristan's root problem, a curse that will afflict him throughout the rest of his life and the rest of this story. The curse that will drive the main plot of this ancient legend. A curse that was written in Caesarian cipher: *PDB KH ORYH DV L GR ORYH.*

You can decipher this plain text if you care to, by replacing letters standing three places further down the alphabet, D for A, E for B, etc. The code was used by Caesar himself. Hence, the name. Thus, the message *Omnia Gallia divisa est enciphers RPQLD JDOOLD GLYLVD HVW.* If you are too lazy to work on it, just go on to the next chapter and see why the Irish are about to make war on Cornwall.

Morhold Arrives

The sun had now passed four times over him in its annual course, and Tristan felt regret of a degree with which he had never been acquainted. He considered how much he might have done. Time had passed and yet left nothing real behind it. Days and years leaked away in common business and amusements. He had suffered his purposes to sleep 'til the time of action was past. Ah, this fleeting world. Time passing by in the blinking of an eye. And like migrating birds, our lives drift away from us, drift away, headed south. Consequently, we are not of the same strength that in olden days moved earth and heaven. We are what we are. Much has been taken. But much abides. Made weak by fate and time—our destiny. It is really not a fair fight, us against entropy, the second law of thermodynamics, wherein things fall apart, have to fall apart. The second law has never been violated.

Tristan measured the four squandered college years with the lifetime of a man. In life, he thought, you can't count the ignorance of infancy or the imbecility of age. The true productive period may be reasonably estimated as 40 years, of which I have just wasted four. So here I am, like Faust, a poor fool as wise as when I entered school. And like Faust, the only thing that I have learned is the impossibility of knowledge. And thinking of knowledge reminded (interesting word re-minded, meaning things brought back into mind) him of his scientific mentor, Professor Flannagan.

One night, Tristan was sitting with Flannagan in the turret of Flannagan's house, watching the emergence of Callisto, one of the 16 moons of Jupiter. A sudden tempest clouded the sky and cut off their observations. Flannagan's plumb, shadowed face, and sullen oval jowl recalled a prelate or scholar of arts in the Middle Ages. He remained silent, immobile, brooding for a time, then, fidgeting with his hands, Flannagan, the Great Man, spoke:

"Tristan, I have long considered you the best of my pupils and thy friendship as the greatest blessing of my life. Knowledge is weak and useless, but integrity, benevolence, and fortitude make character. We used to select for admission to knight school those with the greatest potential and ability. That plan didn't work. Now we look for character first. That is why our knight school out-performs Harvard, where they have plenty of ability but no character to speak of."

Tristan thought himself honored by this testimony, for truly, he considered Flannagan his Yoda. But what was the old man driving at?

"Tristan, you are about to learn one of the most important secrets of the scientific world. Will you keep it to yourself? Or will you demonstrate your immaturity by blabbing it all about?"

Tristan nodded his head hesitantly.

Dance music floated up from the hotel's beach deck below. "Twist and Shout," followed by "Jailhouse Rock."

"Someone is having a good time," said Tristan.

"It's nice to think of them down there, turned out and tipsy, their language apophatic," Flannagan agreed. "But sad to realize that none of them can look up into this night's sky and recount the mythic history of Western civilization as clued through the zodiac."

"I can't do that myself," admitted Tristan. "I can't say what's what and who did what to whom to get where. I've spent my four years learning nothing. All men, by nature, desire to know. That's the first sentence of Aristotle's Metaphysics. I haven't gotten much further. I figure the rest must be out of date by now. However, if the desire to know is so great among men, why can't they name the bushes on their property or the signs of the sky or the three parts of Gaul Caesar spoke of? Why?"

Stale smoke hung in the air of the study, mingling with the smell of the drab leather of the chairs. This was, as it was in the beginning, when Tristan first met him, is now, and will be always, world without end: A scholar's den.

"Mark my words," Flannagan said. "Cornwall is in the hands of Jews. In the high places, they are: finance, press, politics. They are the signs of a nation's decay. Where they gather, they eat up vital energy. I have seen it coming these many a year. They are not like the DAGG, who just want to change leadership. They want to change the form of leadership. They want democracy, not autocracy. That is all very well in practice, but will it work in theory?"

"King Mark is not a Jew. And the Catholic church is everywhere that there is wealth or power. The evidence is more like the Catholics are in control, not Jews. By the way, it is interesting to note—actually striking in the best sense—that precisely those rules that correspond exactly to the church's economic interests enjoy unconditional veneration."

"Catholics are Jews in disguise. Jesus is the most important man here in Cornwall. And he is a Jew and a typical Jew. How do we know? He lived with his mother for over 30 years, he went into his father's business, his mother thought he was God, and he thought his mother was a virgin."

Flannagan looked down and held for a while the wings of his nose tweaked between his fingers. Looking up again, he set them free. He decided not to tell Tristan about Mark's new systematic program of thought control. It was not merely negative, for citizens were also required to subscribe to an official ideology expressed in the triple slogan 'Orthodoxy, autocracy, and patriotism.' Mark had gotten into the habit of tweeting a storm of stupidities every morning before his golf game and never doing any of the real work of governing. One hundred forty characters—that was just about his attention span.

Flannagan: "I'm happier than you are, Tristan. For my sins relate to women. Many errors and many sins. A woman brought sin into the world. Helen caused the ten-year war the Greeks made on Troy. Parnell had a personal downfall. His adulterous relationship with a colleague's wife came to light and was used by his enemies to bring him low. One time, when disturbed with his lady, he beat a retreat down the fire escape. Some wanted to put a fire escape down the back of his statue on O'Connell Street. All that, thank God, is behind me. Happily, history is moving toward one great goal, the manifestation of God and the suppression of women in Islam.

"Before I got on the topic of women and Jews, where was I?" asked Flannagan as he scratched his bald head.

"You were about to recount some secret, one of the most important secrets of the scientific world. You were wondering if I were mature enough to keep the secret."

"Ah, yes. You listen. That is one of your endearing features. So rare these days. Yes, here is the secret: It may come as a surprise to you to learn that I have possessed for 25 years the regulation of weather and the distribution of the seasons; the sun has listened to my dictates and passed from tropick to tropick by my direction. The clouds, at my call, have poured forth their waters, and the Nile has overflowed at my command. The winds alone refuse to obey my authority, and multitudes perish by equinoctial tempests, which I found myself unable to prohibit or restrain. Thus, that recent mud slide in Palm Springs was not my doing, nor was hurricane Dorian. My research will restrain them, O Lord, if only I could unlock the secret of the speed of light and the hidden and concealed superfluid nature of Helium-4 at 2.71 degrees Kelvin."

"You're joking," said Tristan. "No one controls weather."

Flannagan didn't answer. Instead, he resumed the solemn monologue: "You and others have not noticed my powers because this great office have I administered with exact justice and made the nations of earth an impartial dividend of rain and sunshine."

"Perhaps, a vacation in Bermuda would help you," suggested Tristan. "The weather is nice. You could recuperate there and get back your reason."

"Of the uncertainties of our present state, the most dreadful and alarming is the uncertain continuance of reason. Even my reason is in doubt about my reason."

"Professor Flannagan, you speak truer than you think," said Tristan, with a worried mouse-face look, followed by raised eyebrows and a nod.

"Perhaps, if we speak with rigorous exactness, no human mind is ever precisely in its right state. Even I have sometimes suspected myself of madness and should not have dared to impart this secret but to a man like you, capable of distinguishing the wonderful from the impossible, and the incredible from the false. Men like me are very important to the history of humanity. We remain completely unknown to the rest of the world, unknown for we have no apparent power, no money, no honors. Few can understand the pleasures we get from our work. The vast public can't use the work, much less understand it. But in fact, we scientists are the most powerful men in the world. And for one simple reason: we hold the keys to rational certainty. Everything I declare to be true will be accepted, sooner or later, by the whole population. No power—economic, political, or social—can compete with rational certainty. The West will sacrifice everything to this need—religion, happiness, hope. Ultimately its own life."

Tristan wondered if maybe a strong drink would be in order. It might help. F. (Tristan sometimes thought of his teacher as F.) might be anxious about something, and the drink might help calm him down.

Flannagan fell silent, deep in thought. He let his gaze wander around the tables for a moment, then settle on his glass.

"Can you prove you control the weather?" asked Tristan.

Flannagan smiled. "Your skeptical attitude alone demonstrates that your education was not in vain. Yes, Mark is not a Jew, so in a sense, you have shown by counter example that my statement that the Jews control Kanoel is not true, not entirely. Next, you are asking for proof that I control the weather."

"By external evidence, I cannot. But mind you, no one has ever by experiment or observation confirmed the existence of God or Santa Clause. And yet, we know they exist. It is sufficient that I feel this power that I have long possessed, and every day extend. A guardian angel sits on my right shoulder and talks of it with me daily. Yet I cannot prove his existence either for others cannot see her or hear her."

"Which is it? Male or female?" asked Tristan.

"Male or female, what?"

"You said his existence, but you cannot hear her. So, is your angel male or female?"

"Both. Are you stupid? Angels are hermaphroditic according to the Bible. They are male and female both."

"Professor Flannagan," Tristan said sincerely. "Please don't talk about this to anyone. Some at court already consider you insane. The admiralty laughed at your recent grant application to plan a fleet of iron boats. Some even called for your arrest."

"Their ignorance is neither here nor there, for an iron boat will float as surely as the sun will rise tomorrow and the Dog Star, with it, cause the heat of summer. But I feel the pressure, you bet. My arrest is imminent. Plato attempted to disprove the reality of motion. Plato is my friend, but truth is a greater friend. Time is running out, and it is unlikely I will complete my analysis of the 42 books by Hermes Trismegistus."

"But worse than that, the time must come when the regulator of the weather will soon descend the black hole of history and mingle with the dust. The care of appointing a successor has long disturbed me; I have yet found none so worthy as thyself."

Tristan placed his hand on his forehead and ran that hand back through his jet-black hair. Then he pressed both palms tight against his temples but did not speak. Modesty is a fine virtue, though it is more praised than practiced, more often observed in the breach than in the execution. He knew that F. feels age and illness, lost youth, his friends 'all dead,' the passing of time. He knew he (Flannagan) has heard the chimes at midnight and that within the next few pages of this story would come the necessary separation.

Flannagan pointed his left index finger at Tristan and jabbed it back and forth at the young man's chest. "Promise me that you will diligently consider the position of earth and sun, and the axis of earth and the sometimes varied ecliptic of the sun, that you will recognize that all is in place exactly as it should be so that by innovation only the most profound mischief will occur—disordering of the seasons, the robbing of one nation for the sake of another. Special diligence is needed during the ENSO (El Niño Southern Oscillation). And these precepts in your memory: Think while others sleep, read while others play, and never watch TV."

Always eminently sensible, Tristan figured it was better not to trouble the dark water due north of north. Get the big issue out of the way to concentrate on something small, something close. "I promise that should I possess the power to regulate the weather, I will use it with inflexible integrity," declared Tristan, a trace of self-conscious preening in the lift of his well-muscled arms, the rise of his chin, his stare into the middle distance.

Flannagan, overjoyed, raised his voice an octave, pressed his hands into Tristan's. "My heart's at rest. I have found a man of wisdom and virtue, to whom I can cheerfully bequeath the inheritance of the sun. YOU ARE HE."

They celebrated the transfer of power with some Skyy vodka, then moved to another chamber where Flannagan demonstrated the mysteries of the explosive powders, their preparations and ingredients. Flannagan commanded Tristan to memorize the formulae so that their secret would always remain safe within the hollow round of his skull. Nowhere else. The bow was the first way of storing energy to be used later as a weapon. The explosive powders were the second way. These powders will figure prominently in human history. Don't believe me? Look around.

Flannagan did a demo by exploding a bomb in a pressure cooker.

Wow! Such a weapon could injure a lot of people all at once. But to what purpose? Why would anyone want to hurt fellow humans? We are all the same species. Are we not?

In truth, Tristan loved explosive powders. They're real magic.

Who, forsooth, can describe the magic yellow beauty of burning sodium? The rich crimson of strontium, the blue of cobalt, the vert of nickel? One cannot praise enough the esthetic of explosions, the furious, frenetic frenzy of oxidation-reduction.

The tremendous power! The deafening noise! The blinding bright flashes. The sulfur smells. Burning chemicals—enthralling!

Like so many humans, Tristan loved to see things blow up. Afterwards, he liked to savor the ephemeral patterns made by the rising smoke, a series of gray veils suspended in their own doom on the fleeting entropic air. He had a creative drive to build and make, but he also had a darker side that liked to destroy, to kill, to tear down, or tear apart. That this is true of humankind in general, anyone can attest who has watched a child at play at blocks, sandcastles, or anything. They build them, and they knock them down with equal pleasure. The Bible says that humans were created in the image and likeness of God, and the Bible gives many examples of God's interest in destruction. Sodom and Gomorra. The great flood. World wars I, II, III, IV, and finally, V, when everything flamed out. The war thing is probably a natural and expected extrapolation of hunting.

The next day, Tristan, having passed the final exams, was dubbed a knight and armed by King Mark.

The new knight's first adventure resembled those endlessly recounted by Sir Thomas Mallory: He left Cornwall, avenged his father's death, killed some dukes and barons, and many other knights, won back his vassals and fiefs and was re-seized of the ancient wealth of the Lyonnesse. But the Lyonnesse was under the Atlantic ocean still, and Tristan would have to wait for the next ice age to get his estate back.

I could go into all that battle stuff, just like Mallory, but it is not as interesting as the psychological romance that Patten and Bernard want to tell. If you really need that action shit, if that's your bag, if you are an action junkie needing a fix, go to the movies. With CG (computer graphics), you can get all the simulated destruction you need.

Author's sidebar: There are too many fake things out there. Here in this book, we talk only of real things in real life. Things that actually happened. Things that actually matter. If you are looking for fake things, go watch TV.

Once his power was fully consolidated, it occurred to Tristan that he could stay, rest in his own land, forever administering justice in person in a kingdom of modest dimension and seeing all the parts of government with his own eyes. But of course, like most administrators, he could never fix the limits of his dominion. He needed a perimeter to protect his property. And once formed, he needed a perimeter to protect the former perimeter. See where I'm going? Every attempt at protection leads to another attempt at protection and so on down the slippery slope to world domination.

And so, Tristan, just like every administrator, was always adding to the number of his subjects, increasing the burden of their taxes. Excelsior—ever upward, the nature of governments. It won't change for a thousand years. And then it will be worse.

Messengers came twice a week (Moon's Day and Frida's Day—what we now call Monday and Friday) to Tristan telling of how King Mark missed him and the king, for the lack of Tristan's company, had fallen into a serious depression unrelieved by Prozac.

So, Tristan returned to Cornwall to serve Mark as a liege and to have action and adventures there. He followed King Mark in pleas and in saddle and to assizes and to the greyhound races. He advised Mark at council and helped plan festivals, feasts, and fun. By night he slept with the other favored of the court (two hounds) in the royal bed. When the king was sad, Tristan cheered him with harp, jokes, and stories, or funny, silly—but-really-quite-clever poems about the stock market, of which here follows an example:

> Ah somewhere in this favored land
> the sun is shining bright.
> A band is playing somewhere
> and somewhere hearts are light.
> Men are laughing somewhere
> and somewhere kids have dates.
> But there is no joy on Wall Street;
> Greenspan raised the rates.

Such diversions and duties amused Tristan for a time by their novelty and interest, but soon the underlying quotidian boredom began to weight upon him like a rucksack loaded with stones. What people call boredom is an abnormal compression of time caused by monotony. God pity him! He became a rich repiner and a household drudge. He missed adventure, pleasure, excitement, change, and danger—all the things his drab existence denied him. Dyslexia prevented his obtaining harmlessly the things he sought in books the way others do. Deprivation left him with a kind of nameless inner craving that dogged his footsteps night and day. Was this all there is, my friend? Was this all there is? Were there no more goals? Nothing more to obtain? Nothing to conquer? If that's it, if that's all there is, then let's break out the booze and have a ball.

Venerable Bede tells of the king and his people feasting in a great hall. A sparrow flies in one end and exits the other. Get it? The hall is like our experience of life. The darkness the sparrow came from is our experience before birth, and the darkness the sparrow went to is our experience of death. All we know is what's in the hall, the food, the firelit warmth, the fun, and fellowship. What lies beyond is a mystery, unknown, and unknowable.

This is a key point of human existence: We come out of darkness and return to it, with experiences in between. It is highly likely we don't experience the beginning and the end, birth, and death. We are not SUBJECTIVELY aware of them because they exist only in the world of objective events. Don't believe me? Can you recall anything of your birth? And I would bet all dead people don't even know they are dead. They may have known they were headed that way, but when they actually died, nope.

(Ed. Venerable Bede cherished since his death in 735 by the monks of Tyneside and Wear.)

The apple cake Tristan was holding slipped to the floor. He knew there was some sort of risk when he picked it up, so he made the sign of the cross over it. That was the antiseptic of the era.

At last, something happened.

Morhold arrived.

The Morhold, sacker of cities, sailed into Tintagel harbor from Hibernia (Latin name for Ireland) to collect the ransom due. The sky darkened. Was there a certain time when it happened? That the Irish took over? Probably the inflection point occurred decades before when Cornwall lost a war no one remembers. That was a watershed series of events, surely, but the full process seems to have been more like death from a thousand cuts, some self-inflicted. Most of the slavery, in my opinion, will prove to be irreversible. But let us scan the next tableau to see if that poor prognosis comes true. The word is that Tristan will take no shit from nobody. And there is agitation among Cornwall folks for him or Mark or someone "to do something about the Irish exploitation." So, at last, maybe, someone is going to do something. Let's see.

The Irish King Demands 600 Slaves

◆—————————————◆————————————————◆

This year's ransom, tax, and tribute amounted to 300 youthful men and 300 maidens. That makes 300 + 300 = 600 total. They were to go to Ireland with Morhold as his serfs and slaves, nothing else.

(Ed. This is true. In the four-year cycle, Ireland did extract that tribute from King Mark's court, and the person the Irish sent to collect the tribute was Morhold.)

Unless.... Unless some champion killed the Morhold, sacker of cities. Only by the trial of individual combat could Cornwall survive this Irish Exactment.

The trouble was that the Morhold—Mor = Celtic for huge, old = Celtic for hammer; hence Morhold, (misspelled as Morolt by the French) means big hammer or, one could say, sledgehammer—the trouble was that the Morhold, sacker of cities, was fourfold larger than any man and ten times stronger. Rumor had it that since high school, he'd taken human growth hormone and androgenic steroids, as they said about Roger Clements and Lance Armstrong. All previous knights opposing him (the Morhold, not Armstrong) had known a swift vengeance that spoke one last fearsome word to them—and that word was (you guessed it) "death."

Why, O why, O Holy Vesta, Goddess of the handloom, of the hearth, of the home—in spite of clearly reasoned judgment, all the resolutions and promises he had made to himself, the great satisfaction and peace he had once found in turning his back on the madness of war—why in that moment, the moment of the Morhold's arrival, did Tristan experience a frisson shiver of excitement?

Answer: To quote General Patton: "Compared to war, all human activities shrink to insignificance."

The sage Flannagan answered the same question: "Conspiracy and complot are intoxicants more powerful than heroin. They cast a spell over the workaday world and turn common, drab existence into the stuff of Epic Historical Drama. This is why such stuff is featured on CNN. A man who feeds on such soon hungers for more. So mad a diet makes him feel more fully alive even though it may, yea often does, lead him on to death. Woe to you, Tristan! If you fight, you will be annihilated. Who lives by the sword dies by the sword, as said the Savior."

Editor's Note: In that age and in that place, the Irish had an empire. This empire, like all the others you can name or think of, extracted conscription, taxes, and tribute from the vassals who served it. Cornwall, having suffered multiple defeats at Irish hands, fell under the Hibernian yoke. The Irish penalty for defeat was not knout, strappado, or fire. From inception, the Irish empire had been notably more humane. Such barbarous forms of punishment as quartering, breaking on the wheel, impaling, and beheading (for the most part) had been abandoned as had judicial torture, administrative execution, and the punishment of nostril-slitting. What was left was that more modern system of oppression—taxation.

The Irish tax on Cornwall consisted of a four-fold tribute renewed every fourth year: The first year 300 pounds of bronze, the second year 300 pounds of silver, the third year 300 pounds of gold, and the fourth year (as mentioned) 300 men aged 17 or older, selected by lottery from all adult men, and 300 maidens aged 14 or older, selected by lottery from all adult women.

The fourth tax was the most difficult because all Cornwall's subjects, with the exception of the king himself, the clergy (1% of the population), the landed gentry (1% of the population) and children (22%), had a chance of being drafted into slavery.

The Irish high king demanded similar tributes from the King of Leinster, King Maelmora, in Eastern Ireland. But for Maelmora, the tax was less onerous: 300 horses, 300 cows, 300 swords, and 300 cloaks each successive year in the four-year cycle. After payment, each of those subkingdoms received Irish protection and became officially part of Ireland.

(The taxes mentioned are historically accurate, Ed.)

The Morhold, the Darth Vader of tax collectors, whose sister married Brian Boru, the High King of Ireland who wore the torc of gold, and was, by that connection, an uncle of Princess Iseult la Belle, the heroine of this tale, called an assembly of Cornwallians and made the demand.

(Editor's note. Before we go on, let's get this straight: Iseult is the Irish princess and the daughter of the Irish King and niece of the taxman who is called Morhold. In German, Iseult is known as Isolde, in English, Iseult the Beautiful, and in French Iseult la Belle. Iseult will be Queen of Cornwall by marrying King Mark, Tristan's uncle. She is not to be confused with Iseult of White Hands, daughter of King Howith of Brittany. Iseult of the White Hands will enter this story later as a rival for Tristan's affections, eventually becoming Tristan's wife.)

"King Mark, barons, and knights, too long have you delayed the payment of slaves, less than one percent of your total population, a trivial skimming. Hand them over as prescribed by ancient treaty and covenant, and I and my Irish fleet shall depart forthwith not to bother you again."

"Until next year," Tristan shouted, rather impolitely. "You Irish won't bother us again until next year. And then it will be the same thing all over again, a cycle of bronze, silver, gold, and slaves."

King Mark motioned for Tristan to calm down and then addressed the Morhold. "English law requires that we have a tax hearing. Should that fail to mitigate the levy, we get a chance to test the validity of your lord's claim by the trial of combat."

Morhold was underwhelmed, "Good God, Mark, don't you realize resistance is useless. We go through this every god damn year. Every year someone complains about the tax, and every year one of you gets killed. Need I remind you that my Irish fleet lies offshore, nine ships each with a hundred toughs from Dublin. Never give an Irishman an excuse for vengeance. You should have learned the lesson: Don't push the Irish. They push back. Besides, have you forgotten, Cornwall is part of Ireland, so English law does not apply."

"That you prevailed 15 years in a row is a fact, part of the unrecoverable past. But that you will win this year is still part of the indeterminate future," Mark opined.

"So, what!" Morhold frowned. "Your point, please, if you have a point."

Morhold internal dialog: "Once again, my authority was questioned. Once again, the English were to make him work to collect the tribute. One again, the intransigent English (Cornwall being part of Arthur's demesne) were being pains in the ass. Why couldn't the English just give way to tyranny like everyone else? Why did they always have to fight? Why couldn't they be nice like the French and just cave in, capitulate, lay down their arms before they got hurt? Each year it became harder to collect from these Cornwall bastards."

As the above internal dialogue shows, Morhold was getting tired of it all. He had seriously considered early retirement at half pay as part of the new Irish program to decrease costs and ensure fuller employment for everyone. But, despite these qualms, despite his own personal will that there be no more violence, he threw his glove on the bog oak table. In contexts like this, prudence comes uncomfortably close to cowardice.

Tristan picked up the gauntlet. He had spoken himself into boldness. "I challenge the Irish right to tribute. I dispute by combat, my wit craft against his sword."

The Morhold handed Tristan the microphone and said, "Anger, sir, is a bad counselor. For the record, sir, identify yourself and your title. You who are about to die, who are you?"

"Is that scientifically provable or what?" asked Tristan.

"Is what provable?"

"That I am about to die," said Tristan.

"Please, sir," said the Morhold, "Your name and your title, if indeed you have one."

"Sir Tristan of the Lyonness, Tax Protestor."

"You have three minutes, Tristan."

"No, I don't. I shall speak as long as I wish. This hearing is prescribed by Pendragonic Law. I shall have my rights or lodge with King Arthur an official complaint against you and against the Irish king."

These words hit Morhold like bolts of lightning, for he knew all the red tape a complaint would involve. And so, the Morhold collapsed into the Chair of Estate and said, "Speak as you wish and speak as long as you wish."

Tristan's Tax Protest:

"My arguments against the tax are, like ancient Gaul, divided into three parts. The first part is logical, the second is practical, and the last is philosophical.

"First, logic. Logic isn't half as important as love, but it can prove something. What can it prove? It can prove that you lied.

"Your lie: One percent, 600 people, is trivial.

"If it were trivial, why seems it so important to you? If it were trivial, why do you wring it out of us? Why not wring it out of your budget? If it were trivial, why not forget it? The truth is that 600 people is not trivial, nor is it a large amount. It is exactly 600, no more, and no less. That is why we use numbers to count."

Tristan paused and took a slight bow acknowledging various hoots and claps of approval. He soothed his dry throat with a swig of Yoo-Hoo, a sweet chocolate drink of which he had become fond. Too fond. Besides, real men don't drink Yoo-Hoo, just as real men don't eat quiche. Tristan should be drinking Red Bull, not Yoo-Hoo. But the dumb fuck didn't know that because he is just a character in a book and under the control of the author and not under the control of himself. Hence, Yoo-Hoo it is.

Tristan continued:

"Second, the practical solution: FDR, a famous American President, will say in 1932, "You don't cut the deficit by raising taxes. You cut the deficit by cutting the deficit. What did he mean? He'll meant that individuals, families, and, God help us, governments must operate within a budget. The material resources of a nation, the material resources of us all, are limited. There is never enough to do all that one may wish. You have to set priorities and cut things you cannot afford. It is hardly my job to tell the Irish king what to cut. That is his job. As the chief elected official of the Irish State, the king must set appropriate priorities and eliminate what Ireland can't afford."

"If you wish examples, I'll give you some: You yourself bought a hunting park in Wexford that you couldn't afford. I know you couldn't afford it because you had to borrow to pay for it. I know you still can't afford that park because you are still paying interest on the note. Now you who can't afford the park want to make capital improvements in it, construct a jogging trail, dig a water lily pond, lay out a soccer field, all of which you also can't afford. That's like someone who is having trouble paying the note on his Toyota Celica wanting to upgrade to a Lexus because the ride will be better. Yes, the ride will be better. But it just doesn't make good financial sense. You have to get back to reality. You must operate within your individual budget, just as Ireland has to get back to reality by roping in its budget. That done, Ireland will need no tributes."

"Finally, the philosophic—and this is the most important point, the part that you are least likely to understand because it is so super-evidently true: We don't want to pay because we are taxed to the max."

Tristan turned to the crowd and asked them to chant with him. They did in crescendo: "TAXED TO THE MAX! TAXED TO THE MAX! TAXED TO THE MAX!"

And before the echoes (TAXED TO THE MAX! TAXED TO THE MAX! TAXED THE MAX!) settled down, Tristan resumed his relentless barrage.

"Every time we turn around, there is another tax. Studies show that the average citizen of Cornwall must labor 107 days out of the year to pay various taxing authorities. The biggest item in the average family budget is not food, not clothing, not shelter, but taxes. This is because we are taxed on what we earn. That mode is called Income Tax. And the more we earn, the more we are taxed. That is called Progressive Income Tax. We are taxed on what we buy. That's called Sales Tax. We are taxed on what we sell at a profit. Capital Gains Tax. We are taxed when we sell anything. That is called Excise Tax. We are taxed on what we own. Property Tax. And we are even taxed when we die. Estate Tax. Considering the amounts of money involved and the long duration of our taxable lives, it is reasonable to state that most people here spend a considerable part of their existences working for various government taxing authorities. We are truly taxed to the max. Read my lips. NO MORE TAXES!"

Tristan sat, and The Morhold held the microphone and motioned around.

Cowards all!

No other knight or baron wished to speak. In fact, they were relieved that someone beside themselves had volunteered to die uselessly defending Cornwall. They were happy that that someone who would die was not themselves but Tristan.

There being no further discussion, the Morhold, sacker of cities, had a surprise for them and for King Mark and for Tristan too.

"Tristan, you spoke well. I like your style. You talk straight, and you think straight. I am not eager to try my mind against your wit, nor my hand against your witchcraft. Therefore, by the authority vested in me, I do commute the tribute to 50 men and 50 maidens. Take it or leave it."

Mark jumped up and embraced his nephew. "Well done!" he said. "With one brave speech, you saved 500 of my subjects from bondage. Now, as your uncle and as your king, I request that you replace the Morhold's glove and leave off the challenge. Let us accept his gracious offer of a lesser tribute at the discounted market price of 12.5%."

Tristan whispered in Mark's ear, and Mark corrected himself. "OK The price is 18.6% of the old price representing a discount of—of—of—go figure. And yes, it is still an ultimatum. And yes, we are still being treated as the Nazi treated Czechoslovakia in 1938. We are still being treated as a vassal state."

"What's wrong with that?" asked the Morhold. "Hitler offered to guarantee Czech national borders with the military might of the Third Reich. We do the same for you. Besides, we Irish are the master race. Because we are the master race, we are entitled to take slaves and demand obedience."

"Is this the Stone Age? Or what?" said Tristan. "There is no master race. That is just a desperate rationalization for criminal activity."

The Morhold scratched his head. "There's no master race? Are you sure?"

Tristan decided to give the Morhold a lesson in logic.

"Usually, there are two reasons to explain what we do, the stated reason, and the real reason. Often the stated reason is acceptable, and the real reason is not. Because the stated reason is used to camouflage the unacceptable underlying motive or impulse, it is called a rationalization. For instance, an obese man thinks he overate at the party so as not to offend his hostess. When actually he overate because he is a pig. In your case, the stated reason for taking slaves is that you are the master race. Whereas the real reason is that you are criminals engaged in rapine, devastation, depredation, and destruction. You call yourselves the master race in order to justify enslaving others. After all, your argument goes, if there is a master race, that implies there is a slave race. If the Irish are the master race, that implies that they may enslave others. Furthermore, the Irish are not a race in the scientific sense of the word. What you are giving us is bullshit, nothing more and nothing less. Bullshit is something said for effect without due regard as to whether it is true or not."

"Because of that, we don't trust you. We don't trust Brian Boru. And we don't trust the Irish government. Continued violence and a mass of factual evidence, including the Irish fleet that now lies off Cornwall's shores, contradict Irish talk of peace and protection. Show us by your actions that you mean no harm. Take nothing. Sail away. Return empty-handed to the high king. Then we shall be happy and cause no trouble. Otherwise, the opposite. Otherwise, we shall cause trouble. We shall have to."

"Honored king," said the Morhold who at this point looked beat, ancient, and done-in. "I don't know what the devil this knight is talking about, but I do know that it is your duty to instill reason in young upstarts. He prattles on with what I consider to be a terrific act of imagination, giving the impression that he is sure of himself, sure of reasons, and sure of victory. But the last 15 other knights of yours spoke in a similar manner. They speak no more. They went down. They now lie in the unique stillness of death."

Then turning to Tristan: "That's the fact, Jack."

Morhold continues: "Lastly, consider this: What will the world think of you if you permit witchcraft to defend Cornwall?"

"No witchcraft," cried Tristan, aware of the Morhold's louche shot. "I intend to use wit craft, not witchcraft. There's a difference. My power is the power of human intelligence—wit—W-I-T, a mode of mental power which involves the knowledge of matter and the changes that it undergoes, a kind of chemistry that has nothing to do with witchcraft, although it will appear that way to you when you see its effects. Science is real magic. I will win with real magic. Why should I capitulate when I know that, through wit craft, Cornwall will be saved?"

Tristan received a great cheer. Among the other voices, Mark's rang in his ear, crying out his name. The din went on and on. Swords were beaten against shields to produce a deafening clang. The tumult died down, only to spring up again in a great roar that covered Tristan's arms with gooseflesh. The DAGG cabal was cheering too, for a different reason. They thought Tristan dead meat. Considering Morhold's size, strength, and previous record in mortal combat, they seemed to have the odds on their side.

At last, the Morhold looking distressed, disconsolate, and downcast, wondering, at first, if Tristan had packed his partisans into the crowd, stepped forward and raised his hands for silence. Nope, there was no stopping it. No way, José. The ovation continued and was too overwhelming to be false. And why not? Why should it not come from the heart? It wasn't Tristan they were cheering but the hope of freedom.

At that point, the Morhold, like any real Irishman who wasn't getting his way, felt he needed a drink. In fact, he felt like getting stinking drunk. Things had lurched out of control. This Tristan whippersnapper sounded too confident. But what to do? If he did not return to Ireland with the tribute, he would lose his honor, his pension, and, worse, his head. He could hear Brian Boru (the Irish king, remember?) now ringing in his ears: "The fault, dear Jimbo, is not in our stars, but in ourselves, that we are underlings."

After a long pause, the Morhold said in that loud Olympian Zeus voice of his, "There is nothing more to discuss. My deal is my deal. No more doubtful balance of rights and wrongs. No more weary Tristan with his endless tongue. I will not change one iota. Either meet my demands, or I order the attack on Cornwall. My way or the highway."

"Be reasonable, Mark. I reduced the tribute drastically. Why not leave it that way? Order Tristan to withdraw. If you do not, then I demand the full price. There will be physical combat. When I win, you will pay 600. Furthermore, as a private incentive for Tristan to drop his challenge, I offer him my niece Iseult the Beautiful, as bride, under the usual conditions of Irish law. Iseult's pulchritude is known worldwide. The market for brides of her ilk is brisk. Tristan could take her to bed or sell her to the highest bidder or give her away to whom he wishes. Already men have bid her full weight in gold and been refused."

Editor's Note: Yes, ladies, if you want to know the truth of the matter, the real truth, as opposed to the false truth, the shameful truth, the real shameful truth, it is this: In those sorrowful days (fifth century) in that sorrowful place (post-Roman Europe) women were bought and sold on the open market like cattle. In fact, they were considered a form of chattel, moveable property. The going price was one and one-half milking cows, varying a bit depending on the woman. Among the peasants, those women who had good work records commanded higher prices. Among the nobles, a woman of gentle features and gentle touch who could be a companion and intriguing bedmate commanded the big bucks. Remember what Iago said: "If this is not true, then I'm a Turk. Women wake to play and go to bed to work."

To each his own taste. And I know mine.

Of course, the Morhold did not mention that by ancient Irish law, no woman could be sold without her consent. So, this, his most recent bribe to Tristan, was smoke and mirrors. No woman in Ireland could be touched, much less ravished, without her consent. In inserting the phrase "under the usual conditions of Irish law," the Morhold, sacker of cities, was factoring in, on the advice of his attorney, weasel words by which he could weasel out of the contract. Such a defect in the contract was called a "loophole." Many contracts to this day are written that way for the same reason.

King Mark's other nephew, Andread (the A of the DAGG conspiracy) lit a Camel, picked up a cup of coffee, which he sipped, like a grazing dragon, two streams of smoke curling out of his nostrils. Andread smoked like it was the 1940s, and no one had ever heard of lung cancer. As nicotinic spume oozed out of his mouth in a long snake, Andread considered the situation: "What Cornwall really needs is a couple of Haitian hitmen, ex-Tonton Macoutes who'd murder their grandmothers for a quarter. Why not hire them and bump off the Morhold? Wouldn't that solve our problem? As usual, Tristan is being a schmuck, the omega wolf in the pack, always lagging behind, hanging loose from the crowd. Look at Morhold's poisoned sword. Tristan can't even lift it. What will he do when it comes crashing down on his head? He'll fall like a chain-sawed sequoia! Tristan may think he has enough magic to checkmate the Morhold, but the Morhold doesn't need any magic to kill Tristan. Do you think it was by magic that the 15 Cornish champions went down to dusty death? Tristan's a fool, and what a fool says is folly. He tempts God, and he tempts the gods. His death will never save the Cornish folk from becoming serfs and harlots. It will only add a little-bitty small print line to the Morhold's already impressive record of killing Cornwall knights."

Right after Andread finished, deafening boos arose from the women's galleries. The female mind, though cruelly practical in daily life, cannot bear to hear ideals belittled in public. Male and female created He them. Two different types of human animal. Really! And vive la différence!

Previous studies suggest that the relationship between mating and mortality could have been shaped by sexually antagonistic coevolution. According to this concept, the behaviors by which a female can maximize her evolutionary fitness are often in conflict with those of her male partner and vice versa.

But, of course, the female is a better animal, the most fit most times in most places. Women are the future of the human race. Women will figure that fact out when it is realized that men are poisoned by testosterone and should not be left near anything sharp or explosive.

King Mark didn't make direct answer to the Morhold. Instead, siding with the distaffs, he addressed Andread: "Your beard is a qualified success—but it grew in thinly, which makes you look like a dirty old man, a little like Salman Rushdie."

The comment, a direct attack on Andread as a person, was argumentum ad hominem and irrelevant. Mark, like Hilary Clinton, was playing to the gallery, was good at that sort of diversionary line of reasoning. He had not addressed Andread's issues, just ignored them. To make matters worse, Mark continued the ad hominem attack:

"You, sir, are a rogue and a clown, a self-indulgent, impotent whoremaster, a thief, a liar, a cut-purse, a braggadocio, in love with yourself and your own company. You and your companions represent nothing which can uphold or strengthen a country: rather that which can only destroy—disease, lying, cheating, vice."

In the midst of this debate over the life, death, the future of Cornwall, and Andread's character, Tristan received a lascivious love letter from Cato's own half-sister, the wayward Servilia, a perennial source of embarrassment to the great moralist. Was this scene contrived by the Morhold to discombobulate his opponent in the midst of the deliberations? Or did Servilia, pining away in her house, wearing her black leather catsuit and blithely unconcerned about the crisis that paralyzed the whole of Tintagel, simply, that afternoon, crave Tristan's attention with an unusual intensity?

Even the most outlandish writer of romantic comedies would never have dared to introduce into his narrative an intrusion of such pungent absurdity. Such evidence, its presence here, indicates the veracity of this story, confirming the chaotic nature of our daily lives, and its difference from the orderly sequence fabricated by some authors like best-selling Patterson. Real life is full of false clues, irrelevant issues, and fake signposts leading nowhere. It's like the fun house at the amusement park. You're having fun, but the weird mirrors and the slanted rooms and floors unsettle the mind, distort your vision, and make you scared. There and in life, with great effort, we nerve ourselves for crises that never come. Thus, the most successful of us must show a waste of energy that would have moved mountains. On the tragedy of that waste, our national culture is duly silent. It assumes preparation against danger is in itself a good, and that men, like nations, are the better for staggering through life fully armed. The downside of preparedness, the tremendous cost of homeland security, for instance, has been handled somewhat by the ancient Greeks. They knew that life is indeed dangerous, but not in the way our national mores would have us believe. They knew it is unmanageable, but the essence of it is not a battle. It is unmanageable because it is a romance, and its essence is romantic beauty.

Morhold tried for the last word. "Mark, arrest Tristan for treasonous behavior. Send him to Buchenwald, or Sachsenhausen, replacements for the Oranienburg camp of initial infamy near Berlin, or to Ravensbrueck in Mecklenburg. No, No, No, not Ravensbrueck. That's for women. Send him to Mauthausen near Linz or Auschwitz, Belsec, or Treblinka, all too familiar to all the world."

Mark shrugged his shoulders. There was nothing he could do. Secretly, Mark hated people who insisted on having the last word, especially on subjects for which there can be no last word, short of the invention of time travel or communication with the dead. In the scheme of things, history teaches that one concession from a yielding opponent must lead quickly to another, like trying to deal with Karsaid.

Mark didn't want to set in motion a chain reaction of downward spirals. Sometimes you have to take a stand no matter how painful and stupid defiance appears. A nation that refuses to fight soon gets eaten up. Look what all those Albanian and Bulgarian soldiers did to Greece in World War II.

Mark's bland silence had a way of enraging the Morhold, detachment from anger being one part of wisdom. "What a foul mood you dogs are in!" Mark remarked, glancing first at the DAGG and then at the Morhold. "Has your master not fed you recently? Three days hence, Tristan will meet the Irish champion on the Island of Saint Samson in the middle of the river Fowley (pronounced Foy), there to fight until one yields or dies. Until then, Castle D'Or remains neutral, and the Irish fleet stays where it is."

The Morhold emitted the (Olympian) laughter of exhilaration that comes when men give themselves over to pillage and plunder, the cruel, barking laughter at the climax of a chase, in the thick of battle. It turned Mark's heart to stone. It sent gooseflesh over Tristan.

Tristan threw down his gauge and bent his arm toward the Morhold with a be-my-guest gesture. The Morhold picked Tristan's glove up and snapped it at Tristan's face.

"If thou dost not instantly comply with these my just, though revised, demands, I defy thee to single combat to the last extremity." So, saying, the Morhold cast down his warder (a staff carried as a symbol of authority; here used to signal the challenge was final).

Three days was not a trivial amount of time. It was not a great amount of time, either. It was three days, no more and no less. With careful planning, it might be enough for Tristan to prepare. Or it might not be enough time to prepare. Guess what Tristan will use against Morhold. I don't know myself. But I would bet it is one of the feats he learned in knight school or some trick Flannagan taught. Let's see what's what in the next Tableau.

Tristan's Angst

Tristan ignored the woman who, in the ecclesiastical shadows, was squatting down, taking a piss. He gazed at the candles burning in front of the image of Our Lady of Perpetual Succor. He made the sign of the cross, as the last 15 Cornwall knights had done before this figure in each of the last past 15 years. As the last 15 had done before, Tristan prayed for the Queen of Heaven's help. But whoa! Those knights went down to dusty death. Did our Lady of Succor hold a grudge? The evidence was YES.

And did it matter? Did it matter that he must cease to exist completely? Did it matter that all this in this world would go on without him? Did he resent it? The real problem was not saying goodbye to the others (Morgana included) but saying goodbye to himself. How could he stand not existing? How could he say goodbye to Tristan forever and ever? That was the problem, alright. And it frightened him just as much as it frightens me and you.

Everything usually works out when you have a plan. Tristan, his smile spreading wide, his face a bit pale but burning with a ruddy glow, had his, a plan as ingenious and as intricate as a cobweb. Still, there was an off feeling about the situation, the hint of some kind of bad mojo. Was it the August heat, or was it the (very real) possibility that the plan wouldn't work, for cobwebs are fragile? Or was it an adverse effect of the beef tacos he had eaten for lunch? You really have to watch out when you eat Mexican.

Was it one, some, all, or any combination of the above? Who knows? As for me, I think it was the tacos. Indigestion can have an adverse effect on one's mentality and can produce angst.

Angst. That's it. Tristan had angst.

Even the wisest man grows tense with some sort of violence before he can accomplish fate, know his work, or choose his mate. Tristan had angst, anxiety, anguish, neurotic fear, and (let's face it) remorse. Why oh why had he not kept his big mouth shut?

A stroke of lightning fulgurated and splintered just above the spire of Tintagel Minster, casting everything into stark light and shadow. The thunderclap followed without a pause, a booming blast that shook the floor. It quieted to a crackling rumble that rolled around the vacant church like a giant grinding stone. All the candelabras were agitter. The brilliant blue ball of incandescent light had seemed a message from the Virgin herself, an omen from God himself, or both. Was it a good omen or a bad omen?

(Seemed, because, in reality, it was just a close-by lightning strike generated by repositioning electrons. I know what it is like because two years ago, one struck my house just 11 feet from me while I was playing Fur Elise on the piano. The light blinded me for a few seconds. The sound deafened me for longer, and I still have ringing in my ears. All the electrical stuff snuffed, including the garage opener, TV, AC, refrig, etc. Insurance didn't pay, of course. They said it was an act of God and specifically excluded on the homeowner's policy. Ed.)

Lightening portending what? Check the next tableau to find out.

Tristan and the Bat Guano

The next day at first light, Tristan reached the cave, where a great spout of bats was dropping down, thousands of those creatures, and they continued to pour in like that for an hour or more until all had entered.

He left his horse at the mouth of the cave and followed the bats, disappearing from sight and, by short cuts known to him, made his way now through vast congeries of rooms and staircases, past eerie stalactites and stalagmites, through narrow barrel-vaulted tunnels and halls lined with glow worms, to the main bat assembly room, returning an hour later with two panniers filled with that cave's dirt. These baskets he took down to the river. There he built a kiln and burned charcoal, dousing the fire by day and firing it again by night while he leached out the guano with clear, cool brook water and evaporated it in the sun to precipitate the nitrate. By the end of the second day, he had 3.27 pounds of pure crystal sodium nitrate (saltpeter) and about three pounds of fine alder charcoal, which he had ground to a powder so admirable you could make ink with it.

Flannagan had told him of an old volcanic peak, beyond the Mal Pas, with sharp black glass on the edges and sharp flinty stones that could cut Tristan's high leather boots. Although he had led his horse with every care, still the beast was bleeding about its hoofs, so much so that it would go no farther.

Tristan climbed on alone, having reached the rim of the cone, descended into the crater, and chipped away at a weal of pure flowers of sulfur crystal that ringed around the lip.

He chopped it fine until he had about three pounds and then returned to his horse.

Flannagan had been quite explicit about the next step, although, to Tristan, it didn't make sense. He didn't like it, either. He feared it might be wrong. An old man may be so desperate for wisdom he'll make stuff up. He knew him! Flannagan! How deadly socializing with the professor can be to a youngster who believes. Was Flannagan a philosopher, a lunatic, or both? In the long-haul look of history, progress does seem to depend on geniuses, and crackpots and power does seem to pass from old men to their young protected protégées. Most Nobel Prize winners had mentors who won the prize.

So far, Flannagan had been right most of the time. And Flannagan told the truth mostly. He did have some queer ideas about Jewish influence, and Flannagan certainly was delusional about his controlling the weather. That was not possible. Iron boats were a problem also. It was hard to imagine that an iron boat would float because iron is heavier than wood and will sink.

Nevertheless, Tristan did as he had been told. He dumped out the nitrate and the charcoal and stirred them together with his hand as he poured the sulfur in. Then—the part of the process he didn't like—he urinated on the mixture until it was a foul, black dough, which he troweled across the south-facing rocks, spreading it out thin with his knife to let it dry in the sun.

Tristan stared at the black mess in absorption, his powdered power putty. He was taken by a sense of beauty and awe he could not express. This black powder would change the world. With it, walls will crumble, and castles will become obsolete. Multiple young men and women will lose arms and legs and sometimes their lives. Whole cities will be destroyed. No kidding. Just you wait and see. Some jerks will, using black powders extracted from fireworks, even bomb the Boston Marathon.

Ever the good student, Tristan sat down on a cold stone and made notes (as Flannagan had told him to), detailed notes in ink about what he had done, where he had found the ingredients for the explosive powders, the proportions used, and the character and consistency of the resultant mixture. This was real science, a little boring in the manufacture of details, but worth it all in view of the results. If you didn't know what you did, you might not be able to figure out what you did wrong or right. If you didn't know exactly what you did, you might not be able to do it again.

Tristan gathered the dried powder, careful not to strike fire on the stone and filled the pannier. Stage one of the project was finished. Now he had to make the smoke grenades and, if he could, the gun. For it was the property of the powder that, when ignited, it would burn with such rapidity that it expanded rapidly into a gas. If the gas were in a confined space, it could be used to propel a missile or burst a pottery jar.

Working in Flannagan's lab as his postgraduate student, it had been Tristan himself who hit on the idea of using the explosive powder to shoot a lead weight down a metal pipe. More than that: He had discovered that if a spiral groove were etched on the inside of the pipe, a spin could be place on the lead weight, which would impart to it a gyroscopic stability. He called his invention a "rifle" in recognition of the importance of the spiral lining the tube. Improvements on this basic idea rapidly followed so that in the end, he had a helical magazine holding one hundred 9mm bullets attached to a rifle that could fire semi-automatically, that is every time the trigger pulled. There remained but one thing: the name for this marvelous new weapon. Tristan called it after P.J., his favorite cat—the Calico.

The Calico semiautomatic rifle was a marvelous invention. It certainly put that girl in Jean M. Auel's famous novel, *Clan of the Cave Bear*, in her place. A mammoth bone is no match for gun powder.

Ursula Andress jumped up. "Whoa!" she shouted. Her arms sloped upward, palms, and tits facing Bernard, the international "embrace me." Women love imagination but can go only so far and no farther.

Says she: "Did that really happen? In the fifth century, did Tristan really make a gun? Did he really and truly do that?"

A beat and an air of baffled absence. Bernard, the Bardic Narrator, wondered, was she a reality junkie needing a fix? Or was she a detractor? People are as prone to criticize as they are to fornicate, with the difference that with criticism, there is no fear of impotence. Bards work long and hard trying to get their narrative right, fashioning out of chaos, in the torment of their souls, something intricate, intelligent, interesting, and occasionally beautiful. A critic should exercise the same due diligence in evaluation as was exercised in creation.

But, as her question seemed sincerely posed, Bernard decided to answer it sincerely. He pointed toward heaven with the index finger of his right hand and said, "Of course it happened, cutie pie, and I will be pleased to tell you why. How about over drinks later?"

"I already have a date with Patten," said she.

"Break it," said Bernard with wrinkled lip and sneer of cold command. Patten's a smuck."

"You didn't answer my question."

"If I told you something that wasn't true, that's fraud. I could go to jail. Literature is like advertising. The product and all its claims have to be true. It's like promises made in a presidential election. The same body of law applies. Presidential candidates can't lie to you. They just can't make things up or distort the reality. No, ma'am! Politicians just can't promise the moon and deliver the tail end of the rocket. If we didn't have such laws, the bullshit level would be so high around here that we would have to stand on our toes to breathe."

The Ursula Andress look-alike, vintage '64, faced about and looked directly at the audience. She shrugged her shoulders up and forward, arched her eyebrows, quickly inverted her palms, pursed her lips slightly with the corners of her mouth down, and bent her head to the right. All this to say in body language: "What can I do? It's out of my control. This guy is hopeless."

When she sat down, Bernard continued the story.

Tristan had conducted experiments to determine that the lead bullets would not penetrate ordinary armor and certainly would not penetrate the Morhold's Frankish steel, which was thicker and stronger than any other available in the world. But calculations showed that if the Morhold weighed 500 pounds with armor and if each bullet had 936 foot-pounds of energy at the muzzle, a direct hit would transfer all that energy to the Morhold moving him back 1.872 feet.

But why backward?

This was in accordance with the views of Sir Isaac Newton. One of his laws tells us that for every action, there is an equal and opposite reaction. But if the reaction were really opposite, why wouldn't the Morhold move forward? According to Flannagan, this fact might be useful in rocketry, but how the principle applied to rockets was beyond Tristan's ken. A bullet rocket would accelerate so fast humans couldn't ride on top of it.

Tristan knew from observation that what you shot in front moved back. He didn't know why. But he knew it was a fact. The same principle applied to push.

In the present case, if that force were applied through a hypothetical fulcrum at the Morhold's feet through the lever arm of four feet at, say, the Morhold's waist, it would likely tip that stalwart over on his back where (Tristan hoped) he (the Morhold) would lie like a helpless turtle unable to right himself.

Of course, no bullet could strike exactly perpendicular to the vertical axis of the Morhold's body armor. Vector analysis would have to be done to determine the different forces operating at different angles. But, a mass of bullets, fired one after another, by statistical mechanics, would deliver the same force or more. Once Morhold lay on his back, Tristan would try to get him to yield. When Morhold yielded, it would be all over. Cornwall's obligations would remit, and happy days would be here again for everyone, except for the Irish.

But what if? Yes, there's the rub: What if? What if the gun didn't work? What if the physics were wrong and the Morhold didn't tip over? What if the American House of Representatives actually did repeal the laws of physics? What if the Morhold wouldn't yield? What then? This is the exciting thing about battle—the outcome is never known in advance. Hence the narrative interest. The race isn't won until the race is run.

Tristan went to the library. Einstein said the only thing you really have to know is how to get to the library. There he consulted Gustav Fechner's famous book on psychophysics and found sufficient calculus to affirm the hypothesis that several bullets would topple the Morhold over on his back.

We mentioned earlier about Tristan's attraction to violence.

Tristan didn't like thinking about it. So, he didn't. The civilized way to handle that problem, or any unpleasant problem, is to pretend, like most Republicans, that the problem does not exist. How the Republicans handle gun violence and climate change, for instance.

Still, thought Tristan, the discipline of death might be necessary. Studies show that animals that eat their young have fewer disciplinary problems with the remaining siblings. Executed criminals, for the most part, rarely commit other crimes. The death penalty is a penalty all right—pretty permanent too.

It was a mistake becoming a man. I should have become a seagull like Jonathan Livingston. Or a monk or at least stayed home and watched TV. Why can't I be a *hikikomori* and hide in my room for years?

(Editor's note: Hikikomori refers to teenage Japanese boys who refuse to leave their rooms. Because they stay there for years, the medical doctors consider this behavior symptomatic of a new psychiatric condition whose origin is unknown. Japanese entrepreneurs have developed services for these boys. The most interesting service is the delivery of inflatable full-sized dolls dressed to suit the client. The scary thing is that the dolls are rented, not sold, and reused multiple times by multiple different hikikomori. Thus, there might be spread of those social diseases like syphilis and AIDS. The doll is also a bad influence because love is not needed to raise the skirt of modesty.)

Back to story questions:

Item: To kill or not to kill?

The prudent course is to avoid situations like this, which are disagreeable or dangerous. Such a course might get one by the issues of the moment, but it has bitter and evil consequences. In the long days and years, which stretch beyond that moment of decision, one must live with one's self. It's not merely a question of peace of mind, although that is vital; it is a matter of integrity of character.

Item: If to kill, how and when?

How could someone finish off a giant like the Morhold, sacker of cities? It was a giant problem, pun intended. One of Tristan's character defects was that he, through sheer laziness (said some), tended not to plan that far ahead. He liked the drama and adventure of watching problems unfold (said others)—often to solve themselves. He thought that the future was the best time to solve future problems. Problems which loomed large in the present, he had found, time and time again, diminished on close-up inspection. It was bad mental hygiene to worry about contingent events in the future that may or may not happen. As to the gift of strategy, it was his experience that his most carefully planned investments led to nothing. These, his thoughts, drew from an obscure borderland. He could not explain in so many words, but he felt that those who prepare for all the emergencies of life (time ahead) may equip themselves at the expense of joy and (for sure) waste lots of time.

Item: Tristan's bottom-line thinking at the moment: It is necessary to prepare for an examination, for a dinner party, or (especially) for the fall in the price of your stock. But those who attempt human relations must adopt other methods or fail. Tristan summarized his philosophy in what became a famous nursery rhyme: Leave them alone and they'll come home wagging their tails behind them. The laissez-faire attitude became also known as the "Little Bo Peep approach to problems."

(Editor's note: All this shows that, because his mind was not narrowly logical, Tristan would have made a good psychiatrist.)

Some old geezer stood up in the back of the room.

Bernard nodded and let him speak.

Old man: "I must confess a certain sympathy for Tristan's point of view: Trace anything out to the end, and you find yourself in trouble. Life is an interminable struggle—your wants and the world's. But in the end, it's the unbeatable slow machine that brings what you'll get, that brings you down. The real enemy of mankind is time, time the destroyer. The trick is to keep putting one foot in front of the other and not think too much about it or your ultimate destiny. Looked straight on, life looks pretty bleak. Looked askance, it doesn't appear so bad. Denial of reality as a mental mechanism is serviceable."

Bernard took a swig from the Black Bush bottle that he had concealed in the podium. "Thank you for sharing, Pops. What you said is true. A more intelligent discussion of the problems will be found in Cicero's *De Senectute*. But next time, if you don't mind, keep your self-expression to tee shirts, magnetic car ribbons, or bumper stickers. For your information, the "What? Me worry?" attitude had a downside for our hero and explains how and why the subsequent disaster occurred. You don't know that because I haven't gotten to that part of the story. Alas, (as usual) human hope collided with thorny reality, as the next tableau shows."

Tristan and Morhold Fight to the Death

The fatal day arrived.

Fatal for whom? Tristan or Morhold? Or both?

Tristan, clad in mail with steel armor and helm, weeping and praying, bid adieu to the nobility and those of low degree, the young and old, the women and children, to all who escorted him to the shore. In a white-sailed skiff, he sailed alone, arriving at the Island of Saint Samson (sometimes spelled Sampson) in the middle of river Fowley.

(Ed. The island is still there, but only at low tide. See internet for pictures of the river and the ancient church nearby.)

The Irish were camped close to the shore to await the results of combat. Here and there, brunt vast bonfires of cedar and oak lavishly salted so that the flames were of vert, orange, and purple. The folk of Cornwall situated themselves on the bluff in front of Saint Samson Church. A B&B, where my wife and I usually stay, now occupies that bluff.

Saint Samson Church stands about 400 yards south-southeast from the apple orchards of Lantyan and about 200 yards from the outer ditches of Castle D'Or (also spelled Dore), King Mark's winter home. Nice pictures of these places are available on the internet, especially of Castle Dore, which is well preserved as a monument and fortress. The Tristan Stone is there and is grouped with the color pictures of the earthworks that surround the castle proper. Going to the ancient orchards of Lantyan will give you a better idea of where Iseult and Tristan used to secretly meet. It was a romantic place, especially at night. Still is.

French texts claim this famous ancient battle (Morhold, sacker of cities v. Tristan) took place on an island in the Atlantic Ocean offshore from Tintagel. They claim the island appears and disappears with the tides. That's wrong. No such island exists, then or now. The water off Tintagel measures 37.2 feet deep just 10 feet offshore and 60 fathoms just a little farther out. But Samson Island in the middle of the Fowley river does still appear and disappear with the tides.

The locals still know it by its ancient name: Saint Samson Island. And if you don't believe me, go there and talk with them. My wife might have a picture of Saint Samson. If I am nice to her, she might let me put it in this book. Last time we visited there, we had a wonderful dry martini drunk on the veranda of the B&B, watching the emergence of the island at low tide.

All eyes looked, and all ears strained seaward, primed for action. But, within a few minutes, the Irish got bored and returned to their camp to swill dark porter. Not far away, the Cornwall folk sprung for a different kind of consolation: they prayed.

Hope springs eternal within the human breast. Here, however, it seemed to live on lean pasture. It looked likely that Tristan would die. Indeed, the book odds at Dirty Sally's Days-Sinn came in at 9 to 5 in favor of the Morhold, sacker of cities. Heavy Irish betting both ways biased the Paris-mutual pool and rumor had it that the Morhold had bet 600 gold bezants in favor of himself.

Secretly, the Cornwall youths who had already been selected by lot to go to Ireland (should Tristan fail) had resolved to fling themselves over the cliff or fall on gleaming swords, thus ending their lives rather than consenting to live as slaves. "Liberty or death!" they cried. But they crowed this with the usual impetuosity of youth, not realizing that survival is the main aim of existence, personal survival and survival of the race. A suicide is a victory of the lower self against the upper, and a final victory at that. All extremes of feeling are destructive of life, hence allied to madness.

When Tristan arrived at the Saint Samson Island pier, he saw the Morhold's black-sailed skiff moored on the sand. A short way from it was the Morhold himself clad in the full glory of his Frankish armor. A flag close by, planted in the sand, displayed Brian Boru's standard, the three red lions on the yellow silk ground; an Irish High Cross stood near. Irish High Cross: You know, the kind with a circle in the center where the two boards meet. Ancient Irish worshiped the sun, so the Catholic church put a sun on the cross to aid and speed conversions.

On reaching the island, Tristan got off his boat and, with a dramatic flourish, threw the mooring line back into the water. The boat began in the swift river to drift seaward.

(Note inserted by the Monk who copied the manuscript:

Yes, friends the original texts as far back as the 8th century say river. This fact supports Bernard's idea that the battle really did take place in the middle of the river Fowley and not in the Atlantic Ocean off the coast. The excellent descriptions of Cornwall's geography prove that Bernard and Patten visited the area, probably as tourists. Ethel Patten took pictures, which she has let me see. There is no doubt about the Saint Samson island in the middle of the Fowley. Also, if Bernard didn't know what he was talking about, how could he know that the locals call the Fowley river, the Fo or the Fow or the Foy.)

Before Tristan counted to 20, his skiff was out of sight.

The Morhold cried out, "Tristan, you Vassal, why are you letting your boat go?"

"One boat will serve. Only one of us will need a craft to return."

Tristan was trying to act and talk tough, but he couldn't get it quite right. For he had become a new kind of man, a feminine man. Not an effeminate man—there's a difference—but a man in contact with his feminine nature. Interested in cooking and hugging and affection and, yes, even love. Not so much into power or fame, but eager to succor and help. A man who could understand logic and scholarship, but who also trusted intuition and luck. A man who measured his friends, as we measure so many things that we cannot fully define, by his affection for them and not by what they could do for him.

But here, before fatal combat, Tristan had to put on some of the traditional, if false armor of a style of manhood he no longer believed in. He had to talk tough and act rough to try to unnerve the Morhold. He had to unnerve Morhold to gain the psychological advantage.

Using his peat stick, which he'd stashed in his leather pouch, Tristan lit one of the concussion grenades. He threw it at the Morhold. The fuse burned well, but there was no report.

Ugh!

This worried Tristan. It could mean his powder was wet or that the mixture was wrong or his urine defective. Any one of a number of things could be wrong, all of them bad news, bad news for him. But his greatest fear was expressed by the abnormal thought that by a trick of time warp he was back in the old quiet eons when the old quiet chemicals had rather be still and dark in the old quiet earth as they had been before the meddling Flannagan came and dug them up and strained, mixed, and kneaded them into explosive powders.

Undaunted, Tristan lit the other grenade and threw it at the Morhold. He knew, of course, it would do no harm if indeed it went off. His idea was simply to scare the Morhold, throw his mentality off balance.

Blam!

Pottery and smoke scattered everywhere in one tremendous ear-ringing blast. The fearsome air filled with the eerie smell and preternatural taste of brimstone. But instead of frightening the Morhold, the display had the opposite effect:

"Is that your big deal secret, your wit-craft?" asked the Morhold. "No sale, as you can plainly see. That's just a lot of noise and smoke. No real force. Just like you, Tristan. Lots of noise but no force."

Tristan pulled out the Calico and let loose a barrage of five bullets, all of which hit the sand to the right and in front of the Morhold. Firing the Calico had partially deafened him. BEEYOWWW, BEEYOWWWWW! The ricochets slapped some dirt.

"What's this again?" cried the Morhold defiantly.

"More smoke, more hot air, some thrown sand, more bull shit reflecting, externally, your internal fleckless character."

"You mean feckless," said Tristan aiming higher and to the left, letting off another five. "Fleckless is something else. Feckless means weak, ineffective, feeble, futile, valueless, destitute of vigor, energy, or capacity—in a word helpless."

Instantly, the Morhold stumbled as if struck by lightning. He stepped backward, tried to regain balance, tilted wildly, and recovered.

Tristan let him have another burst. This time aimed higher.

The Morhold fell backward and lay in the sand like a turtle on its back, waving his arms and legs, but (quite unlike a turtle) brandishing his giant sword. He was screaming something, but his visor and beaver muffled, and the strong sea breeze scattered the sound. Besides, Tristan was still partially deaf from the ear-splitting noise of gun fire. Tristan lay the Calico down and went over to take a look.

God! It was awful to see a great warrior like the Morhold laid low so easily. Vengeance accomplishes so little. It certainly doesn't bring back the dead. It just makes more corpses. What's the point? Since he is a giant and I am not, this is going to look like a David and Goliath story. Ah! Who cares? This is happening. This is the desired effect. So there!

Tristan took off his armor and sat on a weather-pitted stone, a lithic item rough and huge like the great stone of Fail at Tara. This 5th-century stone is now a Cornwall national monument. But, recently, it had to be moved to a field nearby so that they could construct an 80-home housing project and a park and ride. Locals said the move was the equivalent of Napoleon using the Sphinx for target practice. Nice pictures on internet. Just dial in "Tristan Stone."

But Wikipedia says the stone marks Tristan's grave. Not so. Tristan is buried in Tintagel Minster next to Iseult. Recent archeological digs outside the church next to the woodbine and blackberry bushes confirm two bodies, one male and one female, both carbon-dated to the fifth century."

Tristan put his hands on his cheeks and elbows on his knees. In the pose of Rodin's Thinker, he tried to think. There are times when an inner life actually pays, when years of self-scrutiny, conducted for no ulterior motive, are of practical use. This was one of those times.

What did he think about? Well, he realized that his bladder was full. It's awful hard to do any serious brooding or mulling much less thinking when you have to take a pee. So, he got up, went behind a sand dune, and relieved himself. Ah, what a blessed joy it was to empty a full bladder, he thought, as the urine streamed out. Something about taking care of body functions felt just right, a small pleasure. Life is full of them.

At this very moment, there are ships at sea like the Queen Mary 2 resounding with life, music, excellent foods, and drinks. People are dancing, and lights turned on in all the cities of Europe. Communist chinks and prodemocracy chinks are fighting it out on the streets and in the airport of Hong Kong. Unemployed blacks are pounding the pavements of Manhattan or shooting up in basements in Harlem. Women at their dressing tables in warm rooms are putting mascara on their eyelashes. Adventures and adventurers everywhere. And I am here, wasting my life, writing crap! Why? American Express is on my tail again. The wife says if I don't get them to restore her credit card, she will leave. Doctor Johnson, in that famous life by James Boswell, gives it for his opinion that only a fool writes for anything but money. But I could make more money as a plasma donor or a gigolo. So, I guess that makes me a _____. (reader, please fill in the blank.)

Back to the stone.

There, Tristan thought for only three minutes, but to him, it was like three hours. That there is an extraordinary discrepancy between time on the clock and time on the mind is less known than it should be. Did you ever try to watch a pot boil? It seems to take forever, and yet it doesn't. The matter deserves fuller investigation by neuropsychologists and physicists. There may be a secret here that needs exposure. Any fool with a watch can tell you what time it is, but who can tell you what time is.

Tristan decided that he must get that big sword away from the Morhold. The first rule of combat to the death is to get control of the other side's weapons. Perhaps that blind poet wasn't so insipid after all. The first thing Ulysses told Telemachus was, "Lock up the suitors' weapons. Too bad Bush didn't think of that during shock and awe in Iraq."

Tristan cupped his hands to his mouth and shouted, "Morhold yield. Please yield. Save both of us a lot of trouble."

No reply.

"Look at you, man. You can't get up. No way. Sooner or later, you will die of dehydration or malnutrition."

Tristan thought of something else, "Morhold, you can't live in that metal oven you have on. I'll bet you're suffering lying there in the blatant glare of the noonday sun. It must be hot as Hell."

More sword waving and then, "I can't yield. It would be the disgrace of my life. I couldn't live with the Irish after that. You don't know them. A pigheaded race. Believe me, I know. I'm one of them. Just kill me, P-L-E-A-S-E."

"Morhold, be reasonable. Your situation is hopeless. Give up."

"No."

"Morhold, I want to help you take off some of the armor so that you can cool off. It might clear your thinking."

[It is the well-nourished imagination like Tristan's that is unafraid. As for me, I would be scared stiff to go near the Morhold.]

"All right. Come here."

"Morhold, your sword. Throw away your sword. Then I will come and lift your helm so you may feel the cool sea breezes that might sooth your burning face."

"I can't. They're watching from the shore. It would mean that I'd capitulated. I have lived by the sword and must die by the sword. For so it is writ in the Holy Bible. Nothing could be more logical; more symmetrical, nothing could make more sense. Jesus said it. Give him credit."

"Morhold, drop the sword. I must insist. Otherwise, I shall have to shoot it out of your hand."

More squirming, followed by futile attempts to roll over, followed by sword blandishing, followed by deprecations, which a strange legal requirement prevents Bernard from saying and prevents us from printing. One thing we can print is the Morhold's insight: "The time can't be far off when the strength of a man's arm, and his knowledge of swords and lances, will count for nothing. And I, for one, am glad that I shall be well-beached by then."

"Morhold, your sword makes me nervous. Drop it. Please! Drop it."

Tristan picked up the Calico, counted to three.

"Morhold, I have the Calico. Do you want to taste its fiery breath again?" And (the Morhold, sacker of cities, not having let go of the sword) Tristan shot that implement out of his hand.

The Morhold cried out in pain, clutched his injured palm uttering curses and oaths, which we also cannot print because they include the F word and another expression and another in 12 letters having to do with having sex with your mother.

Morhold started to cry like a two years child and moved arms and legs in a temper tantrum common to that age and not altogether to be applauded, for such acts tend to relax the effort of struggle. And yet, they can hardly be reproved when conducted so honestly. Like those GIs wounded on the beach at Normandy, he screamed for his mama until his voice was hoarse. Then he moaned in a way so unpleasant, repellent, and repulsive that Tristan retreated back to the thinking stone.

Shit! It was getting late. The sun nudged the horizon and as though some mighty artery had burst, stained the world with a crimson light. Soon all the ways would grow dark.

Tristan called to the Morhold. "If I did kill you, how would you like to have it done?"

"Take off my helm. Hit me over the head with your sword. A clean, fast death without much pain."

"Are you shriven?"

"I confessed this morning and received absolution from the monk who lives in our camp. My soul is ready for God's judgment and, hopefully, for heaven."

"You mean you hope for heaven."

"What?"

"Forget it. Many people misuse that word hopefully. Relax, man. I approach, but not to kill you. I will just open your helm so you can get some fresh air. Fresh air, I hope, will help you think more clearly."

Tristan left his own sword at the stone and walked over to the Morhold. Our heroic youth, Tristan, had done some smart things in his life, but trying to cool the Morhold was not one of them. Failure to perceive reality, to understand what the world was really like—ah, that was and is and will always be the most important single stupidity. Tristan had forgotten that the Morhold's character was cold, implacable, and ruthless. Can a tiger change his stripes? Beware tricks!

"How do I get the helmet off?"

"Come over here, bend down, and use both hands under the sides. It just lifts up," said the Morhold. His voice was higher pitched and wavered. And then he repeated himself. Why?

Tristan bent over.

Suddenly, he felt a giant wave seize him and force him forward and under.

The Morhold had grabbed Tristan and pulled him down onto his armor, crushing the youth against him with superhuman force, more or less in sexual position 69.

The Morhold pressed harder, so hard Tristan couldn't breathe. Because of the markedly increased intracranial pressure, Tristan's vision turned red. He knew he would faint, for the filling pressure of the heart depends on negative, not positive intrathoracic pressure. Much to his regret, he now knew directly that tremendous strength that was the Morhold's fame. Consequently, there was no resistance, nor could there be as the Morhold's force was irresistible.

The Morhold pulled harder and repositioned Tristan so that Tristan's head was now trapped between the Irish giant's giant legs. Meanwhile, Tristan's testicles were pressed against the Morhold's breastplate of steel. The pain was excruciating. No question about it: Tristan had lost. He knew that. He wished for oblivion. But his wish was ungranted. Instead, he got yet more pain when the Morhold started biting Tristan's right ankle.

That was a low blow! Biting is not nice. And what is worse, the human mouth is filled with fusospirochetal organisms that can cause a severe infection.

As if he were in positive 4G (that is, four times the force of gravity), which, incidentally, he was—or the equivalent thereof—Tristan's vision reddened out.

(After the cold war was over, American astronauts were able to call this a red-out without much in the way of political recrimination. The excess pressure led to blindness, but the color last seen was red, a vivid dark red the color of oxygenated blood.)

Tristan, blind now, knew he had but 17 seconds left to do something before he lost consciousness and headed down to dusty death. 17 seconds to do something. But what?

Advance to tableau 13 to find out.

Tristan Takes a Stab

Tristan reached for the short sword he carried in his girdle. The ancients called this weapon a short sword. But we would call it a knife, for, though shaped like a sword and sharp, it was only one foot long.

Although he was blind owing to increased venous pressure causing red-out, Tristan was still conscious, able to reach over and, remembering his anatomy mnemonic NAVEL, the order of nerve, artery, vein, empty space, and lymph node, stabbed into the fossa where he thought the Morhold's femoral artery ought to be. Given the occasion, a desperate man will do anything. Who knows? A clever recklessness had always helped Tristan. It might help again.

Pay dirt!

Tristan felt a viscous, warm, pulsatile liquid geysering out. It drenched his linen tunic and woolen cloak as Tristan's world turned black.

Night fell. All the ways grew dark. Stars emerged. Small fleecy white clouds drifted east on high jet stream currents crossing the slivered moon. Four hours ticked by. Tristan awoke. He felt stiff and sore, but otherwise OK His vision was normal. The Morhold's grip had relaxed.

Tristan got up. He was a bloody mess. His right ankle was still oozing where the Morhold had bitten him. He hobbled down to the Fowley to clean the wound. The saltwater smarted (the Fowley is tidal and, consequently, brackish). Because of the pain, Tristan stopped before proper debridement had taken place. Military surgeons know a human bite is just about the dirtiest wound imaginable. It needs to be attended well, lest infection set in. In some contexts and situations, knowledge of medicine is crucial. This present neglect was a grave error, emphasis on the grave. Like so many health problems, failure to get the proper treatment initially would lead to lots of trouble later.

Tristan sat on the stone. As we have seen, he liked thinking and sometimes found it constructive. I mention this because thinking by humans is such a rare event, much more rare than fighting. In fact, most humans would rather fight than think.

For the record, I wish to state that at that moment, Tristan was the only person in all Cornwall who was actually thinking, perhaps the only one in the entire world that was actually thinking.

Let's see. What was he thinking?

He was thinking that there was a fatality and curse on his life, as if God himself were seeing to it that some horrible fate was discharged to the last drop and dreg.

What else?

Tristan screwed his eyes up tight as if trying to work a sum out in his head. The (meager and insufficient) thought that came was: I wonder if the Morhold, sacker of cities, is thinking too. "Yoo hoo. Yoo hoo, Morhold, sacker of cities. How's things? How's things with you?"

No answer.

Tristan ventured closer. With a stave, Tristan tapped the Morhold's helmet. "Anyone home?"

Nothing.

Using the stick to pry open the visor, which had fallen shut when Tristan got up, he found the Morhold's face pale as death, on his mouth the all-purpose grin of a stroke victim. Maggots had already started devouring the face flesh. The air was saturated with flies, mosquitoes, and the smell of rot. Ugh! Morhold was dead, dead for all time, and rotting fast.

Standing there watching this, the results of medieval battle, you get a good look at the competitive aspect of life carried to the extreme. Western culture was to see mucho mas of this scene, as in the battle of Midway where things really got out of control or Hiroshima where things really, really got out of control—142,000 dead in the first six seconds. Nowhere and never is that kind of violence necessary.

"It weren't our fault," said Tristan to the corpse. "It's the fault of this hideous century that we live in, which has denatured humanity and planted death and hate where love and living were. Jesus Christ, if Christ came back, he would vomit all over the place."

Tristan was wrong. There was nothing wrong with his century or any century. Nor could there ever be. The fault lay elsewhere in government of, by, and for the psychopaths.

Note by the Scribe Monk: No one would ever believe how Tristan had conquered the Morhold. Like most story tellers, Tristan understood the inadequacy of language for dealing with the complexity of the real world. If I had read such an account in a book, I would not have believed it myself. But there it was, the true quill. By the by, the French texts ignore the description of the Saint Samson Island combat. They just say that Tristan won and sailed back home. You, dear friend, know the rest of the story. The truth is, as is often the case, too rich and too complex for little (French) minds to comprehend. Fortunately, the world forms its opinions from action rather than from reason in undecided cases, and so selfish are the hearts of poor mortals that they are ready to change as favor goes and believe the victor, not the victim.

Tristan knew that the Cornwall folks, like the very French who snubbed them, wouldn't get it either. He would have to construct a credible story to convince them. He had to claim a fair fight, else he would not be entitled by medieval law to the rewards agreed to before combat. The story would have to be simple so that there would be few questions. But it would have to be true. Tristan was smart enough that he didn't want to get mixed up between fiction and fact. Even modern readers who know about guns and ammo might have trouble believing the role those instruments played in how the Morhold, sacker of cities, died. You can imagine how difficult it would be for the ancient Cornwall rabble, to get the truth, not to mention those malt-addled Irish.

Tristan levered the Morhold's helmet off. He lifted his own sword with two hands and swung with all his might, bringing the blade down on the Morhold's head. The weapon hit the skull with a dull thud. No blood flowed. No cry issued. Four of the great things about the dead are that they don't bleed, they don't feel pain, they keep quiet, and they don't cause trouble. The fifth and most important thing is that the dead make room. Furthermore, according to Siegfried Sassoon in his fictional autobiography *Memoirs of an Infantry Officer,* "The dead are more real than the living because they are complete." That, I guess, is considered a plus in some circles.

Tristan, shielding his eyes from the sun that flashed from the bright blade, tugged at his sword. Ugh! It wouldn't move. It had got stuck in the Morhold's head. Tristan pulled and pulled with two hands, used his foot to lever the weapon out.

Crack!

Tristan succeeded in breaking part of the sword, leaving a three-centimeter scrap stuck in the Morhold's frontal bone. A good and trusted weapon was injured, but that was that. The sword was still an adequate implement of war, well decorated with gold filigree and enamel and worth a fortune even if damaged and still fully capable if properly applied, of reducing the numerical strength of enemy armies. Tristan washed it off with his snot rag (snot rag = old Irish for handkerchief; face rag = face cloth, dish rag—well, you get it).

With a firm pat, he slid the sword back into its sheath. Tristan tried to pick up the Morhold's sword. He couldn't lift it for the weight. The best he could do, using both hands, was drag it along the ground. No way would a sword like that be of any value to him. So, he left it there, on the shelving sand. Many years later, it was rediscovered and made a brief but moving appearance in a gothic romance novel called *The Castle of Otranto,* along with the Morhold's enormous helmet, a hundred times larger than any casque ever made for mere human being, and shaded with a proportionable quantity of black feathers quivering in the wind. The gigantic hand in armour, resting on the uppermost banister of a staircase that appeared in that novel was not, however, the Morhold's. In terms of Whig demonology, so dear to the author Horace Walpole, the armoured hand connotes an arbitrary, executive power. Its appearance in a scene resembling Strawberry Hill implies an invasion into Walpole's affairs. The image was either of unconsciously fabricated origin or of consciously fabricated origin and was, therefore, either way, not real.

Tristan jumped into the Morhold's skiff and steered back to the shore, where the women stood beating their palms in chorus as a sign of support for their hero and champion. Some of these women ululated when they saw, faintly in the distance, the outline of a skiff. It was, however, the skiff with the black sail, the Morhold's skiff. As that skiff came closer, the ululations turned to moans, weeping, and gnashing of teeth. "Oh, God. The Morhold, sacker of cities! It's he that has won."

Some women fell to the ground, hysterically twitching; others pulled out their hair. Others just stood there, silent and immobile, staring blankly into the distance.

Taking that skiff had been a careless, thoughtless deed, but, at the time, fresh with triumph, Tristan was not thinking. He was not thinking of the boys and girls of Cornwall standing on the cliffs. He was not thinking that they, seeing the black sailed boat, the Morhold's boat, might conclude that the Irish guy had won and that they, therefore, were to be sent to Ireland as slaves. He was not thinking that those youths would lose hope and fling themselves over the cliff to certain death below.

What goes around comes around. And so, it will be with a certain poetic justice that Tristan's own death would be hastened (some say caused) by the confusion of black and white sails. About that more later.

Sad to say, the death toll that day was 13. Twelve were suicides.

One involved an accident: An over-enthusiastic, unthinking lad who chased his windblown blue cap, one with a green shamrock on it, whose inside label proclaimed, "this cap brings good luck to him who wears it," over the edge of the cliff. There was no saving him, for a blown away hat be a stochastic event. But the suicides should have waited another few minutes to see Tristan standing on the prow.

Twenty-two boats launched. Men and women swam out to greet the good knight. Flags, pendants, and banners flew in the wind to salute Tristan's victory.

The befuddled Irish were still drinking. Some had fallen asleep. Those awake had trouble understanding that their champion was dead. They began to dispute the idea, then fight. Tristan tried to reason with them. They kept shouting, "Coward! You ran away." And so forth and so on, all blarney. Ah, the Irish had the same faults in those days that they have today: Bless their hearts: They drink too much, they talk too much, and they don't think enough. But that was their problem, for the speeding future will always outlast the past.

Tristan held out his sword to them. "Take my sword. A piece of it lies stuck in the Morhold's head. Take this as tribute, the only tribute you shall get."

The sword was refused.

Then Tristan went up to Castle D'Or.

And as he progressed, the people, he had freed waved green boughs of yew and threw the petals of roses in his path. The bells pealed amid notes of trumpets and horns. The roar of the crowd surged, shouting his name. Weeping mothers collapsed to their knees, caressed and kissed Tristan's shoes.

"Tristan! Tristan! You da Man! Tristan! Tristan! You da Man!"

All that tumult swirled all about him. People everywhere! Dust and dirt kicked up from the squalid road.

Tristan swooned.

He fell limp in King Mark's arms.

Consult the next tableau to find out what the problem was and how it was handled. Some of you who are physicians and were fully awake during the last tableau will have already guessed and know what the problem is and what is needed.

Tristan Sick

The Irish left. Good riddance.

With them, left the Morhold's body. Once home, it was received with honor but no rejoicing. The Morhold's custom had been to take joy from his returns, to greet his sister Maeve (also known as Queen Maeve Iseult), the Irish Queen, and his niece, Iseult the beautiful, Iseult of the red-brown hair, red like sunset at evensong, whose beauty also unfurled like the breaking dawn.

But not this time. This time there was no joy in Ireland. No joy in Tara. No joy no more.

Many times had Iseult la Belle nursed an injured Morhold back to health, for she was a healer passing fair and had great skill in treatments and plasters and surgery. Her magic now was all in vain herewith, for the Morhold, sacker of cities, was sewn in a deer hide and forever beyond the help of potions or of balms or of anything or anyone. He was dead.

Iseult anointed the body and, using pliers, plucked Tristan's sword piece from her uncle's head. She wrapped the fragment of broken blade in a red silk cloth and placed it in her bog oak box while hurling imprecations at the man who had effected her Uncle's demise. She hated the name of Sir Tristan of the Lyonnesse. She thought that she would hate that name forever. Indeed, at her request, after the Morhold had been buried with great splendor, King Brian Boru gave orders that from that day forward, anyone landing in Ireland from a Cornish ship should suffer death.

Meanwhile, talking about Cornwall, back at Tintagel, Tristan languished, his ankle infected with gas gangrene. Wertheimer could do nothing, nor could Lord Godfrey, who was called out of retirement for consultation. This time ,the problem was not HMO or the malpractice situation or administrative restraints on costs or irritating long delays in getting new drugs approved by the FDA (Feudal Drug Administration). This time the problem was real: An infection for which there was no remedy.

An anaerobic bacterium called Clostridium Welchii causes gas gangrene, its putrid pus, its green, yellow swelling, its hateful stench. This was a much worse fate than the fusospirochaetals mentioned.

Tristan's friends avoided him, for they could not stand the fetor, stink, and reek of that disease.

The poisoned wound blackened and festered. The smell grew so sickening that King Mark alone made daily visits (but not without growing nauseated in Tristan's presence at the hideous sight of the poor youth's leg and the terrible foul odor).

Tristan went to the hospital, deposited a stool, which the doctors sent for culture and analysis.

In the hospital, blind men approached, groping with their hands and raising toward him faces pierced with two bleeding holes. Paralytics displayed before him their heavy immobility, the deadly emaciation, and the hideous contractions of their limbs. Lame men showed their club feet; women with cancer, holding their bosoms in both hands, uncovered before him breasts devoured by the invisible vulture. Dropsical women, swollen like wine skins, lay on the ground. Nubians, affected with elephantiasis, advanced with heavy steps, and looked at him with streaming eyes and expressionless countenances. A young girl, who had vomited blood for three days, slept as though dead. The place looked like a conflation of the worst features of the Inferno, Hades, and Hell. People crying and groaning and screaming worse than in Haiti after the earthquake.

Well, what did you expect? It's a hospital.

Yet, despite all these and the encumbered plodding starers doggedly dragging IV's up and down the corridor with plastic sacks of blood-stained urine, the foul smells, the lice, the aching, huddled together, bereft of relief, unwashed bodies of dirty, bewhiskered, verminous men tottering toward the seep of death with wounds hideous enough to turn a conqueror's stomach. Despite all that, Tristan, a sensitive soul wanted to stay at the hospital, wanted to stay with his tatterdemalion sick associates. He felt he belonged there. He felt he belonged there because he was sick. And he had been led to understand from day one of consciousness that the place for very sick was the hospital.

But Tristan changed his mind when his insurance company, Poo-Care, wouldn't certify his admission. In fear of a substantial off-network co-pay, Tristan decided to wait until he had time to work this through the appropriate electronic switchboards.

"I am broken before a frozen false God," he commented cryptically to the Cerberus-like insurance validation clerk in the cool-as-a-vault hospital entrance hall.

"The world around me bears me false witness in the form of my deceitfully denominated Health Maintenance Organization. Everything about them is fake. They are not interested in health. They certainly do not maintain it for me. But oh, they are an organization alright, an organization designed to extract money, lots of it, from their poor unwitting subscribers. Even a knight like myself must fall to them; must have them suck up my life's blood."

Tristan pointed his finger at the clerk, who, of course, had heard all this before many, many times and repeated, "Cleverly designed to extract money and deny care, they are."

For Tristan was that way. He didn't see the small mean modes and practices that tempered a man in life, or a company, for that matter. He did not see the folly or his own devising, for it was he that had signed the HMO contract. Nay, the fault was his, at least in part. Few things come quite up to the representations of them in this wide world. HMO is one of them.

(Author: Oh, I suppose HMO did start out, like so many of our insurance schemes, as a legitimate business before it became a scam.)

Disease control officials ordered Tristan removed to the little hut in the cove below Tintagel. That cove is now known to the locals as Merlin's cove, though Merlin had nothing to do with it.

Tristan, to while away the time, wrote a grant application to the scientific review committee of the castle seeking to get material support to continue his research on explosive powders. In his submission, he put forward the idea that a large rifle might be constructed, which could shoot a bullet, large enough and with enough momentum to knock down a castle wall, blow down a round tower, or penetrate a closed gate and keep. By cogent argument, he proved that such a weapon would make obsolete all the forts and castles of the time, enabling the villages to expand into cities beyond the castle walls. Such decompressing of the population should prevent plagues and most of the other consequences of overcrowding. Thus the "cannon," as he called it, would confer great benefits on mankind.

(Editorial note: Cannon is the Japanese goddess of mercy. Hence, Tristan's name for the weapon that he thought would will merciful peace to the world. The Japanese have named a brand of camera after the same goddess. Takes good pictures, too.)

He was eager to make it. But in times of institutional instability, grants were so hard to get that Tristan's hopes were not high.

He especially considered what had happened to Flannagan's last application and, not to pussyfoot around certain realities, to Flannagan himself. The universe is 100% energy. There is no solid matter, only energy that appears solid. Energy and matter are the same substance, measured differently. Just as space and time are the same physical item measured differently. All that energy doesn't even know we exist. And doesn't care. Poor old mankind is on its own and always has been. Grants or no grants, we all, yes, every one of us, even you, dear reader, God bless, are lost. Anyone who meets students regularly realizes that the ivory tower is more like the ivory emergency room. And if you want to be discouraged about democracy, talk to the average voter for five minutes. "Hopeless it is," says the Yoda. "All is vanity," said someone in the bible.

The powers took away Professor Flannagan's job and his title. Then they made propaganda that Flannagan was the originator of Flannagan's Fallacy, the self-evidently absurd assertion that iron boats can float. As we have seen, Flannagan thought he had invented a boat made of iron, so there is some truth to the matter. The real question is whether or not iron boats can float. Flannagan's grant application specified that boats float not because they are made of wood, but because they displace a sufficient weight of water with their hulls. Thus, a boat could be made of any kind of waterproof material, including iron. The advantage of an iron boat was that it would not rot, could not catch fire, would be resistant to the heavy action of waves, would not be attacked by the sea worms now plaguing wood boats, could carry more passengers, crew, and cargo, etc., etc.

Too bad the committee, an assemblage of cronies, was more than unkind in its review. The official report said it with an otherwise commendable bureaucratic terseness: "The Admiralty opposes Iron Boats because Iron is heavier than Wood and will sink."

By way of *obiter dicta,* they added: "Flannagan must be a seriously deranged man to have thought of such a strange idea. Everyone knows that boats are made of wood. Iron boats just don't float." In fact, as governments often do, the committee hired a PR person to make up a jingle to get the point across to the general population:

(Recitative)	"Oh you can't get to heaven
(Chorus)	Oh you can't get to heaven
(Recitative)	In a Flannagan boat
(Chorus)	In a Flannagan boat
(Recitative)	because the gosh darn thing
(Chorus)	because the gash darn thing
(Recitative)	Just won't float
(Chorus)	Just won't float
(All)	Ain't gonna grieve my lord no more
(All)	Ain't gonna grieve my lord no more."

Lord Barrington, the committee chair, called men like Flannagan a corrupting influence on Cornwall's youth and on boys in knight school. He proposed that Flannagan be committed to the dungeon as an example to others who might try this spurious line of thinking called "natural philosophy." The majority of the committee averred that college, graduate, and postgraduate schooling should from now on be home schooling with government vouchers to parents for their trouble."

Is it not interesting that people who threaten the assumptions of the powerful are always felt to be mad and in need of confinement and punishment? Even before television, people were dumb, but not as much as they are now. Television has made them more dumber. Television = junk food for the mind.

Voice from the audience: "More dumber? You mean more dumb or dumber. More dumber is incorrect English.

(People are too ready to find fault. Julius Caesar is quoted as saying Brutus's was "the most unkindest cut of all." If Shakespeare can take liberties with the language, so can we. Ed.)

Voice from the audience: "Would you please get to the point if you have one. What actually happened to Flannagan?"

Flannagan got no grant. But he did get the dungeon, where no man could live very long as no food or water was supplied to prisoners. On day two of his incarceration, however, something quite extraordinary occurred: Flannagan disappeared in a burst of smoke, accompanied by a sharp sulfuric smell from Hell itself.

Palace guards reported that the wall of the dungeon had been broken down by a dragon who, hissing fire and smoke, ate Flannagan utterly.

Flannagan left a note, which was brought to King Mark who, because he could not read, handed it to Harold, the Chief Druid who read it aloud:

"Lords and ladies and King Mark, forgive me for I am a complete fool and should have known that iron boats cannot float. Now my life is justly ended, for I have been eaten by a dragon. Adieu, /signed/ Flannagan, erstwhile Professor of Alchemy."

Everyone was convinced by this, even King Mark, who was soon smiling and chatting in an empty, pleasant, corporate way of his.

Tristan had doubts. Had he not taken logic in knight school? He knew that the note contained error-in-ratiocination #23: An event cannot follow a prior event if it is impossible for it to occur. Or in plain English, the note could not have been written if the writer, having been eaten by a dragon, were already dead. The sequence was impossible. Therefore, the note cannot be true. If the note could not be true, it must be false. Or the note didn't even say what Harold said it said.

Besides, this note didn't sound like Flannagan. It didn't have his personality, projection, and pizzazz. The note did not have the flavor or tone of discourse that Flannagan would use. In fact, the note sounded more like what the Archbishop thought Flannagan might have said had Flannagan conformed to what the powers wanted him to say.

Bernard stopped dead, looked up, and smiled. "A Freudian slip," says he. "I said archbishop when I should have said, Chief Druid. Interesting slip! Druids and Archbishops should not be compared as one is pagan, and the other represents the true faith."

Later, Tristan got the note from the wastepaper basket where the Chief Druid had thrown it. Here's how it read:

"Goodbye, suckers. God bless. True learning like mine is throwing real pearls before genuine swine like you and has to always go underground. Look for me, not. For I am escaped in my iron boat. Yes, fools. My iron boat does float. Don't follow me, or I'll blast you to smithereens just the way I zapped those donjon walls. Look for me in France, where they respect learning and scholarship.

/signed/ Flannagan

P.S. Fuck you all.

P.P.S. A special note to my dear student Sir Tristan of the Lyonness: Never forget, my dear lad, that the attitude of a man of enlightened ideas, is, and will always be, most comprehensibly expressed by Mercutio's statement: "A plague on both your houses!"

Yes, that was more like it: Flannagan's tone and in the master's hand. The misspelling of dungeon was also vintage Flannagan, who favored medieval orthography over modern. But there was a dash of extra bitterness. Flannagan was usually a happy guy. Unless, unless... Hey, maybe Flannagan was really, really pissed. Two days without food or water will do that to you. If you don't believe me, try it.

Flannagan's note set Tristan thinking.

Could politicians have that much contempt for the public? Could the powers just lie like that? Could they just make up some bullshit thing and pass it off as true? They must, else, why would the Chief Druid misquote a key message and hand out misinformation? Also, if court committees hated Flannagan and his ideas, how might they regard Tristan? Tristan sensed that Flannagan's problems were his problems, too, and would soon afflict him.

Tristan believed that artists were more important than politicians. Who was president when F. Scott Fitzgerald wrote The Great Gatsby? What petty princeling ruled Germany in the time of Bach? Who was the Pope who built the Sistine Chapel and had the ceiling painted by you-know-who?

Oh well, too bad. Tristan's grant application was in the mail and couldn't be retrieved. The moving finger writes, and having writ, moves on, nor all thy piety or wit can lure it back to cancel half a line. Something like that. I'm too lazy to look it up.

The grant system was another problem: Flannagan said the grant system allowed senior, predominantly idea-less, officials to steal ideas from youthful intellects who were predominantly idea-full. If that's true, one of these geezers might make gunpowder and get hurt. The DAGG had already asked for a Committee of Inquiry (equivalent to our modern congressional investigation) into Tristan's behavior. Witnesses had testified that Tristan had attempted to predict the future with a crystal ball (not true), that he did magic tricks (true, but only for the fun), that he had called himself the Patron Saint of the Lost (true, but he was just joking). These things, harmless enough one by one, tended to thicken proofs that did demonstrate thinly. Anything different, unusual, or new in that superstitious age worked against personalities that stood out. Dog ate dog in ancient days, with relish and with ease. Now, we are told, people are nicer. Aren't we lucky?

Tristan's biggest problem was a matter whispered but never stated aloud or discussed publicly until Flannagan's vanishing: The exact manner by which Tristan had killed the Morhold, sacker of cities. Rumor had it that the victory could have been achieved only by the blackest magic.

Andread's envy swelled. By lies, he and the three other base barons angered the chief men of Cornwall against Tristan. To repeat their lies were to do a disservice to our hero and take up too much time and space. So, I give you only a small sample, for it would be too tedious to recount a tenth of them. Similar stuff will assault you during the next presidential campaign:

"There were too many marvels in this man's life," said Andread. "He is too happy, too happy to have achieved happiness by moral means. Men of wit can explain some things, but by what sorcery did Tristan defeat the Morhold, sacker of cities?

Tristan himself admitted that he could not lift the Morhold's sword, even with two hands. How is it possible that a man so weak, without the intervention of tellurian forces or the Devil's aid, kill a man so strong?"

Some people who were listening took out pencil and paper and made a note to look up "tellurian" in the Oxford English Dictionary.

Tristan tried to stand to make an appropriately theatrical Answer Meet, but the poison from the infection was in his blood, and strength failed him. He collapsed back into his seat.

Shit! This looked doubly bad. And, of course, the barons made much of it. The barons were also emboldened against the youthful champion because his power had ebbed. They were beyond the pale as Tristan could not challenge them to trial by combat. Tristan couldn't stand up, much less fight.

Sad to say, it looked like Tristan had had it. Makes of men date, like makes of cars date; Tristan was a 409 AD model: There was now no market for that make. He was an Edsel.

But wait! By a heroic effort, Tristan rose and answered: "My lords and ladies and Mark. Jesus Christ! This is almost impossible to believe. Jesus H. Christ. Holy Mother and Saint Columba! I am a hero, a hero in the mystical Joseph Campbell sense. I left on a journey, I had an adventure, and I came back to give a benefit to all. You should reward me, not question my methods. I said it before, and I will say it again, it was not by witchcraft that I conquered, but by wit-craft. There's a difference, a big, big difference. I understood the Morhold's psychology. He was a big, fat, ugly bully."

"I understood the nature of matter and the transformations it undergoes. By successful manipulation of both those two things—his psychology and my knowledge of science—I won. But the real job was done by my Calico. More than anything, the Calico got the Morhold, sacker of cities, by pushing him over onto his back where he remained helpless and alone."

Buzz, buzz, buzz, a murmur of disapproval spread among the multitudes. The great unwashed rose up. King Mark hastened to Tristan's side to hold them off. With finger pressed tight against his own lips, Mark whispered to Tristan, "Speak no more lest you convict yourself more grievously. Never say anything against yourself for two reasons: One: They might believe it and Two, even worse: you might believe it."

What seemed a confession in open court that Tristan's cat had helped kill the Morhold, sacker of cities, was all the jury needed. They issued a verdict of guilty with (remitting) circumstances. Too bad there wasn't an Emile Zola to go to bat for Tristan.

By the way, in those days, as in Scotland and Ireland today, there are three possible verdicts: innocent, not proven, and guilty. These verdicts result respectively in three different consequences: acquittal, discharge with the possibility of retrial if new evidence arises, and punishment with no possible retrial. As to the punishment, when the case was not entirely clear, or when there were obvious benefits to the community that had accrued as a result of the crime, complete remission of the Irish tax for instance (as Tristan got for Cornwall), the jury would often issue a verdict of guilty with circumstances. This was the signal that the king could give the Punishment of Fate. Which is to say, the king might leave a way out for the convict to escape if the prisoner's luck were good enough.

The Punishment of Fate:

They had a funeral for Tristan at the seashore. It resembled the "American Funerals" that the Irish had for their friends or relatives who were leaving for the States and would never return. Andread gave (with a great deal of schadenfreude) the main address:

"Friends, dismiss these terrors from your minds. The man does not exist, will not exist, and will never be born, who will lay violent hands on Tristan, whose life is charmed. So long as I live and am on earth to see the light of day, I assure you all, and time will prove it—such a man's black blood would soon be gushing round my spear, for Tristan is my true cousin and a friend. Why, he often took me on his knee to put a piece of roast meat in my fingers or lifted the red wine to my mouth. That makes Tristan my dearest friend on earth, and I assure him that he need have no fear of death or any harm should he recover and return here to Cornwall. But there is no escape from what God decrees, and Tristan will probably joint his ancestors by noon."

These encouraging words were on Andread's lips, but death for Tristan was in his heart. Of course, it was all B.S. (B.S. = bullshit, something done for effect without due regard for the truth) as Tristan spent his youth in Loonois (Lyonness) and had no contact whatever with his cousin Andread.

Then King Mark ordered Tristan, with that hateful wound still spreading poison into his blood, put into an open boat without food or water, without oars, rudder, or sails and set loose, as far from shore as one can discern a white shield, to drift in the open sea, the great Atlantic, to face his fate, whatever God might send.

Isn't that beautiful?

Such an exquisite metaphor of life? The Celtic Open Boat floating free. Does it not say that all of us are alone, set out on the open sea, without companions, without rudder or oar, without sail, and under a mysterious sentence of death engendered by our decaying flesh? And yet, there is hope, always hope, if only just a little, if only for just a little while.

Gorvenal, the wise mentor, bade Tristan a sad farewell, throwing Tristan's harp into the boat just before it cast off.

Woe is Tristan. His sad name seems to be working out his sad fate (Tris = sad; tan = child: Hence his name means child of sadness by tradition, though his real Celtic name was (as you scholars know) Dunstan, which is Celtic, meaning child of the fort or fortress child.).

But those of you who bothered to translate Morgana's curse know that this boat thing and infection was not it. The curse is yet to come. Tristan, invincible hero and killer of monsters, is conquered not by destiny, and not by infection, but by love.

That is his sad fate: he dies for love. Nothing else. Morgana's curse sees to that, praying a fierce and hopeless love that causes as much suffering to Tristan as her love for him had caused her: MAY HE LOVE AS I DO LOVE.

Before taking his leave, Tristan said to Mark, "You are not cruel. You would have helped me if you could. Force of circumstance (some might say force of destiny) and your high position prevented you from right action. Kings, too, are constrained by proviso. Even kings cannot always do their will. Real power is purchased at the price of a certain submission. Thus, I forgive you, Mark, my Uncle, and my king. And so, I try the sea. Pray for me, for I would have the sea bear me far off alone, to what land no matter, where that I might through luck find some sweet nurse fair woman to help me to health anew and heal me of my hurt."

Mark beamed at Tristan with an avuncular genial air, incredibly counterfeit. "You know if there is a God, Tristan, he is just like me." Mark lit a cigarette while that sank in. The cigarette tasted flat and unpleasant and made him a little seasick. Mark hated cigarettes, but that was not incompatible with his continuing to smoke them.

Mark took another drag and continued, "I know everything. That's such a fatuous statement that immediately people disbelieve you. But this time, it happens to be true."

"Power corrupts, and absolute power corrupts absolutely," said Tristan. "You sound like Trump."

"Without me, dear nephew, you are just another knight, which I suppose is the operative definition of a man who has no soul of his own."

Reader dear, notice how the above conversation sounds tacked on. It may have been no more accurately recorded than a typical news story in the New York Times, but it did underline a favorite theory about King Mark—that the king was a baffling mixture of the genuine and the sham, as if he assumed instinctively the aspect of his character that pleased him at the moment, a trait reminiscent, not of George W., but of another recent President of the United States, William Jefferson Clinton.

A fog crept in on little cat feet (or was it paws?), hovered over the scene on silent haunches, and soon engulfed our characters. The Cornwall nobles could no longer see, but they heard Tristan as he drifted off. His harp, mellow and low, emitted some of the sweetest, saddest songs that earth did ever know.

"Somewhere
Across the sea
Somewhere
Waiting for me
My lover stands
On burning sands

As I go,
Sailing."

Tristan was improvising the words, some of them, as real poets often do when they have forgotten the text, but the original La Mer by Charles Trenet, *le fou chantant*, melody, complex and haunting, came wafting through and, with its terpsichorean powers, provoked Cornwall men to search for Tristan to take him back to Tintagel. Much is to be forgiven artists for their art. And, of course, all the arts strive for the condition of music.

In vain, the Cornwall men hunted. Tristan was gone. No man knew where.

Fate was about to bring him to another shore. Fate was about to bring him to his true love, to the true love of his life, to his Iseult, Iseult of Ireland, Iseult the Beautiful, Iseult the Fair, Iseult of the red-brown hair.

Meanwhile, his strength was failing. Tristan was close to the final swooning relaxation a man feels when he is being beaten unconscious and no longer cares whether he'll ever get up. Very far away, he could hear the sea howl and the sea yelp, the whine in the riggings, the menace and caress of waves that break on the white sea foams—sea foams that some said were the chalky white manes of the horses of the sea god, MacMannin—the distant rote in Cornwall's granite teeth, the wash and murmur of the swell that is and was from the beginning. And under the oppression of the silent fog, a tolling bell measured time, not our time but a time older than the time of chronometers.

Tristan Meets Iseult the Beautiful

Seven days and nights passed by. Irish fishermen heard wonderful harp music coming from a fog bank offshore near Whitehaven, the beach where the Morhold's body had lain.

An aeroplane overhead flew a banner: Free love, Free trade, Free verse, in a Free Lay State. That beach advertising didn't connect with anything. Advertisements usually don't.

One Irish fisherman to the other: "Now was ever sweeter music heard in Ireland since Dagda herself would be putting men to joy with the charm of her harp?"

They rowed out to see what god or saint made so sweet, strong, living a tune to run above the waves. Music is the proof that the gods love us and want us to be happy. It can do more miracles than a church full of saints.

The fog was thick. They couldn't see it. On that account, they waited with muffled oars for the early light of dawn to burn the haze away. To while away the time, the Irish (what else?) talked. They spoke of many things but significantly of Saint Brendan who had made the trip across the Ocean Sea to *Tir nà Nog*, the Fortunate Isles, returning to tell of that marvelous land, which is now called America.

Yes, it was not Eric the Red, or Columbus, but Brendan, later Sainted Brendan, one of them, an Irishman, who discovered America. Perhaps you did not know that fact. And if you did, it's a conviction of the Irish that you can't hear it too often. *Erin Go Braugh* and all that.

The music came, they speculated, from the Faerie Queene or perhaps from Saint Brendan himself, for to the Irish mind anything is possible, even the fantastic, even the impossible. The Irish live in three worlds: the material world, the spirit world, and the world of the imagination. And of these three, the world that is most real to them is the imaginary world of imagination for that world gives them the most succour. That is the world they can summon anytime they wish. That is the world where most of them would live most of the time.

When the fog lifted, they found not Saint Brendan, but a tired, weak, and very sick Tristan who was languishing in a drifting boat. The fishermen did not dare to interrupt his playings with questions, for the awe was upon them. Instead, they brought him over land to *Cashel* (accent on the cash, *cashel* = Celtic for castle), the king's castle, to the only nurse in Ireland that they thought might be able to help, the sweet and fair Iseult, daughter of Brian Boru, the high king.

At the moment, Brian Boru, the Irish high king, and his men were away on a punitive expedition against the King of Connarach, who had failed to pay his taxes. Therefore, no one who had been with the Morhold, sacker of cities, was at Cashel, and therefore, no one could ID Tristan.

Tristan's role in the Morhold's demise was safe for the moment. Furthermore, he gave his name as Stantris, a silly inversion, but a disguise that the Irish never breached.

When Iseult set eyes on Tristan, the effect was electric; her nipples hardened under the cloth of her gown, and her little button perked up too. She touched him gently, light as the brush of a falling blossom against one's cheek and just as lovely. And as she did, a *frisson* wavered to her deep heart's core, her muscles fell limp in homage to the power of amour. And with the *frisson* (*frisson* = French for a sudden shiver or excitement or more splendidly a small short woman's orgasm), she knew she needed this man, craved him to make her bloom with his magic, to carry her to ecstasy with a fiery carnal love. There is certainly no rest for us on Earth, but there can be happiness. Earth was the right place for love. I can't think of where it's likely to go better. Earth is the right place for death. I can't think of where it is likely to go worse.

Tristan looked at Iseult wistfully. The grace with which she moved, the way her sparkling white dress accentuated the warm colors of her skin and hair, the curve of her cheek, the flash of her smile—all these things had had their effect. But there had been more, much more, things which could never have been caught by a camera, even if it used all the Technicolor in the world. The moment he had seen her, he wanted to marry her. He knew he needed this woman, needed her in a most tremendous way. Her fingers touched his face, and he wanted to lick them and then bite. Just let her stay. Looking at her lips was like spying on her naked through a keyhole. Just let her stay. But alas, he was shy and could not tell her of his desire. He forced his eyes away, though her image would not leave its lingering in his mind and heart. He saw her for perhaps three minutes and would not be able to get her out of his head for the rest of his life. Those of you who have been in love know what we are talking about. Those who have not been in love don't know what we are talking about.

When two hesitate, the love is slight. For whoever loved, who loved not at first sight?

In those days, people fell in love suddenly, as all the ancient romances make manifest. Now, I am told, it often takes lots of back and forth on the internet.

A storm was coming up. It isn't often, in American Lit, that the weather matches human emotions. But in Ireland it often does, and this time it did. The moisture in the atmosphere, the electricity, the fragrant loveliness of the night, connected just right, stirred the youthful lovers strangely, both of them. For the mysteries of love are wrapped in storm and secrets, and, alas, in chaos and in doom. Those of you who have been in love know what we are talking about. Those of you who have not been in love don't know what we are talking about.

"Clearly, this wound is infected," said Iseult, getting down to business in the subsidiary matter of health care. "All such wounds will yield to the red salve, the white salve, and the blue salve, which I shall apply in that order."

Iseult also gave him penicillin, an antibiotic similar to Levaquin (levofloxacin) but more ancient and cheaper. She changed the dressings, cleaned the area with gentle debridement, applied the salves, and offered soothing drinks of herbs to break fevers and give quiet sleep. And so, by her art, after 40 days, she restored Tristan to his manly youth.

[Correction: What I've said is misleading, not quite true. Within a day or two, the red salve had drawn out the poisons and made the sick flesh clean and wholesome again, so there was no need to apply the white or the blue. But Iseult did apply them anyway, as she as a general rule followed protocol. All the rest of what was said was true, though.]

One morning Tristan awoke after a strange dream. He had dreamt that Iseult the Fair had given him oral sex. By way of a kind of joke, he mentioned this to her as she went about her daily ministrations. She blushed and said, "I had the same dream."

Thus, their secret love was no secret anymore. It became revealed to themselves. They had crossed that dangerous threshold to love's other shore, the land of the heart's desire.

One night, Tristan invited Iseult to swim in the small pool by the brook next to the Cashel's southern wall. "You can change into your suit at my place (really the Chief Falconer's hut that had been given Tristan during his recuperation)," he said. But when she entered the bedroom, her eyes showed that she had a more land-based recreation in mind. Truly, passion enters to nourish the soul through the eyes as food enters to nourish the body through the mouth. And in that instant, all was decided without words as the two gazed into each other's eyes. A woman's heart is such a complex thing—the owner thereof is often most incompetent to find what it needs, desires.

Well, it was almost that way. Actually, while Iseult was looking at Tristan's eyes, Tristan's eyes were having trouble staying away from Iseult's bosom, which she had fixed in a beautiful décolletage. Something about cleavage glued his eyes there. Something about cleavage made him wish to touch and pet and suck those gorgeous tits.

Iseult knew this. She had planned it that way. She knew lots about sex. But she was also the kind of woman who went beyond what she knew for she realized that what endeared women to men was not carnality alone but an imaginative play on that theme. Let us say that although she had a dozen medical books on the subject at home, she did not forget to show up for this tryst with a black bra with scalloped straps softly shirred suspended above silk and satin panties half-hidden beneath a sensuous side-slit gown.

Her thigh-high fishnet stockings did not stay put forever, however, nor did her Vee-snap bottom. And so that night, for the first time, the lovers found their bliss. And for the first time, Tristan realized what romance novelists meant by passion, for he had not experienced the true force of cardinal (sic: Bernard the Bardic Narrator probably meant carnal; cardinal love is something else and a persistent problem for the Catholic church, where it often involves boys) love before.

Love enveloped Tristan like a gigantic wave, stronger than the grip of the Morhold, stronger than himself, stronger than any force on Earth (other than itself, that is, for love is an earthy force). Moderation in all things means moderation in all things, including moderation.

Love pulled Tristan down into its clutches (as the Morhold, sacker of cities, did) in position 69. Love pulled him down into the other more conventional positions, as well. This time he would not escape, not even after death, for love is stronger than death, as this story will prove.

Iseult doubled up the fluffy down pillow, the color of barbecued prawns, put it under her chest next to her big breasts and kneeled down, head facing the bed board. She lay her left ear tight against the maroon sheet and wiggled her behind back in the air so that Tristan could easily slip his penis into her, enter the right hole according to Hoyle, enter it from the rear the way she liked, actually preferred, "doggy style," or as the Irish of those old days called it "like a heifer."

Tristan moved forward on his knees, feeling his way, trying to enter, but no luck. He grabbed his erect penis with his right hand and pointed it in the correct direction toward the target, stroking up and down, with overs and shorts like an artillery officer, trying to hit the bullseye, the opening.

Iseult reached behind and put him in.

Suddenly he felt a great soft warmth and comfort. Heaven on earth. Tristan looked down. He saw part of himself amazingly enter the body of another human being. He watched his penis go in and out between the orbic flexes of Iseult's backside. A crazy song began to play inside his head, something about pull it up to the bumper, baby, park it in between. Iseult did have marvelous bumpers, erotic figures of beauty, joys forever. They were buttocks made for sexual drama. But why did they weigh on Tristan? Why did it thrill him to touch them? Why did it thrill him to look at them? Whence came their power? How did they put him in that trance of longing? He hardly knew. He was having the experience but not the knowledge.

Tristan started his rhythmic stroking in and out, in and out, faster and smoother, deeper and deeper, enjoying the erotic pulse and pleasure.

Iseult felt it too. She began to glow down there where a woman ought to glow. She felt the power of love's mystery. She felt love penetrate her, fill her being.

Tristan felt strange like something was about to explode. So, he pulled out and tried to relax. He heard the clock on the wall ticking away, evoking inevitable things, marking the further expansion of the universe after the big bang. Time was recording his own mortality. Love would fade. Grief would come deep and total. His focused attention seemed to make the clock tick louder. With each sound, with each stroke, with each breath, he was nearer death, and love too was nearer death.

Tristan thought: It is the inexorable, unidirectional movement of time that makes life tragic in our human perspective unless one believes in an eternity in which time is redeemed, and its effects reversed. According to Flannagan, the probability of that happening is pretty close to zero. Flannagan had said that time was the fourth dimension. But unlike the three dimensions that constitute space, time can't be explored randomly from point to point. You just experience it sequentially, second after second. This continuous flow from past to the future is the arrow of time. In the time that has passed since you started reading this paragraph, the entropy of the universe has increased, and you are at a different point in spacetime, even if you haven't moved from your chair. Any fool with a watch can tell you what time it is. But who can really tell you what time is? "What is time?" asked Saint Augustine 1,623 years ago. He said, "If no one asks me, I know. But if I wish to explain it to someone who asks, I know not."

Tristan bent down to admire the place where he had been. Driven by natural male curiosity, he concentrated with interest on the object in question. He admired female nature close up, its complexity, the intricate crimson foldings of the labia, like a Georgia O'Keefe flower, beautifully perfecting a design as elaborate as life itself.

Come to think on it, Iseult's pussy looked like a perfect taco oriented vertically. But it was more than that: it was the origin of his magnificent pleasure, the origin of the human world, literally, for from it had come all humankind, even Jesus himself who, although he might have been conceived immaculately through Mary's ear, was born the usual way—out of her vagina.

What in the world did people find debasing about the view between a woman's legs? Why did they pass laws requiring women to hide such beauty?

Tristan dipped again into the origin of the world. He stroked slowly and gently at first, gradually building his pleasure and Iseult's pleasure.

Iseult began to mutter in cadence, "oh god, oh god."

She adjusted the pillow and pushed herself into Tristan with each stroke rocking into his rhythm. She felt herself about to come as if some dam inside were about to burst open and flood an arid plain. With her right hand, she reached behind and between his legs. She pulled his testicles forward and a little down and shouted, "Get ready." Her vagina began to contract. She thrust backward even harder, forcing Tristan to penetrate harder, deeper, right up to the hilt. She felt his tip push against her cervix. She gasped as her own crisis swelled. She yelled, "Now!"

Her orgasm deepened, became a giant tidal wave, a tsunami of pleasure, rushing forward, covering her in quivering tension, sweat, and pink.

Tristan felt her vagina pulsate like a neutron star. He felt sperms on the move, passing out of something down below in him to her, and with a sudden leap, he squirted ahead, lost control, fell forward on top of her. He watched her slide, chagrined and happy, her tripod collapsing, watched her hit her head on the bed board, heard the noise of her impact resound through the room like a percussed Algerian drum.

"What happened," Tristan asked, feeling suddenly spent.

"You came," Iseult informed him.

"I came where? I was here all the time."

"No, silly, I meant you had an orgasm."

Tristan made a vague, boyishly inquiring noise in his throat. He was pretty sure he understood. It was part of the process. But the word discombobulated him as did the fact that she had spoken so freely about it. He was learning that sex is not simply a box that you check M or F on a form. There was more to it, much more.

To her, he still seemed puzzled. "A climax," she added rather sharply. "Do they not teach you that word at knight school?"

"Is this... normal?" He wanted to know, beginning to feel better.

Iseult shrugged. "Not for boys of your upbringing. Not the first time. Appearances to the contrary, you're probably highly sexed."

That evening, Iseult and Tristan did it twice. For a first session, the lovers were passing fair. The fire of him penetrated her, burned down there where a woman ought to glow. Then in a frenzied blast, she quaked (as he had done before her) as she lay beneath him moaning in solid animal health and pleasure. Even then, their first time, they thought their love as a form of holy communion, a new sacrament in some kind of new religion that they were founding, a religion of which they were then only dimly aware—a faith without guilt, without sin, without God, a religion whose ultimate reward was an orgasmic bliss followed by a quiet stall, a restful peace, during which, for a few blessed moments, they weren't even there, on earth, but would lie in a kind of placid, serene ethereal glow, at last, in a true mutual adoration and worship, followed by the peaceful gift of sleep. The sheets were cold. The pillows had no smell.

"Branwen, I am so happy—so happy," Iseult said with a girlish giggle and a broad smile. (Ed. Branwen is her slave maid from Wales. In Welsh, Branwen means White Breasts. Why she was so named no one knows. She may have had white breasts, but as I have not seen them, I cannot say for sure.)

"Branwen, I have to tell you. Tristan is the most amazing man I've ever met— the smartest, the most generous, the most artistic. He's perfect, perfect for me."

From that day forth, neither Tristan nor Iseult felt that they could control themselves. They did not believe what they did was any more a sin than it was sin for snow to cover the ground in forgetful winter or for flowers to bloom and blossom in remembering spring. They were driven by a force of nature beyond their poor power to add or detract.

And so, now you know that the celebrated love potion which I will talk about later when Tristan and Iseult make their famous cruise together to Tintagel was not the cause of their great love. That device was simply an ignorant narrative invention of the French who, in their primitive attempt to explain what they could not understand, once again demonstrated their comical lack of experience with the overwhelming human passion called love.

Tristan and Iseult fell in love not because of some elixir love potion but because of something much more complex and mysterious, so mysterious that poets and novelists are still trying to work it out. It is true Tristan and Iseult did drink together, but what they drank was a pink martini, not a love potion, although some people do consider the martini a kind of love potion because candy is dandy, but liquor is quicker.

The old French texts are also wrong when they call Iseult a blue-eyed blond. She was nothing of the sort. That is just the Gallic projection and interpolation of the French concept of beauty. Iseult was of Hispanic origin, for her mother came from Malaga. Iseult had crimson hair from her father whose red hair was from (what else?) Viking blood. But her brown skin and beautiful brown sultry eyes, eyes that attracted men like magnets, those Spanish eyes suggesting a sun-soaked world of utter decadence that men long for and revere.

Iseult's presence in Ireland reflected a historically important pattern of trade and commerce from the fifth century onward: the Irish traded with Spain—particularly with Sevilla. Spanish princes married Irish girls, and Irish princes married Spanish girls, creating the conjunction of Hibernio-Iberian traits considered then, as it is now, monumentally sexy.

Two days later, messengers brought some bad news. Brian Boru and his men had been defeated. Homeward their footsteps, they had turned. Tristan realized his peril and bade the fair Iseult adieu.

"Life is full of sad partings like this," he explained. "They are but prefigurations of the ultimate departing, which is death."

"That's sad," she said, not knowing what to say, "Sad but true."

Poor Iseult. She accepted Tristan's leaving as traditional (or at least literary) women do because their love is an uncritical love, such as such women usually provide in books, but almost never provide in life. Most men I know complain that they never ever have gotten enough love from women or enough gratitude from their children.

Iseult understood that Tristan needed to travel, to get away, primarily to advance the plot. He was a character, after all, and he was a man. In the direction man-to-woman, the flow of gratitude is never straight, never great, never long. That was the nature of things. The nature of nature. And consequently, the nature of narration.

Night came, bringing foul weather. There was no moon. Rain from Zeus set in, and the wet West Wind blew hard. Tristan rode to the north and arrived at Newgrange, where he figured out the secret message on the entrance stone.

Farther along, Tristan visited Tara, where the kings of Ireland assembled for the Fire on the Hill festival and where every five years they elected their king of kings. Tara was named after Tara, the Irish heaven. That would be a name that figured in a famous novel called *Gone with the Wind*. And like Tara of that novel, Tara of Ireland had fallen into disuse and decay.

That megalithic phallus, the stone of Fail was there, but the banquet hall that had seen so many fantastic feasts, festivals, and fun was rotting in its timbered halls. A constant wind blew through it like a banshee's cry across the hewn ridges and through holes in the roof. *Sic Transit Gloria Mundi*.

After a few adventures not worth talking about, Tristan returned to Cornwall, where he confronted the usual problems. King Mark was overjoyed at Tristan's return and resolved to make him his heir. But Mark's lords did not agree. The DAGG conspiracy was at it again and had, in secret council, decided that King Mark must take a bride to produce a more biologically Kosher heir to the throne. Otherwise, it was fairly certain that Tristan, the much-despised Tristan, would get the nod and become king. One fine day in May, the problem came out in the open in open court:

"Sire, it were a shame that thou should not marry," said Andread while the others of the DAGG nodded their agreement.

"How come?" asked Mark.

"Woman's service," said Denoalen. He was one of those deep ones who know about women. He also knew about stocks and shares. Of course, no one really knows about women, and certainly, no one truly knows about stocks and shares, but he quite seemed to know, and he often said stocks were up and shares were down in a way that would have made any woman respect him.

"I am old," said Mark.

"Not so old that you couldn't marry and beget a son of your own," said Andread.

"I have the son I need, all the son I need. No son of mine could ever be as dear to me as Tristan."

"And thereby produce an heir to Cornwall's throne," said Gondoine. He was off the point a bit, out of sequence, for he had memorized his part. He was going to do his line no matter what.

Mark shrugged his shoulders and shook his head. "What need I of woman's service? Since I have gotten older, I need it less and less. Recently once a fortnight will do me. And at that, it takes all night to do what I used to do all night. And believe it or not, I am beginning to see women as people and not as sex objects. That is one of the great benefits of getting old."

"It's not alone for thyself, we ask this," said Guenelon, the last member of the wicked four. "But for the general welfare of the kingdom."

"The answer is no," snapped Mark. "I'm a king. I'm the one who commands and forbids. I am the decider (like Bush?). I will not accept any criticism of my behavior. All I ask of you is to obey me. You are either with me or against me. My way or the highway."

"Consider carefully, Uncle," whispered Andread. "These barons in secret blood pact among them have pledged to each other their lives, fortunes, and sacred honor.

They have resolved to return to their keeps, issuing forth again to make fierce war against you, should you not agree to marry."

Mark's face looked like a sky threatening weeks of rain. The king turned against them and was wroth. "Don't be so medieval. As long as my dear nephew Tristan be alive, I swear, no king's daughter shall come into my bed."

But Tristan, thinking this might be an opportunity to bring Iseult to Tintagel, sided with the barons. "Mark, if I were you, I would take a wife. Not to do so were to cause too much strife."

Mark was puzzled. Was this some sort of public posture to show the barons that he, Tristan, was not interested in power? "Tristan, you are not me. Therefore, any conclusion from your contrary-to-fact assertion does not follow, for a conclusion based on a false premise must be false."

"You mean invalidly drawn," corrected Tristan.

"What?"

"A conclusion derived from a false premise is invalidly drawn, but not necessarily false. The conclusion could still be true, though the reasoning incorrect. Take, for example, the syllogism: All leprechauns are mammals; all whales are leprechauns; therefore, all whales are mammals. The premises are false, the logic correct because the middle term is distributed at least once, but the conclusion, though invalidly drawn, is true."

"Cut the shit," shouted Mark, turning to leave.

"Not yet, sire. First, your answer. Then you may leave," admonished Andread.

"Gentlemen," said Mark with an upheld finger like a preacher quoting Holy Writ. "I have heard full expression of all relevant opinion. Let me retire and meditate upon our words together. I shall give my answer as soon as I have an answer to give."

Alone in his private chapel on the upper floor, Mark reasoned that getting on in age, he was not really interested in sex. He liked women. That was true. But he didn't seem to like them sexually anymore or at least not as much as he had before. Oh, he still had dreams of naked women. They swarmed through his head while he lay abed. Such visions frequently played on the stage of his imagination after he had looked the day before at a woman, then in the night tried to remember her. Such insubstantial images, as most men know, fond hope all too often scatters to the winds. Strangely, King Mark had noticed recently that the women he noticed were younger than he. The ones he wanted to tell to pull their socks up were precisely the ones he wanted to pull their panties down. Why in the world was he getting interested in girls and not in older, more mature ladies?

Thank goodness, he thought, most of that sex thing is past. Now I can concentrate my energies on important matters like bird watching. But these barons would have me make an effort. Well, they'll have to settle for a token action (for publicity purposes, so to speak), and to that end, I must hit on a reasonable plan.

A man's fate is a man's fate, and none can wipe out the rune written on his forehead. To be human is to drink the cup. It was King Mark's turn.

Mark felt like praying to Saint Bridget, the patron saint of Britain, or to Bridget, the Mother Goddess of Britain in ancient times, the same name, perhaps even the same superfetated idea, but as surely in the mind as the word white evokes the word black, in that instant, the word Bridget evoked Mark's sure-fire plan, a perfect plan that made needless and redundant any prayer to either saint or goddess.

Mark went up to the altar and removed from a small silver box in front of the tabernacle a relic of Saint Bridget of Ireland, which had been kept there and venerated in that box for centuries. In the age of premedieval faith, people believed as fervently in the powers of a saint's hair or bones as we moderns believe in wheat bran or jogging or psychoanalysis or Gatorade® or vitamin supplements.

Holding a lock of saintly hair in his hand, Mark thought he would see if this small token would keep the DAGG away.

Down the staircase, he went, rushing with the hair. And with his clever proposition, which we will learn about in the next tableau or perhaps in the tableau after that one.

Let's see.

The Quest for the Lady with the Crimson Hair

"Lords and ladies," the king announced after taking his position in the estate chair in the great hall. "I have decided to take a wife."

"As I pondered the question of whom, two building swallows came into my room, quarrelling together. Startled, they flew out, but had let fall from their beaks this tuft of hair, long and fine, and shining like a crimson beam of light, the blaze of crimson one sees at early dawn just before the sun rises or at evensong, just before the start of night.

"My kingly intuition tells me that this hair is from a woman fair, a daughter of a great king who will be an excellent wife. You must seek her out, her whom I have chosen."

Ho ho ho. Pretty funny, right? Mark is a politician, true blue. Nothing, but nothing can touch these guys for deceit. The marvel of it all is that they do it so naturally with such a straight face, like Humpty Trumpty (Ed. Donald Trump is the object in question). And what a trick! Substituting the relic of a Saint and instigating a search for the woman of the crimson hair. God himself must have a cosmic sense of humor to put people like Mark in charge of anything.

But, you know, once we start to deceive, a tangled web we doth weave. King Mark thought he was being clever in feigning that he would take a wife. He thought he was setting conditions impossible to achieve. His plan might backfire big time.

"To please Your Majesty," said the barons. "We wish it, all of us do wish it. Tell us who she is, and we will find her and bring her here. Your Highness, her name?"

"Why," said Mark as he gestured with lock-holding hand toward the sky. "She is she whose hair this is, nor will I take another."

"Very well, lord and master and our king," said Andread. "But just tell us whose hair it is and from what land. We need to know. Else we will be wroth and think that you have devised an impossible task to prevent our finding a wife for you and a queen for us."

Mark resisted the impulse to order Andread executed on the spot. Instead, he said, "Indeed, I know her not. See to it yourselves. The birds brought the hair, and therefore she might be near. Who knows? It's your task to find her, and when you do, she will be my bride."

Slick obfuscation and facile bullshit. I love it. Mark didn't tell them anything, but then he probably didn't stir up much new resentment either. He was a real politician. Guys in the U.S. Senate are masters of this sort of thing.

(Here followed a long sidebar about Bernard's experience with the U.S. Senate and the psychopathic Senators that make up the U.S. Senate. As that sidebar is not relevant to the rest of the story, charity demands that it be excluded. Ed.)

"Sire, by my halidome, this subterfuge proves that you refuse to set in motion a rational process that will lead to a new heir for this kingdom, and that you have already prefigured Tristan as the king."

"Tristan has nothing to do with this. Seek you the woman with this crimson hair for I have fallen in love with her tresses. She was born a red head, I can tell. Red more than it is permitted to be, redder than the law allows, red like blood, not just a living orange, but a flamboyant red, a red of rubies, a screaming red, a red of the extreme of evolution, red incandescent, enflamed, startling, fiery, dazzling like the sun, a Viking red so unique that one could spot her anywhere—should she be there. Find her, and her shall I wed."

Andread was underwhelmed. "You beg the question."

"That's my answer. Take it or leave it," said Mark.

"What luck," thought Tristan. Iseult has red hair. Sometimes things just fall into your lap. Probably good and bad luck occur with equal frequency in this indifferent universe, but because, as the psychologists say, we feel a loss two and half times more that we feel a gain, we note the bad more than we note the good because the bad weighs heavier on us 2.5 fold. But, Hell, when you think of it, you just can't keep rolling snake eyes and box cars forever. Seven or 11 has to come up and often does and often come up more often. Therefore, take the risk because the odds are always in your favor until they're not.

Having considered this, Tristan spoke: "Although the way be filled with perils, I take an oath to travel to a foreign land to seek a queen for Cornwall. She will be she whose hair [he whispered to himself the word *closely* (this was his mental reservation taught to him by the Jesuits)] matches this sample."

"There is no rush," said Mark, trying to calm Tristan down. "You all have seven days and seven nights, the time it took God to make the world."

The barons sneered. They thought Tristan was in on Mark's clever trick. But Tristan surprised them by carefully and minutely examining the hair. He looked sincere. He looked sincere because he was sincere. And clever Tristan had a clever plan. I know what it was. Do you?

The barons and Mark accepted Tristan's pledge and outfitted a great ship, putting in it mead, honey, wines from France, 600 gold *bezants*, and all other manner of goods to serve as the bride price for the daughter of an as-yet-unidentified foreign king. For the women of the red hair must be a princess fair.

And so, Tristan, with his faithful Gorvenal, hoisting sails of gold and scarlet as fits a great king's messenger, set out to find the bride for Uncle Mark.

Ah, those men were brave who went to sea in those days. It was as hazardous as going to the moon in ours. For beneath the placid surface of the sea, on the ocean bed, lay skulls without names, green coins that had once been gold, and the old bones of ships forgotten forever and forever forgotten in the silence of the sea.

When Tristan and crew had sailed out, farther than one can see a white shield, Tristan directed the pilot and the captain to head for Whitehaven, in the kingdom of Munster, Ireland.

When the helmsmen heard this, they trembled exceedingly, panicked toward mutiny, for the Irish were their historic enemies, a primitive race that collected heads (I kid you not) and exhibited them at table while boasting of their exploits in battle (no kidding). And the Cornish sailors had heard the news that Brian Boru had ordered all from Cornwall ships who set foot on Irish soil shall be put to death.

Tristan solved the problem by distributing a few silver groats.

A little bit of money will go to change surliness to full cooperation, especially among the poor, for money is not properly divided (radical thought). Among the poor, a little bit of money will work more miracles than deaf and dumb heaven or a church full of saints.

As you guessed, Tristan had it in mind that this would be a good way to bring his beloved to Cornwall, there to share his bed and love. But, as usual, the eager youth had not worked out the subtler points. His vision is notoriously short on detail. His legs fall asleep in the lotus position.

It was not clear if he could convince Brian Boru to part with his daughter. Nor could he think of how to break the news to Iseult herself. Secretly, he hoped Iseult would be content to have him part-time rather than not at all. He had got the idea from reading about time-share condos in Florida. If it worked in Sarasota, why would it not work in Cornwall? His love was blind. Despite his careful schooling, Tristan could not see the defective logic of this, a false analogy. Sharing a wife/woman was similar to but not the same as sharing a condo. A condo is not a wife/woman and vice versa. Because two things share certain traits, it doesn't necessarily mean they share other traits. In symbolic logic: because X had qualities a, b and Y has a, b doesn't mean that if X has c, so does Y.

The 100 Cornwall knights, dressed as merchants, greeted the Irish ambassadors who met them at the beach. The king's Coast Marshal demanded, "Who are you, and where do you come from?"

"Call me Stantris (French texts say Tantris). I and my companions are from uhm, er, (he can't lie, remember—it's one of our hero's character traits; Tristan can't lie)... another land, far away. That's it. We are from another land."

"How do I know you are not from Cornwall?" asked the Marshal, his arms at the ready, for he was suspicious of generalities, and he knew that another land could very well include Cornwall.

"By this," said Tristan pulling a beautiful gold cup in the Breton style from a blue velvet bag.

At the sight of the gold, the Marshal's eyes gleamed like a radium dial. Ah! Handiwork of Brittany! "But this is no proof, for one may buy in one country and sell in another. You still may be bloody, brutal, Sassenachs." [Then as now, "Sassenach" was a disparaging term for Anglo-Saxon.]

"Aye," smiled Tristan. "Take it then as a gift between friends, for yourself."

The Marshal took the cup. "I accept the gift in friendship, and I will speak for you to the king." He went his way but left eight men on guard.

"What now?" asked Gorvenal.

"I have bought us time. Peace in our time," said Tristan misquoting Neville Chamberlain.

"Think you that one will keep faith with us for the sake of a gold cup? He could slit our throats for sport and still keep the bribe."

"Irish cops may take the occasional bribe, but they'll keep their half the bargain. That's why numbers, prostitution, and drugs exist in Harlem. Pay the price, and there'll be no raids. And furthermore, the Irish don't rat. You can torture them for weeks, and they will not rat."

[Editor's Note: An Irishman taking a bribe? This is more wildly improbable than any Roman Policier (French detective novel) you have ever read. An Irish cop could no more take a bribe than a Roman Catholic priest could molest a child.]

[Monk scribe and translator: I have kept silent so far, but here I have to say that I think I might agree that, under most circumstances, Irish cops might not take bribes, and I know for sure a Catholic priest would not molest a child. But it didn't matter. All that is beside the point. The Irish quickly figured out that these were no merchants who did not know the bargain price of corn and who seemed more interested in passing their time playing useless games of chess and dice than in making money by selling stuff. Copying this manuscript has been interesting work. I can't wait to see what happens next. Unfortunately, we are not allowed candles in the scriptorium, so my eyes are suffering when the sun light dims.]

Tristan knew they had been discovered and that soon, Brian would descend on them with a herd of fierce marauders to end their days. Yet he still wanted to complete his mission. He wanted to end the quest. He very much wanted to bring Iseult back to Cornwall.

But how?

As soon as dawn appeared, fresh and rosy-fingered, while he was walking on the beach, Tristan met a young woman who was gathering mussels and cockles from the tidal pools alive, alive-o. Molly Malone, her name was. She was passing fair, despite the bowlegs, scarred cat face, and the shanty Irish look.

Tristan was not distracted, for he was focused on his true mission. He invited Molly into his tent for coffee, nothing else.

Whoa! What the devil am I talking about?

Coffee is a Radcliffe anachronism. Coffee, a Turkish and North African beverage, was not introduced into Western Europe until the mid-17th century. Tristan must have invited Molly in for something else. Coca-Cola? Pepsi? Black Bush Irish Whiskey? I don't know, but for sure, it wasn't coffee. But who cares? Molly was the other kind, for she had "I love you, Rosie Probert" tattooed on her right shoulder. They may be lesbians and into scissoring but, I assure you, they just don't love pussy the way men do. Impossible!

"Brian is wise to you," said Molly as she lit a Marlboro Ultra Lite (0.8 mg tar and 0.6 mg nicotine by FTC method). She blew a smoke ring; the blue white circle rose up boiling within its own form, hovered for an instant, then melted into an entropic weaving strand. It was beautiful, a beautiful thing, but like any beauty thing, it faded and then disappeared.

Molly spelled out a few facts for Tristan's edification: "He knows the men are not merchants, for they have nothing to sell. He knows that they are not from Ireland, for they all speak with a British accent and not a brogue. He is pretty sure that you all are from Cornwall because one of the sailors said so during his visit to our local disorderly house, Day's Sinn. The plan was to do nothing until Brian got back. But he got back last night, and still, nothing happened. The rumor was that Brian needed to rest. The word is that Brian has to deal with a more important community problem—the red dragon."

"He knows we are from Cornwall, but he does not attack?" asked Tristan.

"Too busy with the red dragon."

"Dragon?"

Molly sang, "Oh, Stantris, dear, and did you hear the news that's goin' round? A dragon is forbid by law to burn an Irish town."

Molly took a sip of whatever they were drinking and continued in prose. "Devastates the countryside, it does. And has the people much in arms. It has. Brian tried but failed to kill it. Now he's offered, as reward, the hand of Iseult the Fair to him who can."

Oh boy! Hot dog! Lucky sees as lucky does. This angle greatly interested Tristan. Flannagan had told him that dragons do not exist except in the human mind as a metaphor, a metaphor of evil. Fossil evidence clearly shows that the earth was once populated by a group of giant reptiles, but those animals, according to Flannagan, have long since become extinct. Somewhere in the human brain, however, there might remain some primitive collective memory of such reptiles, a part of the Jungian collective unconscious. These mind-beasts might very well be what we call our Dragons of Eden.

Flannagan said that when we see a statue of Saint George killing a dragon, it means the saint conquered evil. Thus, when we hear a hissing sound, we all keep quiet because the hiss reminds our unconscious memory of times long ago, times out of mind when dragons roamed the earth and sometimes appeared at the cave entrance menacing humans with an eerie "SSSSSSssssssss."

That Flannagan! He had an explanation for everything: "We take consolation from a fire or a candle or the open hearth because flame kept us safe from the wooly mammoth, the saber-toothed tiger, and the Dragons of Eden. And it is likely," Flannagan had continued, "that the flickering of the TV is so similar to a campfire that it, too, gives us this same solace and consolation. I hope that is the reason for TV's popularity, for it certainly cannot be popular on account of people who run it nor the wasteland that they call programming."

Flannagan's point was simple: A dragon was easy to kill, for its sole principal existence was the belief that it existed. End the belief, and the dragon will disappear in a puff.

"Oh no," said Molly. "The dragon is real. I don't know who this Flannagan Mick is, but as sure as you're born, he's fed you a pile of Irish malarkey. The dragon's lair is close by on yon high mountainside. Smoke comes from its cave. The Irish are afraid to approach for fear of being eaten. Risk is one thing, but to be going out against this firedrake is certain death. So it is. The dragon, 'tis real all right, as real as the Blessed Trinity." Molly blessed herself using two, not three fingers.

"You speak truer than you think," observed Tristan while smirking that little smirk of his. For he had studied philosophy in knight school and knew the controversies that surrounded the Trinity. The Father is God and the first person of the blessed Trinity. The Son is God and the second person of the blessed Trinity. The Holy Ghost is God and the third person of the blessed Trinity. So, there you have it. 1-2-3. Muslims say there is only one God, not three. And then there is the filioque problem. In the Western church, the Holy Ghost comes from both the Father and the Son. In the Eastern Orthodox, the Holy Ghost comes only from the Father. Among other things, this super important issue will cause the great schism of 1054. Even the form of blessing oneself had provoked bloodshed. Some thought you needed to use three fingers in recognition of the Trinity, and others thought it was OK to use two fingers. One finger is a no-no of course. History does teach important lessons. How easy it is to screw up your thinking.

Tristan printed the dragon's exact location with his portable Dell computer's program "MapQuest" and called the men to assemble.

"Wait here for my return. I go with Gorvenal to kill the dragon. Fortify the ships and your positions round about in case the Irish strike. If I don't return in three days, sail home without me. That's an order. Now help me with my ringmail and stirrup and plate steel gauntlets. The gods be with you and with me."

Then Tristan armed himself with the same sword he had used to pretend to kill the Morhold, sacker of cities, the one with the bit of blade missing. For the first time in his life, he used his emblazoned shield, the one designed by his mother, Blanchefleur. Its device was a blackberry thorn bush twisted and bent on itself in so true a Celtic spiral that no man could discern its beginning or end. No cross appeared on this coat of arms, for Tristan had grown up. He did not believe in that sort of superstition any more than he believed in dragons. But, he understood the same mental mechanisms that produced a God, produced a dragon. And, sad to say, he also knew that, given human nature, since God and dragons did not exist, it had been necessary to invent them. People create imaginary problems to escape from actual problems they find difficult to escape from. It wasn't like fornication. That did exist. And because it existed, even writers didn't have to invent it. And because it existed, even writers didn't have to invent the problems that fornication caused. Those problems, the multiple ones connected with fornication, exist *sui generic* and are difficult to escape. The problems of fornication will soon form a significant part of this narrative unless Bernard poops out before he gets to that juicy part of the story of True Love: The Romance of Tristan and Iseult.

"You remember much," said Gorvenal.

"I collect ideas. They're cheaper than gold coins and more useful," said Tristan voicing a thought that had just come to him that very moment.

What a fine sight to see, so noble a charger and so fine a knight come from the merchant ships. But Whitehaven was empty of folk, for it was dinnertime, and none of the guards and only a few of the country people saw Tristan in the full glory of his steed, armor, and colors grand.

Soon down the road, from the opposite direction, five panicked knights sped past. Tristan seized one from his full gallop by pulling his red-braided hair as he passed. He swung him down over his mount's crupper and held him fast.

"What's the hurry, friend?" he asked the frightened Irishman.

"God save you, my lord. We flee for our lives. The dragon comes." With that, the man motioned in the direction of the smoky cave that Molly had pointed out on the Google satellite photo of the area.

Tristan began to lose his sangfroid. Talk like that disconcerted him. If a dragon were just a metaphor, why were these knights running for their lives? Can a metaphor be so powerful that it causes the powerful to cower? Could the dragon be real? Tristan was sure of himself and of Flannagan's logic. Still somewhere deep in his heart of hearts, he had his doubts. The reason that that Chicken Little story is so cogent is that all of us are, at the bottom, a little chicken.

A few beats, an interval during which Gorvenal opened and closed his mouth like a fish out of water before he could manage to say, "I ain't drinking the Kool-Aid."

"What?"

"No Jim Jones stuff for me. There are better ways of self-destructing."

"Right," said Tristan. "I shall return with you."

"You can't, old sport. Destiny, man. You can't change it. You {sic} under authorial control. You do as the story says. As for me, I shall decamp to the ships for I have important business there. I need to save the life of a person very dear to me."

"Yourself, of course," sneered Tristan.

"No need to engage in fruitless combat, risking life and limb. Who turns tail and runs away lives to fight another day. Count me out. If I have to die," interjected Gorvenal, "I want to die screwing. Death in the saddle, that's Crossing the Bar for me. Fighting dragons? Forget it."

"OK," said Tristan turning to go. "Scram. And if on the way home you pass some International House of Pussy (IHOP), pull over. Do this in remembrance of me. For where two or three of you shall gather (to make love), I am with you, for love is the whole law and the only profit."

"We shall wait three days and then sail home with or without you and with or without the Princess of the Swallow's Red Hair. Adieu."

"See to it, friend. I feel your fear. But you're right. I must drink this cup."

Proceeding now more cautiously, Tristan approached the smoky mountain. No trees, no lanes, no cluster of cottages or hamlet, but mile upon mile of bleak moorland, dark and untraversed, rolling like something out of T. S. Eliot's wasteland to some unseen horizon. It was a silent, desolate country, vast and untouched by human hands. There is a pleasure in a pathless woods. There is a rapture in a lonely landscape.

On the high tors, slabs of stone leant against one another in strange shapes and forms, massive sentinels that had stood there since the hand of God first fashioned time and them.

When he arrived at the cave's mouth, he saw only steam and sulfur fumes. No dragon. But coming up the trail (with a change of heart) was Gorvenal. Poor Gorvenal! Lonely, as a graduate student without a girlfriend, he had changed his mind.

"Look at this, Gorvenal. Flannagan says the earth is hot underneath. Sometimes this heat comes to the surface as a small fumarole. That's what we are seeing."

"Is it?" asked Gorvenal.

"What luck," replied Tristan. "I imagined this was going to be easy, but it turns out it's going to be easier than I imagined."

They carried sand and stones and all sorts of dirt, muck, and debris to the cave and covered the fumarole so that it no longer vented. Then they constructed a dragon of moderate size using wattles and clay and different animals that they had killed in the forest, including a black bear (no longer seen in Ireland), a giant Irish elk (also extinct), and a wild boar (still around). Tristan let off some stink bombs that drenched the place in an acrid stench. He burned the boar's head and mutilated it (he hoped) beyond recognition.

He had had in mind to carry the head back to Cashel as the proof that the dragon was dead. But then he had second thoughts. Carrying the head was so much work, especially after all the work he had done carting stones and soil. He left the head, *devant* the cave for the forensic team to find.

"Let's think awhile, Gorvenal. For I am a great believer in thinking."

Sure enough, after careful consideration, he decided that things were not quite convincing. Tristan took off his helmet and held it over a fire to blacken it. Brian would think the dragon had vomited from its nostrils two streams of loathsome flame, which toasted the helm like a cinder. Then he mixed iron oxide with linseed oil and dribbled this paint over the scattered animal parts like Jackson Pollack, except that Tristan's work of art looked more like the burned and charred replica of a dragon than an abstract representation of modern complexity.

Most people coming on the scene would quickly conclude that a great battle had taken place and that a great animal had died. In a word, it looked (even without the digital effects) as good as the movie Jurassic Park II, if not better.

Gorvenal was well pleased with his master. "What say we celebrate at Bridey Murphy's Inn?"

"Good idea," said Tristan. "What a better place to discuss our exploits than that local drinking hole. Bridey Murphy, the transmigrated soul who owns the place, will spread the news, for she is a gossip and a tout, not only now in our time, but in centuries yet to come. Within the hour, I predict, we will be summoned out to Cashel Rock for our reward."

(Reader, your experience with this book will be enhanced if, at this point, you look at the amazing internet pictures of Cashel Rock.)

But, you know, when men start to drinking, watch out, especially when they're at a place like Murphy's. Bridey slept with whom she pleased. That is why some called the place Dirty Bridey's. The other theory on the origin of the name was that, i.e., a play on the word "dirty." This matron recently had started giving baths as a service to those who wanted them—a good scrub too with a sauna afterward to get the lice and ticks off. If you go to Cashel now, you will find the Inn still there, next to the castle's south wall. The sign in front reads: "Village Inn" and "Dirty Bridey's" both. And to this day, it is a favorite watering hole and trysting place for the young and the young at heart, who still, believe you me, repeat there every night, except Mondays when the inn bar is closed, the story of Tristan and the dragon as is known by them with all the usual (and unnecessary) Irish embellishments.

(Note: This Bridey Murphy has nothing to do with Viginia Tighe (1923-1995), U.S. housewife, who claimed she was Bridey Murphy in another life. This led to a book by her hypnotist, Morey Bernstein, and an investigation of her claims. Irish records are excellent, and there was no record of a Bridey Murphy born in Cork December 20, 1798 as claimed and no death in Cork in 1864. Virginia called her husband (when she was Bridey) "See-an." That's a give-a-way. In Ireland, Sean is Shawn.

She was just another case of cryptomnesia that came on when she was hypnotically regressed before her birthday. Morey Bernstein, of course, made a fortune on the book and the movie.)

Along the way to Bridey's, Tristan saw a note hanging on a branch of a large birch tree. In those days, even kings could not read, so leaving a note on a tree was as safe as having the CIA encrypt a message. It read:

"Harry, I have been thumbing for four hours and no luck. Consequently, I am in a bad mentality. I will make my way to Dirty Bridey's for a pint or two and meet you there. Brian Boru has interdicted tobacco again, and the poitin (Black North alembic spirits made from potatoes) business is off because of so many raids from the R.I.C. (Royal Irish Constabulary). In addition, a certain Richard Mac Raghnaill, heir to a property in the south of County Leitrim, died from drinking our *uisce beatha* (pronounced 'whiskabough,' *uisce beatha* = Irish for water of life, i.e., whiskey).

"This looks bad when the 'water of life' becomes the water of death for Richard. As if that weren't enough, the high king, Murcheartach mac Earca, while entertaining his chieftains and warriors, as usual, had more than his share of our brew, and the palace was set on fire, and the king, in trying to escape, jumped into a vat of booze and drowned in it. And, intelligence informs me as King Cathair Mor, and his courtiers lay in a drunken sleep after the celebration of Samhain, a thief slipped in and stole the golden crown off the queen's head, for it appears that Her Majesty was just as intoxicated as any of them."

"All this is bad for business. I feel the Irish simply can't handle the creature (creature = Irish expression meaning strong drink) without overdoing and coming to trouble. We should go into another business. I have one in mind. For lack of a better term, I call it 'The Fruit of the Month Club.' Every month we mail some apples or cranberries or some such truck to our subscribers. The markup will be the same, but the product healthier. Think on it. We'll talk." /signed/ David

[The story about Murcheartach drowning in booze is true except the protagonist was just a king, not the High King of Ireland. Brian was high king at the time. Partially inaccurate stories like this have been the bane of Irish Literature from the get-go. The other stuff mentioned is, of course, pure history and fact.]

Tristan decided that Harry and David were on to something. He wanted to invest in the project and would seek them out at Bridey's. Fruit of the Month Club probably has a fruitful future. Don't you think? Personally, I like it better than Cheeses of Nazareth.

Now, the man with the braided red hair whom Tristan had stopped in flight from the cave was Aguynguerran (nicknamed "Red" and also known as "Dragonfly" because his eyes stuck out so). Red was the seneschal (monitor and administrator of spectacles) of Ireland. Red desired to wed (and to bed) the beautiful Iseult the Fair. But when it came to physical danger, alas, he was a coward. He was in the wrong movie.

Nevertheless, such was the power of his passion that every day he went close to the dragon's lair to see if he could muster enough courage to attack. But each day, his courage failed, usually because he thought he heard some sound or other coming from that cave. That sound or other would spook him, and he would run.

For the second time today, driven on by love (and lust), this knight full armed, headed up the mountain to see if he might be pulled together enough for battle. This time, Red found the smoke had stopped, and the dragon was vanquished. Overjoyed, he picked up the monster's head and galloped back to the castle to claim the princess's hand in marriage.

The king was torn between the joy that Ireland was rid of terror and the terror that his daughter must be married to a man she (and he, King Brian) loathed. His promise could not be broken, but Brian was suspicious. He couldn't credit his seneschal's story because the man's armor was spanking clean and nowhere showed even the slightest sign of battle. Besides, even if he had liked Red, Brian didn't like the idea of handing Iseult to a mere seneschal. He wanted to use his daughter the way the other kings did, to cement political and military alliances. For his daughter, a mere knight or seneschal was not enough. Iseult was fit for a king, none less.

To be fair, the king and his retinue rode out to the site and inspected the damage. Their review of the animal there encountered, as recorded in the official annals of the court and kingdom, and recently published in their peer-reviewed journal "Knight Life," led later French scholars to conclude that a dragon is a kind of composite animal consisting of elk, bear, deer, and wild boar. No kidding. I read that in the Bibliotect Nationale. Nor did the French stop there. No kidding. They added creatures of their own imagination, like the griffin. Accounts by Thomas, Gottfried von Strassburg, and Béroul augmented this stupid notion. The French also said that the king found at the entrance to the lair a sign which said: "Faith and Freedom. No Death Panels." That was true, except Faith was misspelled on the sign as Faite and Panels was misspelled Panuls. Details like this are important because they show the ignorance of the tea party people who made the sign.

In its far-back beginnings, Tristan is a Celtic legend woven by harpers round peat fires in live oak groves long before the time of chivalrous knights, fair ladies, and turreted castles in which it is generally set. That is why the French have screwed up the tale so badly. Ignorance, madam, pure ignorance.

How irritating that those troubadours in Languedoc and the Rhineland took the story and embellished it, dressing it in beautiful medieval clothes. Divide the labor, I say. Let each work in what métier he knows best. Troubadours should stick to the things in which they excel: Fine fashion accessories, real estate development, good perfumes, nice wines and cheeses, singing and dancing, and womanizing. They should leave the storytelling to the Irish Bards, like me, who do it best.

Brian declared the dragon dead. Consequently, it was bruited throughout the kingdom that the princess would be wed. The bridal shower was set. The feast was get. And the court prepared to see Iseult the beautiful, the Irish princess, cover her fine red hair with the married woman's wimple.

Ugh! This is terrible. She is to wed a man she does not love. Many women have done that, and some still do. Usually, it doesn't work. But usually doesn't means it sometimes does.

When the bride-elect first heard that she was to wed the cowardly *Seneschal Aguynguerran Le Rous*, also known as Red, she laughed and laughed long and loud. Then, when she realized that this was not a joke, when she realized that her father was serious, she wailed and wailed long and loud, for she had been hoping in her deep heart's core that someday her wonderful Stantris would return and sweep her off her feet to the land of the crystal room (Celtic heaven), there to live for all eternity.

In that instant, came the king's messenger, bidding Iseult come to her betrothal.

Iseult put down the book she was reading, *A Scandalous Courtship* by Barbara (B.K.) Reeves.

"A good story?" asked the messenger.

"I find it highly enjoyable."

A beat as Iseult collects her thoughts.

"Tell my father that I bow to his will. However, I will come down three days hence, not today, for it is that time of the month. A wedding now would be a bloody affair. The bridegroom would get his sword all wet and bloody. Besides, I am weary. I must rest."

"That was clever, Iseult," Iseult told herself. Still, things looked pretty hopeless. Her reverie of marrying Tristan (whom she knew as Stantris) seemed to be a mere pipe dream. But then she ordered Branwen, her trusted maid (the captured slave from Wales) whose name in Welch means White Breast (Bran = breast; wen = white)—remember? To make ready to set out at first light. "Get my Cupbearer, Perenis. Bid him have two horses saddled and posted by the side gate an hour before dawn. I have an idea. It's a little daft, but it might work."

Wow! She did have a plan. A super-duper plan. Check it out in the next tableau. See if you agree.

The Princess of the Swallow's Hair Discovers Truth

The next morning, as soon as Dawn appeared with her rose-red fingers, Iseult and Branwen, cloaked with hoods pulled over their faces, met Perenis at the small side gate. With Iseult riding pillion, they proceeded through town passing a big lot of Texas repos along the highway, proof that quite a number of people thought they could pay a small loan back—no prob—and couldn't do it.

The retinue moved through the Irish countryside, whispering down sandy byroads past worn-out farms, passing cows and sheep that were grazing in the true Irish fashion on the "long meadow," the grass along the side of the road. Irish boys were skimming rocks along the surface of the lake, reminding Iseult of Stantris, her patient-turned-lover, who also liked to skim rocks in water when he sent them skittering over the water. All men and boys do. Men and boys, no difference, except with men, there is no adult supervision.

They ascended the mountain to view the dragon's lair. Suddenly, glancing down at the path below, Iseult had a flash of insight. The hoof prints in the mud she saw there were made by horseshoes never forged in Ireland, a land of saints, sages, and scholars but no blacksmiths. For there is no need for horseshoes on roads of loam and grass.

Farther along, Iseult dismounted and trekked through mud. She knelt close to the putrid (composite) carcass. Damp oozed into her shoes with cold and clammy relentlessness. The hem of her skirt, torn in places, was bespattered with bog.

She looked at a spear lodged in the makeshift animal, examined it with care. Evidence is any sign that points to truth, and this spear was evidence.

"This is no Irish spear!" she shouted. "Some foreign knight has slain the dragon. Not the cowardly seneschal."

Overjoyed, then you, Branwen of the white breasts, shouted, "Mistress, you will not go to his betrothal the day after tomorrow. Hurray! Hurrah! This be the best of Irish luck, thanks be to Dagda."

(Bernard, the Bardic Narrator, really loved Branwen, this character he had created, and here, instead of telling about her, he felt impelled to speak to her directly, as if reminding her of the story.)

"Nor any day," screamed Iseult. "Nor any day. I shall not marry him any day. I feel like I had myeloblastic leukemia and suddenly went into a spontaneous remission."

The sifted evidence amply confirmed their impression: With red paint, someone had arranged a scam to simulate the death of the beast. But Iseult and Branwen couldn't figure out why the smoke had stopped.

"Would Stantris be so clever as to do this thing? Let's seek him out though he be far and wide. A foreign horse and a foreign spear must mean a foreign man is afoot. Let's go get a drink to celebrate and then find him who killed the dragon or seemed to."

They found Tristan and Gorvenal with Harry and David at Bridey's Inn in a stone chamber lined with hangings of brightly dyed wool, eating together and drinking morat, pagment, and claret mixed with Oban Scotch whiskey, Queen Victoria's favorite tipple—a concoction which was regretted by Gladstone not for the violence done to the wine but for the violence done to the Scotch. Morat was made of honey flavored with the juice of mulberries; pagment was a sweet and rich liquor, composed of wine highly spiced and sweetened with honey; the other ingredients like Oban single malt Scotch Whiskey need no explanation.

A turf fire burned in a bronze brazier near their feet. The flame had sunk low in the hearth, and dark shadows stretched long fingers on the wall. The candles, too, had burnt down, and cast monstrous shadows on the ceiling. There was something heavy in the atmosphere reminiscent of the last time it was full, a lingering taste of old tobacco, the sour smell of drink, an impression of warm, unclean humanity packed one against the other on the dark stained benches.

In the middle of the cellar, in the cleared space, a lone couple danced sharpie style, their backsides out, their shoulders moving insolently, as "IN THE STARDUST OF A SONG…"

A couple in the corner had gotten into one of those conversations of the "no-I-didn't; yes-you-did" type, which, though fascinating to those who are engaged in it, neither desires nor deserves the attention of others.

Tristan stepped away from the bar, accidentally colliding with a man holding a glass of beer. When he turned to beg the man's pardon, he received a punch in the mouth. A short while later, he discovered himself in the bathroom in front of the mirror, playing with a loose tooth.

Back at the table, Tristan filled in the details to Iseult and Branwen of the white breasts and Perenis, the cupbearer, after which the group went to the woman's rooms at Cashel where they discussed the situation with Her Majesty, Queen Maeve Iseult herself, who had (impressively) oriental pearls round her neck, Moorish bracelets on her arms, and an aigrette of diamonds on her head.

Unfortunately, there are many Iseults in this story, Queen Iseult, Iseult the Fair's mother, being one. Iseult of the White Hands, daughter of King Howth, whom Tristan later married, being another. Iseult the Fair, also known as Iseult the beautiful, the Irish princess, daughter of Brian Boru, being a third Iseult.

To distinguish Queen Iseult of Ireland (Iseult's mother and sister of the Morhold, sacker of cities), from here on in, we shall address her as Maeve (or Mavis in

English). Incidentally, the juxtaposition of the two women, Iseult the Fair and Maeve Iseult, daughter and mother, appeared to illustrate the interplay of the stochastic laws of heredity and the inflexible law of time.

These two Iseults might have been a single person with her image reflected forward to the future or back to the past, depending on which you looked at first and which last.

"Stranger," said the Queen Mavis. "You slayed the dragon. The reward is yours. Red, our seneschal, a felon, somehow came to the castle with the dragon's head. A mystery we can't explain except that a man might—he just might—come upon the carcass of a dragon slain by another, and cut off its head, thinking to claim the kill. He might then, he just might, present it to the king and claim Iseult for his wage. My husband did not credit this man, a known coward, who had the smell of fear upon him as if he were involved in a willful dissimulation. Accordingly, I shall enter plea for you, giving the usual inducement of my woman's service with Brian to help him decide in my favor and yours."

"Thus, shall you have a chance at trial. Prepare you well. Two days hence, at Hawthorn Mews, make ready to joust."

Queen Maeve spoke authoritatively about the future because she had just come from consulting an astrologer about matters of state. Maeve did that often while she was first lady, just like Nancy Reagan. Someone in government has to know what the future holds. Right?

"Queen Maeve," replied Tristan. "I killed the dragon. Therefore, I have already won Iseult. I have also possessed her in other ways that make her mine. (A beat as Queen Maeve raises her eyebrows and then emits an understanding smile and a side glance at her daughter who turns her face away.)

(Camera back to Tristan.)

"Why do I need to defend my right again in battle?"

"Destiny, my boy. Force of destiny. Thus, is it written," replied Maeve sagaciously.

After the Queen left, the lovers welded together in amorous embrace, but Iseult was worried that for making love, this was not the time or the place.

"I fear discovery for the scandal," she said.

"Not me. I don't care who comes, who knows, or what happens. I'm in your arms now, happy and willing to die."

Faster than you can spell Vercingetorix, Tristan reached in her bra and caressed her warm sienna breasts. Then he slipped the right one out and started licking and sucking the nipple; it got hard and stiff as a Greek olive.

She embraced him back, embraced him passionately. They became oblivious: a thousand eyes, noses, fingers, legs. He can hear not a word because she is beautiful, and he loves her. His only wish is to pour himself into her. Her only wish is to fuse with him. Together their warm bodies collapsed to the floor. Yes, to the cold hard floor, and there, even as they heard the castle cleaning crew coming, they took their bliss and quickly rose again, the sap still oozing from between her legs, a warm feline odor, and her hair, the hair of crimson, in his mouth. For it was that day that something from him blended with her and something from her blended with him, mixed and twisted and became intertwined so like a Celtic spiral it could never be called back again for as long as they both shall live, even longer, if you believe that love is eternal and stronger than death.

They went to Iseult's room, where they discovered that the imposing canopied bed squeaked mercilessly whenever they moved. This brought on fits of laughter but did nothing to diminish their love making and fun.

Iseult awoke at midnight, got up to go to the portchamber. On the way, she noticed Tristan's gleaming sword and decided to polish it at that late hour. She unsheathed the weapon. Truly this is a fine blade, and one that fits a daring baron, she thought. Then she noted the notch and the shape of the dent. Was not this the shape of the piece plied with much effort from the Morhold, sacker of cities' skull? Oh, God. No! Please no!

Iseult went to the place where she kept the piece of steel and matched it to its mark so that no seam showed. Then she ran with the sword to where Tristan lay sleeping, held the sword above his head, and cried: "You are not Stantris! You are Sir Tristan of the Lyonnesse, the same who killed my mother's brother. Prepare you now, in your turn, to die."

Tristan strained but knew he could not resist the blow if Iseult decided to kill him. "Crown princess, go ahead and kill me, for my life is yours. Do with it what you will."

Iseult stepped back, puzzled.

"Doubtless, you'll find it happy to muse on this night of wastage when you are lying in the seneschal's arms."

"No, nay, never. That won't happen. I am known not to take no shit from nobody. There is nothing, neither hate nor love nor filial obligation nor life itself that I'd pay that price for."

"And think of the scandal when they find you killed your guest in your very own bed."

Iseult was silent a long while, staring down at him and mustering her resolve. "An eye for an eye, a tooth for a tooth, your death for the death of Morhold, sacker of cities."

"Did I kill the Morhold, sacker of cities, by treason? No way. Morhold was warned. He wouldn't yield when helpless and hopeless on his back. He brought on his death by his intransigence."

"Intransigence?"

"Obstinacy, obduracy, doggedness, mulishness, stubbornness, pertinacity, pigheadedness, inflexibility, willfulness. You know. He asked for it. He had it coming."

A gale of laughter went roaring through the room, a cloud of dark flame shaking around her head. Tristan sounded pretty funny. Iseult, like most women, had about decided that funny is the best thing in men. I'm talking about aside from money and your basic manageability. Those three things women look for in a mate.

"Pigheaded, aye that's he; that was he," she said. "My uncle, bless his heart, was pigheaded—sure as you're born."

Iseult continued: "Just like me. Just like us, the Irish. I hear strange words from thee. Now I know the plan. You remitted the Cornwall tax but wanted even more. So, you further insult the Irish by planning to bring to Cornwall's shore—myself, the Irish princess, Iseult the Fair, as your serf and slave."

"King's daughter, no," said Tristan, "the way it happened was that one day two swallows flew to Tintagel and bore some of your hair, or some red hair, we really don't know whose hair, but it was red."

"Ca-ca! Pure ca-ca," Iseult screamed out. The echo answered ca-ca, ca-ca, ca-ca, ca-ca. "What idiot would believe such a stupid story? Save your cock-and-bull story, knave, for the devil."

"No, really. The red hair! I have it right here in a leather pocket round my neck. See? This is the hair which King Mark thought belonged to his, to be his intended queen. And so, I came to find her. And I intended that this red hair belong to you. So that I could take you back to Cornwall to be mine."

Tristan might as well have been talking to a cat.

"That's not my hair. You know that! You know that well. Your story is way out there, way out there with fucking Pluto."

Then Iseult put down the sword and, taking up the red hair, was silent a long space. All at once, she kissed him on the lips to prove the peace, and she put rich garments over him. The hair was red, but so was hers, and she knew there would be because there could be a switcheroo.

Now I ask you, dear friend, gentle and great heart, isn't that ridiculous, the last few paragraphs, starting with "She awoke at midnight" and going to "and she put rich garments over him?"

This comes from the French version by Thomas of Brittany (c. 1160), as adapted by the great German poet Gottfried von Strassburg. Permit me to point out some of the many defects in their narrative. Let me prove to you that no such events could have transpired, after which I shall tell you what really happened, the real story. You would like to know the real story, wouldn't you?"

First of all, the tip-off is that the writing is flat. Second, the end is incongruous. Why would Iseult suddenly change? Third, what sleepy woman in her right mind would start to polish a sword in the dark? Knights kept their swords at the bedside, the way Patten keeps at his bedside his Walther PPK 380 semiautomatic pistol, as a protection.

Tristan's sword would no more have been sheathed while he slept than Patten's Walther would have been unloaded. So, Iseult could not have unsheathed a sword that was unsheathed already. When I read crap like that, I know the French are winging it.

Notice also the vagueness and lack of specificity in telling where the Morhold, sacker of cities' steel piece was. We know it was in the bog oak box wrapped in red silk, but the French refer simply to "the place she kept the piece of steel." And there is no way she could have run to Tristan's bedside, for they were in a bedchamber. Anyone who was ever in a medieval bedchamber would know that such a room is cramped and crowded with bric-a-brac and thus does not permit one to run. And how completely out of character Iseult would have been to hold a sword above her lover's head. She loved him. Besides, swords are heavy. All medieval swords, in fact, weigh one kilogram, exactly 2.2 pounds, for that is where we get the kilogram measure. It would be unlikely that Iseult could hold that weight on high, and impossible that she could do so for long.

And wait a second. She's not stupid. Did she not realize that Stantris is Tristan with the syllables reversed? No, that's ridiculous. Iseult never wanted to kill Tristan in the first place. She loved him. Love does not alter when it alteration finds, or bends with the remover to remove; oh no, it is an ever-fixed mark that looks on tempests and is never shaken and bears it out even to the edge of doom. One last thing, for you writers out there, and then I'll let you go back and punch holes in the French text yourself: Notice how stiff, flat, and jerky the dialogue sounds even to Iseult, who knows the truth of it, the real story. It's like a grade B movie. Would two people who had just passed the night screwing, talk to each other like that? No way, José. But I don't mean to be unkind to Thomas or to Gottfried von Strassburg. The criticisms I express refer only to their writing and not to them personally. They were doing their best, and for their time and place, it was pretty good.

Writing what they did, I'm sure it was a great deal of fun, for writing was fun in those days. Thomas and Gottfried knew that they were composing a work of fiction, a piece of literary art, and one that would allow them to take advantage of the novel's capacity for telling the truth while actually concocting a lie. As authors, they were not modern nor postmodern, but pre-modern. So, R.I.P. Let them be. Nowadays, most art aspires to the condition of literature, and most literature aspires to the condition of the novel, and most novels aspire to the condition of the postmodern, metafictional, travel-adventure-love story of the kind and quality that you are now reading.

So, what really happened that night between Tristan and Iseult?

The real story was that Iseult and Tristan, the fury of their passions spent, took a bath together, and slipped into bed to sleep. Iseult, a restless sleeper, arose about 2:00 A.M. to smoke a Winston. After two harsh breaths of nicotine, she felt a solace and surcease, such as smokers do, and went, in a kind of tobacco trance, to gaze out the castle window, past the crenellated battlements and corner towers, across the moat, across the dirt streets to the Village Inn. She recalled in wistful meditation the early rendezvouses with Tristan there when their passion was in its first full flower, and she thought nothing on this Earth can equal her happiness. An immense joy came over her. It was indescribable. It had nothing to do with the effect of tobacco, and most resembled the all-pervading happiness of fine weather. The sun causes fine weather, but Iseult could think of no central radiance here. She stood happy and longing to give happiness. The central radiance, she realized, must be love. Yet, she hardly knew Tristan.

And then, in the same absentminded way, she glanced into the bedchamber to the wall mural of a naked Adam about to stir the passion of his half-awakened madam.

While the fiery tip of her cigarette issued soft blue-white curlicues of smoke ascending to heaven still, she admired the other things in the room, the bric-a-brac, the draped Damask, the magnificently carved English double bed with ornate posts and bed-back and canopy finely embroidered with scenes from the childhood of Christ. There was also a baby's cradle (hers) and a spinning wheel. A throne-type three-legged chair made of turned units and bobbins stood in the corner with a large Rhenish hanging cupboard decorated with elaborate panels of roundel heads. Over the fireplace, a wood carving, probably of Hornberg (German) oak, bore two central allegorical figures of Hope with her anchor and Charity nursing two children. The Leuchterweibchen hanging from the ceiling was one of several of these distinctive German types of flamboyant early chandeliers. The one in her room represented a bare-breasted female figure with antlers sprouting from her back and a fish's tail and bore a shield emblazoned with a lion rampant. The candles, now out, were attached to the antlers. This chandelier, she fancied, was some kind of bizarre symbol of hunting, light, the sea, and female fertility. It didn't make sense, but a lot of perfectly splendid artistic creations don't make sense. So what? Beauty is its own excuse for being. Beauty is truth, truth beauty. That is all you know on earth and all you need to know.

And as Iseult began to suck on the butt end of her smoke in the moonlight, she noted the dent. She got the steel piece from the bog oak box, unwrapped the red silk, and fit the steel piece with Tristan's sword.

Her senses reeled, her very soul seemed to be leaving her body; she tottered and would have fallen had she not braced herself against the wall. With a sigh, she realized that Tristan had killed the Morhold, sacker of cities. But that was long ago in a fair fight, and the challenge was the Morhold's challenge, and consequently, the consequence was the Morhold's. But the dead. Oh, the dead she murmured, one pitied them, one brushed them aside, one had even a little contempt for them. Yes, admit it. The living do have a contempt for the dead. It is a sign of poor character, but a human trait.

Ugh! The dead. Dante was amazed that death had undone so many.

The dead.

They are at our mercy. The dead are at the mercy of the living. The dead are at the mercy of the living precisely because—well—they're dead. Strengthless and dead, the two go together like a horse and carriage, like shrimp and grits, and like I don't know what. In my career as a doctor, I have seen many dead persons. Not a one of them appeared to be having a good time. Is there sex after death? What do you think?

The way that love can disregard things hitherto sacred is an age-old wonder, but it does so all the time. And here is another example:

And so, Iseult kissed Tristan on the forehead, for she had things in her own past that were not so nice. Yes, she had a past. She had been naughty. Iseult had been around. She would tell Tristan about all that... when she knew him better.

Then Iseult slipped beneath the sheets and, navigating by touch alone, found Tristan's thing and with skillful use of her tongue and lips brought him off again with the biggest longest brightest orgasm that he had ever had. Blow jobs skillfully done can do that.

When human beings operate in the force field of love, they try to get something. They also try to give something. This double aim makes love more complicated than food or sleep. It is selfish and altruistic at the same time, and no amount of specialization in one direction quite atrophies the other.

"It is a bawdy planet," says *The Winter's Tale*.

Shakespeare knew his stuff. But I remind you that Shakespeare got drunk and Frederick the Great ran from battle. It's not the depths but the heights that men can reach that count.

Stay tuned for the trial by combat. Our ancient relations sometimes settling things, especially who mates and who doesn't mate, by fighting. Similar behavior occurs among other animals, including deer, elephants, sheep, unicorns, Komodo dragons, and most of the other creatures on this planet. The males are operating under the force field of passion. You might as well talk about photosynthesis in plants. That's what they do. The natural thing. Reproduction is the one veritable transitory power. And what, may I ask, is the alternative? Misogyny? Misanthropy? Isolation? Solitude? Cold heartedness? What? Think about this: If there is no transcendence, then all we humans have is ourselves.

On to combat.

The Trial at Hawthorn Mews

At Hawthorn Mews, the barons assembled with all the lords and ladies of the castle. Tristan wore new armor so no one could identify him. For the same reason, he kept his visor closed. His shield had nothing emblazoned but a large red five, the significance of which few could know. The bend sinister was there, the diagonal band on the heraldic shield, drawn from upper left to the bottom right, usually signifying bastardy.

Too bad that it had come to this, that Tristan would have to fight the seneschal. One or both of them could get hurt. Violence in this wide world is hard to justify, and this particular form of violence, the joust, was stupid.

Tristan hated trial by combat for the uncertainty of the outcome. It was as chancy as rolling dice. Aleatoric really! Lucky for us, modern trials, we are told, are far less risky.

In case the Irish tried to pull an ambush or some other Mick trick, Tristan summoned the 100 knights from the ships to come witness the joust. One by one, the numbered passed along the road to Hawthorn Mews, where all the barons of Ireland stood. They entered in silence, paying no homage to any there; then, they in unison sat in scarlet and purple with gems gleaming.

The Irish, talkative as usual, spoke among themselves. "These are splendid lords! Who knows them? Behold the shimmer of the hilts of their swords, the cloaks trimmed with sable, the golden torques we wish we had. And what about those buckles of solid silver, the emeralds, the many stones the very names of which we do not know."

After much consultation, they could pick out other gems, among them rubies, sapphires (including the rare ink-orange padparadscha type in addition to the lighter and brighter blues from Burma), and of course, diamonds from Golconda, India. They saw opals, cat's eyes, black pearls, and white pearls, the white pearls of perfect color and shape, with matching luster and rich, thick nacre.

By prearrangement, the hundred knights said nothing. Not one moved from his seat, no matter who entered. That built up the tension. The desired effect.

After King Brian Boru took his place in the High Chair of State that had been carried there for him, the wicked seneschal tried to prove by witnesses and by showing the now rotting boar's head that he had killed the dragon.

Before the court, the witnesses looked poor, flimsy, and obviously bribed. One of them was so drunk he kept slipping off his chair to the ground. He had to be carried off.

Then, up spoke Iseult. "My king and my father, this knight with me challenges your seneschal for lies and felony. Promise you will pardon my champion all his past deeds, no matter of what gravity they may have been, for he is the one who did slay the dragon that the people feared. No other. Leastwise, this cowardly seneschal. Grant my man forgiveness and your peace."

The king paused, seeming unable to figure what all this was about. Then the barons and the people cried out in chorus, "Grant it. Grant it for we do desire it thus."

Brian Boru, the Irish high king, looked toward Queen Maeve to get his marching orders. It was the reward of her tact and devotion through the day. Maeve understood why some women prefer influence to rights. Mrs. Simpson, when condemning suffragettes, had said, "The woman who can't influence her husband to vote the way she wants ought to be ashamed of herself."

The king bent his head to indicate assent and kissed Iseult as a sign of peace and forgiveness and that she had her pleasure.

Then Iseult led Tristan on his steed before them and bade him lift his visor and show his war face. When he did, the hundred knights stood in homage. The Irish concluded that he (Tristan) was their lord. Clever they are, the Irish—sometimes.

A few among the Sons of Hibernia were sober enough to recognize the slayer of the Morhold, the Sledgehammer, the sacker of cities. They drew their swords and clamored for his (Tristan's) death, but the king, at Iseult's request, kissed Tristan on the lips, and the rabble toned down, and on that stricken multitude a sickly silence sat. For what but dread held they their peace?

A squire came and brought two good spears. Tristan chose one, the seneschal the other. They spurred their horses to opposite ends of the meadow.

Tristan, awaiting the signal to joust, looked around. He saw the Damsels in white samite and loved them all. He waved to Iseult. She repaid his compliment by smiling in a peculiar, secret way and running her tongue over her lips. It was one of her most characteristic gestures and very effective. It seemed to promise all sorts of undefined intimacies, yet it was really as simple and automatic in her as the word thanks.

As always, Tristan loved being in front of an audience. Yet today, in view of the violence to come, his pleasure was less. Society or fate or something, had roped him into this bullshit thing. He had just had read to him an interesting book called *Life in the Woods,* whose thesis was that men in our society are similarly constrained by circumstance. In America, the book said, it has become impossible, except for the lucky few, to live one's own life: you can be different, but you must pay a price. Accordingly, the poets and the artists tend to move to the fringes. The American Way of Life has become illusory. The real America, the America of our founding fathers, the America of our dreams, exists only in the abstract, a promised land in theory, not in practice. In modern America, according to the author, most men lead lives of quiet desperation. While we boast about free speech, free press, and free religion, none of those freedoms do we actually enjoy in full. Men there, as in medieval Ireland, are trapped, have fences built around them, and are wrapped in chains—albeit in chains of paper and red tape. That ain't right. They need liberation, as do we all. We have become coolies working for a cupful of rice each day, unable to be ourselves. All that will get worse in the future. We are not in the future yet, thank God.

Given his druthers, Tristan would rather not do anything proactively. He still preferred the Little Bo Peep approach to problem solving: Leave them alone and they'll come home. Blunder factor: Sit back and wait for the fascists to louse things up. Believe you me, that will happen, and sooner than you think.

Tristan resisted the strong urge to ride off and join those New England Transcendentalists in Massachusetts, to chuck it all as Thoreau had when he moved to Walden Pond. And if he got bored there, Tristan could move to Yaddo or Holly House at the Cos Cob artists' colony in Greenwich, Connecticut, a fashionable suburb of New York. That thought led to another, and inside his head, as an interior monologue, Tristan heard the voice of William Butler Yeats, a famous future Irish Poet, intone still another set of escapist advice for men: "Arise and go then, and go to Innisfree. A cabin build there of clay and waddles made. Nine bean rows will you have there, a hive for the honey bee. And live alone in the bee loud glade."

Yeat's poem is deliberately misquoted to avoid copyright problems. Innisfree is Irish for Island Heather = Heather Island. When Ethel and I visited, it looked exactly like the picture above, except at noon, the heather had a purple glow.

Across the field, Red, the seneschal, was having no easy time either. The heavy mid-day sun hit directly on his face, beating him down like a club. He hardly felt its blows, however, because he was busy with the stabbing pain in his chest.

King Brian Boru stood up, looking as regal as in the bygone days of King Conor Macnessa (the Strong). "Only a simpleton believes all that he is told. A wise man requires proof. Hence this trial. Two men claim the kill that one has done. Therefore, one must lie. May God protect the killer. And let the liar die."

Then, while Princess Iseult looked, twisting the bracelet on her wrist until it made bloody scratches on her cool sienna skin, at the king's nod, a trumpet blew a sharp, clear blast to arms and charge.

Tristan lowered his helm and leveled his spear. But at the other end of the meadow, he saw something... something really, really strange.

The seneschal was trembling so much his spear quivered like a leaf in a Gulf Coast hurricane. Soon he was on the ground crying out that he could not breathe and that his fingers tingled, and he felt like he was about to die.

"The churlish rogue is having a hyperventilation attack," said Tristan to Gorvenal.

"Aye, a bad one at that. How strange for someone with blood and guts enough to kill a dragon," said Gorvenal the wise.

Ha, ha, ha.

Tristan rode over and tried to get the man to rebreathe into a deer skin bag. The seneschal, quaking with fear and a drenching sweat, rolled down the visor to display his terror-drawn face. It was purple as foxglove in bloom. He would at a future time claim that Tristan had bewitched him, but at this moment, he accepted Tristan's help and began to calm down.

Tristan bent low and whispered to the seneschal, "Friend, the wages of sin is death, but after they take out the taxes, all you feel is a little tired. You're lucky. Unlucky too. If you had been wounded in battle, you would have gotten the ultimate war medal: Being wounded in battle merits the coveted Purple Asshole. And those who die in battle not only get the Purple Asshole, they get a two-man honor guard, a cute aluminum coffin draped with an American flag, and, Jesus, four whole months of combat pay. That's what you get for getting killed that way. Four whole months of combat pay! The lucky stiffs!"

That was it. It was all over. All she wrote.

Because of the anxiety attack, the seneschal forfeited his claim to Iseult.

And so that day there was no great contest, no dressing of shields or splintering of spears, no loud noises so hewed with swords that the cantles flew in the fields; and best of all, where they stood, Hawthorn Mews, would not be overbled with blood. Hyperventilation had saved the day. Hyperventilation had prevented two knights from hurtling together like rams disputing an ewe. Love, say the ascetics, reveals our kinship with animals. One can bear that, but jealousy is the real shame. It is jealousy, not love, that connects us with the beasts. Two angry cocks and a hen: not civilized and not nice. Moonlight and love songs, never out of place. Hearts filled with passion, jealousy, and hate. It happens all the time. But here we have the best. The best battles are the ones you win without going toe to toe.

Tristan trotted back to the stands and addressed the king: "I won Iseult by right of combat with the Morhold, sacker of cities. I won her today by forfeit of the seneschal. I won her by your royal decree for having stilled and killed the fear your people had of the dragon. (Notice he did not say that he had killed the dragon. Our author won't let our hero lie.) Thus, do I claim Iseult the Fair. I claim her as my own property, and with her, I propose alliance. By that alliance, learn these lands Cornwall (here he said it in the Irish tongue, Cornewaille) and Eire (Irish for Ireland) may know no more hatred, but love only, King Mark, my lord, will marry her. These 100 knights are witnesses and will swear on oath on the relic of Saint Bridget, which I happen to have here in my pocket. (Tristan was trying to lie in the very best way he could, yet ironically he spoke the truth for the hair was, as we know but he didn't know, the saint's very own hair.) By this holy relic, King Mark sends his embassy and offer of peace, brotherhood, and good will."

Brian liked the young knight's idea and thought it good to conclude the alliance. He also thought that someday it might mean that he would rule Cornwall. But Iseult trembled for shame and anguish, for Tristan had won her, yet he seemed to be approving her marriage to another. Iseult had always tried to be a girl who understood the complexities that encompassed situations and how everything in life had to be a compromise and paid for in one way or another. Surely, Tristan would discuss this with her on the boat to Tyntagaill (Irish again, this time for Tintagel). She knew that upon the woman depends the whole crushing responsibility for happiness in marriage, just one more unbearable burden which fell to the lot of wives.

All the rest of that morning, Iseult never looked at Tristan, nor spoke one word to him. But by the afternoon, they had made up and were back in bed together. The makeup sex was fantastic, as it usually is.

To allay her fears, Tristan had given her the Claddagh ring, promising his love forever. She put this on with the heart facing in. For an Irish woman, such a ring had a profound importance, a meaning which you will learn in the next chapter where Iseult has three prenuptial parties for both sexes to try to bring her sway of gifts up to Eisenhower-era standards.

The Philtre

Queen Maeve walked in the forest past large fire-ant hills, gathering wild mushrooms, blueberries, twigs, lingonberries, and all manner of herbs and spices. She, thinking she had magic, perfected these in a Brew of Might and poured it into a pitcher.

"Brangien," said the Irish queen for the Irish called Branwen, Brangien, same meaning though now in the Irish tongue: White Breasts. "Go with Iseult to Cornwall. Love her with a good and true love. Take this pitcher. It contains a special love potion which should ensure Iseult's devotion to King Mark. Lately, I have found that Iseult's eyes smile and dwell too long on Tristan. This is not fit for a woman who is to wed someone else. So, when Iseult is alone with Mark, give this to them both to drink, and they will fall madly in love with each other."

(Note: Some texts indicate Queen Mavis as a witch. That is wrong. Her knowledge of chemistry and potions just made her look like a witch to the ignorant and the stupid.)

Branwen hesitated, for she was a virgin and had no experience of love. She had not known that love needed magic drinks to help it flourish. She didn't even know what love was.

Who does? Really, when you think of it, who does?

"But mark me well," continued Maeve. "Give it not to her before she sees Mark, for she will love the first man her gaze falls upon after she has drunk and if she saw someone else than her husband, her life will become a perfect and an absolute all-purpose hell and disaster, not only for her but for all those around her."

Again, Bernard, the Bardic narrator, addressed her directly: And then you, Branwen of the white breasts, said in reply, "A disaster. Aye, madam. That would be a disaster to be married to one and love another."

"Remember that, for this, is this drink's power: They who drink of it together love together each other with their every single sense and with their every thought, word, and deed, forever, in this life and in death."

"In death too?"

Branwen was skeptical. Could love be that strong? That powerful? Last that long? She did not think so. Those with no experience of love never do think so. But those who have truly loved know for sure that love is stronger than death. Many lovers continue to love even after their loved one is dead. Widows and widowers often love the one they loved until their own death. What happens after their death, no one knows.

The undiscovered country from whose bourn no traveler returns puzzles the will and makes us bare those ills we have then to fly to others that we know not of.

To humor the queen, Branwen of the white breasts, you said, "As you say, I shall do, my queen."

And then, Branwen of the white breasts, you put the philter (philter, from medieval French philtre, from the Latin philtrum, from the Greek philtron, philein, to love) in a Florence flask and stored it on the ship in the pantry next to the bottles of French champagne, in fact, close, probably too close, to the Roederer Crystal, or was it too close to the Piper Heidsieck?.

Tristan and Iseult set out on the evening tide on their cruise together. The sinking sun had flushed the horizon to a pretty red orange, like Iseult's lace underthings, which she had purchased from Victoria's Secret.

On deck, just outside Wexford (French texts call it Weisfort, but of course they are wrong: It was Wexford on the southeast side in the estuary of the river Staney) harbor, she explained the significance of the Claddagh ring. "Claddagh, a small town on the bay, six kilometers from Galway, had a goldsmith who had to leave his beloved for a year. Why he left is not clear. Perhaps he was on sabbatical, perhaps he went to Lugestown (Lug's Town, the Town of Lug, the Celtic god of light, now called London) on business. Perhaps he was on the lam for some infraction of guild rules. Perhaps he was on a walkabout, as the men do in Australia. Who knows?

Before he left, he fashioned a special gold ring with a crown held by two hands and a heart beneath. He told his love that he would return and that this ring would be the symbol of his love. If she wore the ring with the heart facing her heart, then she would be his lover, and if she wore it with the heart facing out, his friend but not his lover. To this day, you can tell who has friends and who has lovers by the direction of the Claddagh ring. But due to economic circumstances, gold is too expensive, and most of the Claddagh rings are now silver as pictured earlier."

Iseult double-checked and flashed her ring. Her heart faced the right way toward her heart, and she showed Tristan that. But to make sure that he was on the same page, she asked, "Tristan, do you love me?"

Tristan bent his head into his hands and groaned.

"Do you love me?" said Iseult.

Tristan took off his cloak and hung it over the rail, for the night was warm as heated milk. "I am King Mark's man!" said Tristan, his heart tearing in two. "My duty is to Mark, for he is my uncle and my king."

"But do you love me?"

"He is my uncle and my king, my best friend too. I owe him my loyalty. All my loyalty."

"Stuff the man talk," shouted Iseult, upset that she wasn't getting an immediate, unequivocal answer to the question that women usually pose. "There is no sense in your being more royalist than the king. Besides, love matters more. Love trumps all suits. I ask you again, 'Do-you-love-me?'"

"It is better to love than be loved," said Tristan.

"I must know. Do you love me?"

"People adore flowers without worrying if the flowers love them back," suggested Tristan.

"I'm not a flower. Do you love me?"

"There are all kinds of love. The love I have for my cat is different from the love I have for Beef Wellington."

"DO YOU LOVE ME?" Iseult shouted.

Tristan let out a heavy sigh. He bent his head low and confessed what he, she, and what we all know—"Yes."

"Yes, what?"

"I love you, Iseult. I love you. I love you with my whole heart and soul. Though my love is likely to be the death of us both, I love you. I can't help it. I wish I could, but I can't. And I feel that I shall love you forever. You are the love of my life. I love you so much I am sick with it. Given the occasion and need, a man will do anything."

He turned to leave.

"Stay with me awhile, before we lose each other."

Tristan put his arms around her and held her fiercely close. And she clung to him so tightly that they were as a honeysuckle vine that clings to a hazel tree. Down they went to her stateroom where they passed the night in love's firm grip, taking pleasure from each other and giving pleasure to each other. What they did was essentially devoid of meaning. They were simply doing, from the deepest spurs of their being, what nature impelled them to do. And so, dear friend, are you. Or at least I hope you are. Love makes the world go 'round. Sex gives it the push.

The next day, Iseult packed her bags and moved into Tristan's room, which was bigger and had a larger mirror. For Iseult had discovered that she liked to watch herself being connected to Tristan in intimate embrace. This high-tech enhancement was a new experience for Tristan too. He liked it. But he also noticed that the people in the mirror seemed to be happier than he thought they were. He knew the man in the mirror looked happier than he was. This effect is weird. Try it, and you will see what's what and what I mean.

For the first time, Tristan saw himself have an orgasm. For his mirror image convulsed at the climax of his love grip. He saw his muscles contract in spasm and his face drawn up in a strong contortion that looked as if he weren't he.

From the mirror, the lovers learned that love not only has tremendous psychological power but a physical power as well, powers apparent only from the outside looking in. Generations of humans before them had had similar moments of fun, joy, and intense pleasure. Now it was their turn. But, of course, they made the usual mistake of youth, thinking that they alone knew passion and that they alone had discovered sex.

After sex, Iseult lit up a Winston and inhaled deeply. Tristan was shocked to death when he found out that she smoked. But, somehow, it went with dukes and castles and foreign travel and that sort of thing. She used some kind of musky perfume, and the smell of it and the slight rankness of cigarette smoke in her hair made him dizzy and feverish when he nuzzled with her.

There was something about the smoking that appealed to Tristan. Something about seeing her brown fingers holding that white glowing cylinder that looked right. Something about it that looked just right. And she got such pleasure from what she did, or seemed to, that he wanted to do it too. And that is the way Iseult introduced Tristan to the pleasure of tobacco, indulgence that never quite satisfied, and therefore, a near-perfect pleasure. It was not required to smoke after sex, but it could be a nice thing to do.

From the cigarette, Tristan learned a new metaphor. Life was like a cigarette. When you first lit it, it tasted great. Then you became distracted and thought about something else. Before you knew it, you were sucking on the hot, bitter end, and it was about to go out and die. So, it was with the millions of humans who had lived before him. Their lives were now less than a whiff of smoke. Most of them had lived without much awareness: They were distracted and forlorn. Some had lived without passion, if you can call that living. The poor slobs. So sad. Oh, joyless hearts of men.

Now as to Branwen of the white breasts: She tried to keep her word for she could do no other. For the seas were running high and swift and the rowers fighting the oars, and the salt crusts flew hard back along the decks, and the wheel's kick, and the wind song, and the white sails flying and the flung spume and the blown spray and the seagulls crying.

And when Tristan went to check below, you, Branwen of the white breasts, moaned, "Is the ship sinking?" And when told it was not, you, Branwen of the white breasts, prayed that it would sink. You, Branwen of the white breasts, were too seasick to move, much less give the philter. That's my proof and Doctor Patten's proof that the potion could not have been the cause of the great love between Tristan and Iseult that we see here described. Oh no! How could a potion work if it had never been ingested?

As told, the potion idea was just an invention of the ignorant French who were trying to explain the great aching passion that these two humans, Tristan and Iseult, Iseult and Tristan, had for each other, a passion that the French didn't understand. For no one who had not been through it could possibly believe such passion could exist.

Instead of the potion, Tristan and Iseult drank the Roederer Crystal, leaving the philter where it stood. The champagne made them mellow and put them in the mood again, but it did not cause their fatal love. In fact, Iseult did something with the champagne that I hesitate to discuss lest it offend your sense of propriety. She drank the bubbling wine while Tristan was pounding her from behind (doggy style). She liked the effect, remarking jauntily that that way, she simultaneously had great pleasures on both ends.

Ah, the secrets of lovers. Someone could write an interesting romance about them. Perhaps even Patten could if he knew anything about it. For great abilities are not requisite for a romancer; for in romance composition, all the greatest powers of the human mind are quiescent. A romancer has facts ready to his hand, so there is no exercise of invention. Imagination is not required in any high degree; only about as much as is used in the lower kinds of poetry. Some penetration, accuracy, and coloring will fit a man for the task if he can give the application, which is necessary.

And so on to Tintagel, their bark ran free, bobbing smoothly and smoothly bobbing, under the sheltering sky, the stars, and the moonlight. But it seemed to Tristan that his life had become as an ardent briar, a sharp-thorned blackberry bush, with flowers most sweet smelling that drove roots into his blood and laced the lovely body of Iseult all round about it and bound it to his own and to his every thought and desire, an image that foreshadows their death together and the miracle that happened at Tintagel Minister after the lovers were buried adjacently there together. About that miracle, more later with a picture of Tintagel Minister if I can find it.

Tristan thought about the problems that awaited him at Tintagel, about the DAGG conspiracy of Denoalen, Andread, Guenelon, and Gondoine, felons, who would and who had charged him with every false thing, including coveting King Mark's land and kingdom. Little do they know, mused Tristan. That I am myself indifferent honest, and yet I have more offenses at my beck than I have thoughts to put them in, imagination to give them shape, or time to act them in. What are such knaves as I to do crawling between heaven and earth? It is not Mark's land that I would covet, nor his titles, power, and pelf, (the wretch concentered all in self!)—It is not him or his things that I would covert. Of his wealth, I'll have none of it. NO! It is not his things I covet but his solemnly betrothed wife—Iseult! That crime is what makes me an arrant knave all. It is this conflict between my duty to Mark and my love of Iseult that drives my story. It is this conflict that afflicts me so.

But then Tristan realized that he could share Iseult with Mark. Timeshare her, as they would eventually say. Why not? Mark would be her lawful husband. Tristan could have no complaint of that. Mark would enter her where he (Tristan) had ironed out the wrinkles, made the path smooth and easy for an older man. Why not? A woman can love two men, or three, or four, or any number, no matter what. A woman who shall remain nameless is in the Guinness book of records for having had sex with 235 college boys in 10 hours, an average of 2.6 minutes per boy. She's nameless here (but named in Guinness) because she subsequently got religion and has been traveling around the United States sincerely preaching abstinence as the solution to the problem of teenage pregnancy.

Yes, thought Tristan, there were as many types of love as there are hearts and as many types of marriage as there are couples. Iseult's love for me could be both similar to and different from her love for Mark. A change of sperm might be good for her, the way a change of oil is good for a Chevrolet.

Tristan went to Iseult to explain his ideas. She said to him both humbly and bluntly, "Behold the hand maiden of the Lord. Thy will be done."

"Why do you talk like that?" asked Tristan.

"Two reasons," she said. "One is a literary allusion to the New Testament where Mary consents to being impregnated by the Holy Ghost via the agency of Saint Michael the Archangel. The other sincerely expresses how I feel. Despite what the feminists teach, a woman needs a man, and a man must have his mate. That no one can deny. Thus, I am your slave, and you are my master as I am your master, and you are my slave. That's the way love works, I firmly believe."

"I consider you neither master nor slave, Iseult, but an equal. And I thank the gods that you don't belong to the Gender Club."

"Gender Club?"

"You know, this is male, and that is female, and never the twain shall meet."

"We're the same. Equals," she affirmed. "But I am your slave. You are my master and my slave. The same with me. In both roles, I am well pleased. Both of us are bound together as if married, maybe more firmly. I need you because I am tormented by my love for you. I can do no other. For similar reasons, you need me. Whatever happens I will love you always. I will love you no matter whom I marry. Without love one cannot live. (Actually, she said this in Spanish: *Amor sincero y siempre y no puedes vivir sin amor*).

In reply, he kissed her lips. Then he burst into song: "The Rockies may crumble, Gibraltar may tumble, they're only made of clay, but our love is here to stay, etc."

Tristan then told the story of Gawain's wedding.

What a wedding Gawain and the witch had! Gawain was proper as always, gentle and courteous. The old witch put her worst manners on display. She ate with her hands, belched and passed gas, and made everyone uncomfortable as ever.

On the wedding night, Gawain entered the bedroom. The most beautiful woman he had ever seem lay before him! Gawain was astounded and asked what happened.

The beauty replied that since he had been so kind to her when she was in her witch mood and mode, half the time she would be her horrible, deformed self, and the other half, she would be her beautiful maiden self. Which would he want her to be during the day and which during the night?

What a cruel question! Gawain began to think of his predicament: during the day a beautiful woman to show off to his friends, but at night, in the privacy of his home, an old spooky witch? Or should he prefer having by day a hideous witch, but by night a beautiful woman to enjoy many intimate moments?

What would you do, Iseult?

What would you do, dear reader? What Iseult and Gawain chose follows below, but don't read until you make up your own mind what you would tell the witch.

The answer:

Noble Gawain replied that he would let her choose for herself.

Upon hearing this, she announced she would be beautiful all the time because he had respected her and had let her be in charge of her own life.

The rest of what Tristan and Iseult did that night, I have not forgotten. I omit it, dear reader, out of charity and a due regard for your precious time. But I will mention that at the first light of day, a zeppelin floated over the region with that famous picture on its side of Einstein sticking out his tongue.

Tristan and Iseult were on the path that knew no returning. Love had dragged them already down. Its strength had bound them, their bodies, their lives, their souls, together unto death. They held each other, trembling through their youth with desire. And, as evening fell and all the ways grew dark, they gave themselves up utterly to amour. They didn't know, nor could they have ever guessed what pain and suffering it would bring them. That love. What ache, agony and anguish awaited them in Cornwall, on account of love, that love, their love.

But there is a problem: Iseult is not virgin. So, when the wedding night comes, it is possible King Mark will find her out. If he does find out, Iseult will probably be burned at the stake. So how the hell are Tristan and Iseult going to get around the virginity problem? Take a look at the next tableau and see.

Branwen of the White Breasts Pinch Hits

King Mark met them at the shore and had a seizing at the sight of Iseult. In a heartbeat, she changed his mind about not being interested in women. He, like all men about him, felt her power for she was passing fair, and her acquired name suited her well: Iseult the Beautiful, Iseult la Belle. Her beauty was structural, like a tree. It was not a quality of mind or heart. At the beginning, that's what men always see. And that's what they go for: Structural beauty. Later, they also go for inner beauty, or they should. Some do. Some don't. It all depends on the persons, place, time, and other factors not really known.

Me seemeth that this be the case: Old men, like Mark, believe the fire of their passions dead until the Real Thing comes on the fly and hits them in the eye, knocks them on the head. Irma La Douce said that old men often think their thing dead when all they really need is a jump start.

Old men and sex—the phenomenon has led to some true disasters among them. Nelson Rockefeller, for instance, died in the saddle. Folk wisdom says it all: "No fool like an old fool."

With Edgar's Pomp and Circumstance (Military March One in D Major), King Mark led his new queen off the dock and up the ramp and up the hill to the great castle Tintagel. And, as she came into the great Hall of Estate, her crimson beauty shone as if the walls were lit with dawn.

Tristan, anguished, followed the long and lordly train as the Women's Choral Group sang above them. And then there was a sudden flare, a revivification, an abrupt recovery of vitality and interest in life. For the women's voices enthralled him, transfixed him for a moment, whirled him farther than Uranus flies, and convulsed him like the climax of his love grip. He felt fine again. Women singing always did that to him. How come?

The castle had not changed. It still had that musty smell, as if they were growing mushrooms in the basement. And Tristan realized it was a boring place. In it were no great volumes filled with words and pictures of things dug up by man's relentless curiosity from sand and soil in all corners of the world. No photoplays (ancient talk for movies) that flick like thoughts on a white wall, no phonograph, no machinery with which to achieve the sensation of speed, no diagrams of the fourth dimension, no treatises on the multitude of types and contrasts of life forms, no detailed maps of

Vesta-4, the third largest asteroid in our solar system. Thank God NASA is keeping a close eye on Vesta-4. Larger than Manhattan, if it crashed into Earth—Ugh!

In the castle, the light was weak and episodic, hallways dark, rooms deeply shadowed. The outside world was full of darkness, too, and steeped in gloom. Depressing. But that's the way Castles were. That's their nature in the fifth century.

Mark took the Chair of Estate. "Thank you, Tristan, and thank you, knights, of Cornwall, for your work in bringing such great joy of heart and eye to me."

"Nay," said Andread, who looked at Tristan as if he were a snake that had heard something. (Did that snake, Andread, smell a rat?) "Thank not, Tristan. Thank not the 100 knights. Thank the disputing swallows. It was they who brought the red hair. Which reminds me, I should think that we should check to see that the disputed hair and the hair of this Iseult of Ireland match, else how would we know for sure that she is what Tristan says she is? She may be a counterfeit, a pretender to power, an Irish spy, or just another babe with red hair."

Then as prearranged, Andread led the Women's Choral Group in a song to the tune of Jesus Christ Superstar: "Iseult the Fair, Superstar, How do we know you are what you say you are?"

That reminds me of the C. S. Lewis argument that either Jesus was a lunatic or he was actually the son of God the way he said he was. As he was not a lunatic, he must have been the son of God. The reasoning is defective, of course. It looks persuasive because it resembles the disjunctive syllogism: Either A or B, but not both. Not A, therefore B. Or B, therefore not A. Last Sunday, I had time to go to church or play the piano, not both. I played the piano. Did I go to church? Answer: No!

The C. S. Lewis argument is actually a false dilemma. Do we really know what Jesus said? Did he actually say he was the son of God? The gospels were written long after Jesus' death. Jesus left no records, no writing, no video tapes, etc. So, we don't know if he said what he was supposed to say or he didn't. And if he did say it, we don't know if he meant it literally or figuratively. And so forth. And who said Jesus was not a lunatic? That is a claim that needs support by evidence that is relevant and adequate. Relevant evidence would relate directly to the conclusion, and adequate evidence would be of sufficient weight, kind, and quantity to support the conclusion. As no such evidence exists, a case and often a good case could be made either way.

Take, for instance, this ancient example of another case that could be made either way:

Jim, Jack, and John are in the Sahara and pitch for the night. Jim hates John and decides to kill John by putting poison in John's water bag (his only source of water). Jack, not knowing Jim's plan, also hates John and decides to kill John by putting a hole in the water bag so that the water leaks out. As a result, John dies several days later of dehydration. Now the question is, who is the murderer, Jim or Jack?

Bernard: Jack is the murderer since John never drank the poison and died of dehydration.

Patten: Both Jim and Jack planned the murder, so they are guilty of something, probably intent to murder. My inclination is to call Jim the murderer because he put poison in the water bag, and John would have died had Jack not emptied the bag.

Bernard: You, Patten, are a silly goose. How can anyone in his right mind convict Jim of murder when John never drank any of the poison? If anything, Jack's action removing poison from a poisoned water bag is in no sense killing John. In fact, it prolonged John's life, although this was not intentional because poisoning kills faster than dehydration. Jack saved John's life for a time.

Miss Andress from the audience stands and shouts: "That John must have been one son-of-a-bitch for two men to try to kill him. He reminds me of my ex. He deserved to die. He had it coming. Although I shot him seven times, the all-male jury decided my fate in ten minutes. Not guilty."

King Mark jerked back as if hit by a lightning bolt. In that unguarded moment, he was speechless, full of fear and fright. Andread had reason. After all, the hair couldn't have been Iseult's since Mark knew it belonged to the mother goddess or the Saint: he had forgotten whose hair had actually said to have been in the silver box. But Jesus, logic is logic, and he had to go along. Otherwise, the whole scam would blow up in his face.

"Andread's right," said Mark reluctantly, for he had been thinking that if he married Iseult, he might someday rule Ireland. "How do we know you are what you say you are?"

Iseult seemed puzzled. She never said she was the one whose hair was in reference. And there is a fundamental problem: It is hard to prove what you are and even harder to prove what you are not. For instance, you can't prove you're not a communist. Someone can prove you are by finding the card in your wallet, provided the FBI didn't plant it there. But you can't prove you're not because absence of evidence is never evidence of absence. By the same token, you can't prove you are not a child pornographer. They can prove you are if they find the stuff on your computer. Provided, of course, it wasn't planted there. How can Iseult prove that she is the women whose hair Mark gave to Tristan? Anyway, this is the first time Iseult knew anything about the hair thing or what it meant or didn't mean. Incomplete knowledge is a definite handicap.

Answer: She can't prove the hair in exhibit was her hair because it was not her hair since Mark plucked the hair from the box in the church. Reader, if you are still awake, you know the hair Mark gave to Tristan was the Saint's hair from the silver box. Hence, we and they are now between a rock and a hard place.

Before Iseult could reply, Tristan shouted, "How do we prove anything, sire? We look at the evidence, the evidence of our senses. If the evidence is relevant and adequate, then we accept the conclusion. If the evidence is not relevant or adequate, then we do not accept the conclusion. Relevant evidence relates directly to the issue at hand, and adequate evidence must be sufficient in type, kind, and weight to support the conclusion.

"Get to your point, if you have one," said Andread.

"I have hair right here. Examine it. Is it not like the hair you gave me? I guarantee it belongs to Iseult."

Tristan produced a tress of red hair from his leather pocket. He proved that the hair matched Iseult's perfectly—the sheen, the color, feel, consistency, and texture as well as the spectrographic analysis of the trace metals and finally the DNA tests—everything in perfect order and correspondence. And well it should for Tristan had, the previous day deep-sixed (that is, thrown overboard) the hair that was the first degree relic of Saint Bridget of Ireland, a sin he would confess as soon as he got around to it, provided, that is, he discovered that destruction of Saint's hair is a sin.

Tristan, the clever and wise, then had cut locks from Iseult's brow and stuffed them in the pocket precisely to present to Mark and to the vassals of the court should the need arise. Minor miracles of that ilk were shams and hoaxes, but some said they were needed to confirm the mystical nature of a queen's claim to power and, in this case, to get Iseult off the hook and in the door.

Well, did Tristan plan this design. Well, did he affirm: "The hair matches. Iseult is she! Iseult is the princess of the red hair! As you can plainly see!"

"That this is Iseult's hair. I have no doubts," said Andread looking androgynous and speaking in that special silky way. "That Iseult is a princess with red hair. I have no doubts. But the identity of this hair with her hair merely begs the question. We had the same trouble when they found arsenic in Napoleon's hair. Skeptics say that it is uncertain whether the hair analyzed ever belonged to the Emperor himself. The real question is, therefore, are these hairs the swallows' hairs or are they not? What proof have we of that?"

Mark had a dark thought that came from a recent reading to him of *Alice's Adventures in Wonderland*: There is one thing about power: it can only flow from top down. Little surges of resistance at the middle levels call for more power to be directed downward, to burn them out. At this juncture, why not follow the example of the Queen of Hearts and shout, "Off with his head"? Or why not call him a traitor and prosecute him under the espionage act? And then after a show trial have him executed? What worked for Stalin and Hitler could work for Mark.

"None other," intoned Mark. Then he handed the hairs to Archdruid Gutuart, who examined and approved them and who, in turn, handed them to Mistress Epona, his wife, the archpriestess, who agreed. Neither Gutuart nor Epona had ever seen those hairs before, but that didn't matter. They were, like a couple of Popes, infallible.

There were lots of yes-men like Gutuart and Epona at King Mark's court because those who were not yes-men, more often than not, were no-men. And no-men, having often become, on account of their nos, dead men, were no longer around. The last no-knight, whose name nobody really knew, not even his wife, for she said his name was one thing and his Social Security card said another. And because he was dead at age 45—he ain't saying nothing. So, we don't know.

No non-Hitlerians were tried at Nuremberg. German commanders who had opposed Hitler were by that time six feet under, including Rommel, who was forced to suicide.

Andread threw Epona a harsh look and began like the cast of the original *Planet of the Apes* to snarl, growl, mutter, and grumble. It was as though his anger had reduced him to communicating with the primitive sounds that his first ancestors had used. His rage expanded until it clotted the very conduits of emotion, leaving him trembling with an unendurable wrath. If he had been holding an animal in his hands at that instant, he would have strangled it. He had, in fact, when he was eight years old, due to anger over getting a B+ in third grade spelling, strangled his collie. And at this moment, he wanted to strangle his sometime mistress, Epona, for she had betrayed him by siding with her husband and with Mark and Tristan.

"Funny," Andread said while mentally resolving to have a glorious drunk and soon. "I'm always sure things are going to turn out badly for me and, dang it, they usually do."

In celebration, the court set about to eating roasted beasts, and drinking warmed honey mead, measurefuls, and tills. As usual, as the evening and the drinking progressed, Mark started to feel ever nicer and more generous. Accordingly, he asked, "Tristan, would you have a boon?"

"Yes, my liege, if you will grant whatever I ask."

"Come, come," said Mark. "Too many Arthurian romances have been read to me for me to fall into such a trap. Tell us what you want, and you shall have it even to the quarter of my kingdom. But if it is not as reasonable as that, you shall have it not. After all, we are all part of one big unhappy family."

"Fair enough, sire. I desire that you will allow me now and forever to share the king's cave, its ownership, and use, by right and without question or dispute, and that you should give me sanctuary there for any misdeeds that might have been committed in that cave in the past, or that might be committed there in the future."

Mark was perplexed. There are two king's caves. Mark thought the cave in question was clearly that known for time before our time as the King's Cave, very large cave by the sea in the underbelly of Tintagel. You can see nice pictures of it on the internet. The other King's Cave is on the map a little south of Tintagel on the road to Saint Michael's Mount.

But why would either cave figure in a boon? What misdeed had Tristan done there or anywhere? And what misdeeds did Tristan plan to do in the cave? But wit is not deep in the bottle as they say. On reflection, Mark still didn't get it. So, seeing no objection, he said, "I grant the boon, though it seems small recompense for the service you have rendered."

Tristan jumped up and embraced his uncle and kissed both cheeks.

He had actually had in mind a rather different dark cave, a moist one too, the cave where all love ends, the cave that our Iseult had already let him enter, the cave that would soon by right and rite of marriage become the king's cave. Thus, by crafty and indirect means did Tristan, the clever and wise, secure King Mark's assent for amorous adventures with Iseult. Casuistically accomplished, yes, but accomplished, nevertheless.

None of this had pleased the jealous barons. In secret meeting with the dwarf Focin, court jester, they exchanged a blood oath that at the wedding banquet they would poison Tristan. Poison the one you hate. When shall we see the end of this stupid idea? Fact imitating fiction, fiction fact. Is so little going on out there, such a dearth of original ideas? I mean, do they have to copy? Why not think of a more creative solution? How about a death star? Or why not send Tristan an anthrax laden letter? A suicide bomb? Something new and original. No doubt, the DAGG's original motives were political. But they also are the chorus of the unloved who carry a deep and abiding resentment against those who do love. This jealousy would be reflected in their low-level gossip about a possible affair between Tristan and the new Queen of Cornwall, Iseult la Belle.

The assassins' plan: The DAGG would put the poison in Tristan's goblet. Then as he toasted the new queen and the old king, he would take a sip and fall dead. Some would say of a broken heart. Others of poison. But no matter. The poison they would use would be an alkylfluorophosphate called VX, impossible to trace since forensic medicine had not advanced enough to measure microgram amounts of anything at all, much less a dispersible binary liquid nerve toxin like VX. Of course, a good forensic pathologist would measure the red blood cell acetylcholinesterase, which, after exposure to VX or Sarin, would be zero.

Andread advised the group to adjourn to Dirty Sally's for some stiff ones, for he had need of that. (Same dirty bar and grill but Sally was the new owner. She had purchased it from Bridey Murphy, who had retired to Costa Rica where the cost of living was less and the ratio of men to women more.)

There at Sally's they met a strange woman who wore a black billowing dress, which had not been washed in many a day. She had about her the odor of horses that had carried much weight or run a good course. Her teeth were broken, and she had a strange hideous smile. So, from the looks of her, as you have guessed, she could have been a witch. Or she could have been one of those old eccentric women who roam the streets then and now, usually widows, usually without personal wealth, and usually arrested for one reason or another or no reason at all. This woman, with her glittering eye, held Andread, and raising her index finger, said, "Show me your palm."

"What in Hell for?" said Andread, as he tried to shake off the hag's ice-hard grip. "Who the Hell do you think you are? Dagda?"

(Dagda is ancient Ireland's mother goddess. She may appear in any one of three distinct forms: The girl, the maiden, the hag. It is a Trinity, but in this case, the three persons are the same goddess at different ages. Get it?)

"Thou speakest truer than you think, my lord."

"Well, Dagda, good mother goddess of the cauldron of plenty, you old crone, what's up?"

"I'm here to tell your future to help you understand."

"Understand? Understand what?" replied Andread, a puzzled expression on his face, a pout on his lips, his eyebrows elevated. This crone did look like Dagda, a gypsy, or a witch, one.

"Your fate."

Andread held out his hand and winked to the group. He would go along for the fun.

The hideous hag made a show of inspecting the palm close up in the light of the torch that burned on the side wall of the bar. The whitewashed walls, washed white with quick lime to fend off the plague, reflected the blaze so that the room seemed to glow and glare with an ethereal brightness and warmth.

Without warning, the hag threw off the hand, made the disgust face, and turned away. She held her right hand behind her back, in the waiter's tip position, for payment. And speaking to the opposite wall intoned in poetic chant: "Pay now, my Lord, and I will go my way. Sometimes it is better that the mortal not know what the furies say and what the future holds. Fate is usually swift when she deals a blow. Fear death by water."

Roars of laughter! Ho ho ho. "Big joke!" chuckled Andread. "Just another ruse. You can't fool us. You can't see the future any more than I can. I am an excellent swimmer, and there is no way I could drown."

Whoa! Who said anything about drowning?

(Never tempt the gods or goddesses or Dagda herself.) Andread's hand had shown a movie to the old bag the way an iPad would show a movie today. The movie showed that Andread fell off a bridge into water. Although he was and is a good swimmer, he could not swim with his armor on. No man can. And so Andread was ordained to die by drowning. Death by water was his future. But the dumbfuck didn't know it, Ed.)

Andread slipped a silver groat into her hand, "What's the bad news?"

"Fear death by drowning."

"And?"

"One of your friends will die by the sword. One will perish by an arrow smaller than a fingertip. One will have his head off Celtic style, and a woodsman, your hireling who would hurt Iseult the queen, shall dig his own grave and die in it."

With this, the conspirators burst out laughing, for they knew that they had no hireling that was a woodsman, and they knew how unlikely it would be that one would dig his own grave, much less die in it. And who could die from an arrow smaller than a fingertip? Complete and utter bullshit, the whole thing was!

Editor's Note: In case dear reader you have been dozing off, let me summarize Dagda's predictions:

Andread would die by drowning. That's the A in the DAGG.

1. One of the DAGG would die by sword. This is quite possible. He who lives by the sword will die by the sword. That's Guenelon. His death is too prosaic to mention. He died in a street duel when a man sucked his thumb at him. That's the first G of the DAGG.

2. One of the DAGG will die from an arrow the size of a fingertip. Hmm. I get this. Do you? Tristan will shoot Gondoine with his Walther PPK 380 semiautomatic. The 9mm bullet is what the old lady is talking about when she predicts death from an arrow the size of a fingertip. That's it for the second G of the DAGG.

3. One of the DAGG will have his head cut off. Fair enough. That is Denoalen, who was inspecting Flannagan's guillotine and accidentally tripped the lever while his head was in position. That's the D of the DAGG.

4. A woodsman will dig his own grave and die in it. That seemed impossible because the DAGG had no intention of hiring a woodsman, and it would be unlikely in the extreme for someone to dig their own grave and then die in it. No way such a thing could happen in real life. So, there is no way that such a thing can happen in this book, which is based on real life and real life only.

"Impostor! Leave us!" cried Andread as he shoved the old woman away and motioned for his cup.

The traitors set about drinking hard and fast, for they had need of that. They hoped the whiskey would not lose its power, for they had need of that power as do all men burdened with a bad conscience. But, sadly, whiskey no longer had the same effect as it had had before: They had to drink more of it and got less satisfaction. Perhaps it was because the troubles with Mark and Tristan had multiplied, perhaps they were getting used to the whiskey or perhaps both those two things.

After several hours of drinking Black Bush, even though their blood alcohol levels were sky high, they still felt sober. The panic increased when a Woodsman entered Dirty Sally's and came directly to the table without removing his muddy boots.

"Honored lords, here come I to testify against the queen and Tristan, for a price. For a price, I shall say that I had went at dawn to set the traps when I spied Tristan and Iseult under the apple trees at Lantyan, the orchard adjacent to Castle D'Or. There they were in intimate and shameful embrace. Will I tell the king so these evil ones may be punished as they deserve?"

The DAGG was worried for the woodsman because, in his ignorance, he didn't know "had gone" from "had went." Correct English is "had gone" or "went." I "had went" is incorrect, as is "I gone."

Despite the reservations, they hired him. He would do his false witness at the time and place they wished. But the funny thing was that at the time, the lovers were meeting in Lantyan among the apple trees, so even though the woodsman thought he was speaking falsely, as he had never seen them or anyone in intimate embrace, he was really speaking the truth about Tristan and Iseult. Still, was he lying or not? If you tell the truth but think it is a lie, is it still a lie, or is it the truth? Abraham Lincoln said if a man says something is true but doesn't know for sure it is true and later it is found to be true, that man lied. Get it? You shouldn't say something is true unless you know for sure. Otherwise, you are deceiving the listeners by giving them a false sense of the probabilities that what is said is true.

For the wedding and banquet, protocol specialists were employed in advance, as the Clinton White House would have done to decide what happens to whom and when. And so, on the 18th day, King Mark wed Iseult the Fair in Tintagel Minster. After nuptial mass, the group returned to the castle for more secular festivities, including the banquet.

Tristan, by invitation, sat at the head table with the king, the new queen, and those of the more important lords who were capable of looking powerful but refined, like Arnold Schwarzenegger in a dinner jacket.

Maria, a Spanish maid, served their table and was well pleased that Iseult spoke Spanish. She was not pleased that Focin had forced her to put poison in Tristan's cup. Coming up to Iseult, Maria said in loud, clear Spanish that the DAGG had poisoned Tristan's wine. "*El DAGG enveneno el vino de Tristan.*"

Iseult, shocked, looked up and shot back in Spanish, "You shall be rewarded well this day, a gold bezant and a boon of your desire." "*Seras bien recompensada este dia con una moneda de oro y un deseo de tu gusto.*"

"What's with her?" asked Mark.

"The usual complaints," said Iseult. "Sexual harassment by the men at court, groping by the barons, lewd talk on the part of your nephew Andread."

"That's a relief," said Mark. "Usually, Hispanic maids want more money."

"That too," said Iseult. "I told her now is the time for fair festival, feast, and fun. Later we will discuss wages."

"She'll have a better chance scratching a lottery ticket," Mark observed, as he raised his right hand and signaled for the main course.

After meat, Tristan picked up the goblet and, gazing into the vacant space of the now darkening room, stood there distracted, for he was thinking of something long ago and far away—of his first meeting with Iseult and how she had gazed at him with those eyes of desire, had smiled at him, had given herself to him so freely with such wonderfully mutual pleasure, asking nothing in return, hardly uttering a sound except her animal music of love. Vividly, he felt her nude body pressed against his, her breasts pressed against his chest, his hands tight against the orbic flexes of her behind. It was wonderful and full of wonder. Nothing like it. Nothing can equal it. Our animal consolation. The consolation of being an animal and not a plant. We can't photosynthesize. They can't fuck.

Tristan's preoccupation was an ultra-short-term nostalgia: Homesickness for the extremely recent past.

Mark coughed. Tristan fell out of his reverie, and, with a nonchalance copied from characters he had seen in the photoplays, held his goblet on high and uttered his favorite toast: "To joy and fresh new days of love."

Out of his struggling eyes, tears were flowing, tears that were a veil of desperation through which he saw the dim face of Iseult before him like a phantom in a mist. They are not long the days of wine and roses. Out of a misty dream, our path emerges for a while then closes—within a dream.

Tristan could see deep in the dark wet splendor of her eyes a terror that he knew was more for him than for her.

He sipped and felt a tingling of his lips and then a tingling of the tongue and throat. A sudden nausea seized him through and through. He began to sweat, defecate, urinate, salivate, and twitch, all at once. He fell forward onto the table, foaming at the mouth, biting his tongue and frothing red, his muscles all in the grip of spasm. He convulsed—Grand Mal, followed by another Grand Mal and another and another, without awaking between seizures. In seconds, his respiratory center cut off. He turned blue, and he died of suffocation. His body lay there rigid and immobile, the sardonic grin of Old Mortality upon his face.

Whew!

That was a classic demonstration of death by VX. Just like the North Korean child king's brother.

Now, children, another way of describing what had happened, is that VX inhibited acetylcholinesterase so that Tristan's body was flooded with the neurotransmitter acetylcholine. VX is capable of killing in minutes like that even at small doses, doses as low as six micrograms. Tristan had received 600 times that fatal dose.

Incidentally, the first President Bush once announced that, although the United States had no VX, he had ordered 20,000 tons of it burned. Distracted by the banal? Uncomfortable with that? Uncomfortable with a president's statement? Don't understand how you can burn stuff you don't have? Stuff you never made? Either Bush believes what he said, or he doesn't. I don't know which is more scary, which is more crazy. Anyway, we all know the U.S. government is not bound by strictnesses in logic. It sometimes (thinks it) can do the impossible.

Speaking about the impossible and of the number 20,000. We still have at least 20,000 words to go in this story. The publisher wants a postmodern novel of about 80-100,000 words. No book, no pay. It is hard to get published these days, especially when everyone thinks that your book won't be a bestseller. Conclusion: Tristan can't die here. That's impossible. And the wife is here bothering me about unpaid American Express bills. The story must go on!

Patten gave Bernard the high sign and Bernard pressed the rewind button to the part just before Tristan drank the poison:

Mark coughed, and Tristan fell out of his reverie. Tristan held his goblet on high and gave his favorite toast: "To joy and fresh new days of love."

Tristan stared at Iseult in absorption, caught by a sense of beauty he could not express, a sense of beauty that was ineffable.

Iseult rose to join the toast and with her chalice, pretended to clink Tristan's. As she did this, she "clumsily" knocked the goblet from his hand, spilling poison on his leather jacket and his blue woolen tunic. Some spray also fell on Mark and sprinkled his marshal and even on the seneschal who was two places away, since that tribute to Groucho and slapstick was the direction of spill. Both these men waxed wroth, for they had donned their very best garments for the royal party.

Mark took the opportunity of universal distraction and nudged Iseult. It was time to adjourn to the bridal bower for the full biological union. Mark announced, "Christian marriage takes place in a church. Biological marriage takes place in a bed. This fine night, I will now have my ado."

Fine had been a romantic word in Mark's vocabulary ever since he'd had Hemingway's *A Farewell to Arms* read to him. In that book, everything is fine, especially the drinks. At least fine is better than swell which went out with the Dark Ages.

Iseult had foreseen this event and prepared for it. Branwen, of the white breasts, the Faithful, her gait disturbed and unsteady due to the effect of intoxicating liquors, as though she had not mastered the first principles of walking, entered the bower, unseen by Mark for it was stygian dark. Yes, friends, Branwen of the white breasts, Iseult's maid, slipped into the royal bed. The sheets were cold. The room perfumed with a thousand roses. The pillow soft and pliable of goose down.

And, you Branwen, you were ready. But you didn't know what you were ready for. You had not yet had the experience of sexual intercourse. You had not yet had that privilege. Not yet.

Yes, Branwen, to conceal the queen's indiscretions with Tristan, some would say to conceal the queen's dishonor, you Branwen took Iseult's place on the nuptial couch. Thus, did you, Branwen of the white breasts, save Iseult from premature death. This was easier to do than might be imagined since, in those days, sexual intercourse occurred with clothes on and in the dark, where women, and all cats, are, more or less, the same.

And yes, Branwen of the white breasts, your ardor for lovemaking was brave and strong. Some say it was also sincere, for to brace yourself for the event you, Branwen of the white breasts, had drunk Maeve's potion and then offered it to Mark. Whether it was the potion or the fact that every woman loves the man who takes her first, your debut in the sack, Branwen of the white breasts, set off sparks enough to send the space shuttle into orbit. And from that day forth, you, Branwen of the white breasts, loved King Mark with your whole heart and soul, and he loved you back with his whole animal vigor.

Thus, the loyal maid of the white breasts sacrificed the purity of her body to cover up the impurity of that of her mistress and queen, Iseult the Beautiful. Branwen did this for her friend, out of love for Iseult, and from a sense of duty. The darkness of the night hid her trick as it had doubtless hidden the tricks of many other "maidens." Mark's drinking, which had put him into a stupor, also helped. Whether he also drank the potion, at Branwen's behest, or without her behest, is not known, but it is known that he did drink it. From that day, as mentioned, forward, Mark developed a marked affection for Branwen of the white breasts. And she for him. Some historic documents claim he had loved her often and fiercely thereafter and fathered three children by her. Other ancient texts say that that is not true. Five children is more like it. When Iseult died, Branwen became queen. That is the usual. When the wife quits the scene, the mistress gets promoted.

All five of your children, Branwen of the white breasts, as a matter of fact, do look like Mark.

The net result of this substitution was that Mark thought Iseult had come to bed a virgin and that Branwen was fully privy to the secret love of Tristan and Iseult. For Iseult, of course, had to brief her good maid on the details and necessity of her employment as (so to speak) a pinch hitter.

Uneasy is the head that wears the crown. Iseult was now in constant fear that her dark secret, her forbidden love, might be leaked by Branwen to the court, to the Jerry Springer show or CNN (Constantly Negative News), or might appear on the front page of the Houston Chronicle.

Inferior romancers insist that Branwen gave the potion also to Mark and Iseult and that that was the reason that Mark also loved Iseult and vice versa. Another of their versions has it that when Branwen offered the couple the potion, Mark drank his and Iseult secretly threw hers away.

But why oh why, do these people have to tamper with the tale and render it false? Frenchmen indulge imagination as it pleases them, until at length, it overpowers their reason. The French should stick to the truth. Ye shall know the truth, and the truth shall make you free. The truth is what is as opposed to what is not.

Mark loved Iseult for herself, and Iseult loved him back. Why not? He had made her his queen. He had given her rich gifts, including a princess phone with an extension all her own and a refrigerator in her room filled with soft drinks whose labels boasted they contained no nourishment at all. And last but not least, he gave her money. Money always brings initial happiness, but after a certain point, it just brings more money. Iseult deemed herself happy as a clam. She had the right man, the right outfit, and the right career, plus the additional benefit of the right lover on the side. Many years later, Princess Di was to reprise the same situation, except in Di's case there was not a lover on the side—more like 13 lovers on the side.

Yes, Iseult loved them both, her husband and her ardent knight, both at the same time but for different reasons and in different ways. Iseult, like so many women, was beneficiary and victim of the complexities that encompass the human situation everywhere. The tenderness of her heart moved her to love, and she could no more control it than you or I can fly to the moon by flapping our arms. You will notice, as this tale unfolds, that no matter what anguish, torment, reprisals, reversals, betrayals, agony, distress, grief, misery, pain, sorrow, woe, or wretchedness Mark or Iseult or Tristan garners, none of these three fully expel the other two from their hearts. Neither magic nor potions nor sorcery, explains that only the tender nobility of soul and the human nature of such star-crossed love as faithfully depicted here in Bernard's narrative.

But, Houston, we have a problem. Iseult is paranoid and decides administratively that Branwen must die. The next tableau tells about Iseult's plan.

Branwen Delivered to the Serfs

Iseult lived in the castle as queen. But she also lived, as told, in herself in fear. Fear that her secret might be uncovered. Despite the frescoes, the faience stoves, the floors strewn daily with flowers (roses mainly and some pansies), the jewels, and the fine queen's chamber, a kind of nameless fear, which we would in this enlightened age call "anxiety," dogged her footsteps and afflicted her soul. No wonder Cupid has been depicted as a mischievous child.

Tristan was near. When she needed him, she called him on his portable phone. They loved high and splendidly, as is common among great lords and ladies. They'd meet at Dirty Sally's (the village Inn), usually on a Tuesday at noon. Sometimes they met down by the lake, sometimes in Tristan's office, and sometimes in Iseult's little hackney, which she parked along the roadside or on the castle roof. There in the back of the vehicle, she pulled her dress up, her panties down and rooted her warm bottom into Tristan, quickly pumping him to climax. He came, clutching the orbic flex of her behind with great gasps of pleasure while hoping no one else was hearing. As he came, Iseult had a unique technique of grinding deeper and faster side-to-side. This had the effect of extending and heightening his pleasure. Indeed, Tristan sometimes actually had multiple orgasms, a thing medical textbooks say is unusual for a man, but not impossible.

[A medical note for the physiologically curious: Tristan never had more than three orgasms in a row, so that might be the human male's somatic limit.]

Iseult gave Tristan reports of her infrequent sexual relations with Mark. Tristan never had any pain or objection for a husband is a husband is a husband.

As far as they both knew, no one was privy to their liaison but Branwen. And, because of that fact, Branwen came to seem, in the queen's mind, like a witness spying; for Branwen alone knew what manner of life the new queen led. Branwen alone held her at her mercy so.

One day, Tristan and Iseult met in the watchet-colored chamber to discuss the issue. Iseult was smoking, not holding the cigarette very expertly, but taking appalling inhalations. "Cute" was the word for her as she sat there, blowing smoke from both her mouth and nostrils, wolfing her weed way too fast.

Iseult said to Tristan as she tossed a butt out the oriel window, "I have considerable exposure here. What would a censorious world think of my conduct?"

"You mean we," said Tristan printing a thousand kisses on her clay-cold hands, uttering every expression despairing love could dictate.

"Yes, we. We have considerable exposure here. If Branwen should tire of being my faithful servant and start to make extortionate demands, how could I not grant her wishes? She could easily, so circumstantially, tell about the bed where she passed for queen. What would happen if she did?"

"Are you sure you aren't jealous? Mark and Bran seem to be an item these days. Rumor has it that Branwen's latest pregnancy belongs to Mark."

Iseult lit another Winston and dragged deeply. "Don't divert the argument. Answer. What would happen if she told?"

"Tristan would be in mortal danger," said Tristan.

"And what about myself?" asked the queen as (as if on cue) a clap of thunder, suddenly heard out of the clear blue sky, shook the battlements. Omens from Zeus happen in romances, not just in Homer's Odyssey. But, of course, this thunderclap didn't just happen. It was caused by the natural conjunction of warm and cold air and the electric discharge caused by such a conjunction.

Tristan nodded: "Iseult the beautiful, Queen of Cornwall, wife of King Mark, would be in mortal danger, for the barons might request a trial by fire."

So did the queen meditate her fear. And all that thinking put her in a frame of mind capable of the most fatal excesses. But Branwen of the white breasts was loyal. It was the queen's own guilt that was running and ruining this situation. Guilt is so often shifted onto an external object, in this case, poor Branwen, from its internal intrapsychic origin, in this case, Iseult's conscience. The mental mechanism is called "projection." Its comfort is that it decreases anxiety by placing the problem outside the self where people think it might get handled better or easier.

Fortunately, Iseult could not make up her mind what to do. Indecision is, in this context, rather a good thing. Otherwise, in this wide world of ours, there would be an even more stunning incidence of murder.

One evening, while looking into a mirror, Iseult noticed that, while beautiful still, she had become something she had not been before—infinitely pathetic. It was then, screwing up her courage that she decided what to do. She called before her two serfs, rough and ready men.

"Each of you shall receive 60 gold bezants if you consent to do my will."

The serfs bowed low.

"Branwen has committed a crime against God and the king, a crime that is too vile and tawdry to recount. Because of this crime, Branwen must die."

The serfs said nothing but looked at each other with inquiry faces wondering what the word "tawdry" meant and wondering where this would end. Their resemblance to Rosencrantz and Gildenstern of the Tom Stoppard play was obvious. Like Ros and Gil, they looked and spoke the same except one was taller than the other. And by a strange coincidence, they had the same talent for melodrama, believing the form had a significance, which it does not, in fact, contain. Still, occasionally, you know, from out of this small black hole of literature, there escapes a beam of light that, considered at the right angle, shows us something bright—a highly theatrical exploration of the identity known as "performance."

Iseult gave the serfs her orders:

"Take Branwen to a deserted part of the forest so that none may know what happened to her. Kill her there," Iseult commanded. "To me, bring back her tongue that I may know it will never wag again."

The serfs made three obeisances and retired.

So, three figures marched into the woods. The smaller man in front, Branwen of the white breasts in the middle, the taller serf bringing up the rear. After about 23 minutes, they reached a dark and desolate part of the forest that seemed suitable for murder.

Then you, Branwen of the white breasts, turned to the taller man, for he seemed to be the leader, and asked, "Why stop here? I see no wild mushrooms, blueberries, cloudberries, lignons, or the like."

"May it please your ladyship," he replied. "You caused some serious harm to Mark our king and to Iseult our queen. You have been condemned to death. We are the executioners."

And then you Branwen of the white breasts, sounding much stronger than you looked, asked, "What was my offense?"

"Marry, we know not. It was something against the king. Some sin or crime. That is as far as we know, for the queen told us so. She said it was tawdry."

"Tawdry?" What was tawdry?

"Yes, tawdry," piped up the smaller serf, who was already trembling from the cold or from fear or from both.

"Where and whyfor tawdry?" you, Branwen of the white breasts, asked again.

They replied in unison: "Marry, we know not what tawdry is or means, but we do know Queen Iseult told us to bring you to a dark and desolate place where no one may know what we do, kill you, and bring back your tongue to show that you will speak no more. Tawdry must be a serious offence to merit such, the punishment of death and tongue removal."

"Why would Iseult fear my tongue?" you, Branwen of the white breasts, then asked. Good work! In circumstances like these, Branwen of the white breasts, it pays to keep your cool.

"Maiden," said the taller serf as he pulled out his dirk. "Make amends with God. Prepare to die. But know you well that it is not I who do this to you, for I have nothing personal against you. It's just business, strictly business." [The copycat: He had watched Marlon Brando last week in The Godfather.]

Then you, Branwen of the white breasts, bared your breasts and fell to your knees and grasped the taller serf's two legs. You bowed your head in a sign of entreaty and submission and begged mercy while your arms sought to thrust the knife's point aside, but it was too sharp, much too sharp, and you suffered a bloody cut on your right hand. That cut was, of course, the classic defensive wound seen in knife fights.

"This is no charming adventure," said you, Branwen of the white breasts, trying to staunch the wound. Your voice was so soft and piteous that both the men felt ashamed—as well they should. Speechless, the serfs stood there staring, not at the blood, but at Branwen's white breasts. They had never seen breasts before. Men who are serfs rarely get anything from women but an occasional smile. Consequently, their eyes were glued there on the breasts and the cleavage. Exotic dancers know from their experiences in men's clubs that big tits = big tips.

Believe it or not, some women don't like men who stare at their breasts. These women want men to talk to them, not to their breasts. Perhaps if we invented a breast implant that played a recorded message, the whole problem might be alleviated. That way, women couldn't claim men stared but didn't listen.

What is the real problem?

Lowerings blindly following orders have been the cause of much misery on this planet, then and now. Without the likes of them, a man like Hitler would not have come to power. But notice how romance as social allegory makes the violent actions of the past (and future) at once comprehensible and palatable for the enlightened reader. The problem is abuse of power by those in charge while acting through underlings who think they are doing their patriotic duty.

"Young woman, if Queen Iseult, your lady and ours, wishes you dead, doubtless it is because you have done her some great wrong."

You, Branwen of the white breasts, answered, "Friends, I remember but one misdeed. When we left Ireland, each of us took with her, as the chief of her ornaments, a snow-white shift of samite, a gown for our wedding nights. On the sea, it happened that Iseult's snow-white garment was sullied, tarnished so it never could serve again. Know you well it was not I that soiled her shift, but another."

[Editor: Branwen has altered the facts a little, but the gist is correct. Alteration of facts is common, especially in adventure romance novels when one is speaking metaphorically. The white shift here represents Iseult's virginity, I think, as there is no historic evidence that Iseult's real wedding gown was ever soiled, much less tarnished.]

"Who then? Tell us for perhaps that's the one that we should kill."

"It was a man who lives at court. But who it was, I will not tell. It was he who tore her shift, wounded and reddened it beyond repair. But know you well that Iseult played a role in the tearing, quite a big role too. She participated and willingly, and now she has regrets for once this thing is torn, it cannot be fixed or repaired. Why she might blame me is not clear. But those in power do often blame others for bad deeds that they themselves have done. And it is I alone who knows who tore her shift and that she helped. So perhaps the queen fears that I might tell what I know. But she fears amiss, for I would never ever tell her misdeeds nor of any misdeeds of any others. Jesus said judge not that you be not judge, and that will be my get-out-of-hell-free pass.

"Because Iseult's shift was unsuited for her wedding night, I let her have my own. I did her a favor by substituting mine for hers that been already torn. That is my sole crime. Judge you well and witness if that be worthy of death."

"We learn something new every day, to our cost," cried the serfs in unison, for they were truly puzzled. They were not used to metaphors. They had no idea that the white shift referred to a womanly virginity to which Iseult had bade good riddance long ago in Ireland and not, as the French text says, on the cruise to Cornwall aboard the ship *Young Lover*. Or was the ship's name *The Doomed*? Doomed would be apropos of what happened to Tristan and Iseult later, so I guess that would be the better name. But Carnival is not going to sell many tickets on a cruise ship called *The Doomed*. In my view, a better name for a cruise ship might be *The Titanic*. Yes, sir, that name has a ring of invincibility to it.

The tall serf stood there with bare blade pendent above Branwen's head as if in suspended animation in some cheap technothriller of a movie. Then he lowered the weapon, for it was weighing on him as much as his conscience. He turned to the smaller serf. "You went to law school. How sits this stuff from the point of view of the law?"

The smaller serf looked up and to the left and recited from memory, "Under English law, the punishment must fit the crime. Three elements determine punishment: To wit: The act, the intent, and the contrition. Here, the act were no crime, the intent was to do good not ill, so it is hardly reprehensible, and the contrition, the contrition is...."

"Extreme," shouted you, Branwen of the white breasts, at both serfs. Then in a softer, sweeter voice, you, Branwen, added, "Gentles, if I have offended, by this will it be mended: Since the queen's wish be I die, tell her that I send her greetings and love and that I thank her for all the goodness and honor that she has ever shown me this (sigh) many a day. Tell her that my love lasts although I die. May the Great Goddess in Her Holiness (Branwen still worshipped the mother goddess of the Celts as well as Jesus, and she worshiped fire like the Zoroastrians—she liked to hedge the bets) preserve, protect, and save the queen. Brothers, now strike!"

"Calm down, madam. Not so fast. Let us take counsel among—I mean between—ourselves. You stay here while we go beyond the clearing to yon oak tree."

It was getting dark. The storm-broken limb of the big oak tree was twisted about the trunk like a constricting snake. A plummeting meteor, streaked across the heavens like the spark of a shaken log, vanished. That bad omen means you are gone, Branwen, white breasts and all. Finished. Your doom is sealed. But wait. Let's listen to the discussion between the serfs.

"It seems to me," said the first serf, once they got there by the snarled old oak tree, "that the offence of supplying the queen with a clean white shift for her wedding night is a service, not a crime. And even if it were a crime, it doesn't merit death."

"Only if she had given the queen a dirty gown or if she had soiled the queen's dress herself, might this maid who is, after all, called Branwen the Faithful, deserve some punishment." (The Faithful is Branwen's Cornwall-acquired court name. Her Welch-acquired name is, of course, by now well known to you. Her Welch name reflects the fact that Branwen's breasts were white, snow white. The Cornwall name reflects the fact that she is usually faithful.)

"Aye, that makes sense," said the smaller serf. "There is another thing about this scene that doesn't check out. If the crime were against the king, then why doesn't the king himself take up the matter in open court? Why does he not administer the punishment there instead of by our private agency here deep in the forest where no one else can see? This whole thing smells, stinks to high heaven. I read about Star Chambers in school. Governments can get out of control very easily, for power corrupts, and absolute power corrupts absolutely. Don't believe me? Look around you. In Russia, 3,000 people disappear overnight. Ditto same thing in China. Those are not magic tricks."

"Exactly," replied the taller serf as he reinstalled his dirk in its sheath and lit a *Romeo y Julieta* Cuban cigar, the Churchill deluxe type, which he had extracted from its own sheath, a tubo de aluminio. "Consider also the prize we are to win for this adventure: 60 gold bezants. Now that's real money, enough to buy the services of 100 knights for ten years."

"Aye, so vast a sum must be indicative of something besides a sudden hyper-idealistic redistribution of wealth as suggested by Senator Warren."

"When dealing with such amounts and sums, fellows like us have no idea of what it means. For this is a dimension of money we have never touched, scarce ever dreamed about."

The smaller serf, after lighting a small (*Chicos*) *Partagas*, paused to contemplate the cigar's pale blue vapor and the fine concentric white ash forming on the tip. "If the queen had promised us six silver groats, I would believe her. I could retire on that. Such a sum added to my IRA would suit me fine. It would make up for my cat's lymphoma.

I had to withdraw $4,200 under substantial penalties to get that sucker under control. I'm just daft for cats."

"I love cat stories too," shouted Branwen of the white breasts, who must have pretty good hearing to have caught the serf's drift from that far away. "And I love cats! I'm just daft for cats. I have some cute cat pictures in my pocketbook. Do you wish to see them?"

Yes, Branwen of the white breasts, how clever. You played another card. You identified with your kidnappers. You behaved like Patty Hearst when she was with her captors.

The two serfs paid no attention to her but continued mulling over the situation.

"I've never even seen a gold bezant, much less touched one. How about you?" asked the taller man who had started to trim his fingernails. "Did you know that fingernails grow after death, as does the beard? The nail on the middle finger grows faster than the other nails."

A beat for suspense.

"On guard!" exclaimed the serf who was a lawyer, for he had had a flash of insight. "Fellows like us are often duped by those in power. The powerful use and abuse us. Who sleep with powerful, sleep with tiger."

The taller serf threw his weaponry upon the sward of grass in a swale nearby and sat on a pocked, rough gray stone. "What bothers me is the way women change their minds. Horace or Ovid, I forget which, one of those Latin poets, said what women say ought to be writ on running water. Here in Cornwall, there can be four changes of the weather in a single day, and a woman's heart may change that many times as well. The Mandarin pictograph for "iffy," "not certain," "not reliable" is the symbol of a woman with a mouth. Thus, even in ancient China, it was known what women say is not all that trustworthy."

"Methinks that half of what Iseult told us meant something else, and the other half didn't mean anything at all. She has some free-floating sense of grievance against this woman. That's my diagnosis, nothing more."

"If Iseult changes her mind, what would be our defense? Would anyone believe that she had ordered the death of Branwen, her faithful servant and maid, her bosom friend, and companion? Would our poor wit, contradicting the queen, stand before the king? If we kill Branwen now, she will be dead for eternity. Will you please stop picking your nose, Gil, and pay attention to what I'm saying?"

Gil rolled a string of snot into a ball and flicked it across the mote-speckled clearing. "Eternity is a terrible thought. I mean, where's it going to end? No doubt, though, there's some principle of design at work here, surely you know that. We must play ourselves out to an aesthetic, moral, and logical conclusion, for we believe in the rules of probability, the first criterion of neo-classical criticism, that the reader must credit a fiction in order to be moved or delighted by it. Ultimately, be instructed by it. This rule covers action, characterization, and diction. For the sake of verisimilitude, we must think of something that covers all three conditions and covers them well. Besides, the rumor is that Branwen is King Mark's mistress. If that is true, how's he going to deal with us who kill her?"

"Peace! Blockhead. I am thinking. I am thinking that external events in human history have their origin first in the human mind, and sometimes, sad to say, in the primitive minds of men like us, who are the great unwashed. Men like us made the coup in Russia that toppled the Tzar. Men like us set in motion, the forces that killed six million Jews. Men like us, as members of the Praetorian Guard, determined whether a given emperor of Rome stood or fell. And so on, for human will sets the course of human time. We don't look like much. But we are WE THE PEOPLE. We are the people who get things done. It is we who have the power. We are not of the same strength that in olden days was able to move earth and heaven. We are what we are. Two serfs of equal temper made weak by time and fate but still strong in spirit. Much has been taken from us, but much abides."

The serfs hit on the following plan. They would cover the white breasts and tie Branwen to a tree. Then they would return to the queen to report the dirty deed done. If the queen had changed her mind or wouldn't pay, they would return to release the maid.

"If, on the other hand, the queen really wants her dead, we will return and do our duty just as we have said."

"Right as rain. Let's keep things in proportion. Branwen is mortal. Death comes sooner or later to us all. Consequently, Branwen would have died anyway. We would have speeded up the process, merely. Or look on it from the social-quantitative point of view: Branwen is just one maid among many. The loss would be well within statistically acceptable parameters of reason and convenience. Anyway, what is so terrible about death? Socrates said we don't know what death is, so it is illogical to fear it. It might be very nice. Besides, we can sure use the money ever since we hit that bit of a snag with our dot com shares in the stock market."

As they turned to leave, you, Branwen, helpfully, reminded them that they needed a tongue as a token that they had performed their mission. Positive thought, that was. The will to live cannot be overly estimated. Ninety percent of all deaths are suicides. Persons who lack curiosity about life, who find minimal joy in existence, are all too willing, subconsciously to cooperate, and attract disease, accident, and violence. Bad personal habits cause heart disease and stroke, bad industrial habits cause cancer, and bad political habits cause war.

So, along the road to Tintagel, the serfs killed a wild boar and cut out its tongue, placing that object in a basket of straw as a present for the queen. Then the serfs headed back to the castle. Along the roadside, they stopped to rescue a bull who had gotten stranded in a swamp because he had thrown his stifle out. Thus, the serfs were delayed. When, eventually, they appeared before the queen, she was frantic.

"Did she speak?" Iseult inquired anxiously.

"Yes, my queen, she spoke before her death."

"What? What did she speak?"

"Words, my queen. She spoke words."

"Don't be funny. You fellows read too much Shakespeare. I swear that lately, the toe of the peasant comes so close to the heel of the courtier. Something like that. Now to it again. She told you what?"

"She told us that you were angry with her for one wrong and one wrong alone. That was that she had given you her precious white shift for your wedding night because yours had been sullied."

"What the devil did she mean by that?"

"We don't know. She also expressed her thanks to you for all that she had received from you, and she prayed to the Mother Goddess to protect your honor and your life. She closed her last speech with parting sentiments of love. No more will she speak. Oh, great queen, here is her tongue."

The serf searched his kirtle flap but found no tongue. Then he recalled that he had not put it in his kirtle but instead in the straw basket. With a flourish of his hand, he held the bloody mess out to the queen. Glue-like clotted blood dripped red onto the parquet floor.

"Murderers!" shouted Iseult. And echoes answered the same. "Give me back my beloved maid. She was my only female friend, my trusted companion, my chaperon. FFF (First Female Friend). Or as Cosmo has it, my BFF (Best Female Friend, or is it Best Friend Forever, or is it both?). Give her back!"

The two serfs flinched at the queen's rage and with knowing eyes, looked at each other. The leader replied, "Queen, it is said in sooth, the woman of the species changes her mind in but few hours. She laughs, weeps, hates, and loves in a kaleidoscope of emotions. We killed her as you bade. Now we request the wage that's due."

"Go to, you two," screamed Iseult turning crimson with rage, coarse drops of spittle floating on her harsh hot breath. "Go to Hell. Are you simpletons? I sent her into the woods to gather wild mushrooms and blueberries and cloudberries and blackberries and lignons. And I sent you two to protect her from the riffraff and wild beasts, and you return to tell me that you killed her? Prepare by earnest prayer for your reward and wage. You will burn on hot coals as preparation, I hope, for your eternal torment in Hell. I sent you with her as her protection. And you killed her? Outrageous! I shall tell, and I shall tell the king of your most grievous crime."

The serfs decided that things were getting out of hand. Soon the queen's guards might come and dispense with them then and there. The serfs, therefore, announced what they had rehearsed: "Branwen lives. We will bring you safe and sound to her."

Bernard, the Bardic Narrator, stopped and stared into space. He shook his head. "All the ancient texts say the same. This was sometime a puzzle, why Iseult should change her mentality so quickly. Now we know that she herself may have been a victim, a victim of premenstrual syndrome. PMS afflicts women just before and sometimes during their menses. The existence of PMS may have an evolutionary reason. The female of species during menses is not fertile. So, the purpose of PMS could be to save mating for the time that would give a better chance of producing offspring. Science has documented that some women, not all, may undergo profound personality changes during PMS and then revert to goodness and niceness when the menses is over."

Iseult did not believe such knaves. Nevertheless, she set out right quick to the place where Branwen was still tied to the tree.

"Mistress," said Branwen of the white breasts. "The Goddess answered my prayer, and now I find myself reunited with yourself. Pardon my faults, as indeed you should."

Iseult could not make answer speak. And feeling very weak, she fell to her knees in front of Branwen and quite swooned away.

Tristan Tries Escape

Tristan and Iseult; Love pressed them hard as a force of nature, as indeed love is, like the hawk as it sweeps down upon its prey, or the dying stag that seeks the stream to drink, or the raccoon that washes and then devours the fish it has caught.

There were those at Tintagel who had dark suspicions. The barons thought they saw Love terrible that rode Tristan and Iseult. The women at court caught queen and knight chattering intimately, looking at each other too long or smiling too much. It is true that no one discovered the lovers in each other's arms or heart on heart, mouth on mouth, all that mingling of breath in those old vehement bewildering kisses. Not Branwen of the white breasts, who tried to know nothing and who was faithful anyway, had the lovers to fear, but themselves. Yea, hearts so stricken may sometimes lose their diligence. A secret love will not be hidden. Rumor, the old messenger, had spread the word. The chorus of the unloved sang their song.

The wish to exhibit one's lover must be a tribal feeling; the wish to be seen as loved is part of one's self-respect. Alone, one has a rather incomplete outlook. One is not sure what is funny and what is not. One solid pleasure of love is to check up together on what has happened to view life's events together.

The DAGG, with evil joy, watched the queen and thought they saw the lineaments. They decided to tell the king. They hoped that Mark's tenderness would turn to torment, then to fury. But things could backfire. They knew that well. So, screwing up their courage, they requested audience with Mark. Andread, as usual, did the talking.

"Sire, there is too much prattle about Iseult the Fair and Tristan."

"To your shame, Andread, for it is you who are doing most of this prattling, none of it good."

"Sire, we know this is an unpleasant topic. We mourn ourselves to speak of it."

"That's well. Very well. So shut your trap. Zip it! Go your way. I've had too much of late, too much of everything, people, events, problems, conflicts. Intelligence reports that rogue Flannagan has built iron boats for the French of Normandy and will soon lead an expedition against us. Lutetia (Lutetia = Paris, where it is said no whore is too old or too ugly to survive) backs them and so does Lugdunum (Lyon), formidable foes, not to mention the Arverni, Hadui, and Helvetii, ancient Celtic tribes eager to regain their antique glory after their miserable defeat at the hands of Julius Caesar at Alesia. For the first time in history, Celtic Gaul, Iberian-influenced Aquitaine, and Germano-Belgic Gaul appear united. They even plan a common currency called the

Euro. Meanwhile, here in this little section of merry old England, I'm having a terrible time trying to organize the Celts and Saxons into a united front of the willing."

"Sire, our duty is to you. We would not see you mocked by your nephew, nor by anyone else. You have placed great trust in Tristan. Yet Tristan would shame and stain you with his unholy love of your wife."

"It's too bad, Andread, you live now and not in the future. In the future, say about 1941, there would be a nice position for you in the Gestapo. Tristan loves Iseult, and she loves him. That is meet, for Our Savior commanded that we love our neighbor as our self. It's a Christian value, and some people still follow it, and some of them that do follow it are, believe it or not, Christians, though not that many."

"The controlling word in what I said, sire, was unholy. This couple mocks the ties of marriage and insults, thereby, the court and the church and my kingdom."

Mark, now crimson, shouted at Andread, "Fool, I'm not a simpleton. You wished me to take a wife. The problem here is your fault. Beauty bewitches even the wisest man. When its power strikes, even the bravest and most robust knight must fall. Iseult is a lusty woman passing fair. She may well need another man beside myself to share her love. As long as I get my due, this bothers me not at all. For I have learned that in this earthy vale of tears, we must each of us learn accommodation and accord."

The DAGG brought in the woodsman who claimed to have seen Tristan and Iseult in carnal embrace in the woods. Mark reproved this vile man with a seemingly precognitive proleptic autogenic curse: "He who speaks against my nephew, now my son, will dig his own grave and bury himself in it. Wretched woodsman, you are he. And doomed you are."

The other witness was Focin the Jester, who described a foot-fondling incident he'd once noted upon entering Iseult's room to complain to her of sourness in his breakfast milk. Mark's reprove was brief: "Fool, you've got a brain so full of helium, I'm surprised you're not stuck to the damn ceiling. Why would a jester complain to a queen about sour milk?"

A note of hand was introduced: "Do not quarrel with your governess for not employing the rod enough." This was, of course, irrelevant evidence. Irrelevant evidence and side issues are common obstructions to reasoned discourse.

Students of seventh-century literature know this forgery as the only written evidence supporting the array of psychoneurotic suppositions that have since been made about Tristan and Iseult, exciting charges of corporal discipline. Unimaginative clods! The exact same silly and irrelevant forgery was used to accuse Dr. Johnson and Mrs. Thrale.

King Mark shifted his weight in the Chair of Estate and rose stiffly to his feet, poising the scepter above the heads of the felons. The seneschal told them to kneel.

"What wicked thoughts you felons have. Where were you when the Morhold, sacker of cities, wanted the maidens and the boys? By force of arms, Tristan saved us. You might profit from the Morhold's example. No knight of the round table, not even

Lancelot himself, would dare to challenge Tristan, nor will you. What fools you be to bring such accusations here. Your lives may not be long unless you still your tongues. You trembled before the Morhold, sacker of cities, and were dumb. Prepare to tremble threefold more before my nephew, now my son."

The reiterated news of Tristan's adoption hit Andread like a sledgehammer. Desperate men do desperate things, so Andread said, "Tristan wants a general election. He questions the divine right of kings. He feels we should try a new form of government, democracy."

"Rubbish! All that has the sound of unconvincing horse shit. You have been coached," said Mark. "Every country has the government it deserves, and we have a government by cliques, oligarchs, hot-heads, malignant psychopaths tempered by revolution now and then. A very good government it is, in harmony with the physical conditions of the country and the national temperament. It's true I am king. But I am merely a figurehead. Real power is reserved to the barons and to the people. General election? Who cares? There will always be kings, whether elected or not (look at George Bush and Obama and, God help us, Trump). Kings and oligarchy, on and on, there will always be that stuff until our galaxy goes supernova. Beware that green-eyed monster, jealousy, that cruel emotion. Psychiatrists tell us its origin is in a decreased sense of self-esteem. I cherish Tristan more than I do you. I have told you so before. That is why you hate him. There is no reason other."

"*Ne dump pas on moi*," came Andread's reply. "I have my own demons. Don't trivialize them with your crap from Psych 101."

Mark signaled that the audience had ended.

"With respect, sire, while there still is time, look, and listen. The evidence is there all around you, which your own eyes can see, your own ears hear."

Andread, irresolute, striving in vain for utterance, his complexion pallid as death, his knees beating one against another, slowly obeyed the mandate and withdrew, leaving the king to taste the poison.

Mark could not shake off the evil spell. Most aggressions in this time and in times to come were and will be caused by jealous minatory men like the DAGG. Men willing to kill to abate their jealousy.

Mark sent for Tristan.

"Tristan," said Mark. "May I have a word with you in private?"

They adjourned to a bridge over the river Flowey where the sounds of the swiftly flowing waters obscured their speech and made it difficult for any other to hear.

Mark continued, "Tristan, rumor at court has it that the queen has a lover. Since you are the only one here that I know I can trust, I want you to follow her and tell me who it is, if indeed the rumor's true, so that I may seize the disloyal felon and burn him at the stake."

Tristan made no reply. Nor could he reply he was so choked up. He just stared at Mark.

"Felons have charged the queen with awful treason but ask me nothing for I could not speak their words without shaming us both. Originally, I had thought of banishing her from Tintagel, forbidding her to repass its moat or boundaries. But evil men with evil words charge the scroll with new punishments, so I have concluded that the only way to assuage the situation and ease my problem-weary soul is to have you investigate and gather evidence. Report back to me, and we shall take it from there."

"Is this your decision alone, or has a group concurred?" asked Tristan.

Sensibly Tristan wanted to know who the enemies were and how many.

"Top secret," so I can't tell you.

"You really love her, then?"

"I was born when she came. I live while she is with me. I will die if she leaves. She thrills me to my deep heart's core. Just touching her backside sends frissons of pleasure down my spine. You can imagine the pleasure I get when I'm in herself."

"Iseult is loyal," said Tristan.

"If you say so, I believe it," said Mark reassured.

"Leave her alone, sire. Banish me instead. Make up some excuse, and I will go."

"The scientific review committee says your grant application has serious defects. Not only did they not approve it, but also they disproved it as unscientific."

"You mean they disapproved it, not disproved it, for to disprove it would require considerable evidence, evidence that would have to be relevant and adequate. Adequate evidence would have to be sufficient in kind, number, and weight to justify the conclusion. That would require research, real investigation, which committees are incapable of doing," said Tristan.

"Nope," said Mark waving a dismissive hand. "They said they disproved it. And that's a fact, a final fact."

"Mere assertion doesn't make it so, sire. And repetition is no proof. Committees here proved by fiat that iron boats can't float. Yet a fleet of iron boats now approaches our shores from France. Fact defeats all arguments to the contrary."

It was at this moment that Tristan acquired a disrespect for all experts who equate pessimism with wisdom. He told Mark so, but the king was unmoved. Mark's anger was mounting. The politics here were bad. If he didn't do something about Tristan, the DAGG wouldn't support him, and the French might attack Cornwall.

"Furthermore, those experts concur that your grant showed a mind deranged and that you, like Flannagan, are a persistent corrupting influence on our youth. So, I have to banish you for national security. Get it?"

Mark, like so many people in power, was getting carried away by his own rhetoric. Leaders actually start to believe their own bullshit. Why this happens, no one knows. But it is common enough. Il Duce (Benito Mussolini) invented the Italian 11th Army and then wondered why it didn't answer call up when he needed it. Il Duce learned the hard way: Imaginary armies don't cut the mustard.

Tristan's hand gravitated to his sword hilt while Mark continued, "Ideas of fantasy such as rifles and powders that blow down gates are in the minds of children and mad men only. Double shame on you for such poor work indeed. The group recommends that you be killed."

Tristan was speechless, awed that it had come to this. Tristan restrained, no doubt by his permanent moral standards, a very pure and laudable impulse to spread his huge fat hand over Mark's red, sweating face and push, push hard such that Mark would flop into the Flowey and the swift running waters. (They are on the bridge, remember?)

"Despite the punishment I am about to inflict, I want you to know you are still dear to me. I respect and love you as a son. It's just that people in my position have to make... difficult decisions. Eliminating you has been the most heart-wrenching decision of my career," said Mark. "I only hope you regret the anguish you have caused me."

King Mark turned and, with a gesture of his right hand, summoned his retainers to arrest Tristan.

[Poor Mark—he frets over this Tristan/Iseult thing, thinking he's making a disposition. The dumb fuck doesn't realize that he is just a character selected by the author to become the shapeshifter, the person who changes in order to alter the direction of the story at this point, which is, for your information, plot point two. Some of you readers may think Mark's change of mind and heart occurred too fast, but who knows? The poor guy is under pressure from the DAGG, and he thinks Tristan is screwing his wife, and he has a bad case of indigestion from the rotten oysters he ate. Some shapeshifters do seem to act too fast and in opposite to everything expected. That Judas Iscariot character is an example. Right out of the blue, he kisses Jesus goodbye. Then Judas shapeshifts again by hanging himself. Go figure.]

Tristan broke away and jumped down the stairs in his patented "Hero's Leap™®©" to the main guard. The moat bridge had already been drawn up.

With so many fully armed men close by, Tristan decided he would have to cross the moat via the secret steppingstones that he learned about from the master of the hunt. He ran to the northeastern tower while the castle crew heated hot pitch and oil to fling at him through the murder holes. Several crossbow arrows streamed by his right ear, so Tristan knew he must find the hidden path now or go down now to dusty death. There was one problem: He had forgotten the combination. He was sure of the number 169, for he had used the sexual mnemonic after he learned about 69. Yet, he could not recall whether the second step was to the right or left. A mistake here would be fatal. He reasoned that much clearly, but for the life of him, he was not sure how to proceed.

"The logical thing is to take one step forward and then six to the right." He spoke this to himself aloud as he glanced back at a bristling company of fully armed knights, a fearful sight, ten feet from him and closing fast. Tristan knew that the swift vengeance of their gleaming swords might at any moment whisper a last word to him—and that last word was "DEATH."

Somehow in his mind, Tristan heard the slogan: "Right is wrong." At the last moment, he took the one step forward and six to the left, running straight ahead the last nine steps and into the forest green. Knights pursuing him couldn't cross the moat, for they were not privy to the secret of the stones. They could not and would not risk falling into the water while fully armed.

Naturally, the miracle of Tristan's walking on water set in motion rumors, the most interesting of which was that he was a Christ-like figure, perhaps even Jesus Christ himself. Multiple learned papers have been written about this idea and published in peer-reviewed journals. The truth is that no one can walk on water, not even Tristan or Jesus. And no one can change water into wine or raise the dead. Those things are just impossible. About ascent to heaven, I am not sure. I can jump about three feet toward heaven, and a trained high jumper can do more. Assisted by rockets or air balloons or wings—Hmmm, that's a different story.

News, spreading fast, soon reached Andread, who was down there in the Chthonic Bar and Grill with his friends drinking. Andread said in an unusually loud voice, "I don't mind Jews, Pagans, or Negroes or even a few people with leprosy. They have souls, the same as you or I. But when a man goes to his pub, he likes to think he's going to associate with human beings. Not some form of reptilian life."

Andread was referring to a group of Irish Catholics from Dublin who were over in the corner listening to Father Coughlin on the radio.

As usual, the booze had decisively loosened Andread's tongue: "I've heard, on good authority, that Mark has even had a couple of very white little bastards off that slut Branwen, whom people around here call The Faithful. But that I ain't going to vouch for. All I can say is that he keeps putting bills through to make the Welch slave a queen. Jesus! He's doing that for a good reason. That woman is running the whole kingdom and its labor movements. The king is being influenced every time she wiggles her slit. She's no better than I am. Her shit don't smell like ice cream. Just because in that leopard skin bikini she looks like Raquel Welch doesn't mean Mark has to go ga-ga."

Though his sentence-structure had faults, for a man imperiling himself Andread was feeling exceptionally good. The whiskey had filled his body with a rosy sense of complete wellbeing. Vague lewd sensual images stoked his mind. Images of Branwen in the nude. His groin filled, became tumescent, and his nose quivered with excitement as he recalled the ferny sweating smells of a woman in heat. "Branwen's some dish. Nice bumpers, and even nicer white breasts," he announced to no one in particular. "I'd give anything to be loving up to such a tidbit now. Pull it up to the bumpers, Andread. Park it in between."

Then a notion hit him that he thought was funny, which he said aloud, "I always made sure the current victim knows, before she takes off her clothes, the difference between coupling and marrying."

Those thoughts set off a recitation of Shakespeare's sonnet 130. And when he got to "My mistress when she walks treads on the ground, and yet, by heaven, I think my love as rare as any she belied with false compare, on unsteady feet," Andread rose. He walked over to the old Emerson table model and changed the station from Father C's sermon on the benefits of sanctifying grace to "Make Believe Ballroom."

The Catholics had no serious objection. They started dancing. Saved by an evil chance, the good are always the merry and the merry love to dance.

Gondoine laughed. "That's it, Andread. Keep the flags of discontent flying."

"And never trust anyone over 30," added Denoalen.

The DAGG were happy when they heard the news of Tristan's flight. "That Boy's gone forever," Andread gave it for his opinion. "Probably he would travel far away, perhaps to France, where he will seek a professorship at one of those newly organized guilds of scholars, the Cities of the Universe (Universities), that we all know have no future. *Et tu in Arcadia vixisti...* That's Latin, a language of scholars. Latin also has no future either. And thou in Arcadia I saw."

The others of the DAGG, Denoalen, Guenelon, and Gondoine, were of the opinion that Tristan would stick around and cause new trouble. They thought Tristan would try to see Iseult. But they didn't know how that could be possible since the castle was well guarded.

Meanwhile, on the lam, Tristan indeed stayed in town. At first, at Dirty Sally's. But it became too hot there (no AC). So three days later, he lodged with his trusted mentor, Grovenal, in a burgess' house by the rising of the waters. For in that town that very week, a miracle had occurred. Water, lots of it, suddenly rose from the land, creating two large rivers, just like Cong, Ireland where there is the famous Ashford Castle and where The Quiet Man was filmed.

Wherever water breaks from the earth or issues from a rock, that place is sacred ground, often with its own goddess, god, nymph, or elf. Because of the new rivers and the publicity they had received, the streets were loaded with Japanese tourists with please-don't-murder-me smiles and lots of cameras.

"Notice that," said Bernard, the Bardic Narrator, "though the events I described were miraculous, my description of them was realistic. My effect here was similar to that obtained by the artists of the Middle Ages, who, when doing a subject like the raising of Lazarus from the dead or Christ walking on water, were careful to keep all the details intensely real."

How did Tristan go undetected in that town so close to a castle, all of whose guards were looking for him? Simple. He changed to common clothes. We may explain it biologically by Darwin's phrase "cryptic coloration," survival by learning to blend in with one's surroundings. Why stand out when you can blend in?

But poor Tristan. Protected or not, he did brood and fret and grieve and mope and sulk. For he was more wounded than he had been when he languished from the Morhold's bite. Sure, he was disappointed in Mark that the king's love had turned to hate. But his main concern was Iseult. He wrote and wrote, sent many letters, but received no reply. And then he found out why: Iseult was under house arrest.

Whoa! Some of our readers may be wondering why Mark turned against Iseult. Can you think of some reasons? I can. She was unfaithful. She has been accused of adultery and must stand trial. Mark has a thing for Bran. They drank the love potion together, remember. Maybe Mark likes white tits. And of course, Bran loves Mark. When a woman loves a man intensely, the man usually responds and follows up. But the real reason is that all the ancient texts say so and use this element of plot structure to drive the narrative forward to Iseult's trial.

Iseult's case awaited disposition by King Mark. The barons had requested trial by fire, as was their right in indictments for adultery. The theory was that everyone knew God would not permit fire to touch, much less burn, a woman who was pure. So, the procedure (I am not making this up) was to put the woman among lots of twigs and branches and light her fire. If she burned to death, she was guilty, and if she did not burn, she was innocent. Later, during the time of the Inquisition over one million European women were burned at the stake. Some towns and villages in Germany were completely depopulated of women by this method. We know this for a fact from the Catholic church's own records. Conclusion: There must have been many, many impure women in the old days. Now all that has changed of course. Modern women are as pure as cough drops. It is of historic interest that the women who were burned at the stake had confessed that they were witches and had had sexual intercourse with the devil and had the ability to change into black cats or black crows and that they could fly around on broomsticks. As I said before, as versatile as women are, we now know such things are impossible. Remember that.

The reason for the signed confession was that if they didn't sign, then the church could take away their husband's property, and their children would consequently starve to death. Salem witch trials, same thing. We have to watch out, remain forever vigilant against religion gone haywire.

Tristan would have to think of a plan to save his beloved. But not in that town. The atmosphere was too tense for sustained thought. Not there. He sought shelter elsewhere.

Wonderfully wild was his way through the wood, through the forest of Morris (in the French version, *forêt de Morrois*) to the hut of Orri the hermit. Hermits, whether faithful to the true religion or necromancers, is not certain. Orri's quiet place could be his place to think, his zone of meditation. And think he must.

Iseult was thinking too. What to do? What to do together to remedy the problem.

The lovers hit on a most ingenious plan. Nor was there ever known a more subtle ruse of love. The device would make history and show how clever lovers can be. Let's turn to the next tableau and discover the plan.

Tristan and Iseult,
Part Deux

For those of you who fell asleep during that last chapter, let me bring you up to speed:

Tristan escaped and is now hiding out in the Forest of Morris, where he has taken up residence in the hut of the Hermit, Orri.

Iseult languishes in castle Tintagel under house arrest for adultery. The disposition of her case awaits her husband, King Mark.

The evil barons of the DAGG have proposed the trial of fire, the usual sorter-outer in cases of suspected adultery.

For reasons of political expediency, it is likely that Mark will accede to their request, in the which case woe is Iseult.

Today we join Perenis, Iseult's cupbearer, as he runs through the woods carrying a missive. I think the message is from Iseult to Tristan, but let's see.

TABLEAU TWENTY-FOUR

Iseult and Tristan Prepare for Trial

Secretly, Iseult sent her cupbearer running through the woods, avoiding paths, until, except for a slight delay, he came to Orri's hut.

Out of breath, Perenis puffed, "Good morning, my lord. How does your honor for this many a day?"

"I humbly thank you, well, well, well."

"My lord, the queen, has remembrances of yours, which she has longed long to re-deliver. Pray you now, receive them."

Tristan put down his latest book, *Animal Heroes of the Great War* (dogs mostly but some camels—some even got the Purple Heart, dogs mostly). The stories were more interesting than any of the articles in the recent edition of *Bondage Babes*. "I never gave her aught," he said, suspecting Perenis of spying for the king.

"You know right well you did, my lord," Perenis replied. "And with them, *bis* (*bis* = French for kisses. It is pronounced pretty close to the English word bees) of such luscious taste composed as make the things savor of honey sweetened or so the queen said to me. But, behold another bee of these self-same gifts." Perenis produced from his pocket the blue bee (that Tristan had given Iseult) and held it up on high for Tristan to plainly see. Then he pocketed the bee again as if it were a clandestine thing, which, incidentally, it was.

Tristan hastened to open the letter, for a note from Iseult was a rare event. The queen preferred not to write lest her screed be discovered and serve as evidence against herself. It is an old Irish axiom: Never write what you can say. Never say what you can wink. In point of fact, she often wrote to Tristan, sealing the letters with a kiss. But she wrote for her own completeness, never mailing the letters but guarding them closely. Some day she might show them to him. Oh, yes, something else. Iseult, like most real writers, found that nothing arrives on paper quite as it started. And much arrives that should have never started at all. If you don't believe me, take a look at three better sellers from the New York Times:

1. *Return to Tradd Street* by Karen White (New American Library). Struggling to finish renovations before her baby arrives, a psychic realtor faces the possibility that her home is haunted.

2. *Vampires in the Lemon Grove* by Karen Russell (Vintage Contemporaries). A century-old marriage between two Vampires (who favor lemons in lieu of blood) suffers because the husband had developed a fear of flying.

3. *Fear Nothing* by Lisa Gardener (Dutton). The Boston Detective D.D. Warren, seriously injured at a crime scene, is treated by a pain therapist whose father was a serial killer.

Hmmm… How can people read such crap? The whole publishing thing = hopeless.

"Friend," the letter said. "The date is near. This is serius. I bargained this: That the day of the ordeal King Arthur and his court including Lords Gawain, Girffet, Kay the Seneschal, and 100 knights, at the Sandy place called *Mal Pas* by the ford of the river Avon that separates the two kingdoms, Cornwall on the west and Camelot on the east, shall assemble. The tent with the holy relics of the saints and the holy books shall be on the Camelot side. The iron forge will stand there. It will heat the iron poker white-hot, and I will be required, to prove my innocence, to carry it in my hands 60 feet and throw it in the sand. No blemish must appear on my skin, and in every way, my flesh must remain intact. That failing, my fate is sealed. They will burn me at the stake.

"I told Mark that I could not swear before his barons alone, lest that they should demand some new thing, and there should be no end to my trials. If powerful Arthur with his knights is there, by arrangement, the Cornwall barons, especially the evil DAGG, will not dare to dispute a favorable judgment. Know you well that of late Arthur has often had his eye on me and given sweet talk. During jousts, especially the recent one at Lonezep, he did not cease to gaze, after each event, at my box, hungering for my nod and noise. And once, to my nod, he did puff his chest and raise his chin to heaven high, a sign that he did flirt, methinks.

"After the tournament, Arthur came to dine with us. He made show of kissing me before the rest, a kingly privilege I did not resist. And as he kissed, his hands did slip down to lightly touch my breasts—a kingly privilege and Celtic tradition, which I didn't resist. Thus, with a woman's wisdom, know I that Arthur will his best to win, in the ordeal, a decision for me, though by what means I can neither say nor guess."

At this point, Tristan dragged his eyes from the large childishly formed immature letters, with the mistaken spelling ("serius") to find that Perenis wore a worried, malcontented look. Perenis, the cupbearer, had lit a Cuban cigar, a *Romeo y Julietta*, and had faced the wall where he remained silent for a moment, the way people do when they first light up. Or was he reading the trophies of campaigns for limited monarchy that Tristan had arranged around the room? A copy of the Magna Carta graced one side of an aperture, the warrant for the execution of Charles I the other. It was a great progress of history that a ruler must be bound by a written document; that no one is above the law, not even a president of the United Snakes.

"Anything wrong?" Tristan asked.

Perenis' color changed. "Nothing." Perenis glanced away.

"Out with it, man. Come on," insisted Tristan.

Perenis took a puff and came over. Smoke exited his mouth as he spoke: "On the way here, while I was trying to avoid detection by taking side paths and hidden routes, I came to a small clearing where the woodsman, the one who had betrayed you and the queen, was busy making a fossa as a trap for the hart.

The spy saw me, grew frightened, stepped back, and fell into the hole. He screamed. I ran to the edge to help. He had impaled himself on the spikes of wood made to kill the animals he hunts. Blood everywhere. His shirt and trews were drenched. A most disgusting sight! I bent over the edge to hand him my stave, but the main supports, agitated by his struggle, and my weight, collapsed. With that, the whole hole caved in, burying him injured but alive, in the grave that he himself had dug. A most disgusting death!"

Tristan believed him. The story was sufficiently weird and irrational to be true. "That's not your fault," said Tristan, soothingly. "Bad things happen to bad people."

"Still, I'm worried. The goddess Fortune has frowned so persistently on me at Hazard and that I have begun to worry about... about...."

"About what?"

"Among other things, what history might think. People talk, you know. Once the rumor mill gets started, it's hard to stop it. They might start a rumor that I killed the man with my stave for such was written by Béroul in his *Romance of Tristan*. The same error repeats itself in *Recollections of Tristan of the Lyonesse* by Sieur Louis de Conte, who says he was your page and secretary."

"An obvious fabrication. That fancy name. I never had a page or secretary, much less him. Misinformation is everywhere," observed Tristan. "A real bummer. I swear the level of bullshit in our society is getting so high we will soon have to stand on our tip toes to breathe. People are stuck in it, sucked in it, confined by small ideas and lies. The internet has given us lots of information, but very little knowledge and even less wisdom."

"Aye. It hurts to think on it. Most of us don't mind the bullshit because we are used to it and think we can handle it."

"And most of us contribute our share, myself included," added Tristan. "But I find the major fault is with our journalism that it forces us, every day, to take an interest in some fresh triviality or other, whereas only three books in a lifetime give us anything of real significance. Wouldn't it be great if every morning when we tore the wrapper of our newspaper with free hands, a transmutation were to take place, and we were to find inside it—I don't know, shall we say Pascal's *Pensées* or James Joyce's *Ulysses* or Woolf's *To the Lighthouse* or Faulkner's *As I lay Dying* or Garcia Marquez's *One Hundred Years of Solitude* or Defoe's *Moll Flanders* or Sterne's *Tristram Shandy* or Laclos's *Les Liaisons Dangereuses* or Balzac's *Pere Goriot* or Melville's *Moby-Dick* or

Dickens's *Bleak House*? Light reading is as unwholesome as cakes and candies. TV is worse: Junk food for the mind."

(Trump: I'm for a free press. It's the newspapers I hate.")

"Listen to this:

'Stormed at with shot and shell

Boldly they rode and well

Into the jaws of Death

Into the mouth of Hell

Rode the Six Hundred.'"

"Your point?"

"No one knows the guys killed in this battle, but the guy who wrote this poem gets to be a legend."

"Jesus, Tristan, in your old age, you're getting discursive," Perenis the cupbearer remarked.

That was true, Tristan knew, but what could he do?

He'd felt he had something to say. Besides, why worry about what a character (like Perenis) in a story, a minor character at that, a mere cupbearer, why worry about what the likes of him might think? Anyway, unlucky at chance, lucky in love. He should look with confidence for the smiles of the goddess of beauty and not worry about his loses at Hazard.

Tristan didn't apologize. Instead, he expatiated further, "You know, I never heard of a character like you in a story like ours worrying about what future people might think of him. It's just not done. If Hamlet had worried about such things, he would have been paralyzed into inaction. He would have with his dying breath asked Horatio to tell his story, because he couldn't do it himself."

"Well, as to Hamlet," observed Perenis, "for all we know, that could have been the case. For all we know is what that London cad did say, writing of him. As for me, I believe there is a secret history in everything that it would be interesting to know if only it could be authentically told."

Tristan made the give-me sign with his right hand, and Perenis, Iseult's cupbearer, passed him the cigar. Its pale blue vapor relaxed Tristan. It was nice to know that some nicotine delivery devices still did deliver nicotine without the hazard sometimes associated with electronic devices made by Juul. And as usual, the cigar smoke conjured a bit of philosophy: "If I cannot smoke in heaven, I shall not go."

A beat of silence ensued as Tristan paused and puffed. He was disappointed that Perenis didn't recognize the quotation from Mark Twain.

"Two hundred years from now, we will be nothing but bones and dust, oblivious to all, as thin and as insignificant as this smoke," said Tristan. "So, let's concentrate on today's problems today. The future takes care of itself, come what may."

"Easy to say, and poetic in its way, but hardly consoling," said Perenis, motioning for his cigar back.

Perenis had a tidbit to recount: "The Category of Hardly Consoling Knowledge reminds me of that court astronomer. Remember him? The one who hung himself from the castle gate? His name slips my mind. First, the mind goes, then the pecker. It will come to me after a while. No matter. The guy had discovered, by careful research, that Uranus had five moons, Miranda, Ariel, Umbriel, Titania, and Oberon. And amazingly, this guy had observed that there are moons around Jupiter. Then he happened on a fatal knowledge: that our sun is cooling and in the process expanding into a red giant that will soon leave the main sequence of star evolution and start to die. Think on it: Five billion years from now, our sun will die, and all on Earth will die with it."

"That is in so remote a future that it interests me not," said Tristan.

"Nor me. But, that poor astronomical soul, tortured by the idea of the preprogrammed mass extinction of the human race, suspended himself at the palace door, a great disgrace."

"Had he received Christian burial?" asked Tristan.

"Alas no, for he was dead," said Perinis with a smirk, for the strengthless dead, in a certain sense, can't receive anything.

Tristan reframed the question and got this answer: "Nor did his body receive Christian burial, for the church claimed it was a pagan thing to kill himself and a grievous sin."

"The church does beg the question. For I would think the question was whether this man was in his right mind or not. The question was not whether he had killed himself—for surely he did. Further, what role, and therefore what fault, lies therein with God, who did reveal this fatal knowledge to a poor soul that he (God) must have known that he (the astronomer) could not abide or brook. And what of Christ?"

"Christ? What's Christ got to do with it?"

"Christ was certainly not murdered. You can't murder God. Ergo, Christ killed himself or went along with it, the same thing. He hung himself on the cross, permitted it to happen, as surely as the astronomer hung from the castle gate. If Christ, the son of God, can kill himself, then suicide can't be a sin. God doesn't sin. God is perfect."

Perenis puffed again, considering the logic. He couldn't find a defect, so it must be so: Ergo Christ killed himself. Then Perenis observed, "God can't be Japanese because they killed priests and nuns at Pearl Harbor.

The muscular dystrophy telethon was on, and little children were being exploited, coming out with the little crutches. Tristan shut it off with the remote.

"Friend," said Tristan. "Beware the black hole of self-absorption. It is bottomless. On my advice, think no more of the death of that genius who hung himself or the dolt who died in his own grave, else, you too may do yourself some harm. For to worry about the many that death has undone were to worry too much. *Un bateau prend l'eau par les cales,* which is to say a boat leaks/takes on water through its holds, that is, to speak yet more plainly, an accumulation of grief will sink a man. Rest, rather, with your cigar. Find consolation in it, for tobacco is the solace of a troubled world."

With that, Tristan turned back to Iseult's letter. He had never expected to have a destiny like those in a Greek tragedy, but he did—and it was beginning to unfold. He had, like all men, always wanted to rescue a Rachel or a Laura or some woman, *n'import*. He would see. His chance was coming. He, like so many characters in books, seemed surprised by the extended opportunities offered, and a little unsure of what to make of them. Breathing through this burgeoning mass of chance is a whiff, sharp as wood smoke, of mortality and impending darkness, but even that proves welcome in its time. A story that gave no hint of danger, no hint of fatal end, would be no fun. With that insight, Tristan turned back to Iseult's letter:

"My lord, fail not. On that day, the day of trial, at that place, Mal Pas, come you dressed as a monk or pilgrim, so that none may know you. Come unarmed so that none may challenge you. Keep your head low and shoulders bent so that none may see your face to recognize you. Wait on the Camelot shore for my arrival by skiff. For I must cross the Avon from the Cornwall docks to the beach at Mal Pas on Camelot's muddy shore.

[Monk A: Iseult's geography, like that of most women, was off. Mal Pas is on the estuary one mile southeast of Trufu (modern Truro) and just north of Old Kea in Cornwall. Tristan thought he knew the place she meant, though. In fact, he was sure he knew it. Mark and he had hunted ducks and swans in that very place.]

"I dread the day of my judgment, but I know by my love, I have done nothing wrong. I hope to think of something, some trick or scheme to get us out of this alive and free. Doubtless, you will be of use. Right now, I can't say how.

"My trust is in the courtesy of the White Mother Goddess (Bridget), who has helped and saved me many times before."

The letter was signed "Diana Garcia," the code name that the queen often used to rent rooms at Dirty Sally's.

P.S. "I'm pregnant. It must have happened last time when you came so hard the condom broke. I was in mid-cycle then and felt your warm sap drench me inside and knew what must be so. We have created new life together. This is the one veritable transitory power."

Tristan wrote in reply:

"My love, yes, yes, and yes. Roger, Wilco. Your fool will do as you command and more. Take these gloves of silicon dioxide fiber called asbestos. Wear them, and the heat of iron, no matter how severe, will not transfer to your skin. Thus, does science make a mockery of the pretensions of religious rite. And thus, you may hold the white blistering incandescent light, the fiery metal, white hot like a rivet, without pain or injury. Flannagan, my mentor, the old man with the plus ten diopter lenses, taught me such. And for his knowledge much thanks. But what is knowledge compared to love? What is knowledge compared to the marvel of us, our power! Together to create new life. Life! Pure, sparky, intrepid new life. So tiny and so utterly without fear. Lucky for us, you have been having sexual intercourse with Mark. He'll think the child is his; he won't know the child is ours. Our kind are immortal, though we are not.

/signed/

Red five.

P.S. I wrote a poem in your honor. Believe it or not, it was inspired by Mark:

Iseult my breath, my life, my death:

I was born when I met you,

I lived when you were with me,

I will die if we part.

And so, on the appointed day, a day of gray frost, King Mark and Queen Iseult la Belle and the barons of Cornwall, having ridden as far as the White-Sands, arrived in fine array at the river. They camped two miles south of the Ford of Chances on a bluff known to the locals to this day as King Mark's Rest.

Massed on the other side, on the chalky shelving shingle beyond the muddy flats, the hosts of Arthur bowed to them Camelot's brilliant standards of azure and vert.

Just before Arthur's tents and pavilions, sat on the shore, a man dressed as a poor unarmed pilgrim, with brown hood and wrapped in cloak, so no one saw his face, with wooden platter in hand. From those who passed, he begged, in piercing mournful tones, charity and alms.

Woe unto Sir Tristan should his disguise be discovered! Double woe unto the queen should she forswear herself!

The Ford of Chances

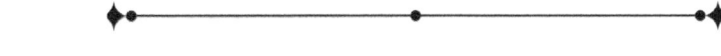

Tristan lifted his hood and saw, in the shadowy miasmic vale, something like the bitter purlieus of Styx, awaiting the sempiternal dawn.

Day began to break with a haze like cigarette smoke in a closed political caucus room. A feeling of big events hovered there.

Arthur's fine array: 400 tents and pavilions, a marvelously great number of knights, squires, nobles, retainers, and, in the foreground, a riffraff of commoners, about 400 strong.

Across the shore, through the gray mist that hung over the water this triple brrrs morning, Tristan saw Iseult boarding the skiff. So beautiful was the queen that the glimpse he had of her reminded him of captive beauties in fairy tales. I would rather have her safe, he thought, than all the gold in the Vatican. She is more precious than the four treasures of ancient and modern China: Ink, brush, paper, and ink stone.

Tristan smiled. His teeth were as white as the pearl of a gun butt, the result of some new light white technique his dentist has learned. A gust of wind combed the thicket and bent the stretch of high ornamental red grass that separated him from her.

As the skiff came closer and closer, Tristan felt himself grow more and more esurient, hungry, a hungry lion.

He decided that if this turned out right he would, he would… Yes, that, he would that—that for sure, but also he would write poems to her, each poem would be a flower praising her beauty, charm, grace, mirth, spirit, and disports. One particularly good poem immediately came to mind, a poem by Emily Dickinson:

> Futile the winds to a heart in port—
> Done with the compass,
> Done with the Chart.
> Rowing in Eden!
> Ah, the sea!
> Might I moor
> to-night in thee!
> Wild Nights!
> Wild Nights!
> When I'm with thee;
> Wild nights
> Shall be our luxury!"

Something like that, a shocker expressing yearning for reunion with a lover. Something which so perfectly captured his present mentality. That's what he would write. The sexual imagery is astonishingly explicit, but not for a woman, not for the women he knew at court. Remember that first party. But she—she must be in Hell, not Iseult, the poetess Emily D. The poetess must be in Hell if she can't keep her meter regular. What anguish lies in that startling analogy comparing making whoopee with sailing? Just to make sure that we don't misread her intentions, Auntie Em Dickinson repeated *Wild Nights* twice and added an exclamation point. It must be nice to have memories like that filed away and revisit them now and then.

No question, the port, and the moor are clear sexual images. So even if love cannot return people to paradise, it can offer sanctuary to exiles who row in Eden. The poem was so good Tristan was jealous that he had not written it. But what was the point about White Nights? They occurred, of course, and he had seen movies about them (mainly movies that took place in Russia). There during a certain time of the year, he wasn't sure, but he thought that time was summer, the sun doesn't set, and the sky is white all night. Many people can't sleep because of the light, and so they just stay up and screw.

As for Iseult, she was being rowed too, but not in Eden. And the grinding of the low sounds of the oars in the rowlocks grew and swelled with the same rhythm as the blood in her head, a terrible rhythm, pressing, mounting, menacing. And suddenly, Iseult herself was stunned. She could hardly speak for everything seemed intensely real.

(Nothing like being on trial for your life to sharpen the mind, as so many death row inmates have experienced on their long walk to the execution chamber.)

And never had so many gathered for such a test as this with so many pendants and banners of so many colors: Maroon, lavender, indigo, lilac, inky magenta, heliotrope, and vermilion glistened, glinted, and glimmered in the early rays of the first morning sun.

Well, the great thing about life, in case you haven't learned it yet, is the unexpected stuff that happens along the way. When the crowd realizes it's she herself, the real Iseult, the famous Iseult the Fair, Iseult la Belle, they go bonkers as if she were an underfed, overhyped Hollywood actress. And come to think on it, the Iseult show is about to start.

Before her boat beached, she told one of the knights, "Call that man dressed as a pilgrim. Order him to wade into the water to carry me to Arthur's shore, for there is no dock, and I don't want to soil my houppelande."

[Monk B: The houppelande, Iseult's dress, was a surcoat, sideless with the skirt made of separate material than the bodice. Her hat (while we're at it) was a cute purple chaplet, thick, padded, round, and embroidered, set on top with jewels.]

"Churl, come here," the knight shouted, motioning with his sword and pointing to the queen.

Iseult held down her head and said no more.

Tristan held off, pretending he had not heard.

The knight hailed the pilgrim again, "Friend, truss your coat, and try the water; carry you the queen to shore unless you fear the burden."

But as Tristan took the queen in his arms, she whispered to him, "Friend." And then she whispered to him, lower still, in that voice he loved so well, that voice so sweet and low, "Stumble upon the sand when we reach the shore. I will fall with you to the ground."

Safety first as they say, but with Tristan, Iseult comes first. First Iseult, then love, goodness, beauty, truth. Safety may have been back there somewhere. A little voice inside his head talked to him and said: *Dans le doute, absteins-toi.* It was the voice that argued with himself, his interior dialogue, what some might call the voice of conscience: When in doubt, don't. Caution of the kind meant (by his inner voice) was important in investments and science, but unimportant in love. Why should he stumble with the queen? It didn't make sense.

"I will," he whispered to Iseult, even though he had no idea what she had in mind or why she wanted him to stumble and fall, much less why she must fall with him.

So, as they touched the shore, Tristan fell with the queen and uttering, at impact, an ineffectual little grunt of alarm followed by a gigantic scream. (Real men can never learn to give a full-bodied scream like a woman. It's a pity.)

Microseconds later, Iseult collapsed herself into him and let out a high-pitched yelp, which the barons mistook for a scream, but it was her cry of pleasure for at that moment she had a small orgasm, the kind she sometimes experienced just holding Tristan in her arms before her clothes were off and before they had even really started to make love. Such orgasms, rare as they were, as rare as Tristan's multiple orgasms in her, often rather annoyed the queen because they made it more difficult for her subsequently to have a Big One. But this time, she rejoiced at the coming, for the pleasure gave her release from tension.

And then she smiled, no, let's get this right—it was more a smirk than a smile, a smirk that exactly duplicated that of the Mona Lisa, for at that moment she felt the flat of Tristan's hand light and fleeting on her behind.

For a few wonderful seconds (five? seven? Surely no more than ten), nothing happened. She didn't move. But then she felt another warm glow down there. It spread flooding her body, so she thought she might faint. The glow continued, and she actually felt Tristan was in her down there where she wanted him to be.

Weird, right?

But that's what Iseult felt.

The boatmen with their oars and boat hooks drove the poor pilgrim away.

When she saw Tristan assaulted, Iseult's stomach seemed to drop from her down, down, down, 135 feet.

"Let him be," cried the queen. "For great travail and long journey may have weakened him, and I am unharmed." Her face was flushed. Her dark red hair, parted on the left side, then swept over her right temple, was somewhat tousled, for her chaplet had fallen off. Her heart was beating faster than it should since the promise of violence hung in the air like static electricity. Despite that, she wore the sea wind like a jewel. It caught her dress, molded it against her body. Fingers of wind teased and skeined her long, silky hair around her neck or across her mouth, causing trouble, delicious trouble for Tristan, and delicious trouble for quite a few of the other men around.

Iseult looked ravishing, quite like a Renoir for, as she aged, her curves are filling out, and it is inevitable that she will go through the wide white world like a butterfly.

[Monk C: "Wide white world like a butterfly"—Patten, the producer should beg your pardon for the dubious imagery of our otherwise excellent Bardic Narrator, Bernard, who obviously has read many (perhaps too many) Russian novels. All literature, in my opinion, should aspire to the condition of the novel, and all literary novels try to approach the condition of the Russian novel. That is just my opinion. Monk B disagrees. Monk A is sleeping.]

Iseult looked better than the Pieta, or the Winged Victory of Samothrace, for hers is the eternal, full female form. A divine nimbus exhales from it head to foot. And it attracts with fierce undeniable attraction. This is the female form, and it attracts with an undeniable attraction.

Woe is Iseult. Great beauty seems ever to portend some tragic fate. Great beauty is a great calling card in this wide world, but it often causes great problems.

There was a silence. Iseult's eyes, it seemed almost against her will, rose to meet Tristan's. Those eyes of hers said something beyond the present situation in a much older language than that of words. Poor Iseult! She could not see the objective truth: That, though men may do deliberately unjust things to each other, destiny is mainly hazard. A life without risk is without drama. Her life was not like that. Life was not like that. Her life was real.

Iseult picked a loose thread from the hem of her tunic and threw to the pilgrim her torque of gold. Then she distributed among the poor many silver Ecu coins and some gold bezants. This had the magnificent effect of biasing the crowd most favorably on her account.

No, wait a second. Considering the historical and cultural significance of what was about to happen, it is better to be less cynically clear: The crowd favored Iseult from the start, for Iseult received everything as homage due to her rank and to her beauty. For beauty is more lofty in its exactions than rank. Beauty is in the eye of the beholder all right, but it also exists out there in reality (as does truth). Luckily for Iseult, she had it. That is, she had beauty. And her beauty was structural. As to truth. Who knows? That's what the trial was about. All trials are attempts to get at the truth. This trial may get at the truth, or it may not. Let's see.

"What is truth?" asked the Ursula Andress look-alike.

Bernard, the Bardic Narrator, smiled at her. The relief of comedy at this point was welcome. "A famous question, my dear, that Jesus didn't answer. So, I will answer for him. Have you forgotten? This was mentioned before. Are you ready? Got your notebook out and pencil?"

"Here it comes: Truth is what is as opposed to what is not."

The look-alike licked and smacked her lips as she wrote it down in Gregg shorthand. She shook her head, knowingly.

Then, Iseult gave to the poor her precious stones, her purple mantle, her surcoat, even her low-cut leather shoes. But she did not part with her love ring, the Claddagh, nor her (special) gloves, nor did she part with the golden bees that Tristan had given her.

Immediately before the tent of Arthur, there had been spread upon the grass a great Nicean cloth, the same that held the body of Christ himself, which cloth had been brought to England by Joseph of Arimathea. Upon this cloth lay the holy books and relics of the saints, which had been removed from their covers, shrines, and reliquaries. Around these stood the special guards, which Iseult had requested for her protection, including Lord Garwain, Sir Girflet, and Kay the Seneschal.

To Iseult, the relics, reliquaries, and books seemed nothing more than wretched junk, but she bowed down before them in recognition of the superstitions of the time and kissed the holy books one by one. Then, with only the sleeveless tunic, her arms and feet quite bare she faced east, toward the rising sun which hung below the smoked glass of the lower atmosphere—orange, oblate, distended, more color than light and, for the nonce, bearable to look at. The sun—ancient symbol of truth, light, and life. Irishly, she hoped for something dramatic to happen and was want to play her part.

Then, lifting her arms to the level of her shoulders, palms facing the favonian wind, those special gloves still on, she prayed as the ancient Celts had prayed before, for untraceable centuries, prayed the ancient ways, in ancient days, facing the sun, the most ancient royal and godly power, prayed to Lug:

"I swear by Holy Vesta, Goddess of the handloom, hearth, and home, by Apollo the physician, and Aesculapius, and Health, and Panacea (All-Heal), and all the gods and goddesses, especially by the mother goddesses Tanit, Tophet, Ishtar, Allet, Isis, Astarte, Ashtoreth, Innana, Cybele, Hecate, and Dagda."

Here, Iseult took a breath and resumed.

"I swear by famous ancient couples, Poseidon and his consort and charioteer, Amphitrite, Scylla and Poseidon, Madareus and Canace sister and son of Aeolus who committed incest and then suicide together, Radna and Krishna, the gopies and Krishna, Parvati (Kali) and Shiva."

Another breath.

"Hippolyta and Theseus, Phaedra and Theseus, Phaedra and Hippolytus, who died falsely accused, Rhea and Cronos, parents of Demeter, Medusa and Perseus, Hera and Ixion, Persephone and Hades, Venus and Vulcan, Leda and Zeus, Phoebe and Zeus,

Helen of Troy (whose name signifies the quintessential power of a woman's beauty to change the course of history) and Paris, Helen of Troy and her husband Menelaus, Venus and Mars, Juno and Jupiter, Ashtoreth and Baal, Atalanta and Hippomenes, who, with the apples of the Hesperides, tricked her into becoming his wife, Cybele and Attis, Isis and Osiris, Diana and Callisto (that is, Jupiter in disguise as Diana), Aurora and Cephalus, Ganymede and Jupiter, Flora and Zephyr, Cyrene and Ares, Pleione and Atlas, Pomona and Vertumnus, Omphalia and Hercules, Europa and Jupiter, Andrometer and Persus, Latone and Jupiter, Calliope and Apollo, Epimetheus and Pandora, Penelope and Ulysses, Venus and Adonis, Arthemis and Actaeon, Psyche and Cupid also known as Eros, Pyramus and Thisbe, Tethys and Oceanus, Oenone the nymph Paris abandoned for Helen and Paris, Iris and Mercury, Semele and Zeus, parents of Dionysos, Arane and Bacchus at Naxos, Syrinx and Pan, Antiope and Jupiter, Fauna and Faunus, Gaia and Uranus, Thea and Hyperion, Galatea and Pygmalion, Pyrrha and Deucalion, who cast the stones that reconstituted the human race, Alcestis and Admetus, Aphrodite and Anchises, Andromeda and Cassiopeia, Antigone and Haemon, Aphrodite and Hephaestus, Andromeda and Cassiopeia, Antigone and Haemon, Aphrodite and Hephaestus, Andromeda and Cassiopeia, Aphrodite and Hephaestus, Aphrodite and Zeus, Aphrodite and Hermes, Aphrodite and Ares, Aphrodite and Dionysos, Aphrodite and the mortal Anchises."

"Whoa! Am I repeating myself?"

Iseult looked around. I nodded, but she continued.

She was making a point that history, particularly literary history, often consists of the stories of famous couples. The names of the couples might produce a mental association among those in the know the way the mention of Levin and Kitty or Anna and Karenin or Anna and Vronsky might produce mental associations (ideas of certain kinds of love) in the minds of those who have read Tolstoy. All of these couples have attached to them tales told by idiots signifying nothing. But tales told by idiots, signifying nothing, as we all know, signify a great deal and are at the heart of Western literature. There is repetition, of course. What's wrong with that? Think of King Lear saying "Never, never, never, never, never," or old Walt Whitman saying "Death, death, death, death, death." When words lose their denoted meanings, they can become sounds of themselves, and still open into deeper connotative meanings.

"I swear by Aurora and Orion, Aurora and Tithonus, Coronus and Apollo, Arethusa and Alpheus, Doris and Nereus, Gudrun of Teutonic legend, daughter of the King of the Nibelungs who eventually murdered her husband, Atli, which reminds me of Delilah and Samson, Diarmid and Grania, Deirdre and the Sons or Usna, whose ancient Celtic legend is the story of Tristan and Iseult."

Here, an enormous aspiration and a sad, resigned sigh.

"I swear by more famous couples, ancient and modern, Sapphira and Ananias, Rebekah and Isaac, Medea and Jason, Glauce and Jason, Jocasta and Laius, Mary and Joseph, Mary and the Roman Centurian Panthera, Mary and the Archangel Michael,

Mary and the Holy Ghost, Portia and Bassanio, Queen Antea and Bellerophon, Beatrice and Benedick, Rachel and Jacob, Potiphar's Wife and Joseph, Judith and Holofernes, Herodias and Herod Antipas, Hero and Leander, Hecuba and Priam, Andromache and Hector, Bernie and Ethel, Allegra and Tad, Craig and Michelle, Hans Castorp and Clavdia Chauchet from that very famous novel by Thomas Mann—*The Magic Mountain*—and I swear by Clavdia Chauchat and her unnamed husband who lives in Daghestan, her travel companion Mynheer Peeperkorn (the money magnet, or is it the money magnate? Who killed himself), and Clavdia Chauchat's Doctor lover Director Behrens, known to his patients as Rhadamamthus, who runs the Berghof sanatorium and prescribed her treatments."

Breath.

"I swear by Sappho of Lesbos, poetess, who in despair over her unrequited love for Phaon, the boatman whom Venus had made young and beautiful, threw herself from a cliff into the sea. She loved a man with her whole heart and soul, though history ironically records her as a prominent lesbian."

Quick breath and a head shake.

"Artemisia and King Mausolus, Queen of Sheba and King Solomon, Susanna and the Elders, Jane and Tarzan, Thaïs and Alexander, Thaïs and Paphnutius, Brynhild and Sigurd, Astree and Colador. I swear by the goddess Inanna and her brother, the sun god Utu, and her true love and lover, the shepherd god Dumuzi."

Pause and a sip from some bottle, which, from where I stood, looked like Diet Coke, but it could have been beer or the V-8 that Iseult liked so much.

"I swear by Niobe and Amphion, Hagar and Abraham, Sarah and Abraham, Electra and Orestes, Jezebel and Ahab, The Witch of Endor and King Saul, Endymion and Selene who proved a thing of beauty is a joy forever, Silas's daughter and Godfrey Cass, Rebekah and Isaac, Queen Vashti and King Ahasuerus of Persia, Esther and King Ahasuerus of Persia, Eurydice and Orpheus."

Breath.

"I swear by all those Shakespearean couples starting with the bard himself who, when 18, married Anne Hathaway, eight years older than he and already pregnant. Six months after the wedding, their daughter Susanna was born. They had twins two years later—Hamnet and Judith.

He wrote 37 plays. Let's start with the first and work forward in time, passing famous couples in review.

Titus Andronicus: Tamora, Queen of the Goths, vows revenge on Titus because he sacrificed her son to the gods. So, her two other sons rape Lavinia, Titus's daughter, and cut off her tongue so she can't talk and cut off her hands so she can't write. Titus finds out and kills Tamora and the sons, after which he is himself stabbed to death by Saturninus, the corrupt emperor of Rome. Tamora's Moorish lover Aaron is then buried alive.

Two Gentlemen of Verona: Valentine loves Silvia; Proteus loves Julia. Proteus becomes infatuated with Silvia, betraying his friendship with Valentine. In the end, their original friendship is reaffirmed, and they are untied with their original love-partners.

King John: The characters are pasteboard, but I do like the speech by Constance about her son Arthur, who is to die, beginning, 'Grief fills the room up of my absent child.'

The Taming of the Shrew: Petruchio wins Katharina in what is perhaps the most famous play ever written about the battle of the sexes. The idea of a man taming a woman has been popular since the time of the Greeks. Both the *Shrew* and Shaw's *Pygmalion* were adapted into celebrated musicals: Cole Porter's *Kiss Me Kate*, and Lerner and Loewe's *My Fair Lady*, in which Professor Higgins tries to turn a cockney flower-seller, Eliza, into a lady and falls in love with her. And then there is Lili (also known as Lilith) Adam's first wife, according to some Hebrew Bibles. She revolted, said women were equal to men, and was sent out of Eden, exiled. Subsequently, God made Eve, who accepted Adam as the bossman.

Romeo and Juliet: Passion is destructive. It destroyed Anthony and Cleopatra, Tristam and Isolde, Parnell and Kitty O'Shea, R&J. And if it does not destroy, it dies. Thus, the essence of the play is that the lovers are doomed. It is ironic, and perhaps significant that their names the world over have become a symbol of ideal youthful passion.

Henry VI parts one, two, and three: Part two starts with saintly and young Henry meeting his future queen, Margaret of Anjou. He and the whole court greet her with the words 'Long live Queen Margaret. England's happiness.' No words are to prove more ominous. For it is the fierce and subtle Margaret, later called the 'She-Wolf of France' who is the mainspring of Henry's tragedy and who plots a welter of hate and greed. Margaret and her lover Suffolk bring down the king's protector, Duke Humphrey of Gloucester. Then Margaret teams up with Richard, Duke of York, and Cardinal Beaufort. Later, the relation with York sours and Margaret has him beheaded. At a later fight, Henry loses his crown and is made prisoner by York's son, who then becomes King Edward IV. Part three ends with Edward rejoicing with his queen. He is all unconscious of his brother Gloucester's plots. 'Here,' he says, 'begins our lasting joy.'

Richard III: Richard's over-vaulting ambition and loves are too many and too well known to require comment.

Love's Labor Lost: A show of adolescent, high-spirited men and girls playing at love. The youthful King of Navarre and three courtiers swear to fast, pray, and study for three years, completely giving up the company of women. Fat chance that. Almost at once, they find they are forced to break their vows. For when the princess of France and her court arrive to discuss matters of state, the king falls in love with the princess and his three courtiers with her ladies.

The Comedy of Errors: Here, we have the adventures of two pairs of twins (two masters and two servants) who are confused for each other. The story, says John Masefield, "shows for the first time in our theater a lively sense of the natures of woman." Shakespeare gives us a crazy magical Ephesus where men may re-find their brothers and find themselves and where women may re-find their husbands and learn about themselves. The city and the people of this play and this Ephesus may be highly improbable, just like this story of Tristan and Iseult, but they are infinitely desirable, a triumph of imagination over life.

A Midsummer Night's Dream: It is likely that the first performance was to celebrate a noble wedding, of the Earl of Derby to Elizabeth Vere in 1595, with the queen and the entire court present. Comedies at that time largely depended on the falling out of lovers. But to have such a falling out motivated by failure of affection in the lovers themselves, or indeed produced by any human agency, would be indiscreet in a wedding piece, so Shakespeare introduces the fairies—who are tough and dangerous demons more than figurines in ballet shoes, not essentially malevolent but, to use the theological term, uncovenanted powers.

The play starts with Theseus, Duke of Athens, speaking with impatient love of his forthcoming marriage with Hippolyta. It ends four days later with the wedding night, at which an unwittingly comic interlude, in the form of a so-called tragedy, Pyramus and Thisbe, is acted by Bottom the Weaver's group of rustics to entertain the pair.

The time between is occupied with the adventures of four court lovers. Hermia and Lysander leave Athens because their love for each other is opposed and are followed into the woods by Demetrius, who also loves Hermia, and Helena, who loves Demetrius.

There, Oberon, King of the Fairies, angry with his queen, Titania, and wishing to punish her with a trick, commands Puck to fetch for him a magic juice which, dropped into sleepers' eyes, makes them fall in love with the first being they see when they wake up. Bewitched by this juice, Lysander falls in love with Helena, and Titania falls in love with Bottom, whose head Puck has transformed into the likeness of an ass. Eventually, the spells are lifted. The lovers are united with their true partners, and Bottom and his friends speed to court to do the wedding play."

Patten interrupts. "What's the point of all this?"

Author: Demonstration by fact that magic realism was alive and well in Shakespeare. If he can do it, so can others, myself included. All these stories explore the problems of humans and deal with interesting, if somewhat bizarre, human actions and concerns. The lessons derive from the opinions of the audience and from the reactions of the readers for better or worse.

The Merchant of Venice: (Iseult stopped the Shakespeare stuff here because she saw that most people were bored with it.)

"And yes, I swear by Iseult and King Mark, Iseult and Tristan, Branwen and King Mark (Iseult knew that Branwen and Mark had a history and probably had children together. But she didn't know how many. Iseult also knew or felt she knew that Mark preferred Branwen, though for what reason he preferred her, she knew not, and she cared not)."

"I swear by Melisande and Golaud, Pasiphae and the Bull, Grushenka and Dmitri Karamazov, Solveig and Peer Gynt, Tammy Faye Bakker and Jim Bakker, TV evangelist arrested for indecent exposure, Gertrude and Claudius, Regan and Edmund, Goneril and Edmund, Miranda and Ferdinand, Mattie and Ethan Frome, Zeena and Ethan Frome.

"I swear by Molly Bloom and Leopold Bloom, Molly and Stephen Dedalus, Pamela, attractive servant girl who struggles against the advances of her employer, Mr. B, until he finally pops the question, Clarissa and Lovelace, Anna Karenina and Alexei, Anna Karenina and Count Alexey Vronsky (if only Anna had known that Vronsky had a toothache that fatal day, she might not have thrown herself under the train), Nicolette captive Saracen and Aucassin Count of Beaucaire."

Pseudo-summative break and breath.

"I swear by Becky Thatcher and Tom Sawyer, Bathsheba and David, Tinker Bell and Peter Pan, Wendy Darling and Peter Pan, Eustacia Vye and Clym Yeobright, Xantippe and Socrates, Yum-Yum and Ko-Ko, Yum-Yum and NankiPoo, Dido, who committed suicide when Aeneas left."

Iseult now turned and addressed Arthur's tent directly. "I swear by Queen Guenevere and King Arthur (Arthur smiled and nodded). I swear by Queen Guenevere and Sir Lancelot du lac (Arthur frowned and shook his head). I swear by Dame Elaine (the Lily Maid of Astolat) and Sir Lancelot (Arthur smiled, Guenevere frowned, and history does not record Dame Elaine's reaction). I swear by Dame Elaine and Gawain (Lancelot frowned)."

Iseult returned to face the sun. "I swear by the Queen of Hearts and the King of Hearts, Katisha and Ko-Ko, Vivian, the Lady of the Lake, and Merlin, Lydia Languish and Captain Jack Absolute in his alter ego form of Ensign Beverly, Catherine Barkley and Frederic Henry, Francesca de Giocondo (Mona Lisa) and Leonardo da Vinci, Beatrice and Dante, Bice Portinari who, at age nine, conquered the heart and soul of world-class poet Dante to become his Beatrice, Diana and Red Five, Desdemona and Othello."

"I swear by future couples, Jessica (Shylock's daughter) and Lorenzo, Ma Joad and Pa Joad, Fernande Olivier (née Amélie Lang) and Pablo Picasso, Eva Gouel and Pablo, Matilda and Theodore and Isabella and Theodore from Walpole's masterpiece *The Castle of Otranto*, Isabella and Frederic, Isabella and Manfred, Hippolita and Manfred all from the same gothic work, comatose wife and Claus von Büloe, who was also known as Ducky by the children because of the way he swam with his head above water when his hair transplants were new.

"I swear by Andrea Regnolds and Ducky, Louise and Scobie and Helen and Scobie and Louise and Wilson and Helen and Bagster from *The Heart of the Matter* by Graham Greene, Jean Marais (who said without Cocteau I am nothing) and Jean Cocteau (who said I am her slave and her king), Pat Paterson (British born actress) and Charles Boyer, Boyer the French actor who committed suicide soon after Pat died because he (Boyer) said he couldn't live without her, Madeline Bray and Nicholas Nickleby, Jay Gatsby and Daisy Buchanan, Nora and Torvald Helmer, Titania and Oberon, Judith (Bluebeard's last wife according to Bartok) and Bluebeard, the seven murdered wives and Bluebeard, Monica Lewinsky (who seemed notable for being so generic a victim and provocateuse but who also scored the biggest governmental intern romantic coup of the century) and President Clinton, Paula Jones and President Clinton, Genifer Flowers and President Clinton, Senator Hilary Rodham Clinton and President Clinton, partners in crime, Bonnie and Clyde, Luana and Tomak from *One Millions Years B.C.*, multiple women and Don Juan, part of the Italy of the imagination that guaranteed the most complex delight to English audiences and the British imagination, a response to literary stereotype so satisfying that it was impervious even to Byron's skillful mockery in Don Juan: 'What men call gallantry, and gods adultery, is much more common where the climate's sultry.' Evidently, Byron didn't realize that it isn't the climate; it's the Italian wines."

"I swear by Maria Prophetissima and Duke Morgan, Laura (real identity unknown) and humanist poet-scholar Petrarch, Chandra Levy (who may have learned the hard way the wisdom of the ancient Chinese maxim 'who sleep with powerful, sleep with tiger') and representative Gary Condit, Jeanette MacDonald and Nelson Eddy, Mrs. Bardell and Mr. Pickwick, Bessie Bighead, hired help, in the White Book of Llareggub and Gomer Owen, who kissed her when she wasn't looking because he was dared.

"I swear by Scarlett and Rhett, Scarlett and Ashley, Pompeia, wife of Caesar and Clodius, Camille and Armand Duval, Carmen (whose name in Latin means verse) and Don José, Polly Peachum and Macheath, Portia and Brutus, Priscilla and speak-for-yourself John (he did, and the two were married), Priscilla and Miles Standish, Clara Peggotty and Barkis, Scheherazade and Emperor Shahriar, La Belle Sauvage Pocahontas and Captain Smith, Pocohontas who later married another Englishman John Rolfe, Nancy and Slugo, Lois Lane and Clark Kent, Lois Lane and Superman (strange visitor from another planet who came to Earth with powers far beyond those of mortal men and who disguised as Clark Kent, mild-mannered reporter for a great metropolitan newspaper, fights a never-ending battle for truth, justice, and the American Way)."

"And talking about radio, I swear by Margo and wealthy man about town Lamont Cranston, who years ago in the orient learned the secret of how to cloud men's minds so that they cannot see and who now is the one who knows what evil lurks in the heart of men, the Shadow, Caroline and Julian English, Esmeralda and Quasimodo, Josephine and Ralph Rackstraw, Caracas (which is to be, unless I am mistaken, the Capital of Venezuela) and Gogol, also known as Nikolai Vassilevitch, Little Red Riding Hood and the Wolf, Lucretia and Sextus son of King Tarquin who wrought the deed of shame, Pussum and Gerald, Gudrun Brangwen and Gerald, Ursula Brangwen and Birkin, Katherine O'Shea and Parnell, Lady Godiva and Earl Leofric, Charlotte van Kalb and Friedrich von Schiller, Evangeline and Gabriel, Jane Eyre and Rochester, Fata Morgana, also known as Morgan le Fay, and Demogorgon, Rima and Mr. Able, Mrs. Ramsay and Mr. Ramsay, alias Julia and Leslie Stephen, parents of Virginia Woolf, Abigail and Nabal, Abigail and David, Ozzie and Harriet, Lucy and Desi, Andriana, Foscarini, Leonilda, Marina, Morosini the nun, and 122 other women and Casanova."

A much-needed breath.

"I swear by Olive Oyl and Popeye, Donna Elvira or Donna Anna and Don Giovanni, Sarah Woodruff and Charles, Sarah and the French Lieutenant, Ernestina and Charles, Lily Tomlin and Peter Lynch, Edith and Archie, Nancy and Ronald Reagan, Orra and Wiley Harvard, seniors in an almost classical mode, Jack and Jill, Isabella, sister of the man Angelo condemned to death measure for measure for fornication, and Angelo, Clotilde de Vaux and Auguste Compt, Montana Wildhack and Billy Pilgrim, Betsy Rath and the man in the gray flannel suit, Tom Rath, Maria (his mistress) and Tom Rath, Gretchen and Faust, Beauvoir and Sartre, Beauvoir and Nelson Algren, Sophie and Stingo, Sophie and Nathan in Sophie's Choice.

"I swear by Eva Braun and Adolf Hitler, Mrs. Simpson and Hitler, Mrs. Simpson and King Edward, Mrs. Simpson and John Thompson, Zuleika Dobson and the duke, Zuleika Dobson and all the Oxford undergraduates who fell in love with her, but whom she cannot love, Dulcinea del Toboso and Don Quixote, Eliza Doolittle and Henry Higgins, Sister Carrie and the flashy, boyish, and utterly superficial Charles Drouet her first lover, Sister Carrie and George Hurstwood her second lover, who, as a result of his affair with Carrie, lost his reputation and self-esteem, ends his life as a sordid suicide in a flop house, Catherine Earnshaw and the brooding Heathcliff, Lilith, Adam's first wife, and Adam, Else and Lohengrin, Lolita and Humbert, Lot's wife of salt pillar fame and Lot, Lot's daughters and Lot, Maid Marian and Robin Hood (she loved him when he was still Earl of Huntington and then she followed him into the forest when he was outlawed. She lived with him chastely until their marriage.)"

"Who else? I swear by Lucie Manette and Charles Darnay, Lucie Manette and Sidney Carton, Eve and Adam, Miranda and Ferdinand, Victoria and Albert, Alonso's son and Alonso's daughter, Alonso's daughter and the King of Tunis, Estelle and William Faulkner, Sylvia Plath and Ted Hughes, Trilby and Svengali, Alison and Nicholas, Lilly's identical twin sister June and Nicholas, Jojo and Nicholas, Kemp and Nicholas, Mrs. De Seitas and Maurice Conchis, Adelia and Ronny in A Passage to India, Tai-yu and Pao-yu in the *Dream of Red Mansions*, Salome and John, Constance Baker Motley and Thurgood Marshall, The queen and Rizzio, Esperanza and Zorro, Elena and Zorro, Lily and Henderson the Rain King."

Pause and deep breath. Even Iseult seemed to be getting tired of reciting all the famous couples that she could think of. The display did prove that couples do play a major role in the consciousness of Western culture. No question about it. In fact, there may be more famous couples than there are famous individuals. But how could that be? Easy—the truth of the statement turns on the definition of famous.

"I swear by Princess Di and Dodi, Di and Charles, Di and Squidy (car salesman), Di and her personal trainer Lieutenant Kelly Flinn, Di and the mysterious neurosurgeon, Di and the heart surgeon whose name I have forgotten, Camilla Parker-Bowles and Charles, Donna Rice and Gary Hart, The babysitter and Michael Kennedy, Kimba Wood and Frank Richardson, Francesca Johnson, wife and mother, and the photographer in Bridges of Madison County, Heloise and Pierre Abelard, Marilyn Monroe and JFK, Marilyn Monroe and Joe DiMaggio, Marilyn Monroe and Arthur Miller, Barbie and Ken, Ivanhoe and Rowena, Mamo Ocllo and Marco Càpac, Aztec sister and brother, also husband and wife, Emma Bovary and Charles, Emma Bovary and Leon, Hester Prynne and Arthur Dimmesdale, parents of Pearl, Hester Prynne and Roger Chillingworth, incarnation of evil and vengeance who returned after he was thought dead."

Quick breath. Oh God! Iseult has hit her stride.

"I swear by Mary Magdalene and Jesus, Lady Capulet and Tybalt, Odette de Crécy and Swann, Agrippina the Younger, niece and third wife of Emperor Claudius who poisoned him with his favorite dish of mushrooms, Germanica and Tacitus Agricola."

Breath-ette and a smile.

"Furthermore, I swear by Yün and Shen Fu (from *Six Records of a Floating Life* in which is told the true love story of Shen Fu and his wife Yün. It is set in a traditional Chinese society—and thus their love coexists and intermingles with Shen Fu's affairs with courtesans, and with his wife's attempts to find him a concubine. And yet for all that, what he feels for her and she feels for him is, none the less, love—true love."

"And I swear by Cleopatra and Anthony, Cleopatra and Julius Caesar, Tess of the d'Urbervilles and Angel Clare, Tess and Alec whom she murdered, Octavia and Anthony, Columbine and Harlequin, Becky Sharp and Rawdon Crawley, Minnie Mouse and Mickey, Nova and Taylor from *Planet of the Apes* (original and best version, 1967)."

"I swear by Katrina Van Tassel and Icabod Crane, Katrina Van Tassel and Abraham Van Brunt, also known as Brom Bones, who resorted to playing practical jokes on his rival."

"Brom Bones always laughed when his wife, Katrina, told the story of the Headless Horseman who threw his head at the schoolmaster. I swear by Dame Van Winkle and Rip, a loafer hero appealing to our taste for irresponsibility, which balances our dour puritanism, Cora and Hawkeye, Virginia married at age 13 to Edgar Allan Poe, her cousin, Ligeia and Guy de Vere, Lady Rowena Trevanion and Guy de Vere, Emily Dickinson and Reverend Charles Wadsworth, Emily Dickinson and Judge Otis P. Lord, Zelda and F. Scott Fitzgerald, Nicole Warren and Dick Diver, Emily St. Aubert in the *Mysteries of Udolpho* and Valancourt (sympathetic characters wildly anachronistic for the period during which they are supposed to be living, just like you-know-who), Emily and the evil Signor Montoni, Queen Azura and Emperor Ming the Merciless, Queen Azura and Flash Gordon. Some of you may be old enough to remember Queen Azura and Flash."

Genuine summative breath. The end is near. Thank Dagda. She tried but failed to cover all couples. She can't. There are just too many. She knew more, but people can take only so much. So, she had to stop.

"And finally, I swear by Maud Gonne and W.B. Yeats. He was only 23 when he first met her and, as he said, 'the troubling of my life began,' Constance Gore-Booth and W.B. Yeats, and speaking of them reminds one of Ballylee and Blind Raftery, the renowned 18th-century harper who had sung the praises of the beautiful Mary Hines, 'a girl whose skin was so white it looked blue.' Raftery was blind. How did he know?

And may these couples remain,

when all is ruin once again."

Iseult took a breath and break and looked around to see if the throng was listening.

They were not.

And who could blame them? Her list of couples had been almost as extensive as the credits at the end of a digitally enhanced modern movie. But, of course, her list is incomplete. I can think of other couples, like Mae West and those 13 Columbia undergraduates, for example, who "made Mae West," but charity demands that we and Iseult stop after we recall some presidential couples.

Presential couples:

The liaisons of the present president of the United States, Agent Orange, are too well known to list. They include playboy bunnies and porn stars who got paid off to keep their mouths shut. Naturally, they didn't keep quiet. Consequently, Agent Orange is mad at them.

(Note: Agent Orange is Bernard's name for Trump, Ed.)

JFK heads the passions parade. He learned how to swill the babes from his father, Joseph, whose greatest preoccupation was women. The most famous of Joe's many mistresses was Gloria Swanson, star of the silver screen. He took her on many luxurious trips to Europe, along with Rose his wife. Rose didn't mind. "As long as he provides for me and the family and it doesn't interfere with my personal life."

"I swear by JFK and airline stewardess Susan Imhoff who complained in her memoir that JFK made her do all of the work. This was way before his back injury. And I swear by JFK and Danish journalist Inga Arvad, who was being trailed by the FBI on suspicion she was a German spy. Official FBI reports confirm JFK traveled to Charleston with her and spent every night with her in her hotel room and had engaged in sexual intercourse with her on 'numerous occasions.' I swear by JFK and Hedy Lamarr, Angela Greene, Susan Hayward, Joan Crawford, Lana Turner, Sonja Henie, Peggy Cummins, Olivia de Havilland, and her famous sister Joan Fontaine. Gene

Tierney became a serious romance object. She said JFK had "the most perfect blue eyes I have ever seen on a man." For Gene, it was love at first sight. She divorced husband Oleg Cassini to marry JFK. But Jack finally told her marriage was out because of his presidential ambitions. That relationship ended with her abrupt departure."

Next came Pamela Farrington, who was in the habit of sunbathing in the nude. When JFK ran for the senate in 1952, a photo circulated of him next to a nude Pamela. His comment: "Yeah, I remember her. She was great."

"And I swear by JFK and Jackie Bouvier and of course, JFK and one of the most beautiful, glamorous, and well-known women of the century, Marilyn Monroe."

Iseult stopped and looked around.

Most of the members of the court, despite the importance of the present trial, had fallen asleep. Others were on the nod. A few were thinking about their next meal, their next fuck, their next car, how the stock market might do that day. Two men in the rear ranks were drinking vodka and discussing Butkov's novel. They were West Indian Negroes, immaculate in their personal habits, and of accent quite entertaining to listen to. The one spoke, "Mon, what de Hell awr ye tawkin' boot? You don't speek de king's hinglish."

Another man altogether in white spats scratched his head, for he was trying to make sense out of certain radical reforms in the laws of inheritance recently passed by the United States Senate. He was beginning to wonder if we were electing the right kind of people to the Congress. A little girl about four years old tugged her mother's hand and announced, "I want to go poo poo." What can you do? They were the average human article, nothing more.

Seeing that no one was paying attention to her and that most had, in fact, forgotten her, Iseult decided to skip Harding and the fact he made love to his mistress in a closet at the white house. And Iseult decided to skip JFK and Blaze Star (engaged at the time to Louisiana Governor Earl Long), JFK, and Pam Tuenure (his secretary), who subsequently became Jackie's secretary. JFK lost interest in Pam and began sleeping with her roommate, Mary Meyer.

"Stop!" Cried Patten. "Iseult, darling, and dearest, enough is enough. You made your point. Couples make history. So what? Refer interested readers to Sullivan's excellent 1991 book *Presidential Passions: The Love Affairs of American Presidents*, Shapolsky Publishers, 136 West 22nd Street, New York, NY 10011. And get on with your trial. People are beginning to think you are stalling because you know you are guilty and want to buy time."

"OK, Patten, you are the producer, and what you say goes."

And then, perversely, Iseult resumed the solemn oath:

"I even swear, if I must, by that old gray bearded peevish male god of the Bible and the Old Testament, the one who seems so trivial, trifling, forgetful, and lowdown, the desert sky god who inhabits some part of heaven just beyond the other side of the moon, the old man without wife or consort, the jealous god who has caused so much distress and strife in this wide world."

"Come on, Iseult," yelled Andread. "You're stalling. Get to it. You can't avoid punishment forever."

Iseult gave him the up-yours sign with the third finger of her gloved right hand while simultaneously sticking out her tongue. Then she smiled. Take my word for it, that smile was simply stunning. I will never forget it. And it was that moment that I realized I too was in love with Iseult and that I would love her forever, though she would never love me back. Some loves were never meant to be. Sad but true.

"And I swear by the Nine Worthies: Hector, Alexander, Julius Caesar (pre-Christian pagans), Joshua, David, Judas Maccabaeus (pre-Christian Jews), and Arthur, Charlemagne, and Godfrey of Boulogne (Christians)."

Patten and Bernard shouted in unison to awaken the audience: "OK, here it comes! Here it comes!"

"My lords," Iseult said, trembling and shouting to wake them up. "My lords, kings of Longress (this is the ancient name of England), and of Cornwall, I swear, by these ancient things, and by all the holy things of earth, by all the couples, married and unmarried, burning aflame or calm in respiration, those that are touching and sighing right now and those that are not, couples, that have, do, and will always interest mankind now and forever:"

[Monks A, B, & C: And here followed the meat of her oath:]

"(I swear) that no man has held me in his arms or has lain with me, saving King Mark, my husband and my lord, and this poor man dressed as a pilgrim who only now took a fall with me as you did plainly see. He carried me over the water, and I did lay with him as you all do know. He and King Mark are the only ones I have lain with, so help me God."

Iseult turned to Mark and screamed above the din of the riffraff who had now become aware that the real action was about to start, "King Mark, will that oath stand?"

Mark nodded assent as he simultaneously drew his pocket-handkerchief out of the basket-hilt to drive off a fly that buzzed about his nose. What had he been thinking about? Oh yes, a glass of water. When one is thirsty, whether one be king or commoner, it's part of our animal nature. One thinks of drink.

"Yes, queen," King Mark said, clearing his dry throat. "And God see to it."

"Amen," said Iseult.

Then Iseult and the crowd waited for any instant vengeance that might fall upon her should she be forsworn. But the earth did not rip apart to carry her to Hell. The skies remained clear and bright. No bolts of lightning fell. In fact, nothing happened, nothing at all.

Yes, she was terrified here, like a bird astray in a room, a bird already stunned by dashing itself against mirrors and panes. She hesitated; then, the queen went by the brazier, pale and stumbling. With her gloved hands thrust among the coals, she grabbed the white-hot iron and held it high above her head, glistening and glinting incandescent, smaller than the sun, but, close up, it was just as radiant, effulgent, and bright, a single flash, dilating fixed, immense and blinding, an intolerable, lacerating light!

She carried the iron 30 paces, hearing only the sound a person makes who is walking through sand, then with flourish, she threw it in a dune.

Iseult showed her palms for all to see, and she began with deliberate gesture in the stylized manner of a Noh drama to take her gloves off. Triumphant, she showed palms of lily-white wide-open skin, clean and fresh and cool, unscathed, uninjured, unhurt hands. She was transfigured.

At that great sight, the kings and the barons and the people stood still for a moment, silent in awe, the ladies astonished, the men with lumps in their throats. And then, after a long silence, there arose a clangorous tumult, a jamboree of capriciously clashing cries.

Iseult tried to understand what she was hearing. Beneath and outside the bare acoustics, there is a code in even the simplest conversations that tells us **What's Going On**. And the things Iseult now saw seemed doubtful, changing, metamorphosing. The thing, the trial, was becoming something else.

But what? And what? And why?

Andread stepped up, bowed to King Mark and the other lords and ladies. He didn't look good. Worse for wear. Yellow, downright sick. This morning, he had had an attack of quartan fever, in all three stages (chill, hot flush, sweats) that always left him exhausted. His condition was made doubly worse by the now unpleasant consequences of drink. "I overdid it last night," he announced. "No! permit me to say—overdid it badly."

Then he, wicked Andread, walked, or staggered, with legs spread wide, jerking now and then from one side to the other, presumably still drunk, suspecting some kind of trick, stumbled to the iron and seized it to pull it from the sand. Although it was cooler now, the iron metal still retained quite a lot of heat and a vaster law (of thermodynamic transfer) here expressed itself in a particular apodictic truth, a clear demonstration, established on incontrovertible evidence, the kind of thing Kant applied to a proposition enouncing necessary and hence absolute reality.

As Andread recoiled in pain, his velvet glove burst into flame, his face contorted in anguish and, with a terrible scream (not bad for a man, in fact so good I retract what I said previously about men never, like women, learning to give a full-bodied scream).

Andread dropped the red-hot iron like a hot potato. The air filled with an excessively unpleasant smell, the stench of sizzling flesh, the stink of a third-degree burn. Then a stone like silence bore down an impenetrable silence of men with stern, tight-drawn lips. Their anger, like the wrath of God, directed against Andread for what he did.

We recount the fact, indifferent to the danger of conservatives at court, to rearrange things to suit their ideas and convenience, by creating fake news and stupid stories.

And so, with that detail, the "pyre of vanities," as Andread's burns would be known to future generations, the magical illusion planned by the lovers looked even better than could have ever been imagined. But here, as everywhere, due to over exposure to Hollywood action movies, popular amazement was quickly exhausted. And the din dimmed down.

Woe unto Andread; his death is near. He tried to escape in a rowboat and got unbalanced and fell overboard. The armor weighed him down, and he drowned. Vengeance is mine, saith the Lord. And while vengeance in real life may safely be left to Him, what a pleasure it is to give the bad guys and gals what they so richly deserve in our fictional stories. Thumbs up for heroes; thumbs down for villains, kin or not.

May God be more merciful to Andread than just.

"See how my innocence protects me," shouted Iseult while passing her hands outward from her breasts toward the group and to the confused cries of the cynical and the suspirations of the rest.

Thus, did the queen certify herself.

And the world voted of the kings, earls, barons, counts, vice counts, and knights that she had proved herself innocent, virgin-white and pure, and was now "quits."

Of course, it wasn't cut and dry as all that. There were some objections, some minor bickering, so often that is the way of those who build up, like a card-house, to a pack of truth. Yet neither Arthur nor Mark nor any of the other grandees or peons there assembled succeeded in formulating an even remotely tenable hypothesis as to the true nature of what they had witnessed. When I say formulate, I mean expressed in terms which would be at once rational and accessible to all. Instead, they called it a miracle.

Of course, about this marvel, there was no love in Mark's eyes, but cold silent anger like a plaintiff's attorney who had just lost a major Class Action Lawsuit, which he had taken on with the usual shark contingency fee. Mark's white face had gone whiter still. It was like a death mask upon him, for now, the rumor mills buzzed that he had falsely accused his queen. False accusers in post-Roman Europe were routinely put to death—no kidding. Any leader, pasha, king, emperor, prince, satrap, etc. who made a treaty with Rome and then subsequently violated the treaty routinely suffered death. Example: Mitredates. Mark might escape the penalty for accusing falsely. Then again, he might not. Mark's immortal soul was also in danger because he had bourn false witness, a mortal sin. But that might be forgiven in his next trip to the confession. Or it might not. Forgiveness depends on the priest. Whose sins you shall forgive, they are forgiven them. Whose sins you shall retain, they are retained.

Iseult felt relief, but also she thought her life a little empty, for never again could there happen to her anything so dangerous, exciting, so sublime. Further, she knew her position was destined to be even more untenable now that she had been found in the right. Whenever one is in the right in relation to government or the powers that be, watch out (cf. Voltaire, Private Manning, Julian Assange, Edward Snowden, former U.S. Ambassador to Ukraine Marie Yovanovitch, and many others).

The trumpets blew "unto lodging," and they rode to their pavilions, unarmed themselves, washed their faces and their hands, went to dinner, and were seated at tables to eat the meat and drink the ales and mead.

Not wanting to introduce even the slightest element of uncertainty into this true story, I must warn you that, while you might have thought that supper that night would have been a hilarious affair, it somehow was manqué.

King Mark and Iseult—both parties felt wholly in the wrong. Each repented the impulses of what, in retrospect, seemed to each a kind of momentary insanity. Yet neither had an inkling that the other felt the same. Thus, each waited for the other to show signs of forgiveness and remorse, signals that never came.

Holding to our principle of not making things look any better or worse than they were, we quite refuse to let ideas out of novels undermine the reality displayed here. Iseult, instinctively annoyed by Mark's attitude, made one or two pointed remarks she let slip, and which we may insert at some juncture. Mark, in turn, rejoined her comments showing he wouldn't let his relationships undermine justice, nor would he let things in his kingdom be determined by a woman. If this couple appeared for marriage counseling, even the psychologist's secretary would, with a glance, know just from body language alone that the situation was hopeless.

Tristan made his way back to Orri's hut. A smoke detector was sounding off, signaling its batteries were dying. He walked from alarm to alarm, unable to find the right one.

Water dripped in the sink, so he tightened the tap.

A nail in the heel of his right shoe was digging into the flesh. To Hell with it. A good start is a good beginning. Flannagan proved with his probability calculus that you can't throw snake eyes all day. Boxcars won't jump up in your face every throw. The trial was a natural for us. And there are more 7s and 11s up the road. There have to be.

He took off his pilgrim garb. But, preparatory to hanging it in the armoire, while emptying the pocket, he found a note.

Iseult must have put it there when they fell together:

"Dearest Friend, If I should acquitted be, come to Lantyan Orchard a fortnight hence. Near the ancient apple tree, meet to get your recompense:

Wild Nights!

Wild Nights!

When I'm with thee;

Wild nights shall be our luxury!"

And so, they were, for a secret and clever recklessness always helped them.

To celebrate, Tristan and Iseult decided to travel together to Castle Pleure. Their weird adventure there is recounted in Mallory.

God protect the lovers.

God protect all lovers.

God protect us, everyone.

Time flowed on. Time, the real enemy of mankind.

Tristan and Iseult had many happy times together and some adventures which you may read about in the official versions of this tale. If you do follow up, you will find that Tristan married another Iseult, Iseult of the White Hands. She was passing fair and a good wife. But on his death bed, he asked Iseult of the White Hands to send for Iseult la Belle, for he loved her still. There is a wonderful display of this scene in the 1981 movie *Lovespell* with Richard Burton (King Mark), Kate Mulgrew (Iseult), and Nicholas Clay (Tristan).

Would she come?

His message was about black and white sails. If she has come, display the white sails, and if she has not come, show black.

On the way back from Kanoel to Saint Jean de Didonne in Bretton, the white sails were torn in the wind and unthinking, and out of necessity, the black sails were set out. So, when Tristan saw the black-sailed ship move along the crested and scallop-edged waves, his heart squeezed tight and would not move.

Yes, he literally died of a broken heart, a death more common than you might think.

Iseult la Belle came. The skin around her mouth was twitching, and her lower lip looked like it was going to melt on her chin. She turned pale as a scallop. Like a snowflake that had melted away: much beauty was gone.

She rested her head on Tristan's chest, for she loved him then and still. She moved the body and lay down next to him the way she had so many times when he was alive. She noted with regret the nonresponse. And from that place, she rose no more. For her heart squeezed tight and would not move.

Thus, she also and quite literally died of a broken heart.

Sleep on, Tristan. Sleep on Iseult. Sleep on, you fools. The barons have you where they want you. Europe needed your corpses, not your ideas of love. You and your ilk are dead. So, sleep on. Sleep on. You have fallen into a deep black space worse than tears, deeper than regret or pain or sorrow. It is an abyss where there is no climbing out, no ray of light, no sound of human voice or touch, smell, or taste, and all the worse for you—no love. The unromantic live on; their lives punctuated by screams, by imbecilities, by agonies, but you, you fools, have died, died for all time. Farewell, Tristan and Iseult. Your story is over. We have told it to your end. We told it for its own sake, not yours. It was neither short on diversion nor long on boredom. And it was hermetic.

King Mark breathed like he had bad, bad asthma. "I have seen plenty of tough titty in my day, but this is the toughest." Was he crying? It sure looked that way.

Mark ordered both Tristan and Iseult buried at Tintagel Minister outside on the south side of the church where their graves remain today. Pictures are available on the internet.

A blackberry thorn bush, twisted and bent in so true a Celtic spiral that no man could discern its beginning or end, grew out of the ground at Tristan's grave and wrapped around a woodbine (honey suckle with flowers white and fragrant) that grew from Iseult's grave.

Isn't that romantic! Literature has the ability of art to gloss over the crude horrors of reality. Picture coolly and calmly what actually happened here. Two people are buried like Aida and Radames. Decay is doing unspeakable work on their bodies until they become two skeletons, each indifferent to whether it lay there alone or with another set of bones. That, sad to say, is the real factual side of the matter.

The royal gardener tried but failed to separate the two plants and reported the situation to the king.

Mark ordered the bushes cut back to the ground. But there they sprung again. This time faster and more entangled, their limbs so intertwined that when the damp wind blew, not a breath could pass between them, not the rays of the sun penetrate their shade, nor rain soak through.

Mark ordered both ardent plants uprooted.

And they were.

But this did no good for the vines grew again and embraced themselves again, interlacing so closely and tightly that they seemed one living thing, not two.

King Mark, Queen Branwen, and the entire court declared the miracle. Archbishop Wilson said that this miracle proved their love innocent. What was the reasoning to declare a miracle? That's easy: There was none.

And so, by royal decree, and with the official blessing and sanction of the One Holy Apostolic Catholic Church, the lovers were never again to be parted and would live on happily together forever as woodbine and blackberry in fond embrace.

Their tombstone reads the truth they both knew their whole life long:

LOVE IS STRONGER THAN DEATH

FINIS OPERIS

Here ends the most noble tale made by Patten, the producer, and Bernard the Bardic Narrator.

Adieu, friends, and good luck to you.

Postscript by the Bard

Looking back, like Sir James Frazer, at the melancholy record of human error and folly, which has engaged our attention, I too welcome the displacement of religion and myth by science, and I don't know why I have wasted so much time writing this piece. And when I was wasting time, time was wasting me.

For it is a silly tale, really, a tale of the eternal triangle of two men in conflict over one woman and the poor fit between moral and erotic love. The things, characters, deeds and events bound up with coincidences, which are essentially the same as those found in life, cannot but baffle people who, like myself, wish to follow the dictates of common sense, yet, who would like to think there is an order to the universe and an order to our lives.

Perhaps love and the meaning of love, if there is one, is just a riddle that we cannot understand, a riddle, it is a pity, that we modern people have relegated with the ancient myths to the kindergarten. Perhaps it is a pity to know, find out, as I have in my research in Ireland and Cornwall, that for the seers and the sages of old, these riddles enshrined the deepest wisdom.

Our opinion: Love is always simply itself. It is philosophically correct to distinguish between sanctity and passion in analytical matters. But the result is ambiguous, for love can't be disembodied in its sanctified form, and it is not without sanctity in its fleshy form. So, we leave the question open, unresolved, irresolute. Unable to get to the bottom of the mysterious question, Bernard and Patten apologize to readers who may have worried about this issue. To think too much about defining love is like trying to square the circle or reduce pi to a rational number. It can't be done because love is both flesh and soul.

And now dear friends, return to your mundane lives—to the parking lots, the streets, the supermarkets, the television shows, Facebook, tweets, iPhone, all life's distractions and hubbub.

The story is behind you, reflected for a few moments in your rearview mirror, a holiday souvenir, a curious edifice, leaving a fugitive impression of an encounter with something out of balance and harmony.

But wait. Perhaps, my friends, you have passed through too quickly... and will visit again.

Shy and secretive, the basilica does not reveal itself to the hurried or inattentive visitor. Return to wander around. Take several hours, sit down inside, tune into the vibrations of light and color, listen to the voices echoing from the arches to the roodscreen, from the dungeon to the stained-glass mullioned windows, from the Last Judgment fresco to the tabernacle lamp. Feel this great mass tremble with life. It has been erected by the faith of its people, fashioned by a multitude of ardent souls, of craftsmen and artists, of prayers and hymns, a vessel of certitudes, masterpiece of grace and strength, of vigor and poetry, of inspiration and craftsmanship, of silence and jubilation.

Then go out and sit on a rock. Think! Yes, go ahead, think. Think about all those things you read in high school and have forgotten. Know that unity is not uniformity, liberty is not anarchy, and that success lies in convergence and communion.

Your task, our task, is to master matter and technique and make them sing:

Man is not diminished when, at the height of his possibilities, in his fervent quest for beauty, he acknowledges that he is but a pilgrim and a mendicant.

Note by the scribe A (translation from Latin by B. Patten):

> "I who have copied this story
> Or, more accurately, fantasy
> Do not credit the details
> Of the story or fantasy.
> Some things in it are devilish lies
> Some poetical figments
> Some seem possible
> And others not
> Some are for
> The enjoyment of idiots.⊕
> Adieu, God Bless Love Always,

⊕ This was copied directly from a handwritten note left in the margin at the end of the Tristan story in the Book of Kells, the only book most tourists see, which along with the bible, is one of the most revered and least read books in the world.

The scribe, an Irish monk, remains anonymous because he didn't sign his note. How do you interpret the God Bless Love Always?

Is it God Bless Love? Or God Bless and then Love Always? Or is it God Bless Love Always? Or is it_____? (Reader fill in the blank.)

Humm, we'll never know.

www.ingramcontent.com/pod-product-compliance
Lightning Source LLC
Chambersburg PA
CBHW050349190726
48284CB00007BB/2209